AVEREE

Stephanie Phillips
with Dave Johnson
Writers

Marika Cresta
Artist

Andrew Dalhouse
Colorist

Saida Temofonte
Letterer

Joseph Illidge
Editor

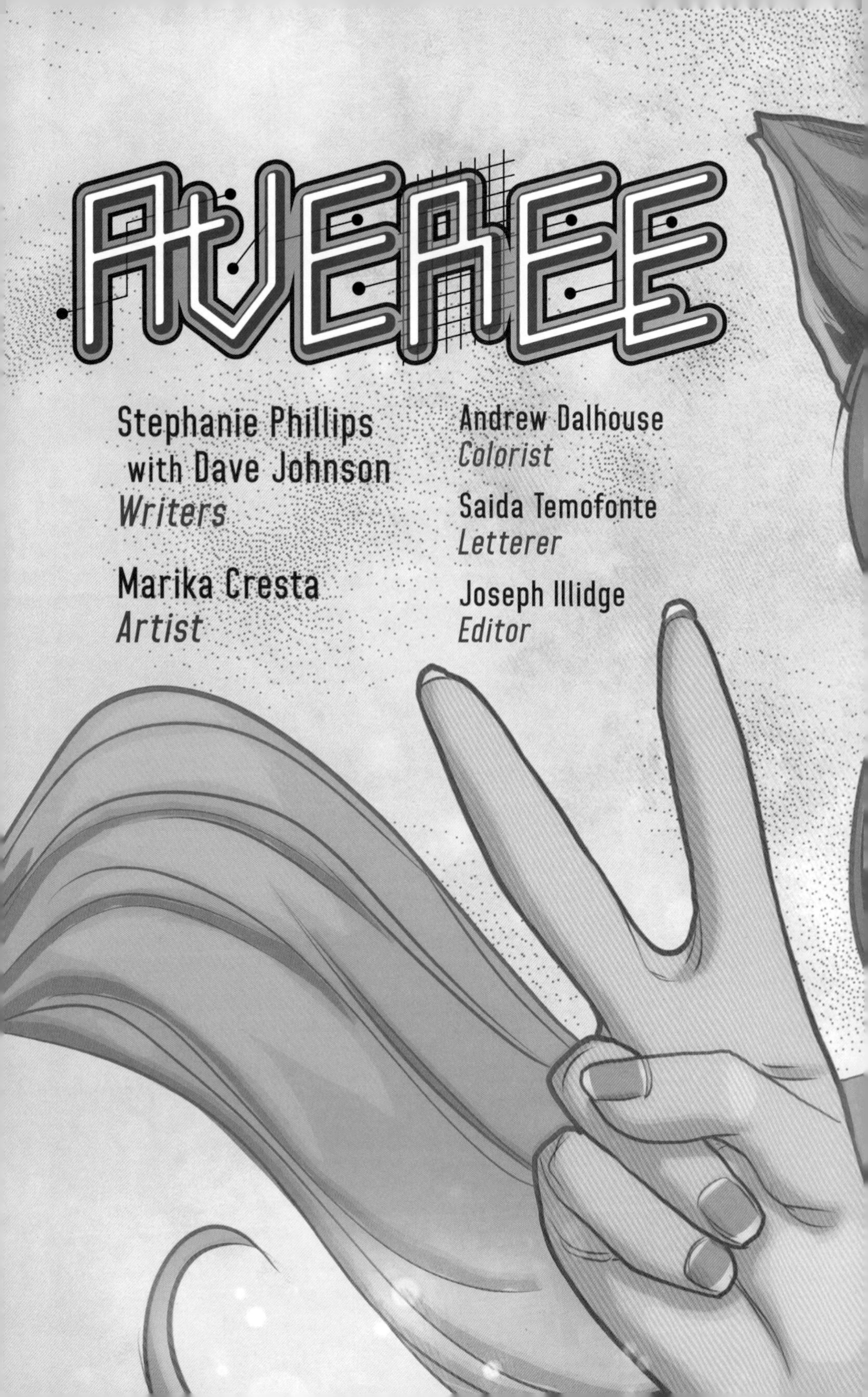

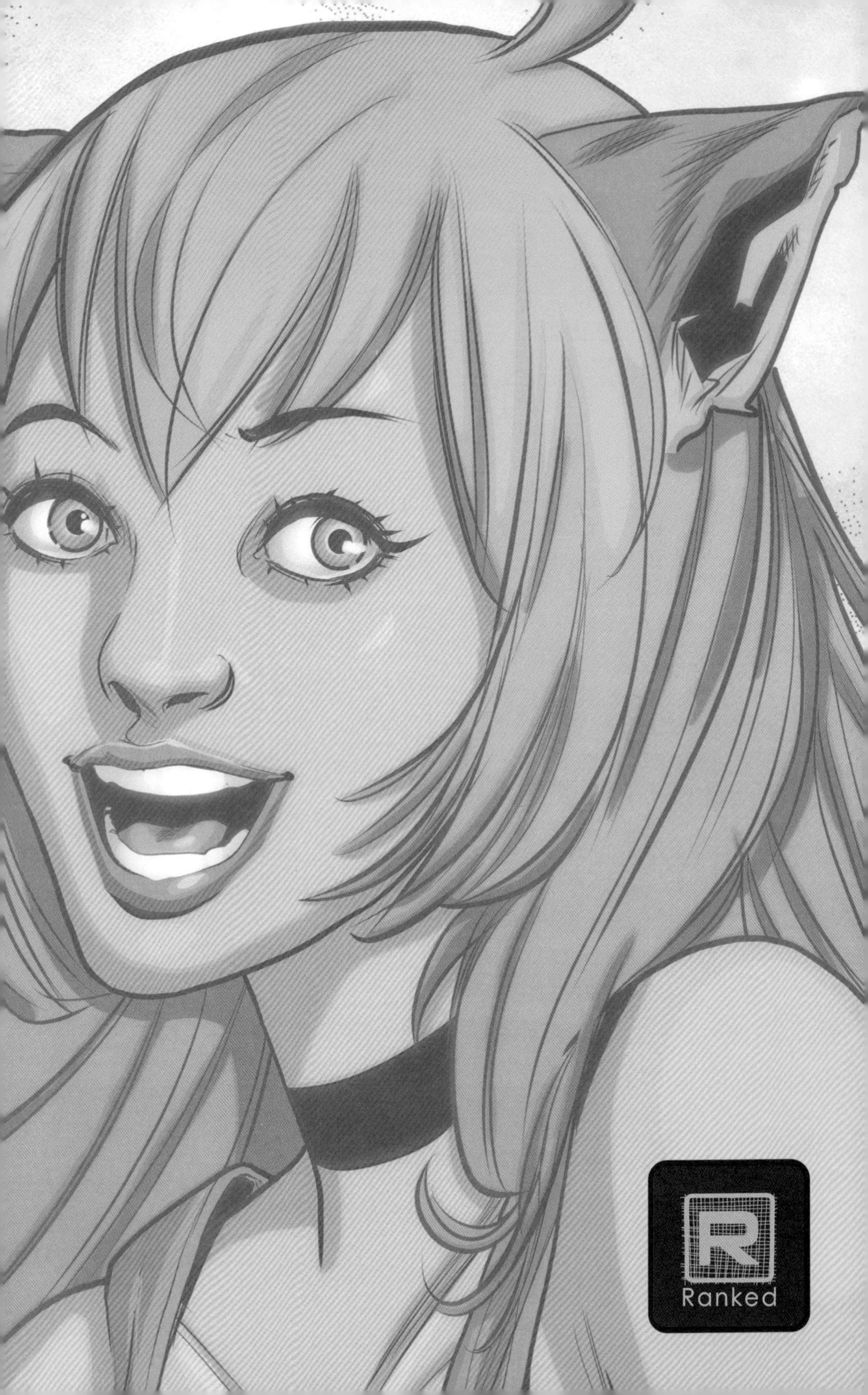
Ranked

Cover Illustration:
Marika Cresta and Andrew Dalhouse
Logo:
Phil Smith
Book Design:
Pete Carlsson

Tyler Chin-Tanner:
Co-Publisher
Wendy Chin-Tanner:
Co-Publisher
Justin Zimmerman:
Director of Operations
and Media
Pete Carlsson:
Production Designer

Diana Kou:
Director of Marketing
Jesse Post:
Book Publicist
Hazel Newlevant:
Social Media Coordinator
Erin Beasley:
Sales Manager

Publisher's Cataloging-In-Publication Data
(Prepared by The Donohue Group, Inc.)

Names: Phillips, Stephanie, 1991- author. | Johnson, Dave, 1966- author. | Cresta, Marika, illustrator. | Dalhouse, Andrew,
    colorist. | Temofonte, Saida, letterer. | Illidge, Joseph, editor.
Title: Averee / Stephanie Phillips, with Dave Johnson, writers ; Marika Cresta, artist ; Andrew Dalhouse, colorist ; Saida
    Temofonte, letterer ; Joseph Illidge, editor.
Description: First edition. | [Rhinebeck, New York] : A Wave Blue World, Inc., 2021. | Interest age level: Teen. | Summary:
    "Averee is one average girl's mission with her BFF through an unnerving world of near-future tech to take back
    control of their lives from an all-knowing social media app..."-- Provided by publisher.
Identifiers: ISBN 9781949518122 (trade paperback)
Subjects: LCSH: Social media--Comic books, strips, etc. | Social classes--Comic books, strips, etc. | High technology--Social
    aspects--Comic books, strips, etc. | Friendship--Comic books, strips, etc. | CYAC: Social media--Fiction. | Social
    classes--Fiction. | High technology--Social aspects--Fiction. | Friendship--Fiction. | LCGFT: Graphic novels.
Classification: LCC PZ7.7.P5213 Av 2021 | DDC 741.5973 [Fic]--dc23

ISBN: 978-1-949518-12-2   Printed in Canada

AWBW.com

To my sister, Bailey.
-Stephanie

To Stephanie, without her this project never would have become a reality.
-Dave

To my husband Diego, who is my rock and to my parents Antonella and Marco, who have always supported me.
-Marika

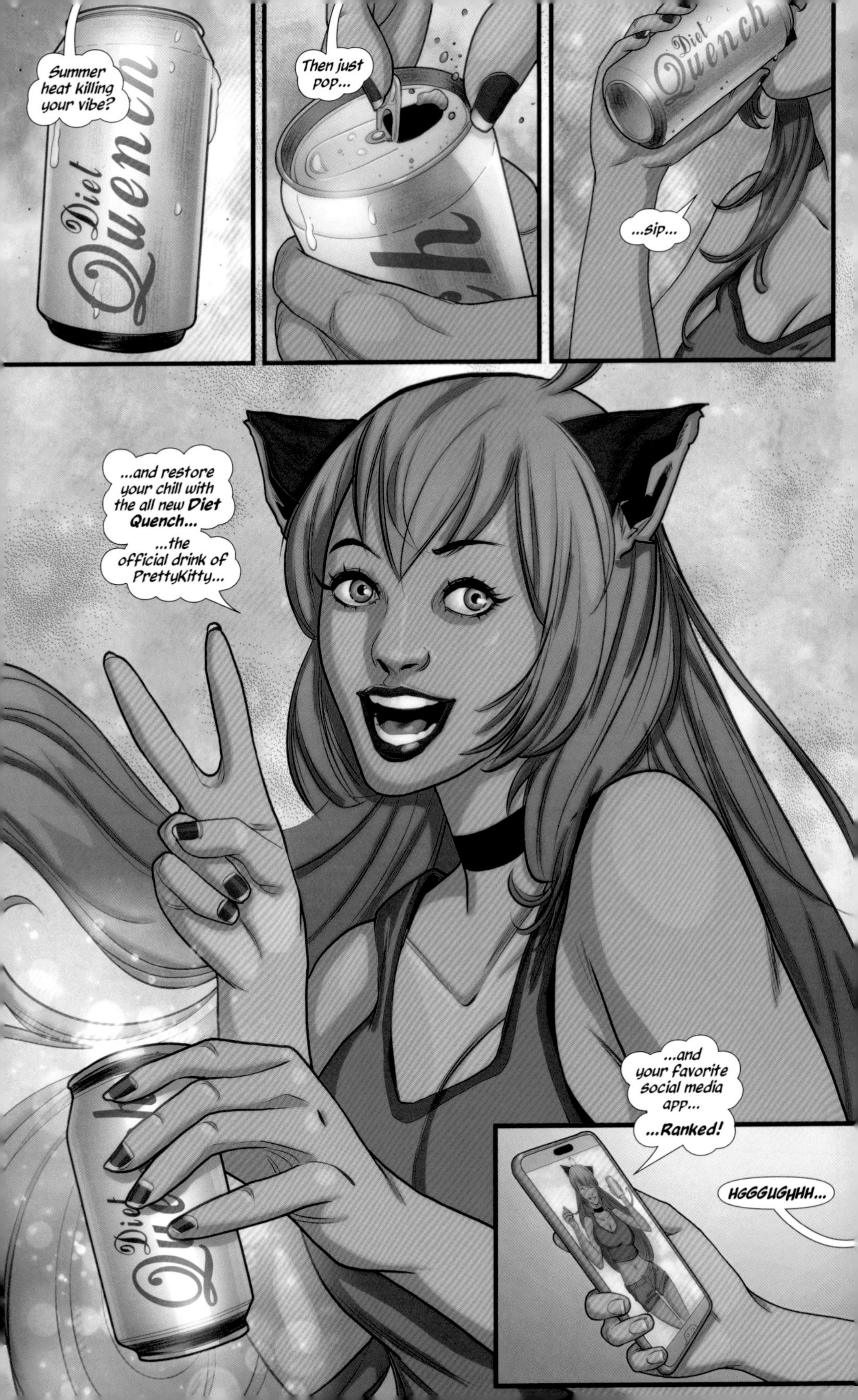

Summer heat killing your vibe?
Diet Quench
Then just pop...
Diet Quench
...sip...
...and restore your chill with the all new Diet Quench...
...the official drink of PrettyKitty...
Diet
...and your favorite social media app...
...Ranked!
HGGGUGHHH...

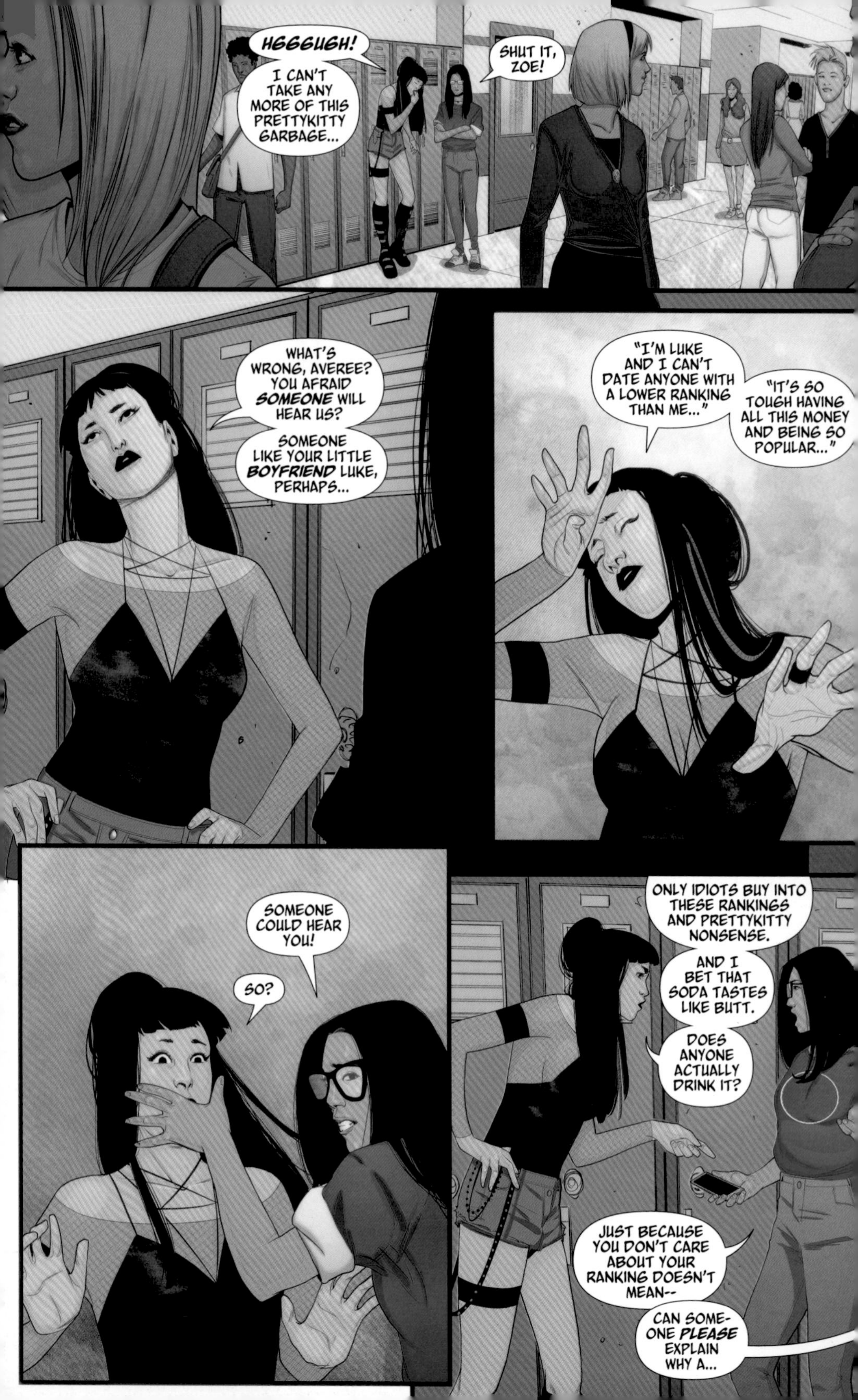
HSSSUGH!
I CAN'T TAKE ANY MORE OF THIS PRETTYKITTY GARBAGE...
SHUT IT, ZOE!
WHAT'S WRONG, AVEREE? YOU AFRAID SOMEONE WILL HEAR US?
SOMEONE LIKE YOUR LITTLE BOYFRIEND LUKE, PERHAPS...
"I'M LUKE AND I CAN'T DATE ANYONE WITH A LOWER RANKING THAN ME..."
"IT'S SO TOUGH HAVING ALL THIS MONEY AND BEING SO POPULAR..."
SOMEONE COULD HEAR YOU!
SO?
ONLY IDIOTS BUY INTO THESE RANKINGS AND PRETTYKITTY NONSENSE.
AND I BET THAT SODA TASTES LIKE BUTT.
DOES ANYONE ACTUALLY DRINK IT?
JUST BECAUSE YOU DON'T CARE ABOUT YOUR RANKING DOESN'T MEAN--
CAN SOME-ONE PLEASE EXPLAIN WHY A...

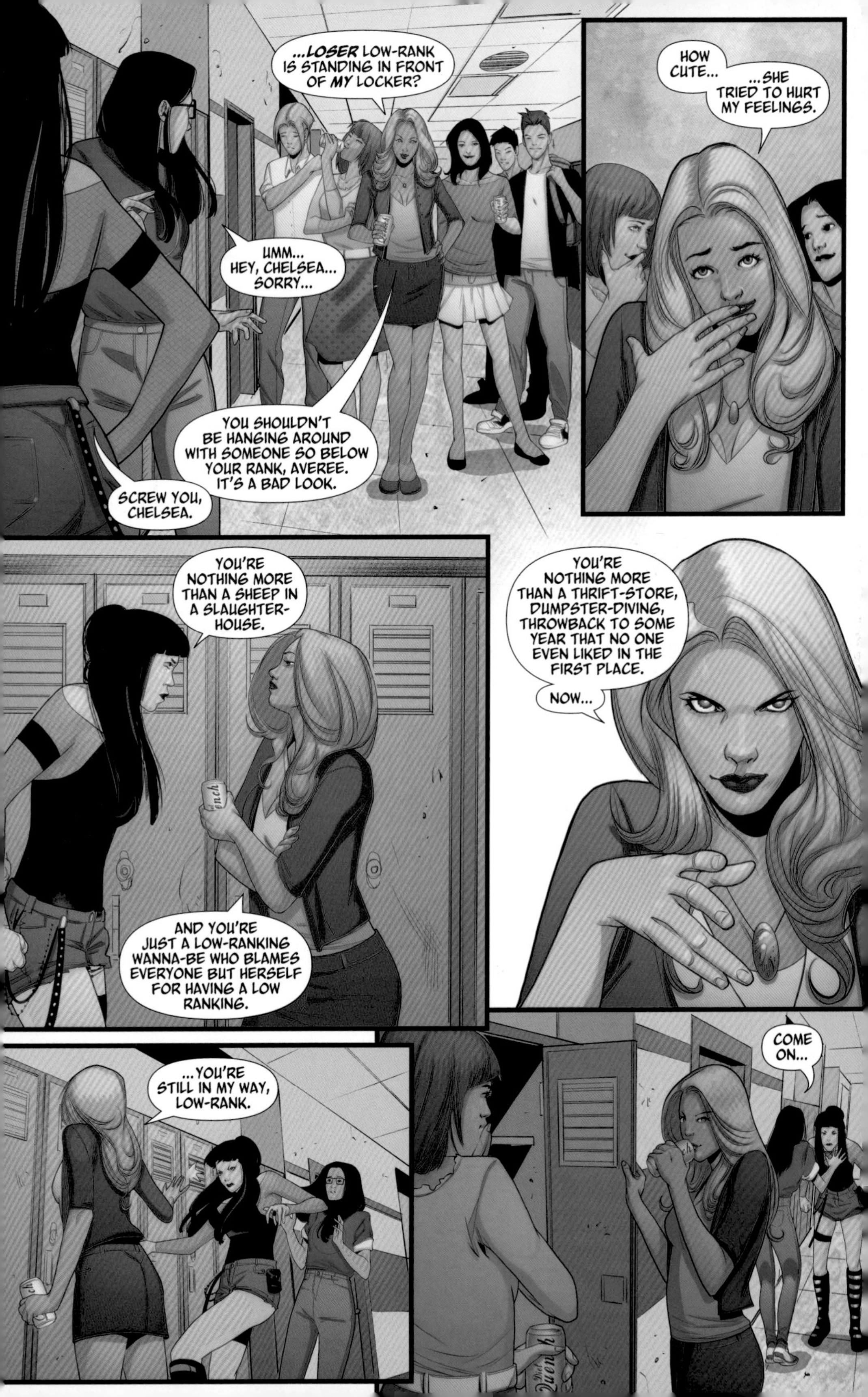
...LOSER LOW-RANK IS STANDING IN FRONT OF MY LOCKER?
UMM... HEY, CHELSEA... SORRY...
YOU SHOULDN'T BE HANGING AROUND WITH SOMEONE SO BELOW YOUR RANK, AVEREE. IT'S A BAD LOOK.
SCREW YOU, CHELSEA.
HOW CUTE...
...SHE TRIED TO HURT MY FEELINGS.
YOU'RE NOTHING MORE THAN A SHEEP IN A SLAUGHTER-HOUSE.
AND YOU'RE JUST A LOW-RANKING WANNA-BE WHO BLAMES EVERYONE BUT HERSELF FOR HAVING A LOW RANKING.
YOU'RE NOTHING MORE THAN A THRIFT-STORE, DUMPSTER-DIVING, THROWBACK TO SOME YEAR THAT NO ONE EVEN LIKED IN THE FIRST PLACE.
NOW...
...YOU'RE STILL IN MY WAY, LOW-RANK.
COME ON...

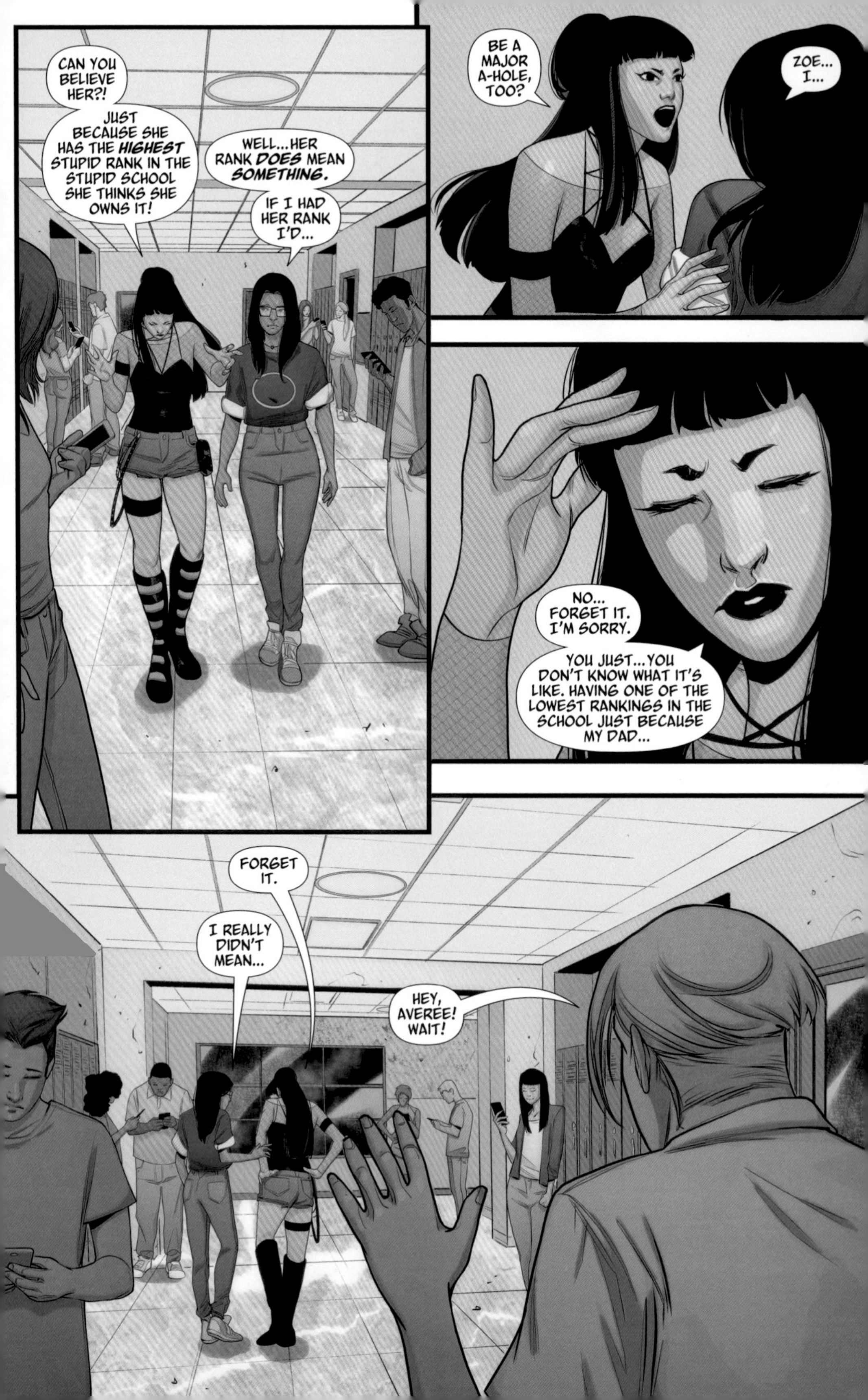
CAN YOU BELIEVE HER?!
JUST BECAUSE SHE HAS THE HIGHEST STUPID RANK IN THE STUPID SCHOOL SHE THINKS SHE OWNS IT!
WELL...HER RANK DOES MEAN SOMETHING.
IF I HAD HER RANK I'D...
BE A MAJOR A-HOLE, TOO?
ZOE... I...
NO... FORGET IT. I'M SORRY.
YOU JUST...YOU DON'T KNOW WHAT IT'S LIKE. HAVING ONE OF THE LOWEST RANKINGS IN THE SCHOOL JUST BECAUSE MY DAD...
FORGET IT.
I REALLY DIDN'T MEAN...
HEY, AVEREE! WAIT!

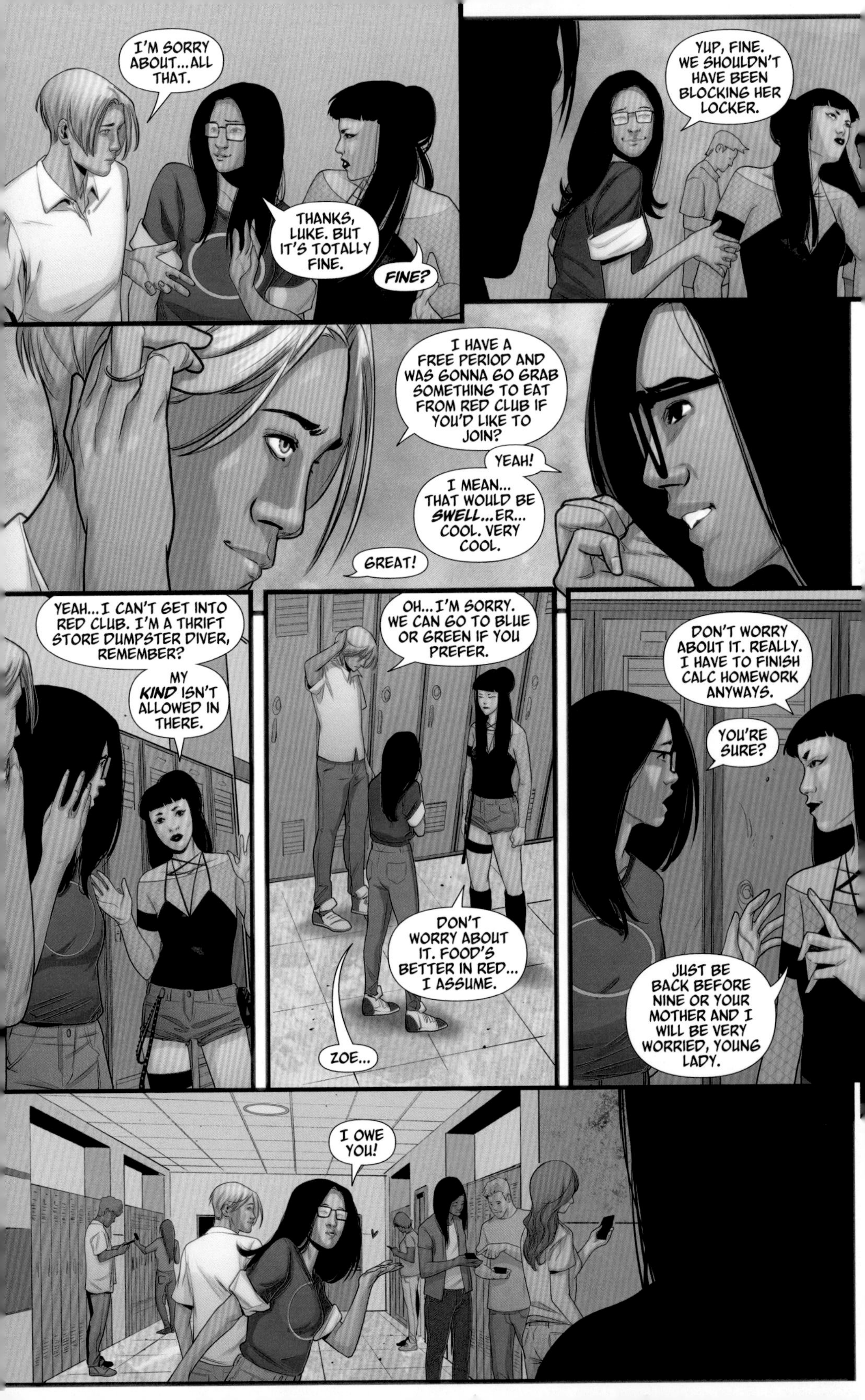
I'M SORRY ABOUT...ALL THAT.
THANKS, LUKE. BUT IT'S TOTALLY FINE.
FINE?
YUP, FINE. WE SHOULDN'T HAVE BEEN BLOCKING HER LOCKER.
I HAVE A FREE PERIOD AND WAS GONNA GO GRAB SOMETHING TO EAT FROM RED CLUB IF YOU'D LIKE TO JOIN?
YEAH!
I MEAN... THAT WOULD BE SWELL...ER... COOL. VERY COOL.
GREAT!
YEAH...I CAN'T GET INTO RED CLUB. I'M A THRIFT STORE DUMPSTER DIVER, REMEMBER?
MY KIND ISN'T ALLOWED IN THERE.
OH...I'M SORRY. WE CAN GO TO BLUE OR GREEN IF YOU PREFER.
DON'T WORRY ABOUT IT. FOOD'S BETTER IN RED... I ASSUME.
ZOE...
DON'T WORRY ABOUT IT. REALLY. I HAVE TO FINISH CALC HOMEWORK ANYWAYS.
YOU'RE SURE?
JUST BE BACK BEFORE NINE OR YOUR MOTHER AND I WILL BE VERY WORRIED, YOUNG LADY.
I OWE YOU!

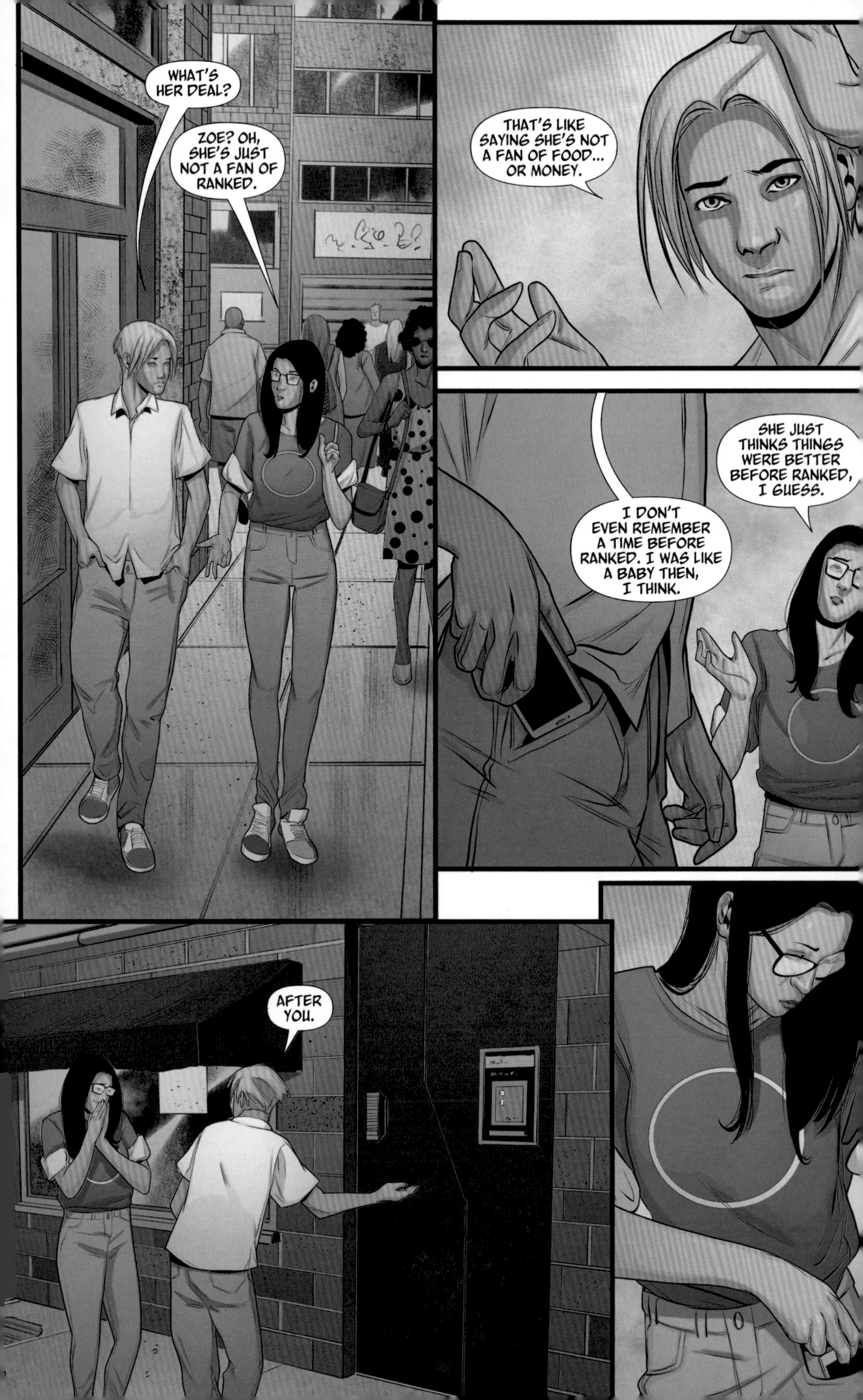
WHAT'S HER DEAL?
ZOE? OH, SHE'S JUST NOT A FAN OF RANKED.
THAT'S LIKE SAYING SHE'S NOT A FAN OF FOOD... OR MONEY.
SHE JUST THINKS THINGS WERE BETTER BEFORE RANKED, I GUESS.
I DON'T EVEN REMEMBER A TIME BEFORE RANKED. I WAS LIKE A BABY THEN, I THINK.
AFTER YOU.

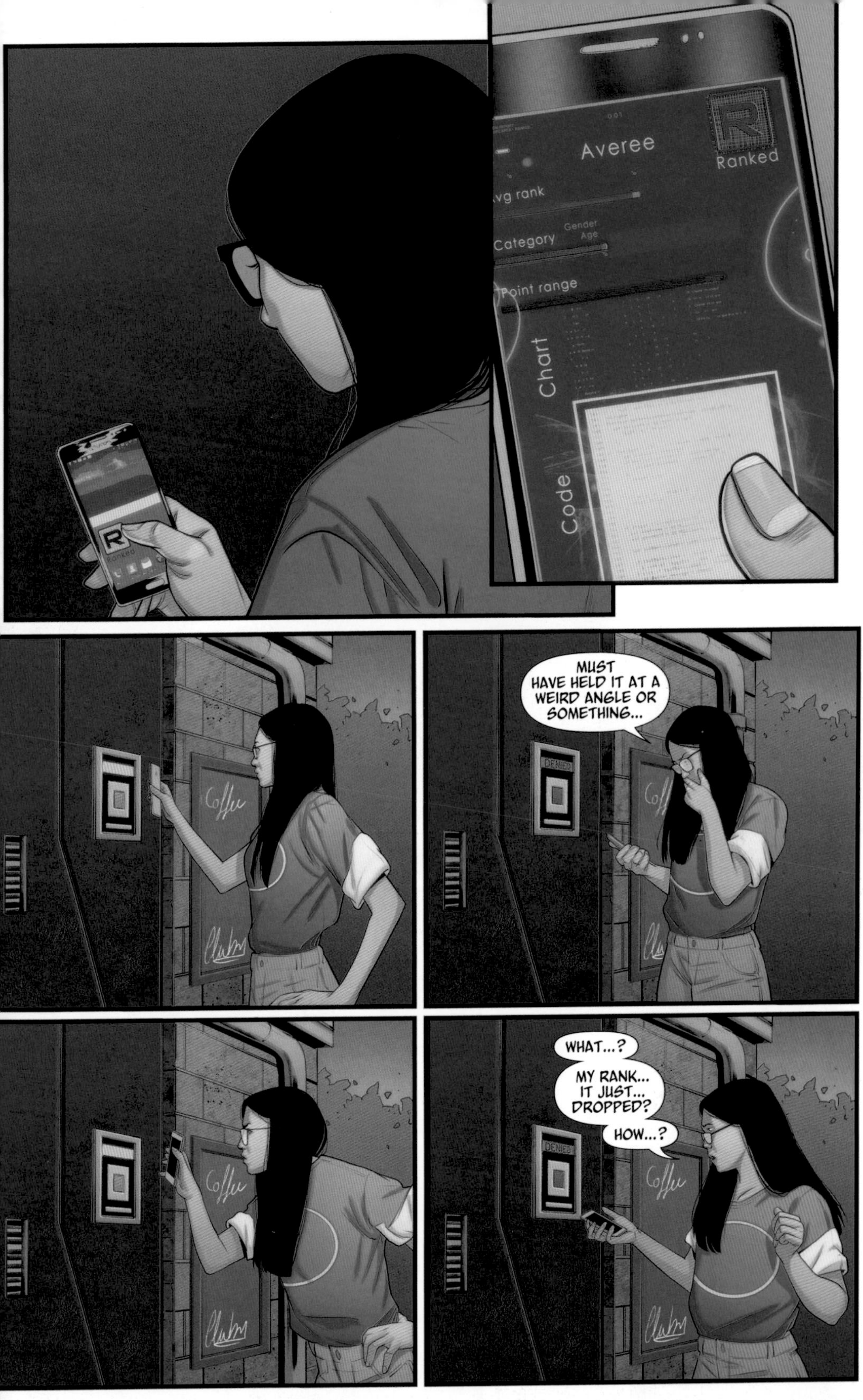

Averee
Ranked
Avg rank
Category
Gender
Age
Point range
Chart
Code
DENIED
MUST HAVE HELD IT AT A WEIRD ANGLE OR SOMETHING...
DENIED
WHAT...?
MY RANK... IT JUST... DROPPED?
HOW...?

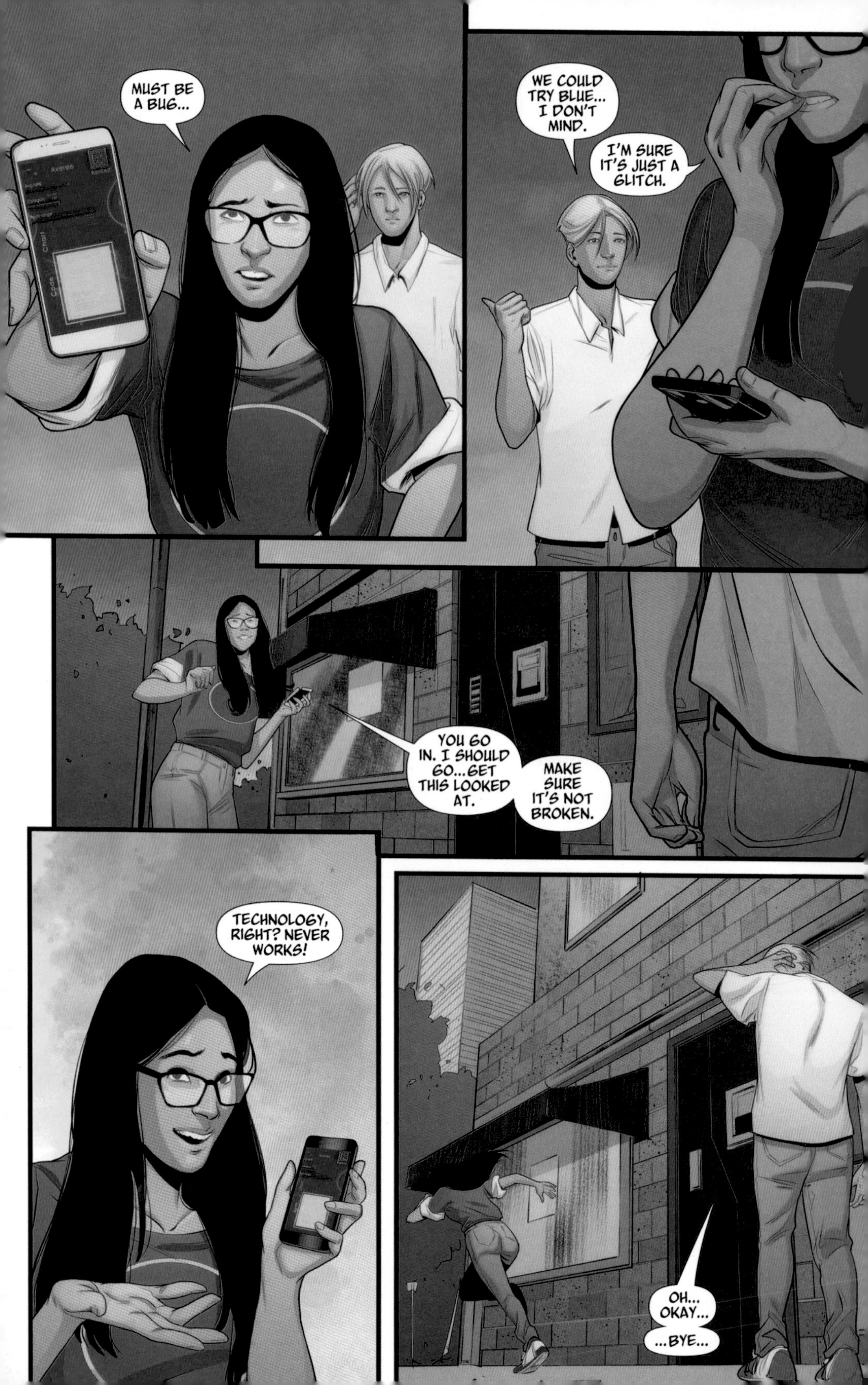
MUST BE A BUG...
WE COULD TRY BLUE... I DON'T MIND.
I'M SURE IT'S JUST A GLITCH.
YOU GO IN. I SHOULD GO...GET THIS LOOKED AT.
MAKE SURE IT'S NOT BROKEN.
TECHNOLOGY, RIGHT? NEVER WORKS!
OH... OKAY...
...BYE...

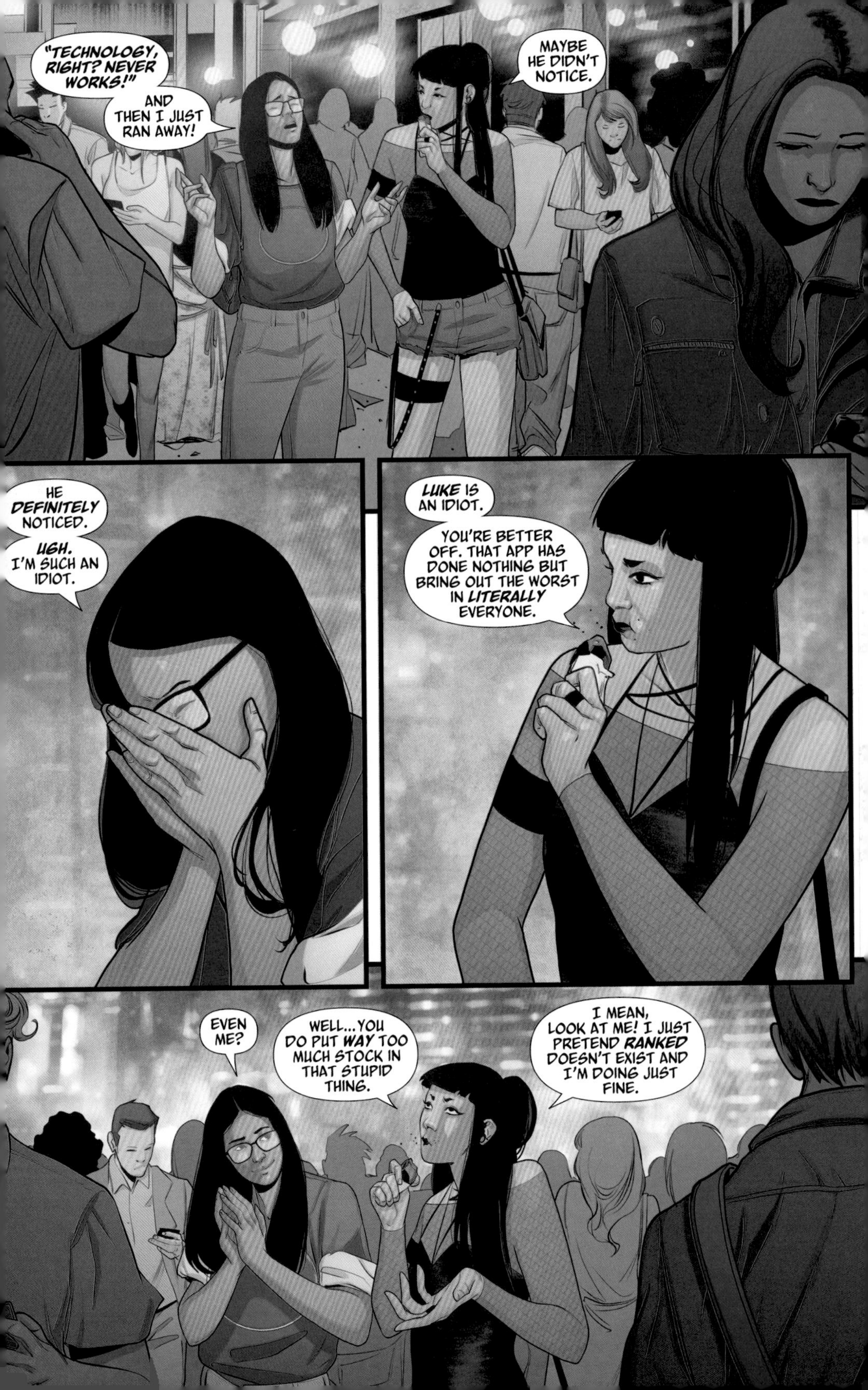
"TECHNOLOGY, RIGHT? NEVER WORKS!"
AND THEN I JUST RAN AWAY!
MAYBE HE DIDN'T NOTICE.
HE DEFINITELY NOTICED.
UGH. I'M SUCH AN IDIOT.
LUKE IS AN IDIOT.
YOU'RE BETTER OFF. THAT APP HAS DONE NOTHING BUT BRING OUT THE WORST IN LITERALLY EVERYONE.
EVEN ME?
WELL...YOU DO PUT WAY TOO MUCH STOCK IN THAT STUPID THING.
I MEAN, LOOK AT ME! I JUST PRETEND RANKED DOESN'T EXIST AND I'M DOING JUST FINE.

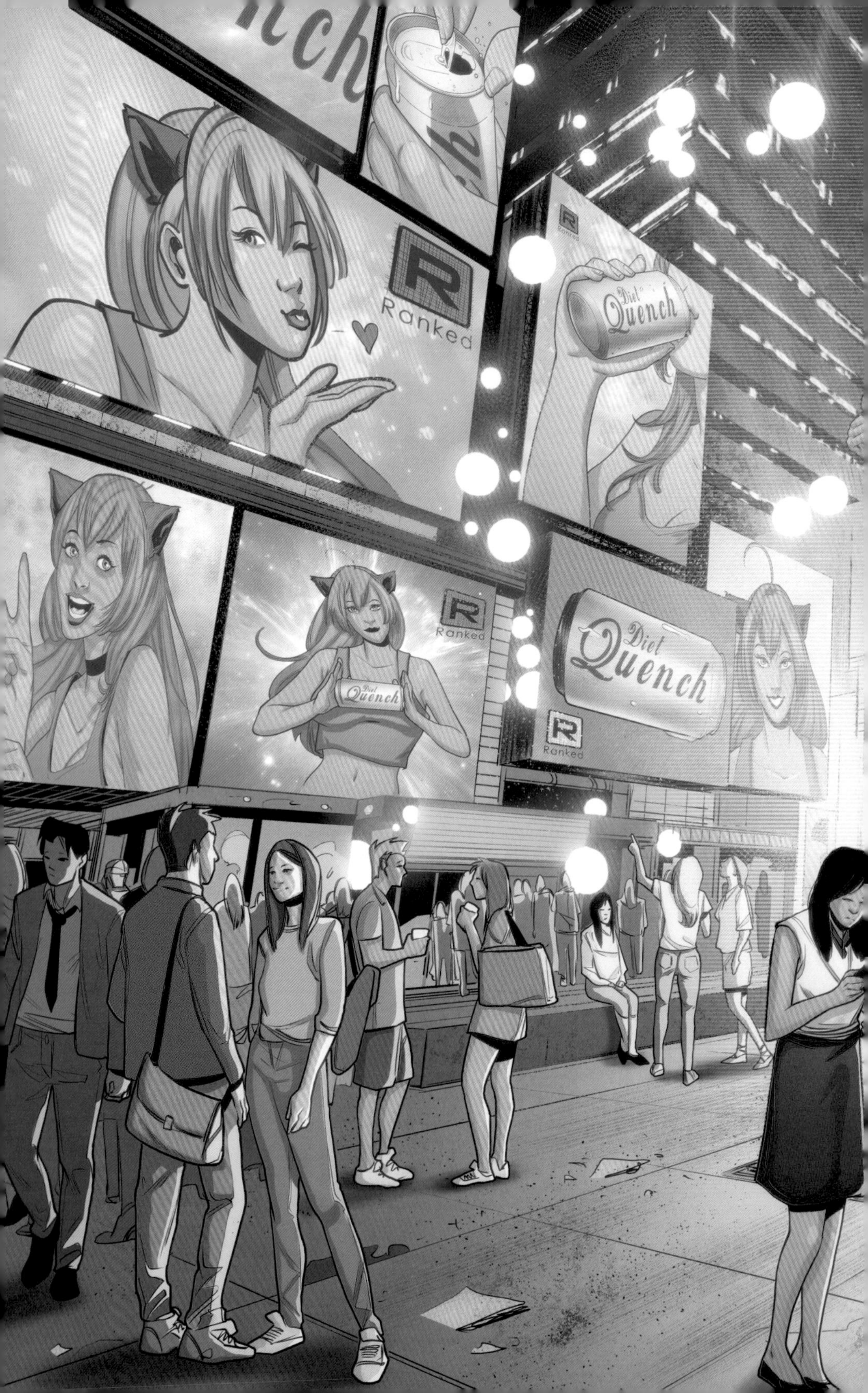
Ranked
Diet Quench
Ranked
Diet Quench
Diet Quench
Ranked

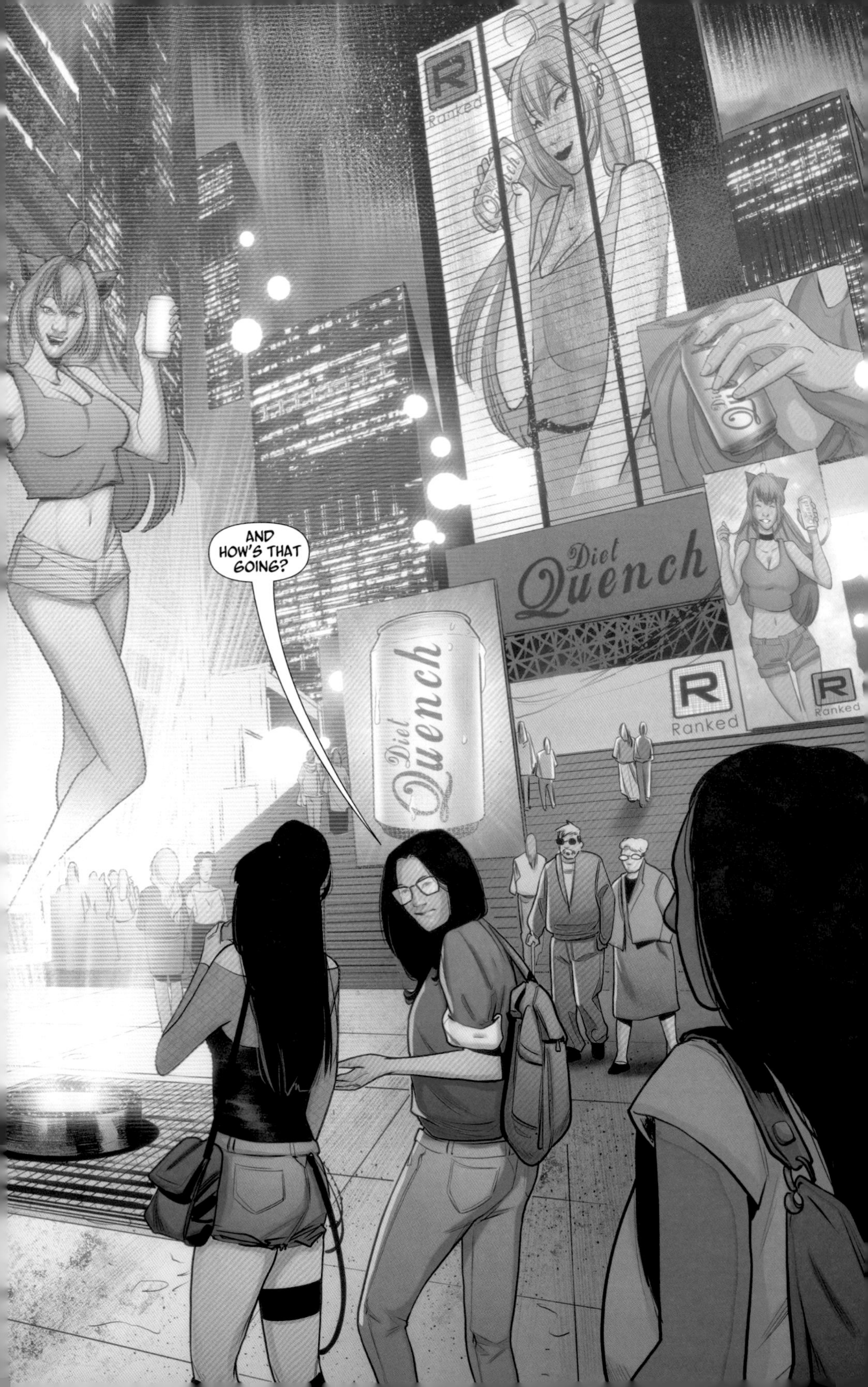
AND HOW'S THAT GOING?
R Ranked
Diet Quench
Diet Quench
R Ranked
R Ranked

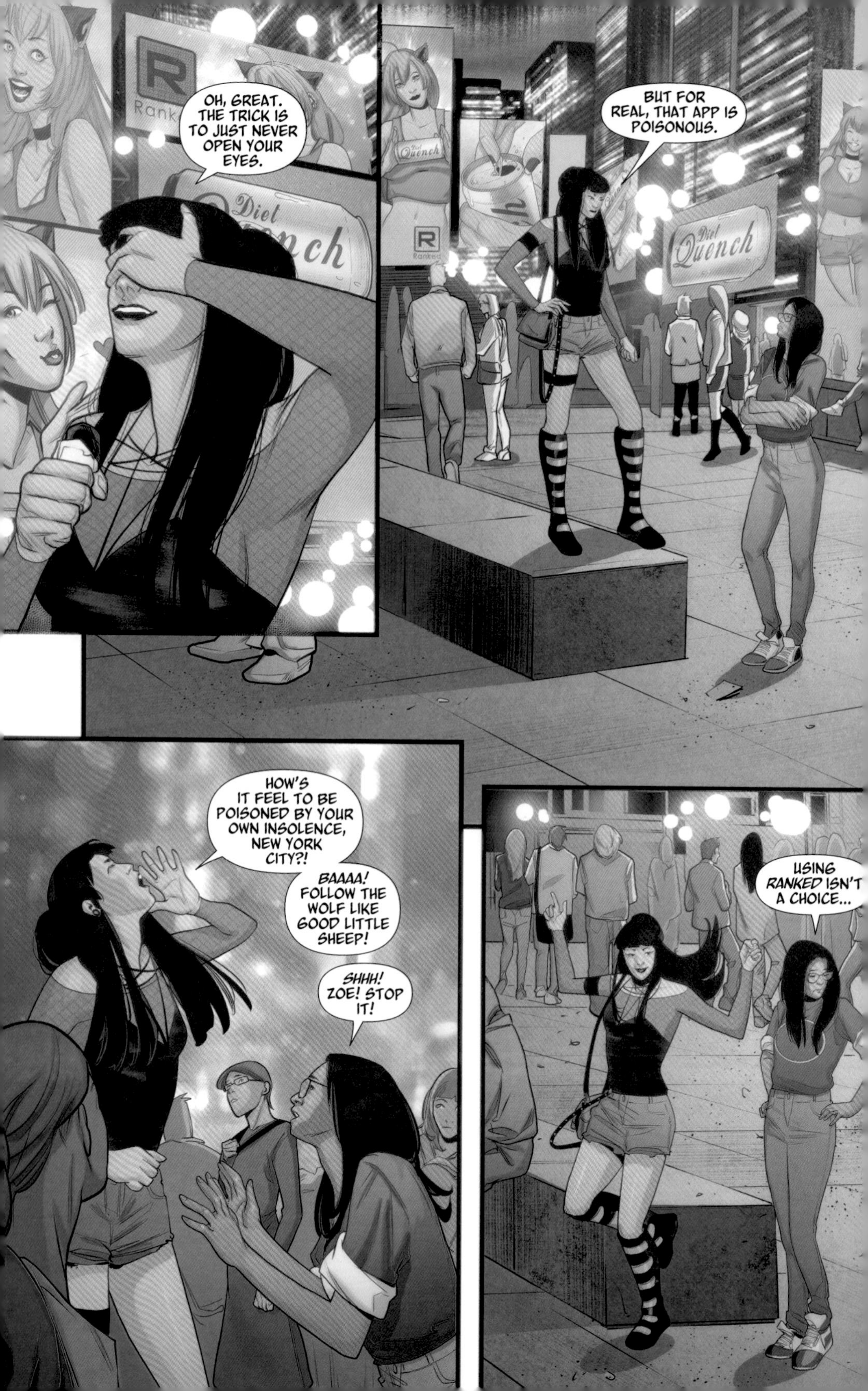
Ranked
Diet Quench
OH, GREAT. THE TRICK IS TO JUST NEVER OPEN YOUR EYES.
BUT FOR REAL, THAT APP IS POISONOUS.
HOW'S IT FEEL TO BE POISONED BY YOUR OWN INSOLENCE, NEW YORK CITY?!
BAAAA! FOLLOW THE WOLF LIKE GOOD LITTLE SHEEP!
SHHH! ZOE! STOP IT!
USING RANKED ISN'T A CHOICE...

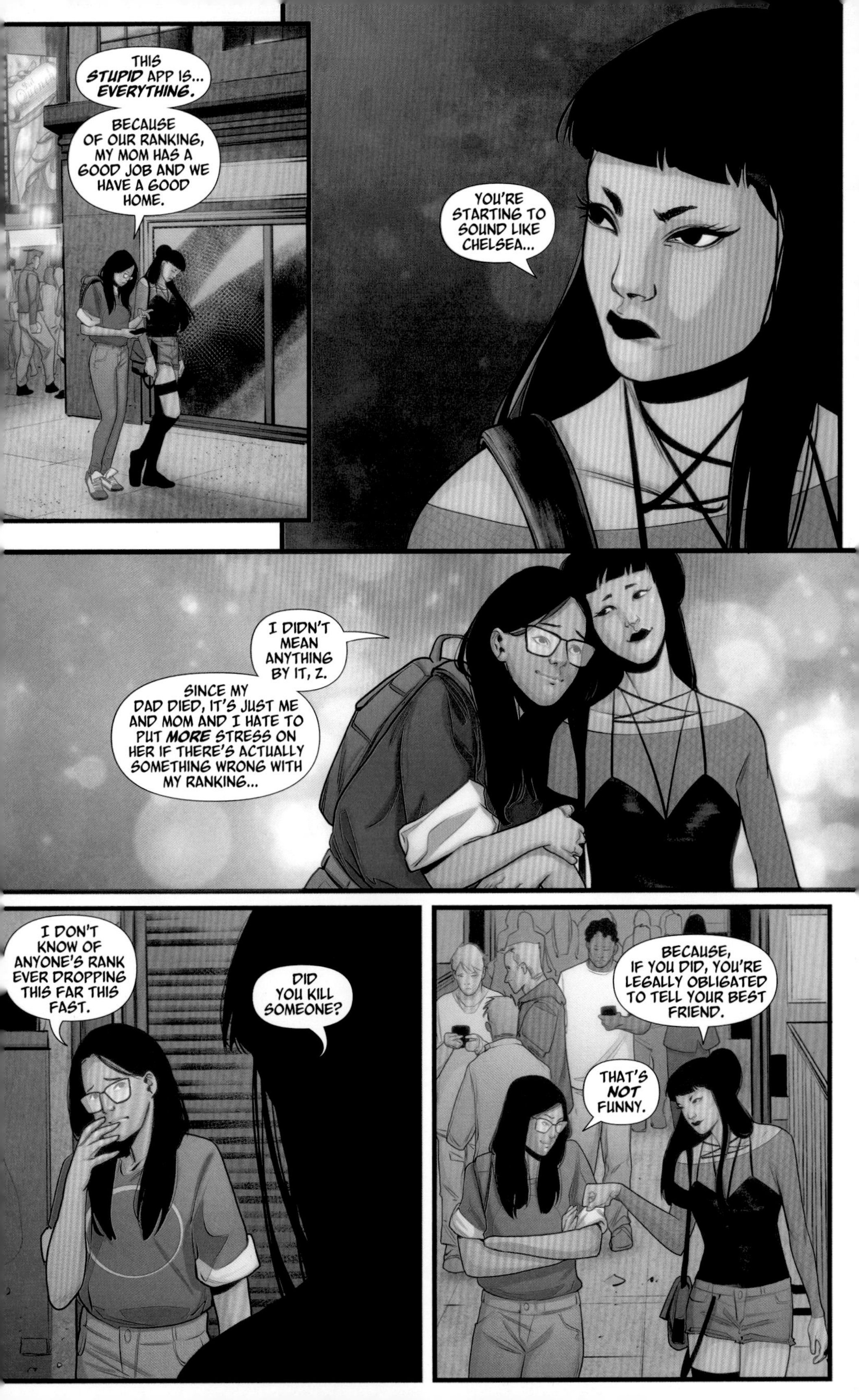
THIS STUPID APP IS... EVERYTHING.
BECAUSE OF OUR RANKING, MY MOM HAS A GOOD JOB AND WE HAVE A GOOD HOME.
YOU'RE STARTING TO SOUND LIKE CHELSEA...
I DIDN'T MEAN ANYTHING BY IT, Z.
SINCE MY DAD DIED, IT'S JUST ME AND MOM AND I HATE TO PUT MORE STRESS ON HER IF THERE'S ACTUALLY SOMETHING WRONG WITH MY RANKING...
I DON'T KNOW OF ANYONE'S RANK EVER DROPPING THIS FAR THIS FAST.
DID YOU KILL SOMEONE?
BECAUSE, IF YOU DID, YOU'RE LEGALLY OBLIGATED TO TELL YOUR BEST FRIEND.
THAT'S NOT FUNNY.

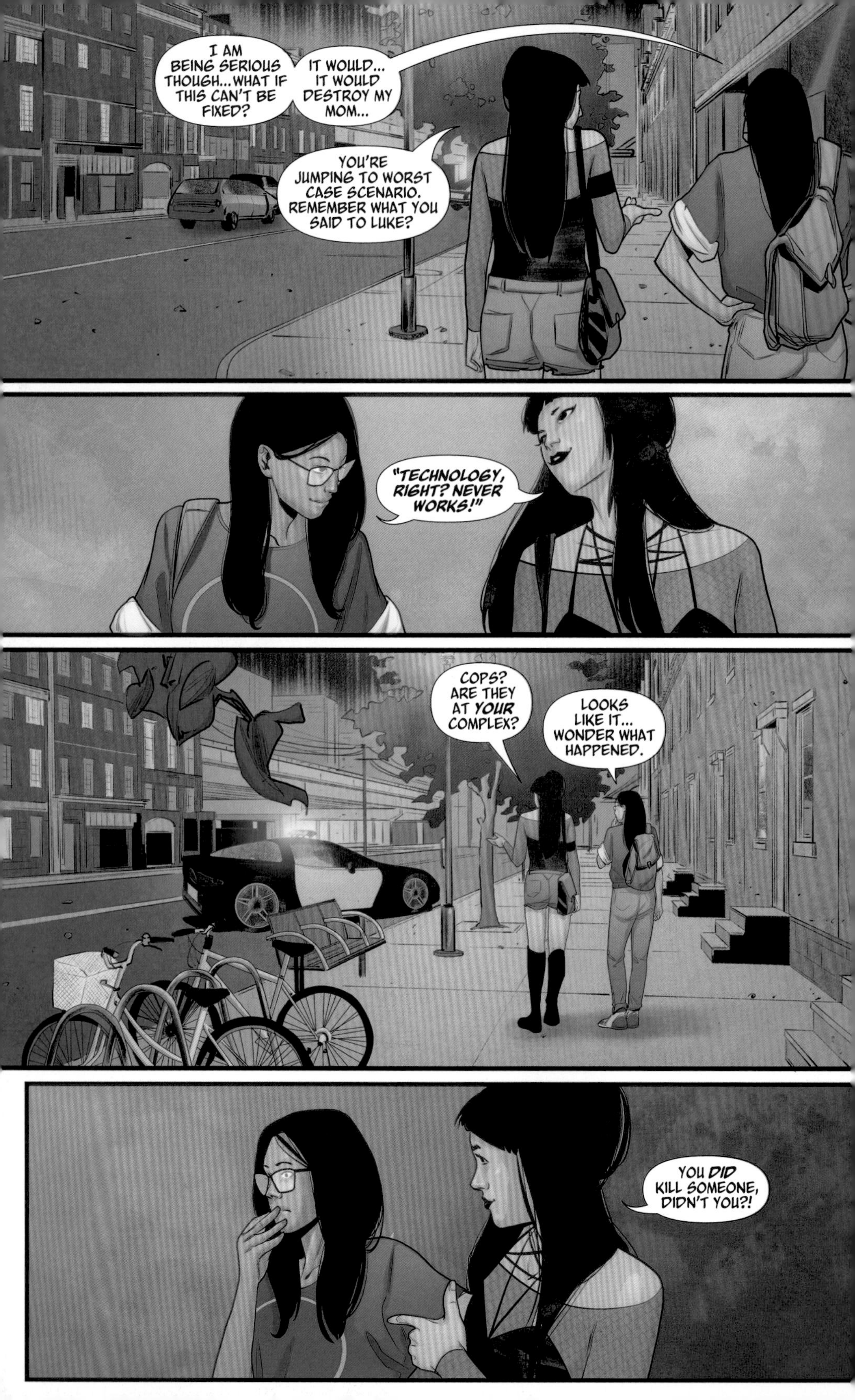
I AM BEING SERIOUS THOUGH...WHAT IF THIS CAN'T BE FIXED?
IT WOULD... IT WOULD DESTROY MY MOM...
YOU'RE JUMPING TO WORST CASE SCENARIO. REMEMBER WHAT YOU SAID TO LUKE?
"TECHNOLOGY, RIGHT? NEVER WORKS!"
COPS? ARE THEY AT YOUR COMPLEX?
LOOKS LIKE IT... WONDER WHAT HAPPENED.
YOU DID KILL SOMEONE, DIDN'T YOU?!

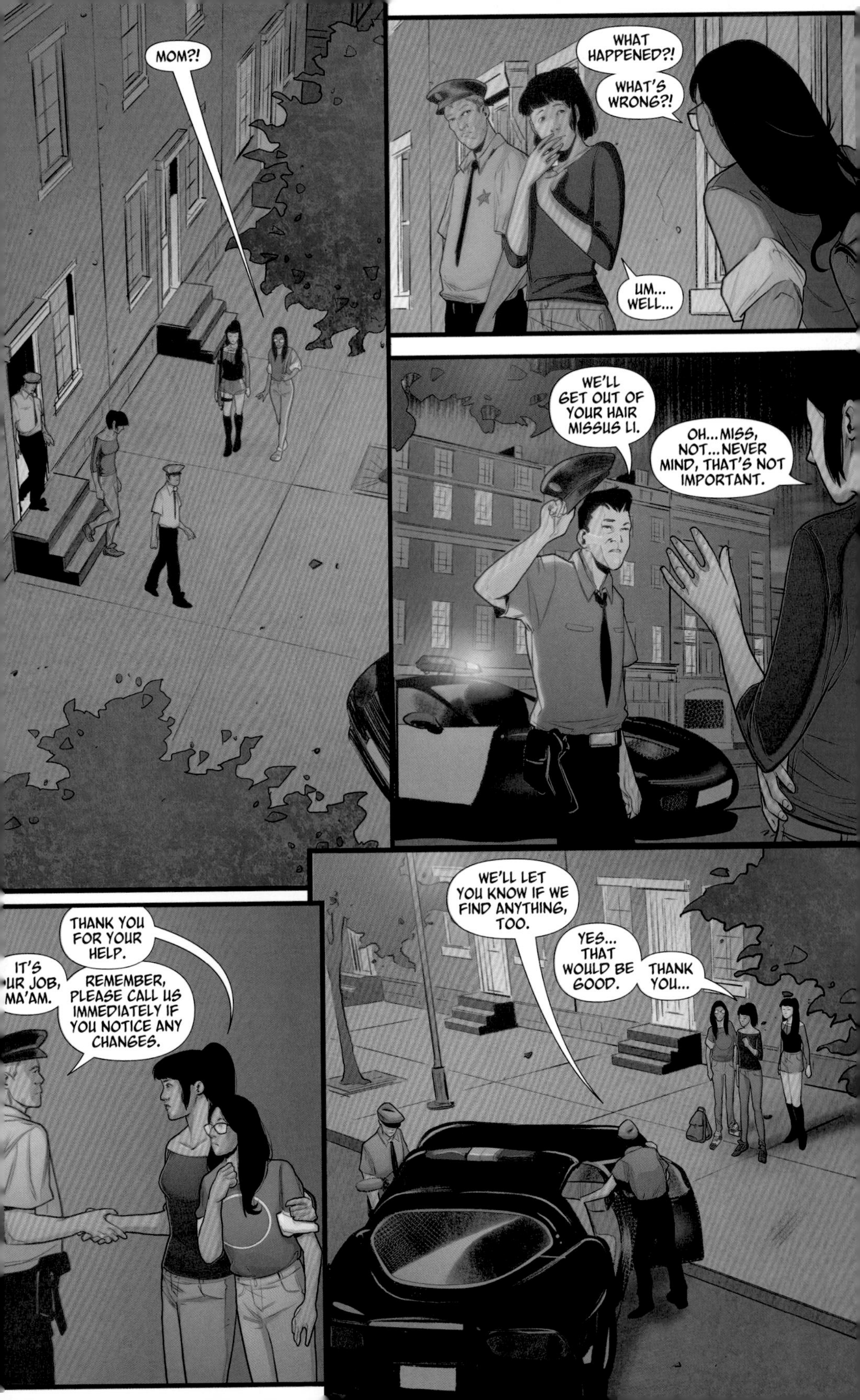
MOM?!
WHAT HAPPENED?!
WHAT'S WRONG?!
UM... WELL...
WE'LL GET OUT OF YOUR HAIR MISSUS LI.
OH...MISS, NOT...NEVER MIND, THAT'S NOT IMPORTANT.
THANK YOU FOR YOUR HELP.
IT'S UR JOB, MA'AM.
REMEMBER, PLEASE CALL US IMMEDIATELY IF YOU NOTICE ANY CHANGES.
WE'LL LET YOU KNOW IF WE FIND ANYTHING, TOO.
YES... THAT WOULD BE GOOD.
THANK YOU...

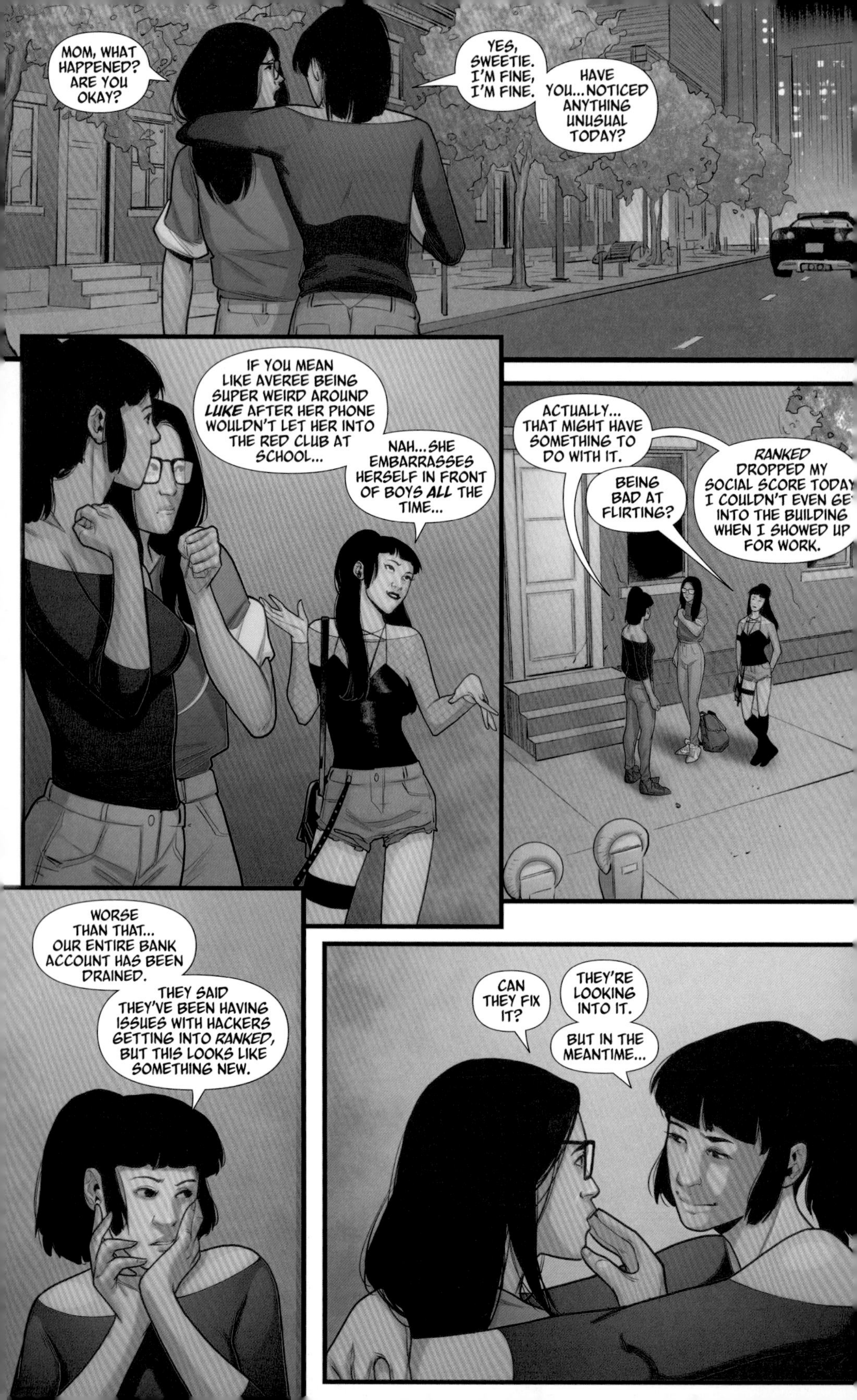
MOM, WHAT HAPPENED? ARE YOU OKAY?
YES, SWEETIE. I'M FINE, I'M FINE.
HAVE YOU...NOTICED ANYTHING UNUSUAL TODAY?
IF YOU MEAN LIKE AVEREE BEING SUPER WEIRD AROUND LUKE AFTER HER PHONE WOULDN'T LET HER INTO THE RED CLUB AT SCHOOL...
NAH...SHE EMBARRASSES HERSELF IN FRONT OF BOYS ALL THE TIME...
ACTUALLY... THAT MIGHT HAVE SOMETHING TO DO WITH IT.
BEING BAD AT FLIRTING?
RANKED DROPPED MY SOCIAL SCORE TODAY. I COULDN'T EVEN GET INTO THE BUILDING WHEN I SHOWED UP FOR WORK.
WORSE THAN THAT... OUR ENTIRE BANK ACCOUNT HAS BEEN DRAINED.
THEY SAID THEY'VE BEEN HAVING ISSUES WITH HACKERS GETTING INTO RANKED, BUT THIS LOOKS LIKE SOMETHING NEW.
CAN THEY FIX IT?
THEY'RE LOOKING INTO IT.
BUT IN THE MEANTIME...

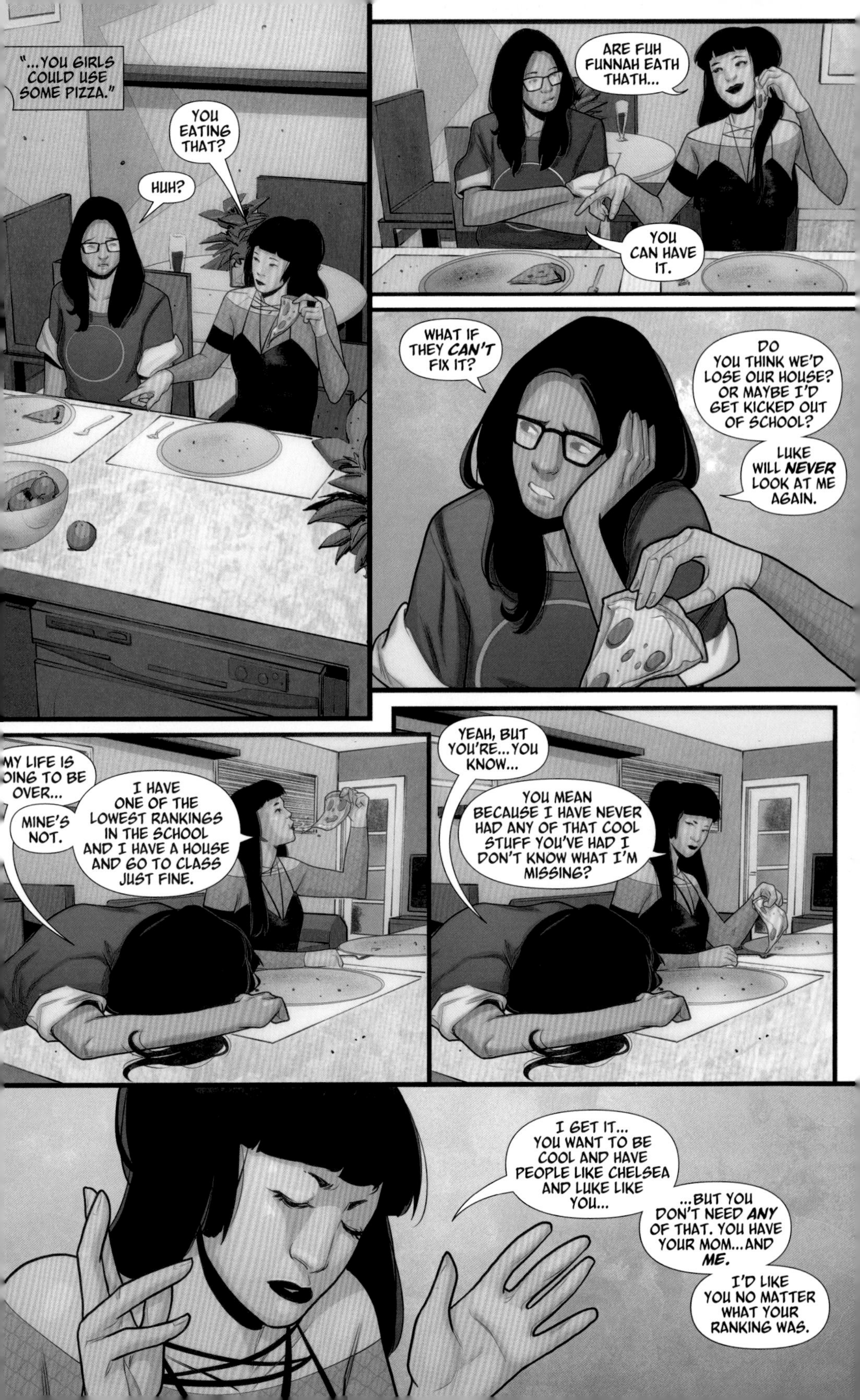
"...YOU GIRLS COULD USE SOME PIZZA."
YOU EATING THAT?
HUH?
ARE FUH FUNNAH EATH THATH...
YOU CAN HAVE IT.
WHAT IF THEY CAN'T FIX IT?
DO YOU THINK WE'D LOSE OUR HOUSE? OR MAYBE I'D GET KICKED OUT OF SCHOOL?
LUKE WILL NEVER LOOK AT ME AGAIN.
MY LIFE IS OING TO BE OVER...
MINE'S NOT.
I HAVE ONE OF THE LOWEST RANKINGS IN THE SCHOOL AND I HAVE A HOUSE AND GO TO CLASS JUST FINE.
YEAH, BUT YOU'RE...YOU KNOW...
YOU MEAN BECAUSE I HAVE NEVER HAD ANY OF THAT COOL STUFF YOU'VE HAD I DON'T KNOW WHAT I'M MISSING?
I GET IT... YOU WANT TO BE COOL AND HAVE PEOPLE LIKE CHELSEA AND LUKE LIKE YOU...
...BUT YOU DON'T NEED ANY OF THAT. YOU HAVE YOUR MOM...AND ME.
I'D LIKE YOU NO MATTER WHAT YOUR RANKING WAS.

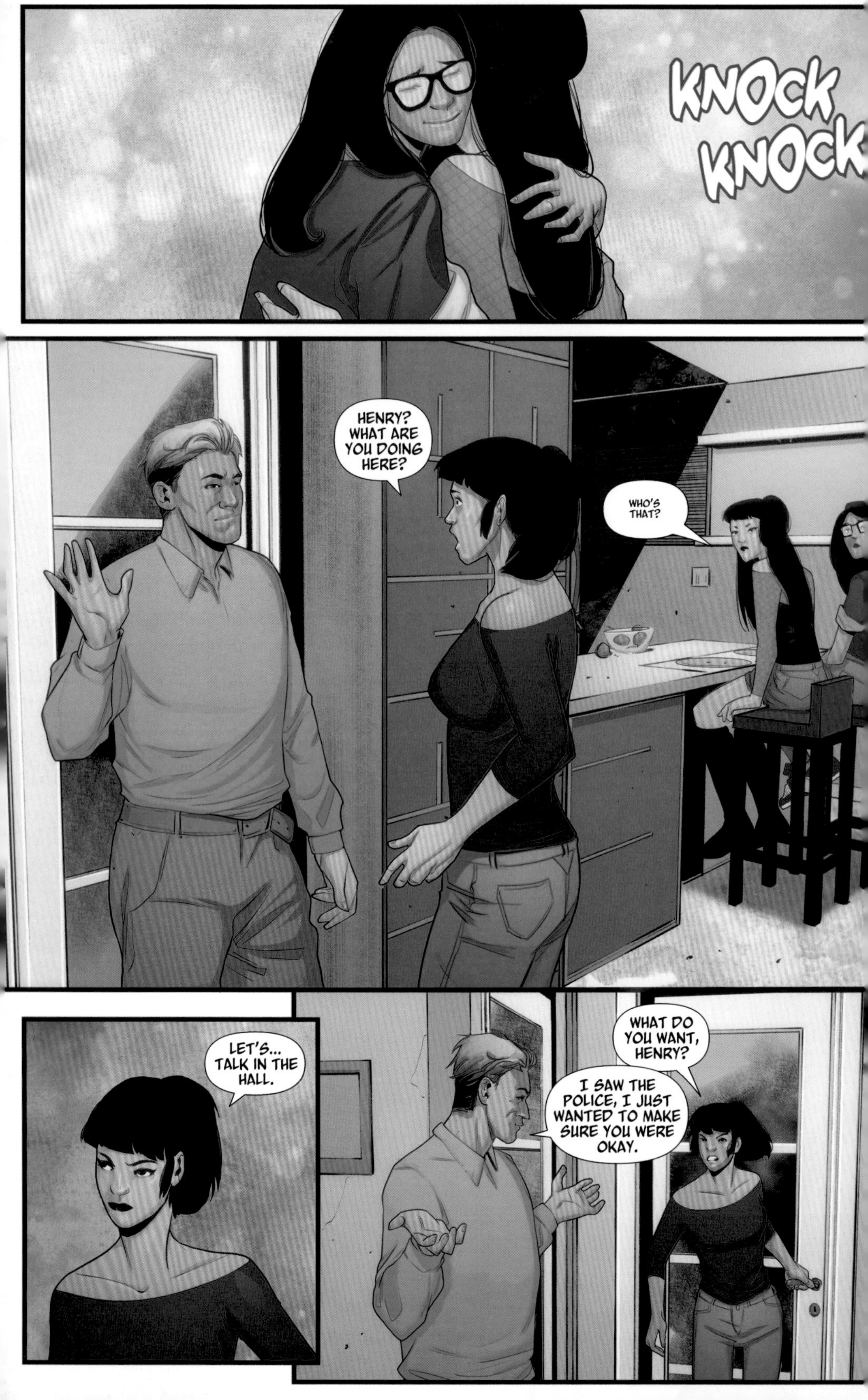
KNOCK
KNOCK
HENRY? WHAT ARE YOU DOING HERE?
WHO'S THAT?
WHAT DO YOU WANT, HENRY?
I SAW THE POLICE, I JUST WANTED TO MAKE SURE YOU WERE OKAY.
LET'S... TALK IN THE HALL.

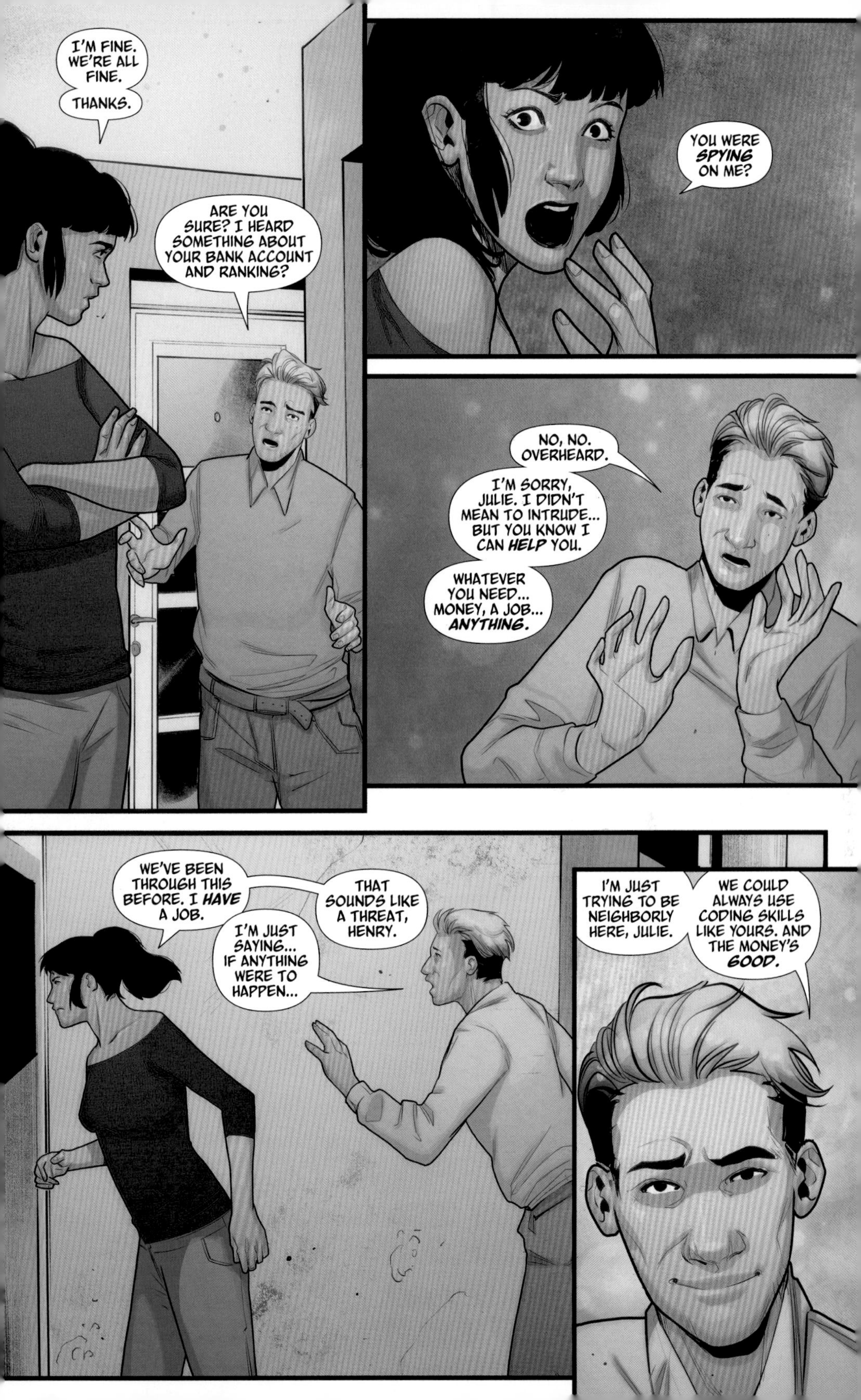
I'M FINE. WE'RE ALL FINE.
THANKS.
ARE YOU SURE? I HEARD SOMETHING ABOUT YOUR BANK ACCOUNT AND RANKING?
YOU WERE *SPYING* ON ME?
NO, NO. OVERHEARD.
I'M SORRY, JULIE. I DIDN'T MEAN TO INTRUDE... BUT YOU KNOW I CAN *HELP* YOU.
WHATEVER YOU NEED... MONEY, A JOB... *ANYTHING*.
WE'VE BEEN THROUGH THIS BEFORE. I *HAVE* A JOB.
I'M JUST SAYING... IF ANYTHING WERE TO HAPPEN...
THAT SOUNDS LIKE A THREAT, HENRY.
I'M JUST TRYING TO BE NEIGHBORLY HERE, JULIE.
WE COULD ALWAYS USE CODING SKILLS LIKE YOURS. AND THE MONEY'S *GOOD*.

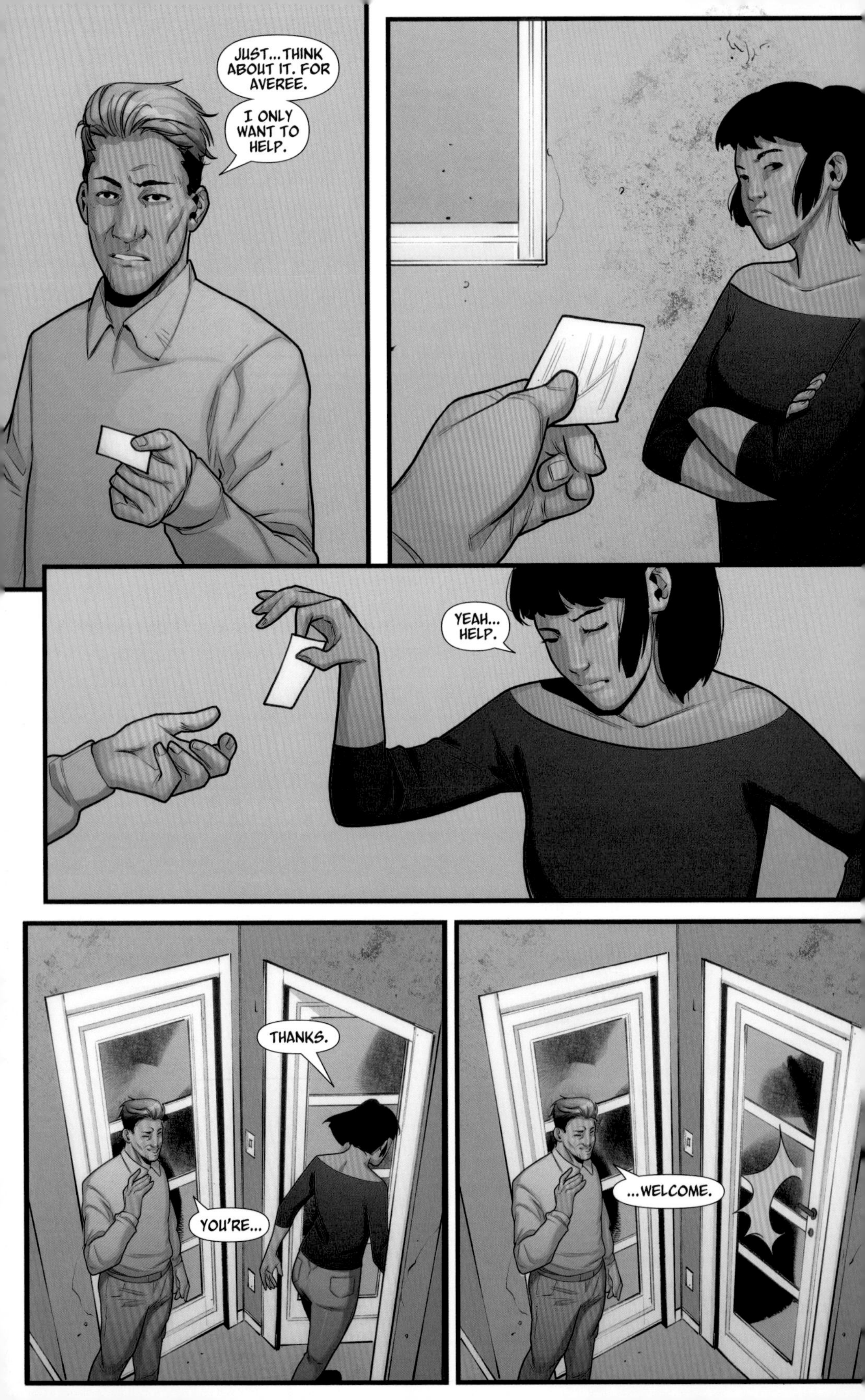
JUST...THINK ABOUT IT. FOR AVEREE.
I ONLY WANT TO HELP.
YEAH... HELP.
THANKS.
YOU'RE...
...WELCOME.

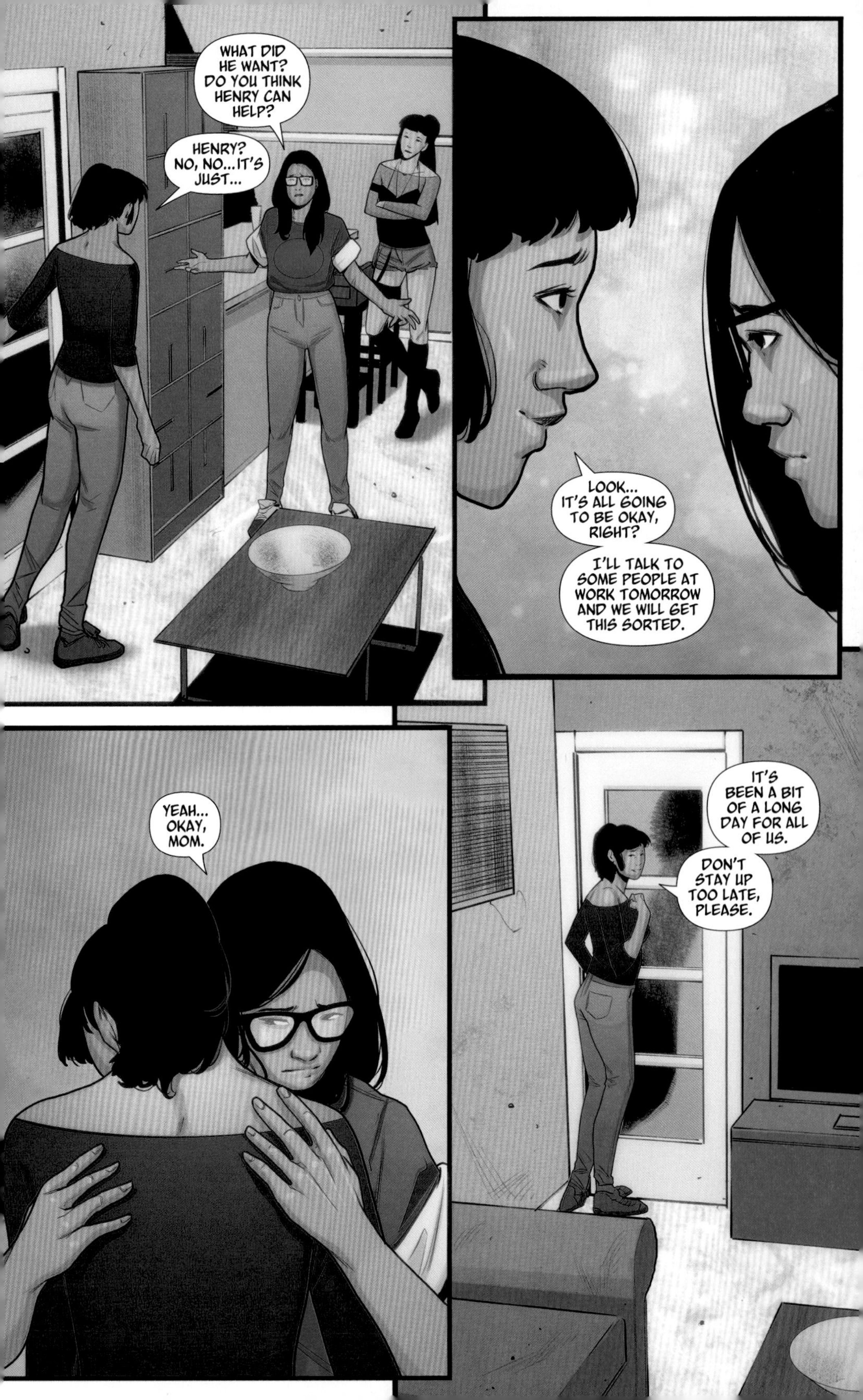
WHAT DID HE WANT? DO YOU THINK HENRY CAN HELP?
HENRY? NO, NO...IT'S JUST...
LOOK... IT'S ALL GOING TO BE OKAY, RIGHT?
I'LL TALK TO SOME PEOPLE AT WORK TOMORROW AND WE WILL GET THIS SORTED.
YEAH... OKAY, MOM.
IT'S BEEN A BIT OF A LONG DAY FOR ALL OF US.
DON'T STAY UP TOO LATE, PLEASE.

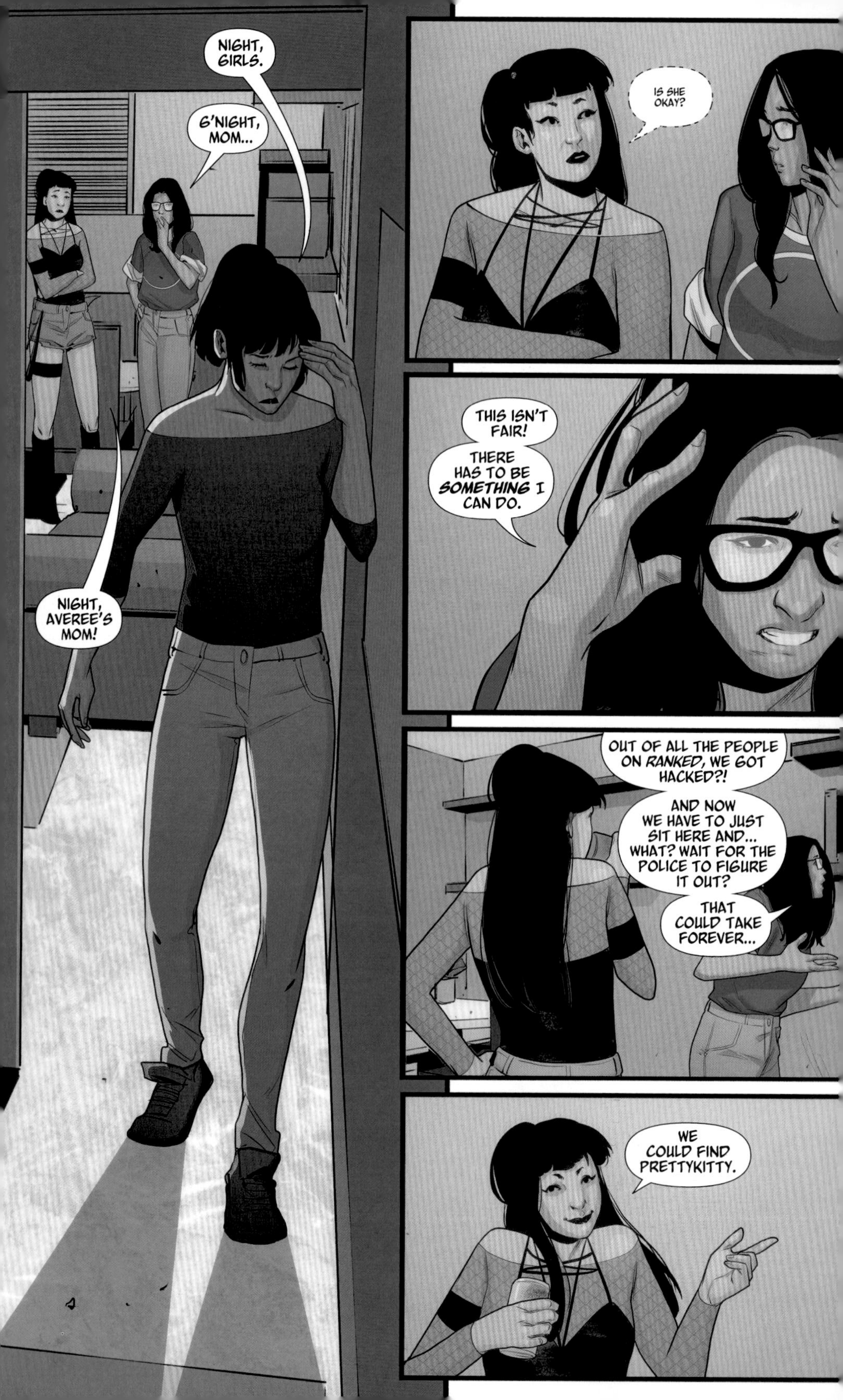
NIGHT, GIRLS.
G'NIGHT, MOM...
NIGHT, AVEREE'S MOM!
IS SHE OKAY?
THIS ISN'T FAIR!
THERE HAS TO BE SOMETHING I CAN DO.
OUT OF ALL THE PEOPLE ON RANKED, WE GOT HACKED?!
AND NOW WE HAVE TO JUST SIT HERE AND... WHAT? WAIT FOR THE POLICE TO FIGURE IT OUT?
THAT COULD TAKE FOREVER...
WE COULD FIND PRETTYKITTY.

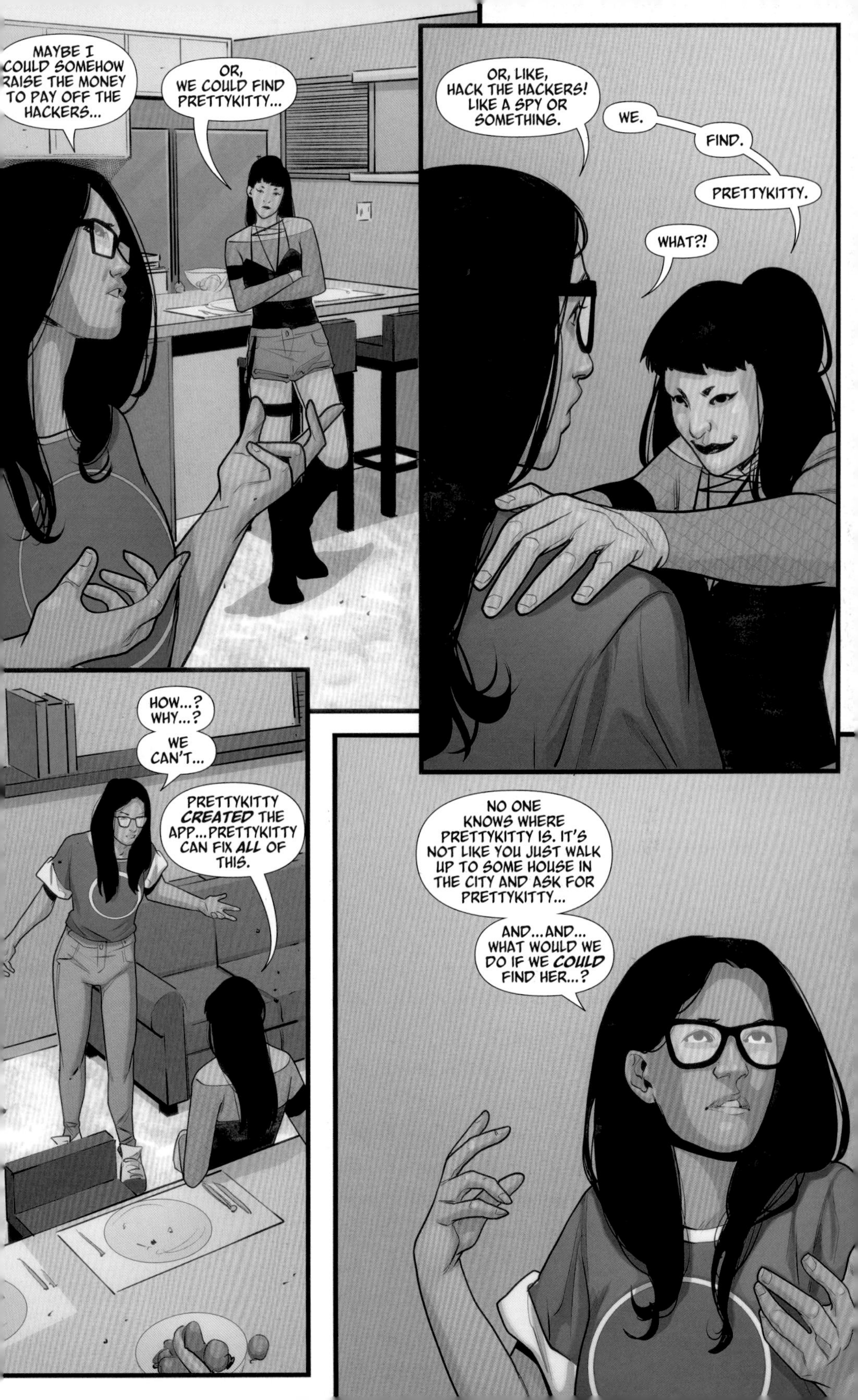

MAYBE I COULD SOMEHOW RAISE THE MONEY TO PAY OFF THE HACKERS...
OR, WE COULD FIND PRETTYKITTY...
OR, LIKE, HACK THE HACKERS! LIKE A SPY OR SOMETHING.
WE.
FIND.
PRETTYKITTY.
WHAT?!
HOW...? WHY...?
WE CAN'T...
PRETTYKITTY *CREATED* THE APP...PRETTYKITTY CAN FIX *ALL* OF THIS.
NO ONE KNOWS WHERE PRETTYKITTY IS. IT'S NOT LIKE YOU JUST WALK UP TO SOME HOUSE IN THE CITY AND ASK FOR PRETTYKITTY...
AND...AND... WHAT WOULD WE DO IF WE *COULD* FIND HER...?

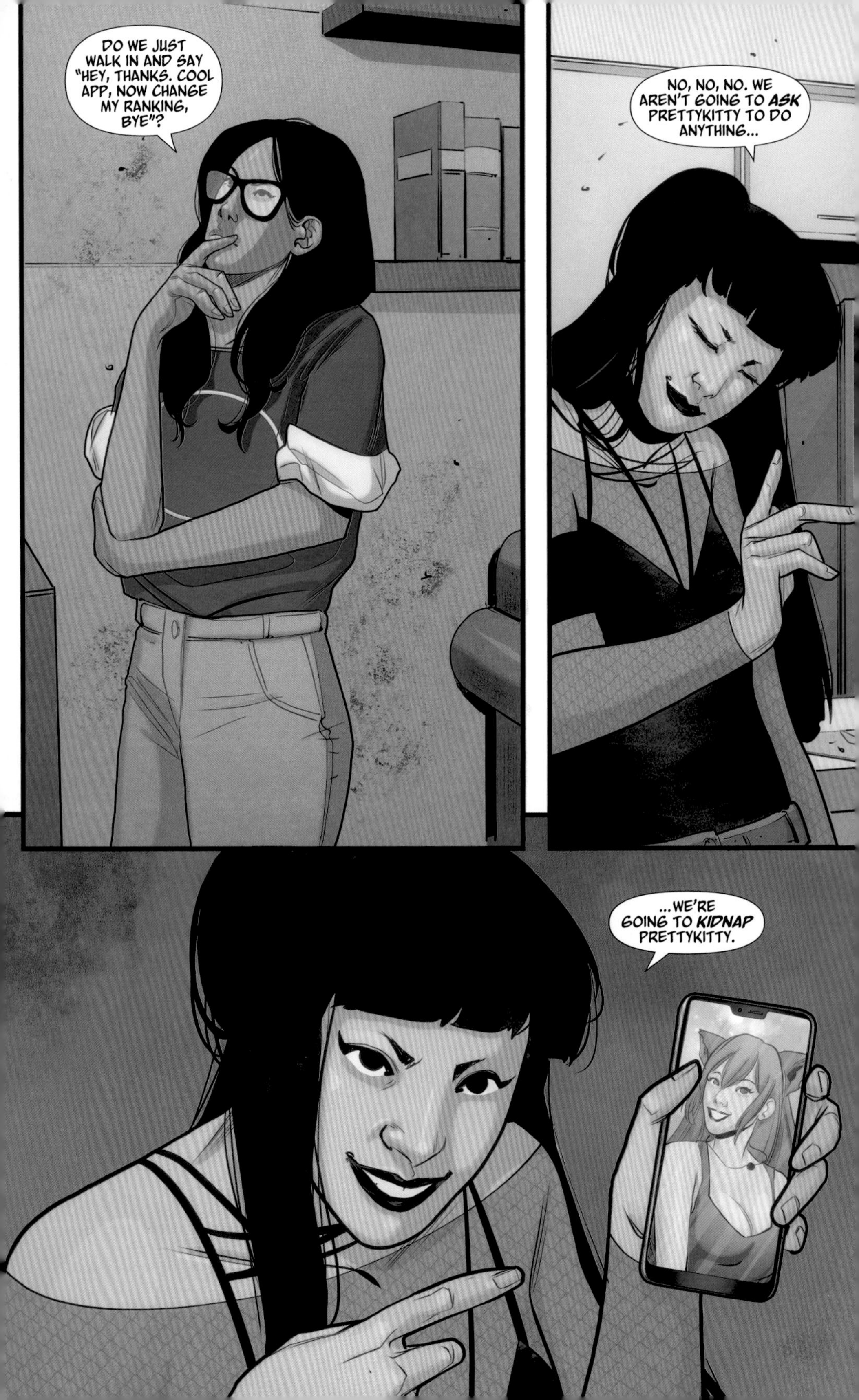
DO WE JUST WALK IN AND SAY "HEY, THANKS. COOL APP, NOW CHANGE MY RANKING, BYE"?
NO, NO, NO. WE AREN'T GOING TO ASK PRETTYKITTY TO DO ANYTHING...
...WE'RE GOING TO KIDNAP PRETTYKITTY.

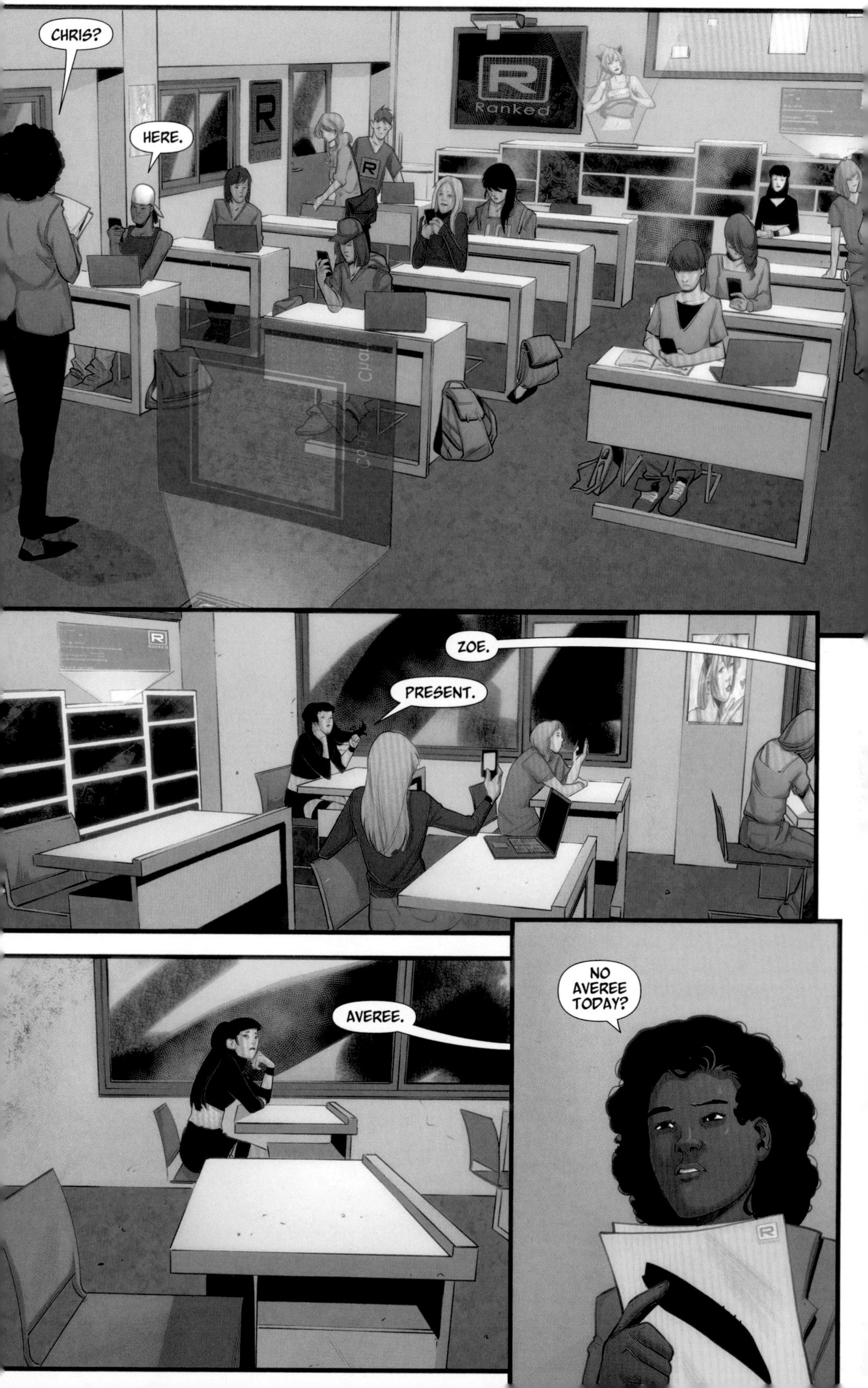

CHRIS?
HERE.
ZOE.
PRESENT.
AVEREE.
NO AVEREE TODAY?

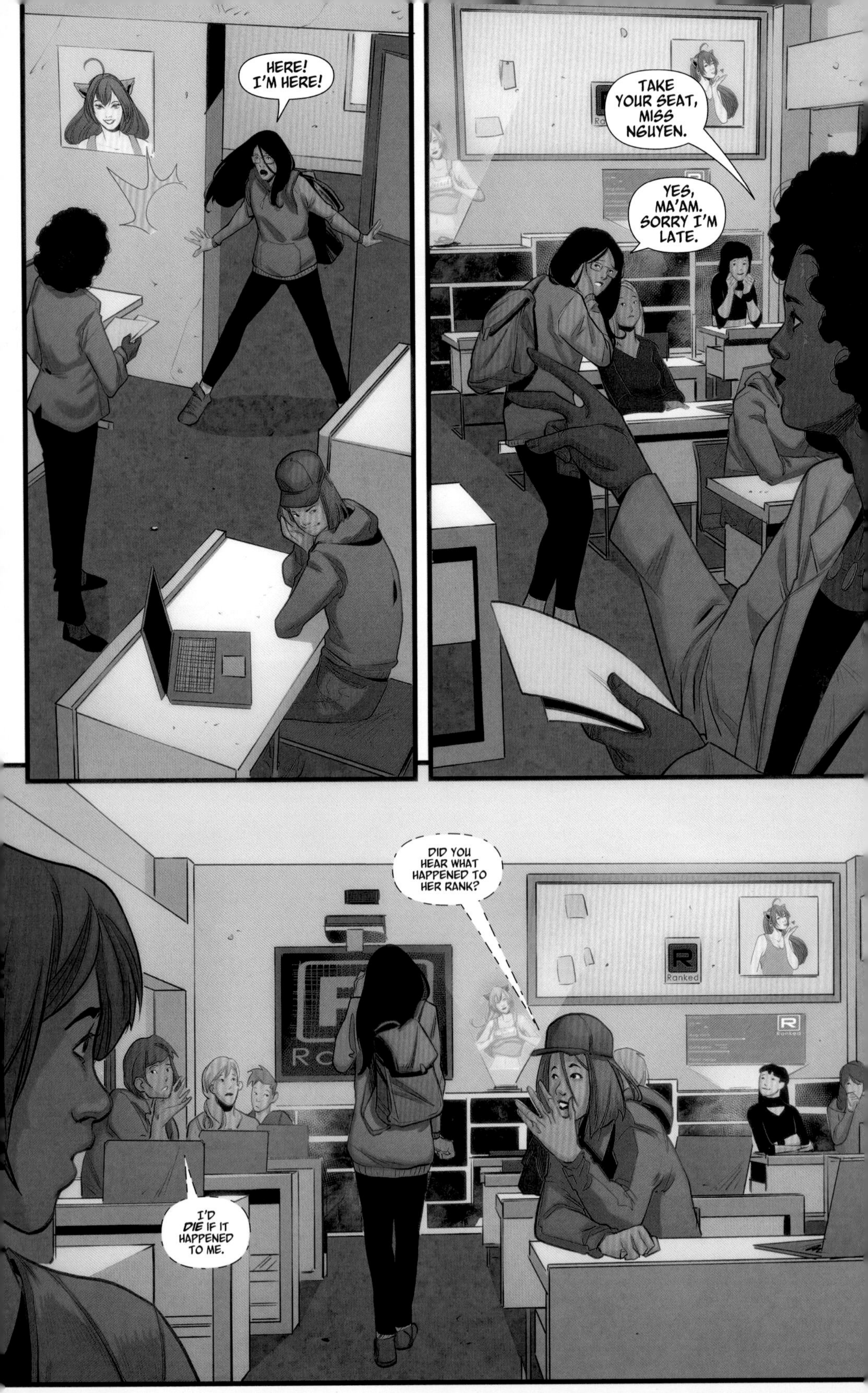
HERE! I'M HERE!
TAKE YOUR SEAT, MISS NGUYEN.
YES, MA'AM. SORRY I'M LATE.
DID YOU HEAR WHAT HAPPENED TO HER RANK?
Ranked
I'D DIE IF IT HAPPENED TO ME.

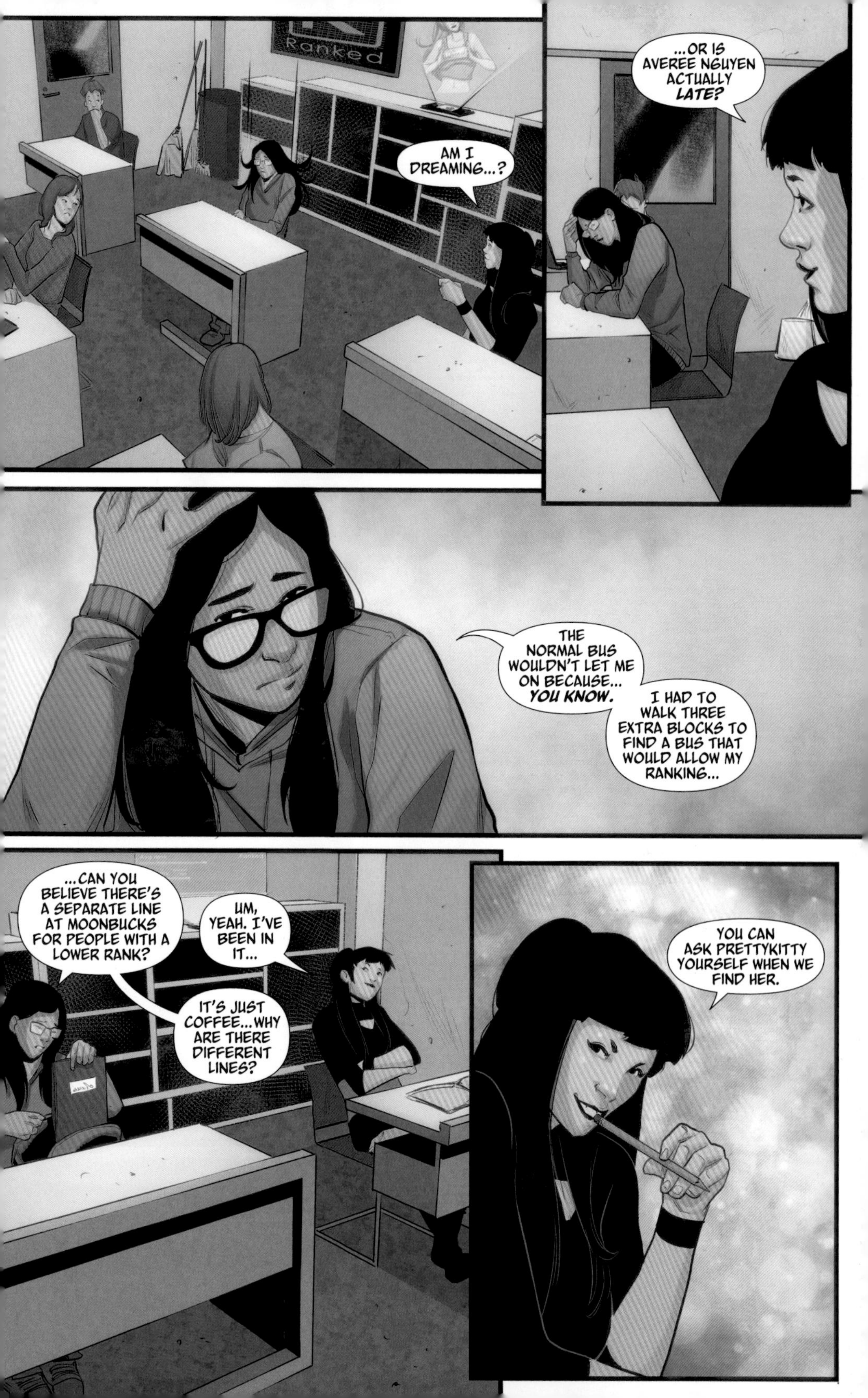

Ranked
AM I DREAMING...?
...OR IS AVEREE NGUYEN ACTUALLY LATE?
THE NORMAL BUS WOULDN'T LET ME ON BECAUSE... YOU KNOW.
I HAD TO WALK THREE EXTRA BLOCKS TO FIND A BUS THAT WOULD ALLOW MY RANKING...
...CAN YOU BELIEVE THERE'S A SEPARATE LINE AT MOONBUCKS FOR PEOPLE WITH A LOWER RANK?
UM, YEAH. I'VE BEEN IN IT...
IT'S JUST COFFEE...WHY ARE THERE DIFFERENT LINES?
YOU CAN ASK PRETTYKITTY YOURSELF WHEN WE FIND HER.

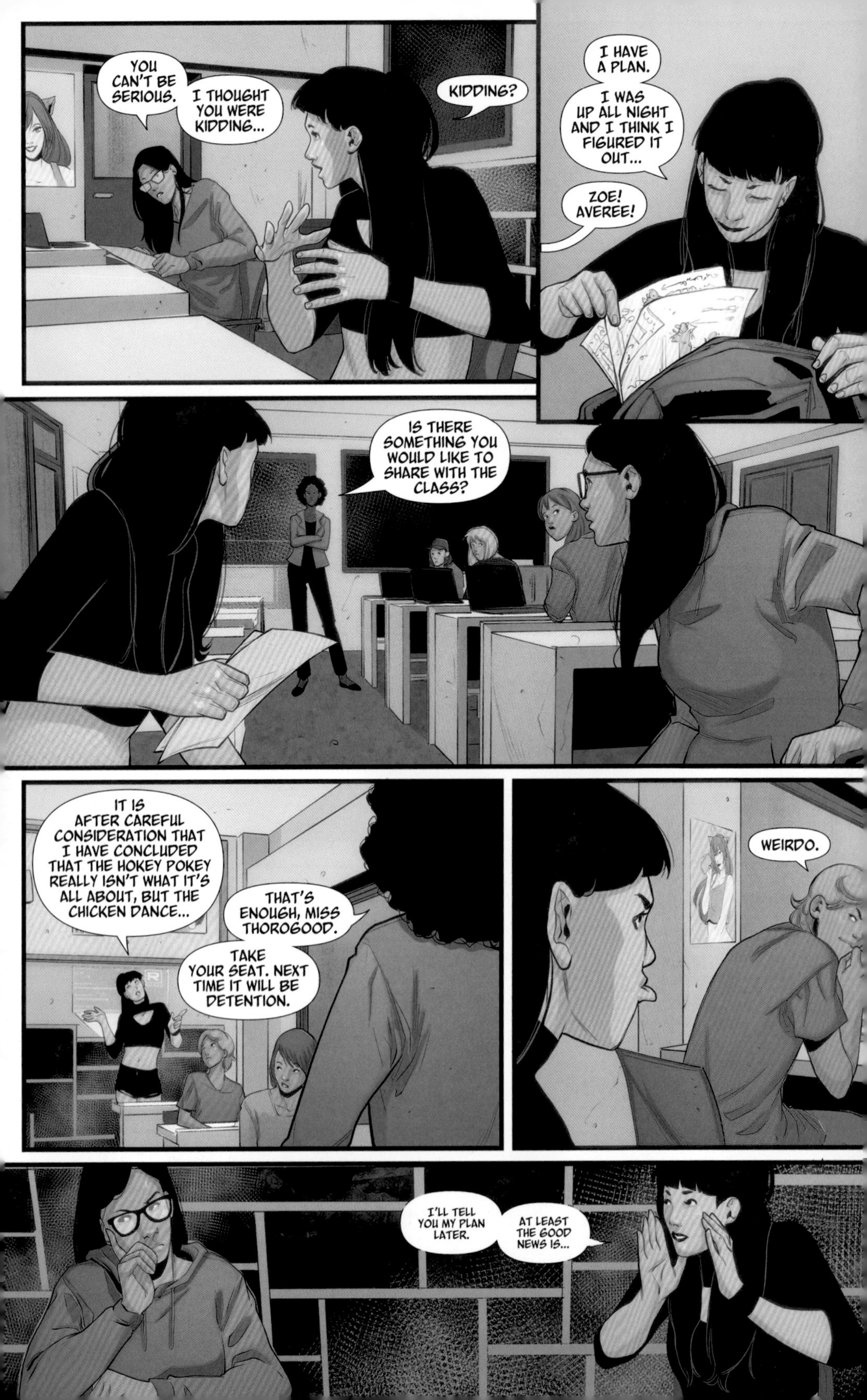
YOU CAN'T BE SERIOUS.
I THOUGHT YOU WERE KIDDING...
KIDDING?
I HAVE A PLAN.
I WAS UP ALL NIGHT AND I THINK I FIGURED IT OUT...
ZOE! AVEREE!
IS THERE SOMETHING YOU WOULD LIKE TO SHARE WITH THE CLASS?
IT IS AFTER CAREFUL CONSIDERATION THAT I HAVE CONCLUDED THAT THE HOKEY POKEY REALLY ISN'T WHAT IT'S ALL ABOUT, BUT THE CHICKEN DANCE...
THAT'S ENOUGH, MISS THOROGOOD.
TAKE YOUR SEAT. NEXT TIME IT WILL BE DETENTION.
WEIRDO.
I'LL TELL YOU MY PLAN LATER.
AT LEAST THE GOOD NEWS IS...

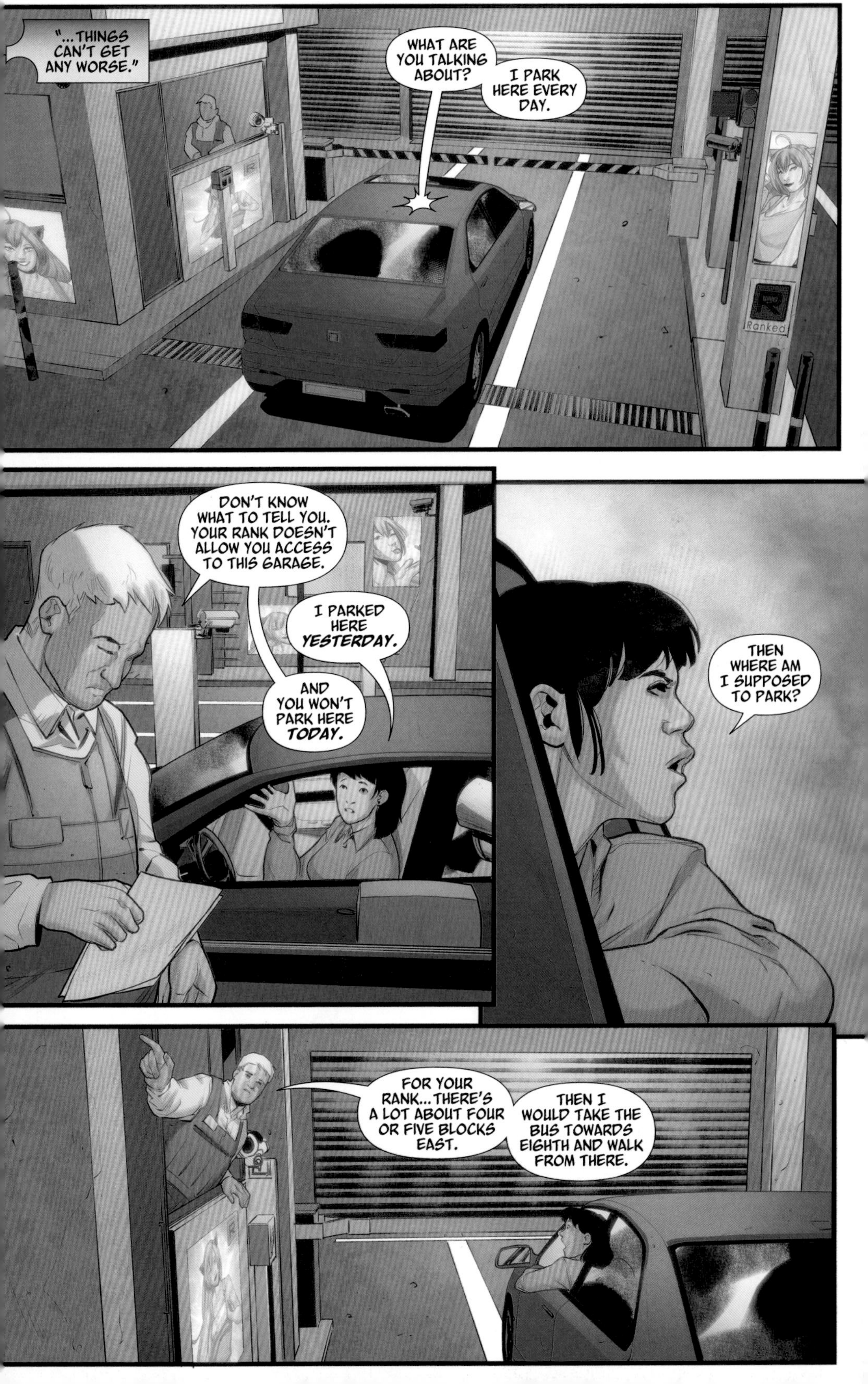
"...THINGS CAN'T GET ANY WORSE."
WHAT ARE YOU TALKING ABOUT?
I PARK HERE EVERY DAY.
Ranked
DON'T KNOW WHAT TO TELL YOU. YOUR RANK DOESN'T ALLOW YOU ACCESS TO THIS GARAGE.
I PARKED HERE *YESTERDAY*.
AND YOU WON'T PARK HERE *TODAY*.
THEN WHERE AM I SUPPOSED TO PARK?
FOR YOUR RANK...THERE'S A LOT ABOUT FOUR OR FIVE BLOCKS EAST.
THEN I WOULD TAKE THE BUS TOWARDS EIGHTH AND WALK FROM THERE.

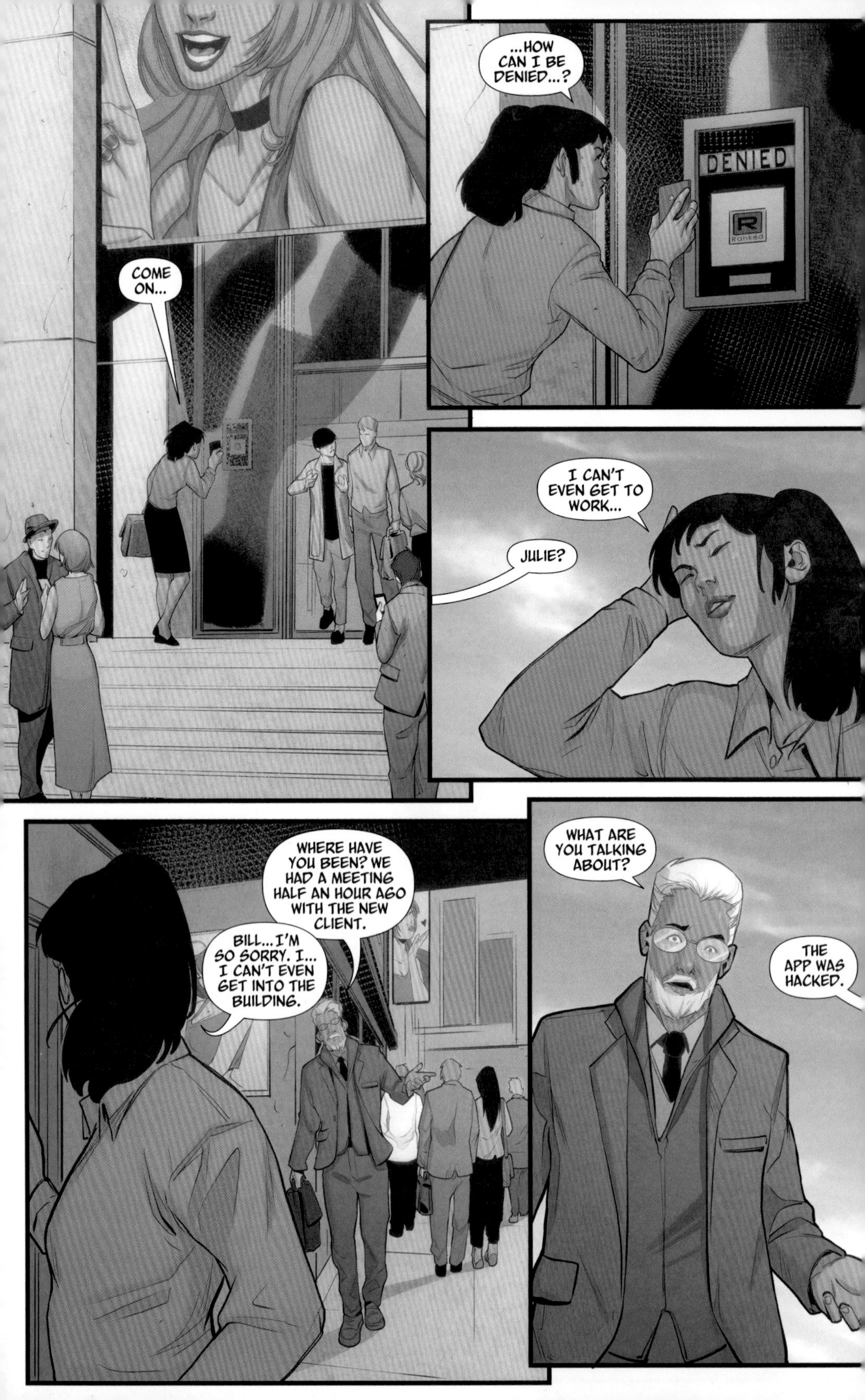
COME ON...
...HOW CAN I BE DENIED...?
DENIED
Ranked
I CAN'T EVEN GET TO WORK...
JULIE?
WHERE HAVE YOU BEEN? WE HAD A MEETING HALF AN HOUR AGO WITH THE NEW CLIENT.
BILL... I'M SO SORRY. I... I CAN'T EVEN GET INTO THE BUILDING.
WHAT ARE YOU TALKING ABOUT?
THE APP WAS HACKED.

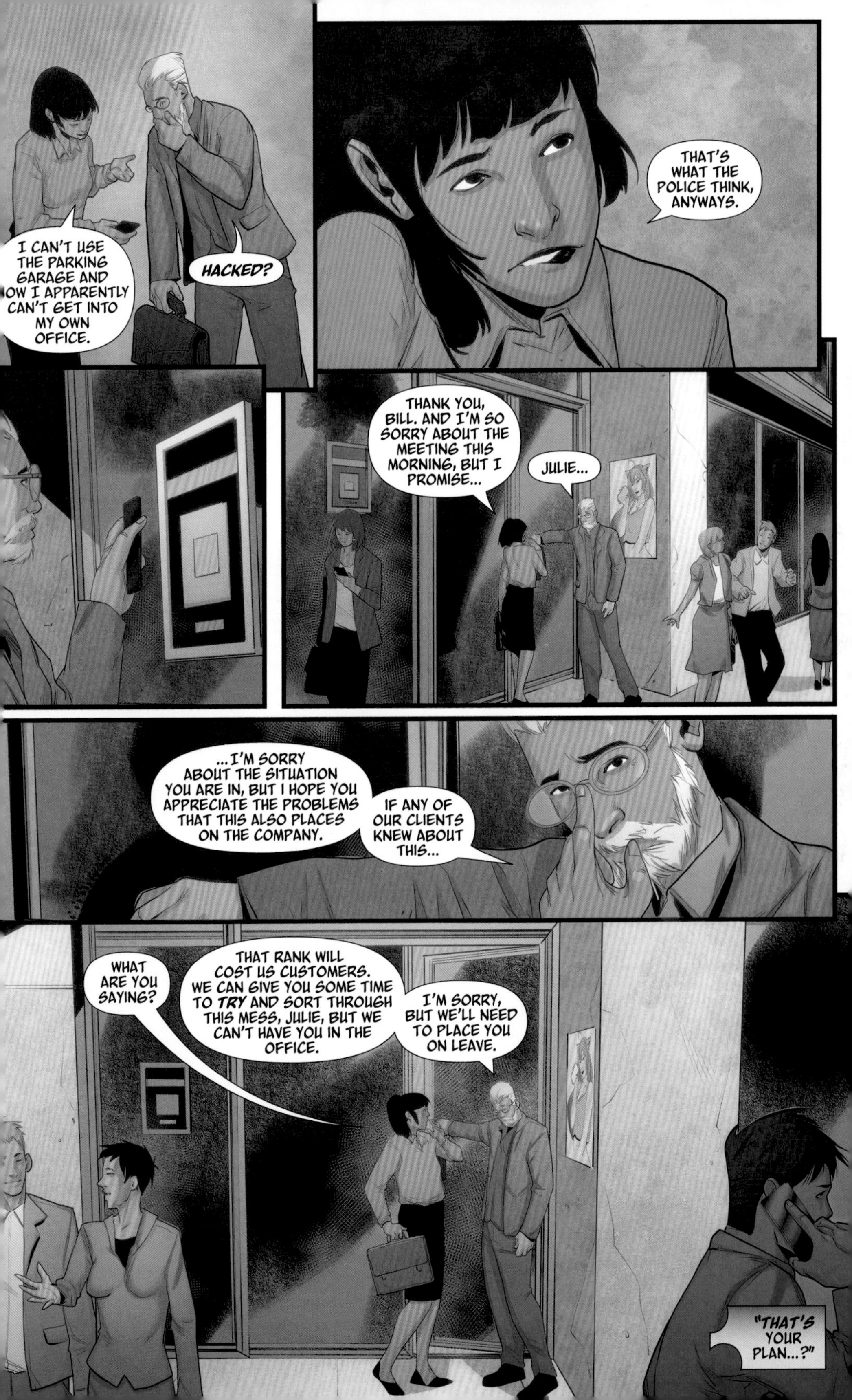
I CAN'T USE THE PARKING GARAGE AND OW I APPARENTLY CAN'T GET INTO MY OWN OFFICE.
HACKED?
THAT'S WHAT THE POLICE THINK, ANYWAYS.
THANK YOU, BILL. AND I'M SO SORRY ABOUT THE MEETING THIS MORNING, BUT I PROMISE...
JULIE...
...I'M SORRY ABOUT THE SITUATION YOU ARE IN, BUT I HOPE YOU APPRECIATE THE PROBLEMS THAT THIS ALSO PLACES ON THE COMPANY.
IF ANY OF OUR CLIENTS KNEW ABOUT THIS...
THAT RANK WILL COST US CUSTOMERS. WE CAN GIVE YOU SOME TIME TO TRY AND SORT THROUGH THIS MESS, JULIE, BUT WE CAN'T HAVE YOU IN THE OFFICE.
I'M SORRY, BUT WE'LL NEED TO PLACE YOU ON LEAVE.
WHAT ARE YOU SAYING?
"THAT'S YOUR PLAN...?"

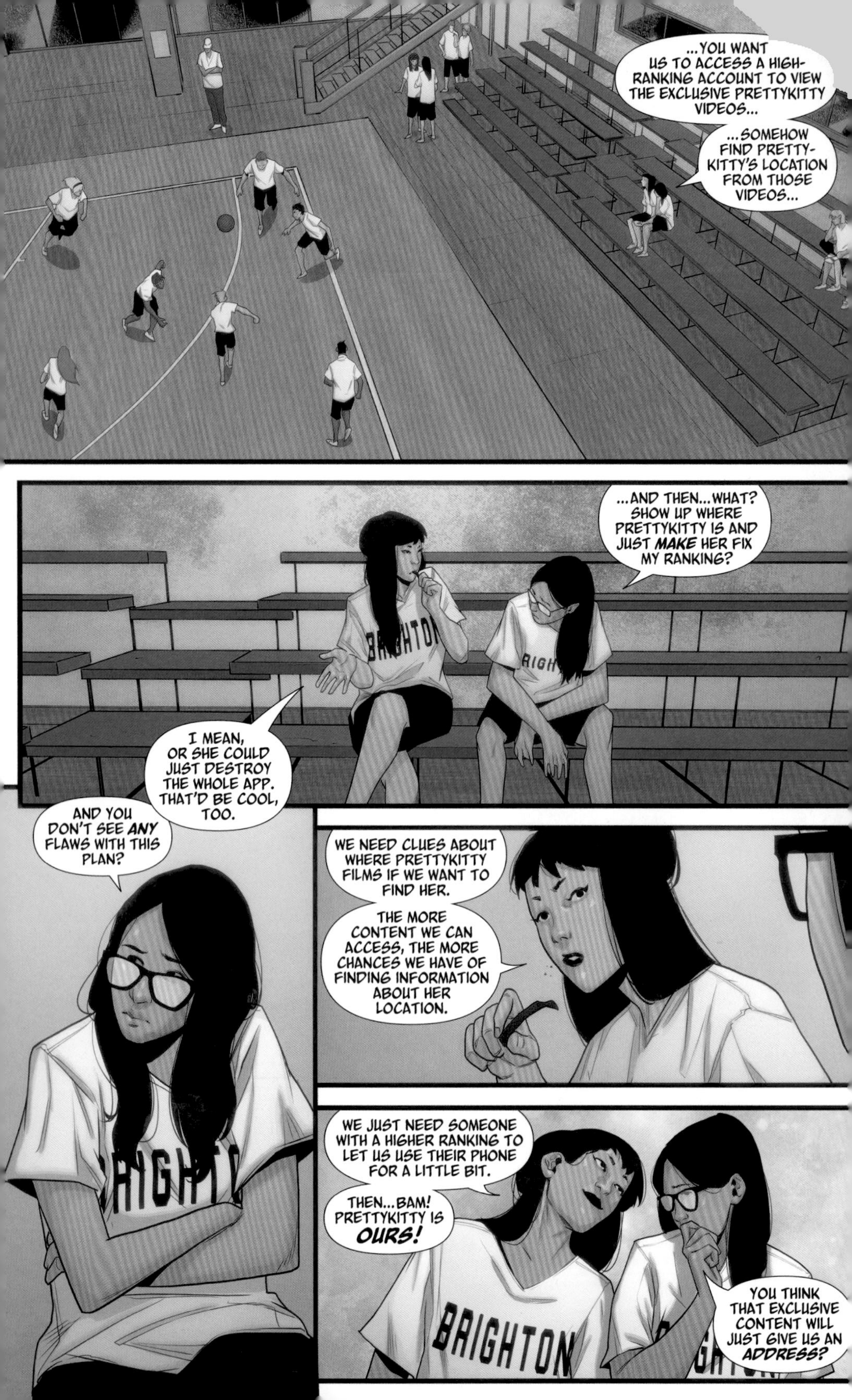
...YOU WANT US TO ACCESS A HIGH-RANKING ACCOUNT TO VIEW THE EXCLUSIVE PRETTYKITTY VIDEOS...
...SOMEHOW FIND PRETTY-KITTY'S LOCATION FROM THOSE VIDEOS...
...AND THEN...WHAT? SHOW UP WHERE PRETTYKITTY IS AND JUST MAKE HER FIX MY RANKING?
I MEAN, OR SHE COULD JUST DESTROY THE WHOLE APP. THAT'D BE COOL, TOO.
BRIGHTON
AND YOU DON'T SEE ANY FLAWS WITH THIS PLAN?
WE NEED CLUES ABOUT WHERE PRETTYKITTY FILMS IF WE WANT TO FIND HER.
THE MORE CONTENT WE CAN ACCESS, THE MORE CHANCES WE HAVE OF FINDING INFORMATION ABOUT HER LOCATION.
WE JUST NEED SOMEONE WITH A HIGHER RANKING TO LET US USE THEIR PHONE FOR A LITTLE BIT.
THEN...BAM! PRETTYKITTY IS OURS!
BRIGHTON
YOU THINK THAT EXCLUSIVE CONTENT WILL JUST GIVE US AN ADDRESS?

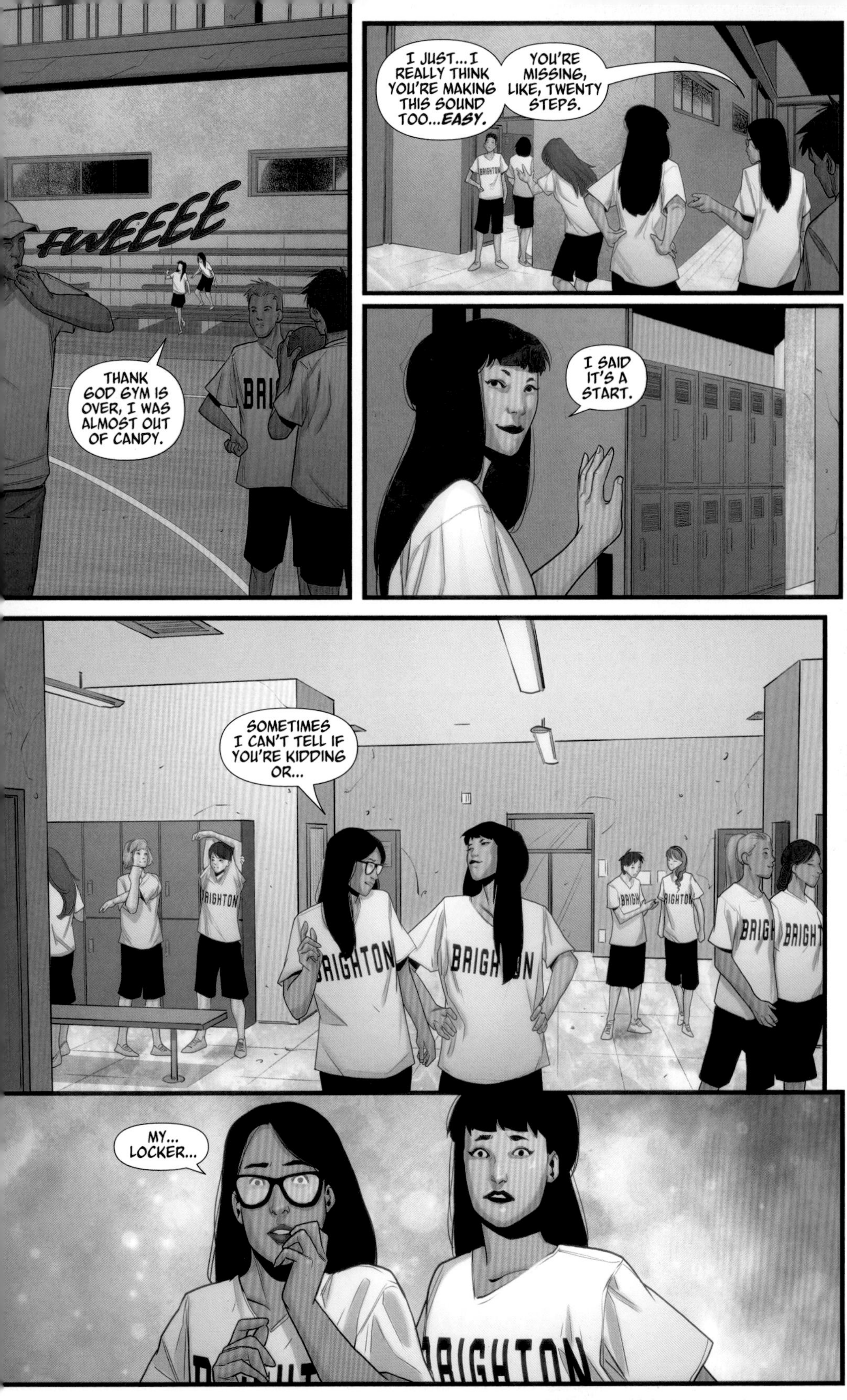
FWEEEE
THANK GOD GYM IS OVER, I WAS ALMOST OUT OF CANDY.
BRIGHTON
I JUST... I REALLY THINK YOU'RE MAKING THIS SOUND TOO...*EASY*.
YOU'RE MISSING, LIKE, TWENTY STEPS.
I SAID IT'S A START.
SOMETIMES I CAN'T TELL IF YOU'RE KIDDING OR...
BRIGHTON
MY... LOCKER...

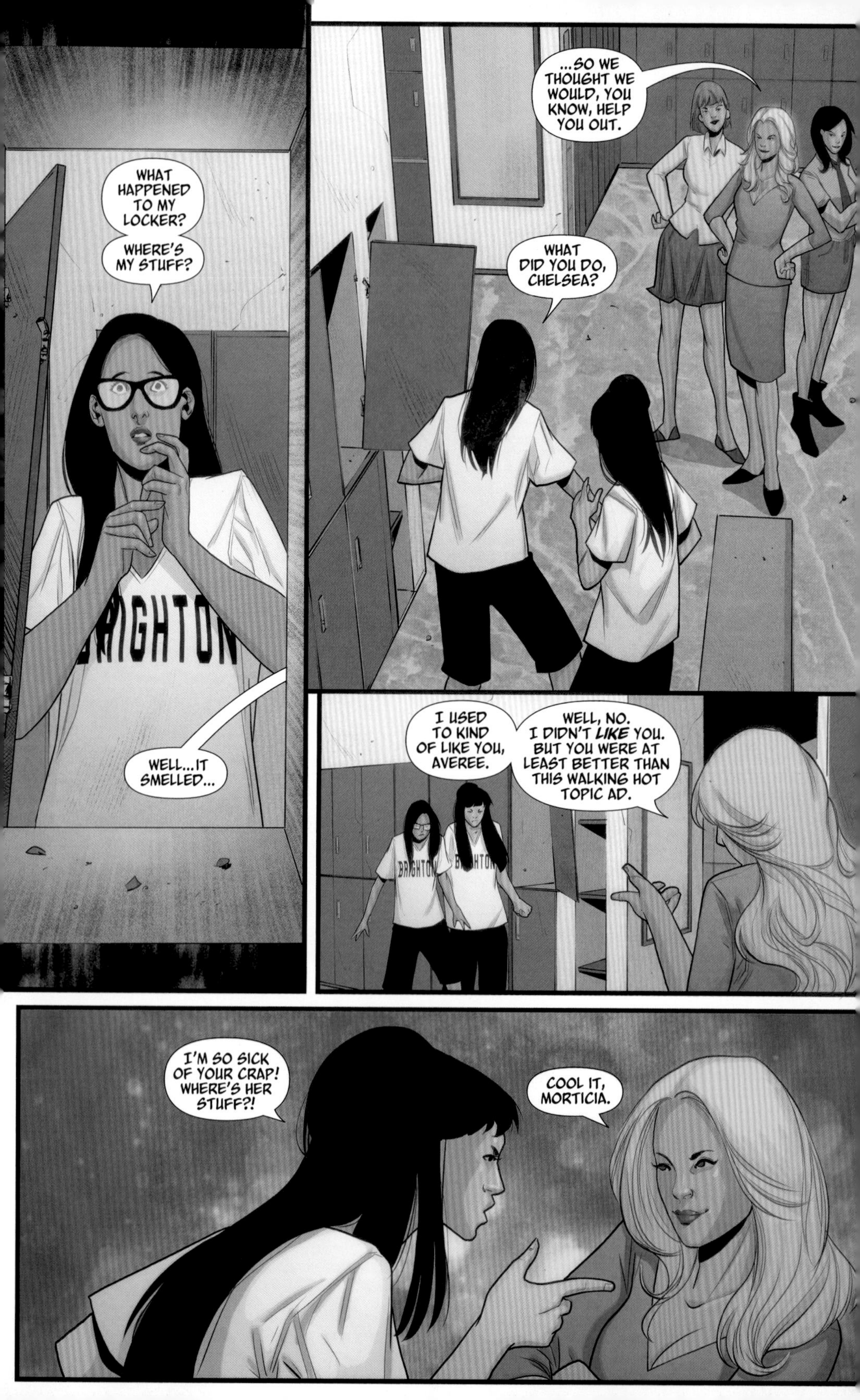
WHAT HAPPENED TO MY LOCKER?
WHERE'S MY STUFF?
BRIGHTON
WELL...IT SMELLED...
...SO WE THOUGHT WE WOULD, YOU KNOW, HELP YOU OUT.
WHAT DID YOU DO, CHELSEA?
I USED TO KIND OF LIKE YOU, AVEREE.
WELL, NO. I DIDN'T *LIKE* YOU. BUT YOU WERE AT LEAST BETTER THAN THIS WALKING HOT TOPIC AD.
I'M SO SICK OF YOUR CRAP! WHERE'S HER STUFF?!
COOL IT, MORTICIA.

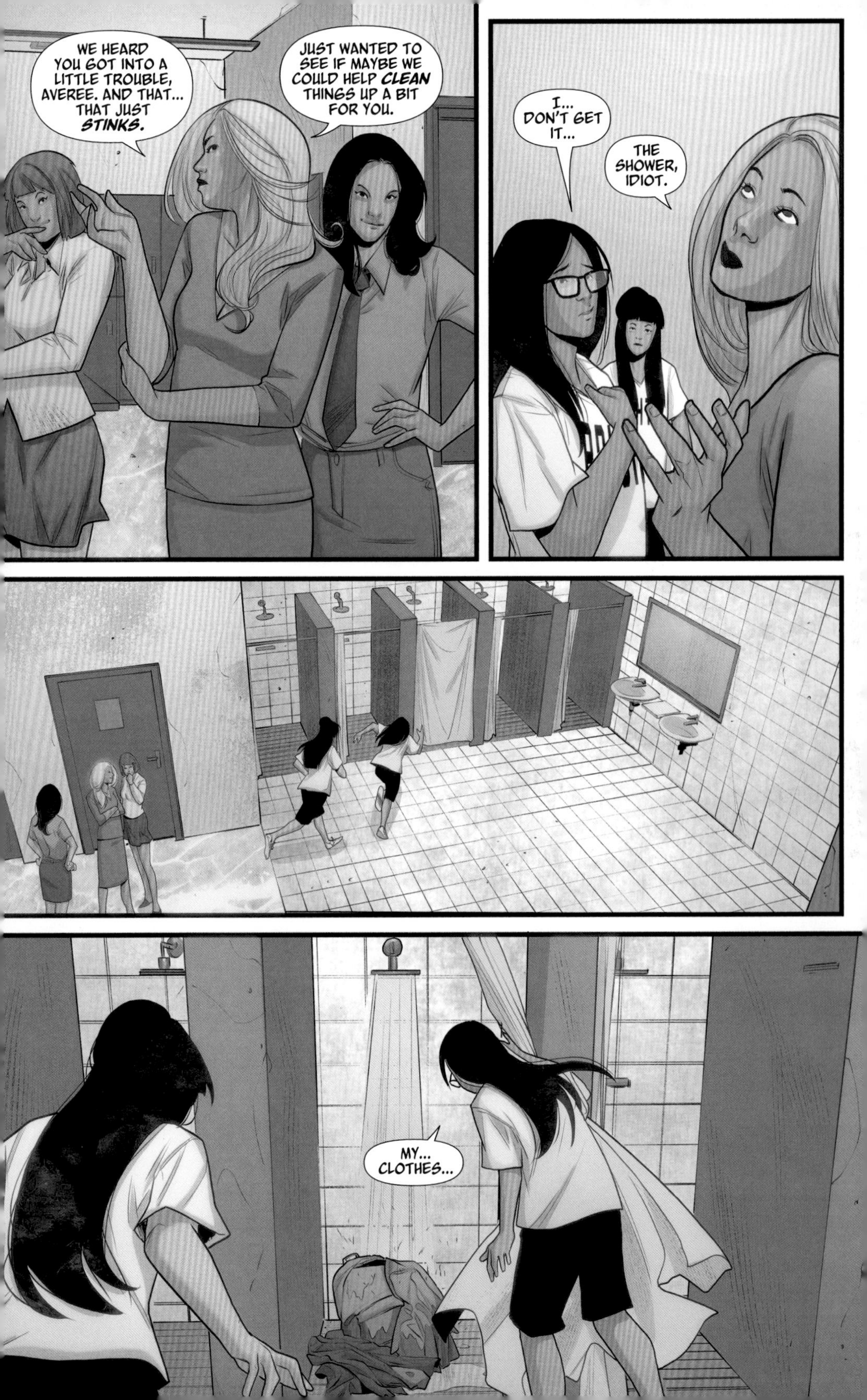
WE HEARD YOU GOT INTO A LITTLE TROUBLE, AVEREE. AND THAT... THAT JUST STINKS.
JUST WANTED TO SEE IF MAYBE WE COULD HELP CLEAN THINGS UP A BIT FOR YOU.
I... DON'T GET IT...
THE SHOWER, IDIOT.
MY... CLOTHES...

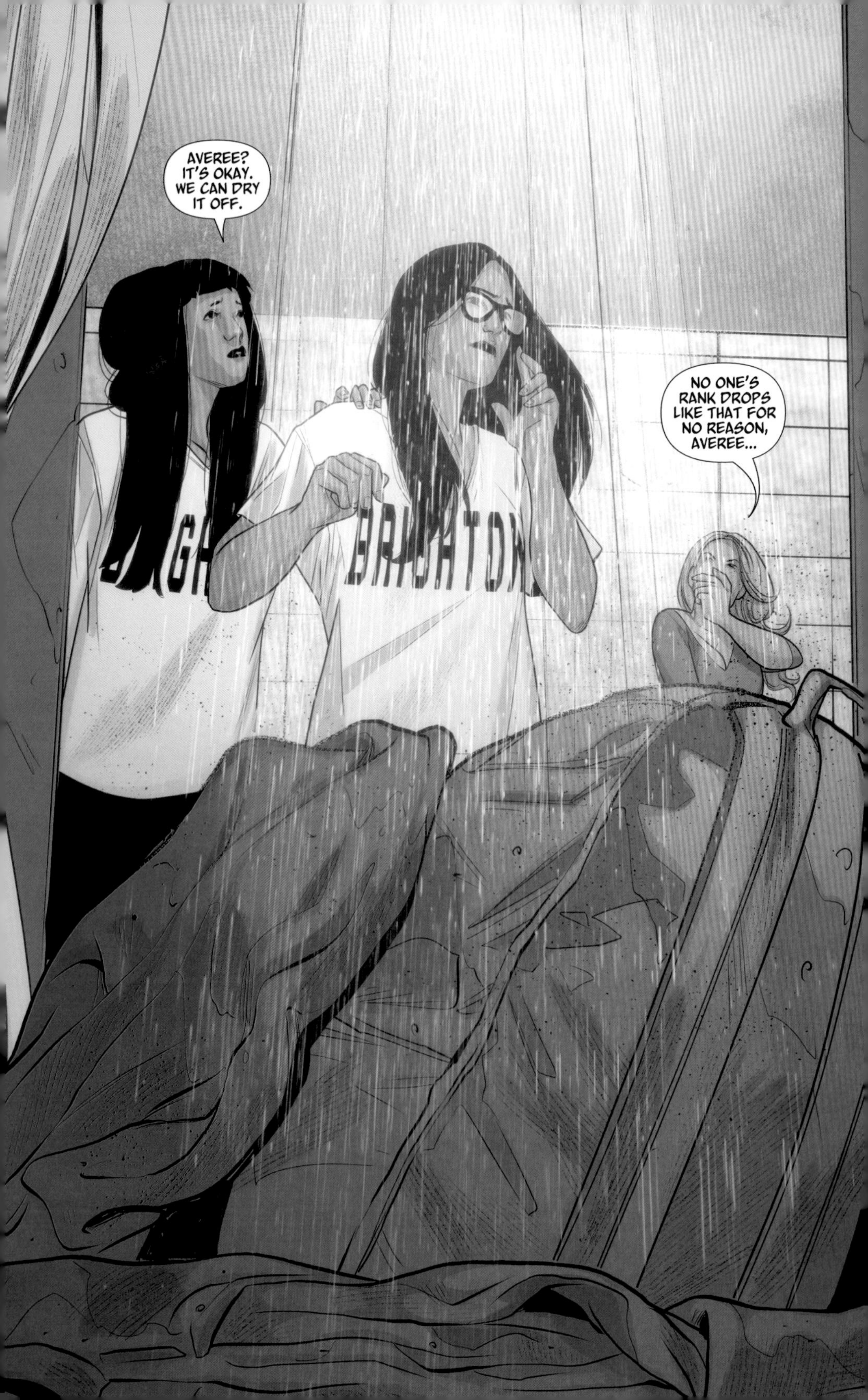
AVEREE? IT'S OKAY. WE CAN DRY IT OFF.
NO ONE'S RANK DROPS LIKE THAT FOR NO REASON, AVEREE...

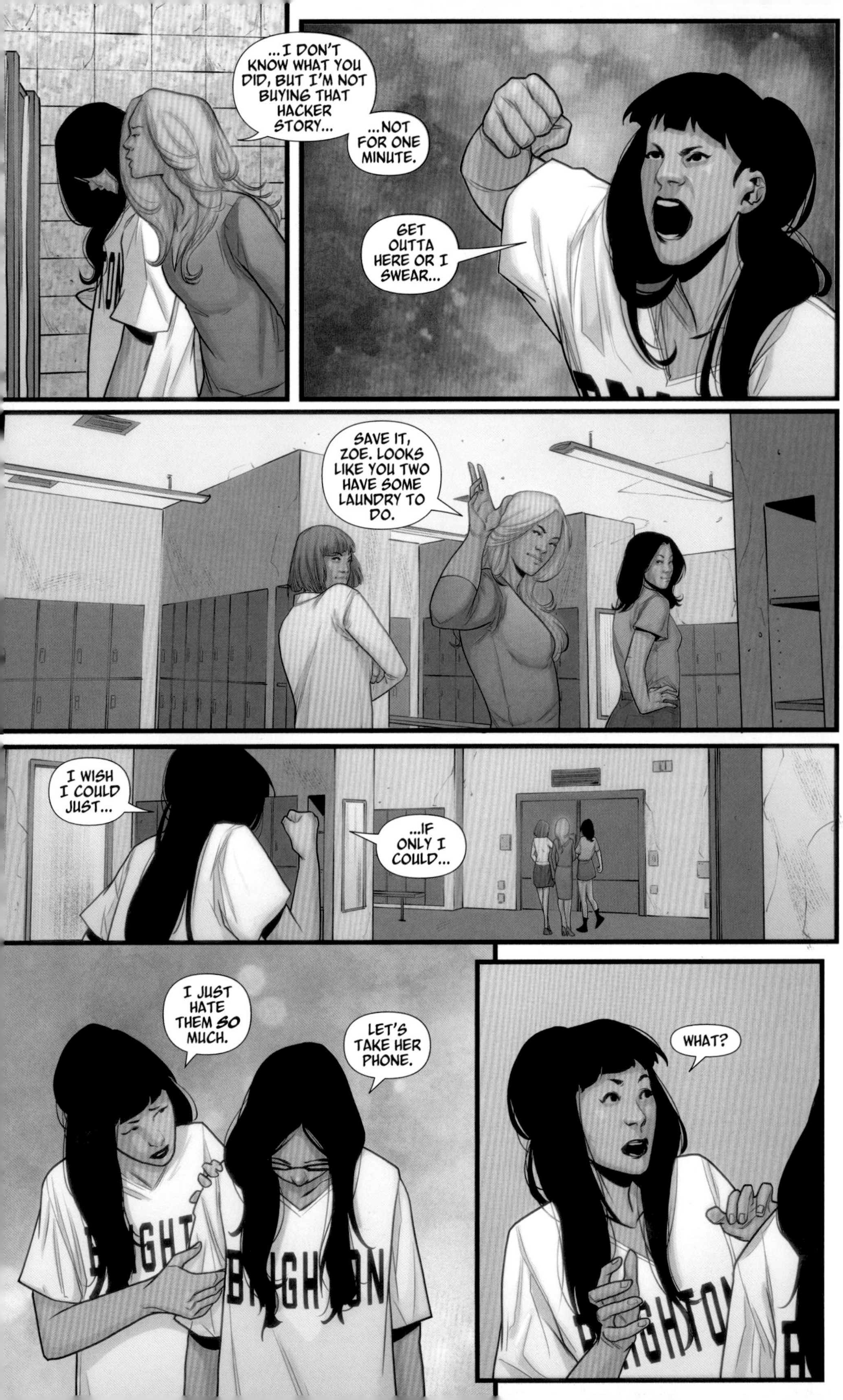
...I DON'T KNOW WHAT YOU DID, BUT I'M NOT BUYING THAT HACKER STORY...
...NOT FOR ONE MINUTE.
GET OUTTA HERE OR I SWEAR...
SAVE IT, ZOE. LOOKS LIKE YOU TWO HAVE SOME LAUNDRY TO DO.
I WISH I COULD JUST...
...IF ONLY I COULD...
I JUST HATE THEM SO MUCH.
LET'S TAKE HER PHONE.
WHAT?

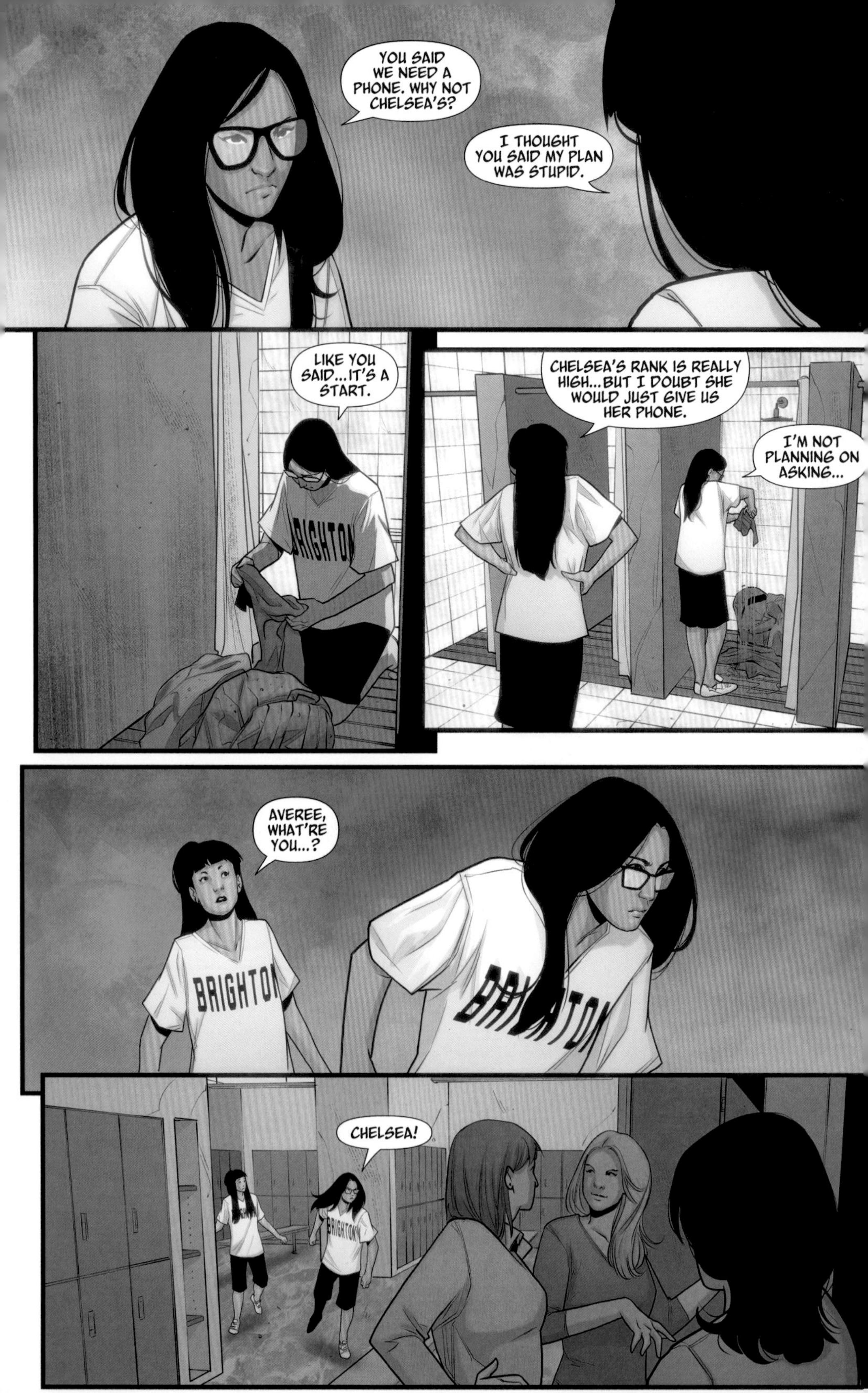
YOU SAID WE NEED A PHONE. WHY NOT CHELSEA'S?
I THOUGHT YOU SAID MY PLAN WAS STUPID.
LIKE YOU SAID...IT'S A START.
BRIGHTON
CHELSEA'S RANK IS REALLY HIGH...BUT I DOUBT SHE WOULD JUST GIVE US HER PHONE.
I'M NOT PLANNING ON ASKING...
AVEREE, WHAT'RE YOU...?
BRIGHTON
CHELSEA!

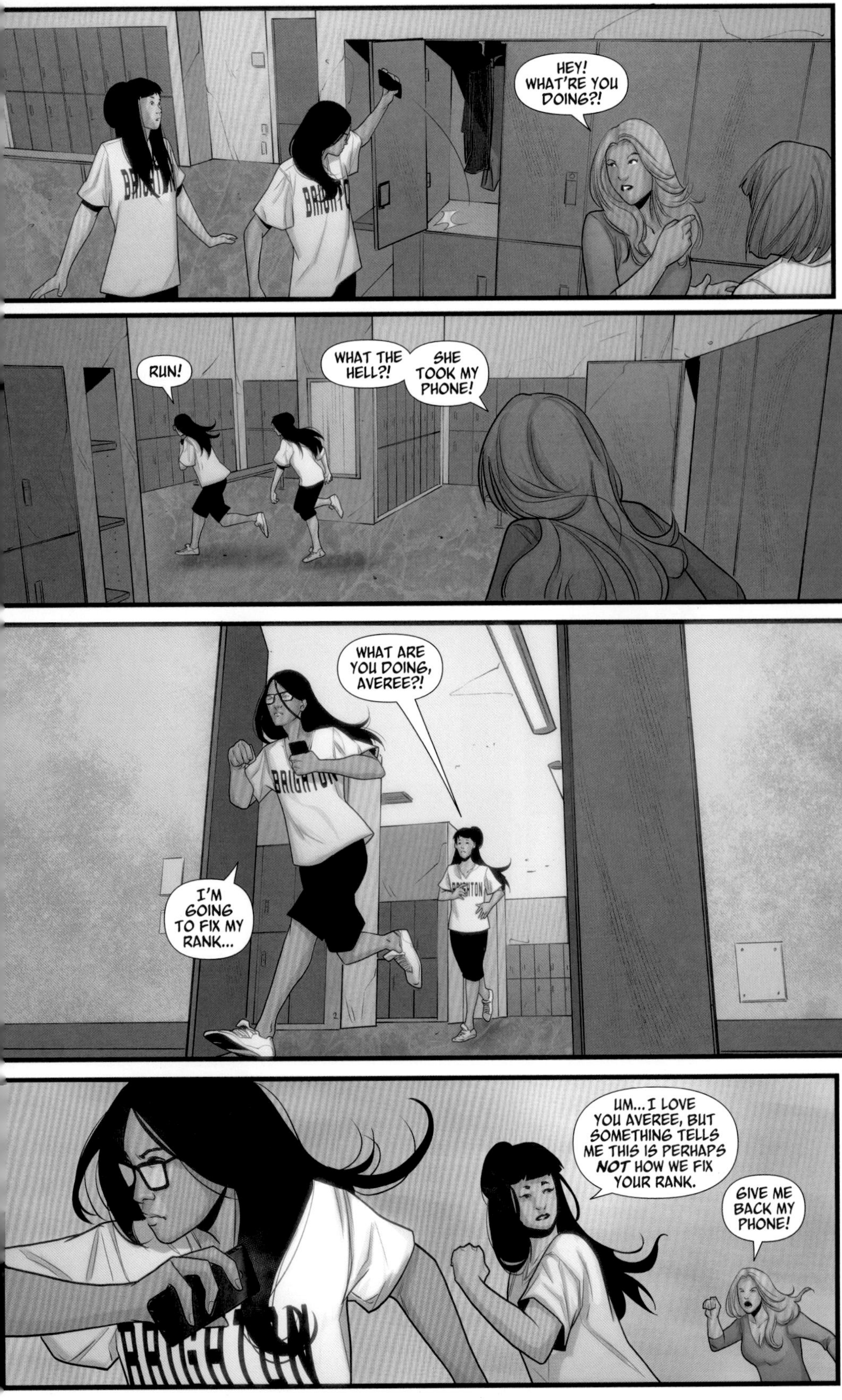
HEY! WHAT'RE YOU DOING?!
RUN!
WHAT THE HELL?!
SHE TOOK MY PHONE!
WHAT ARE YOU DOING, AVEREE?!
I'M GOING TO FIX MY RANK...
UM... I LOVE YOU AVEREE, BUT SOMETHING TELLS ME THIS IS PERHAPS NOT HOW WE FIX YOUR RANK.
GIVE ME BACK MY PHONE!
BRIGHTON

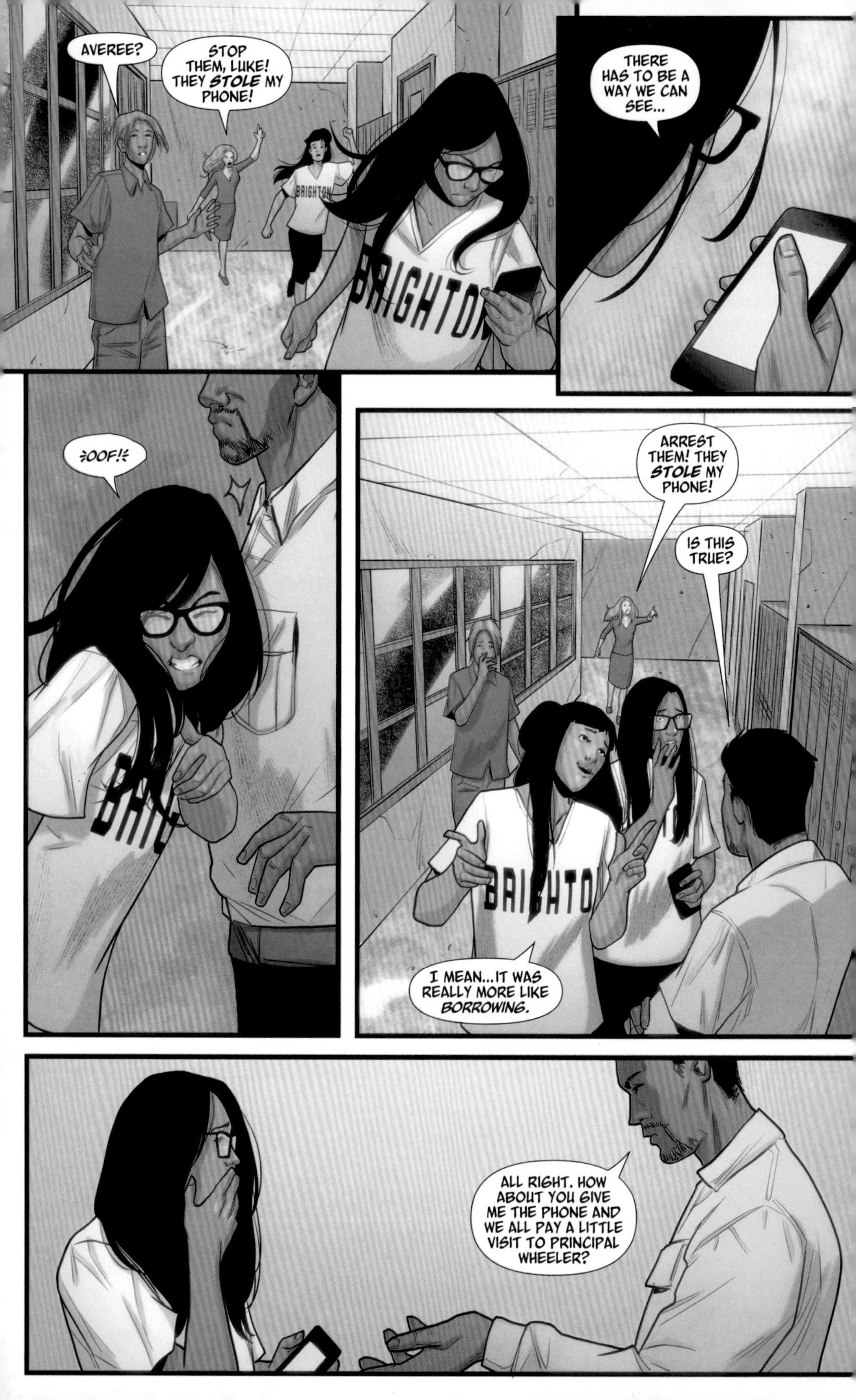

AVEREE?
STOP THEM, LUKE! THEY STOLE MY PHONE!
THERE HAS TO BE A WAY WE CAN SEE...
OOF!
ARREST THEM! THEY STOLE MY PHONE!
IS THIS TRUE?
I MEAN...IT WAS REALLY MORE LIKE BORROWING.
ALL RIGHT. HOW ABOUT YOU GIVE ME THE PHONE AND WE ALL PAY A LITTLE VISIT TO PRINCIPAL WHEELER?

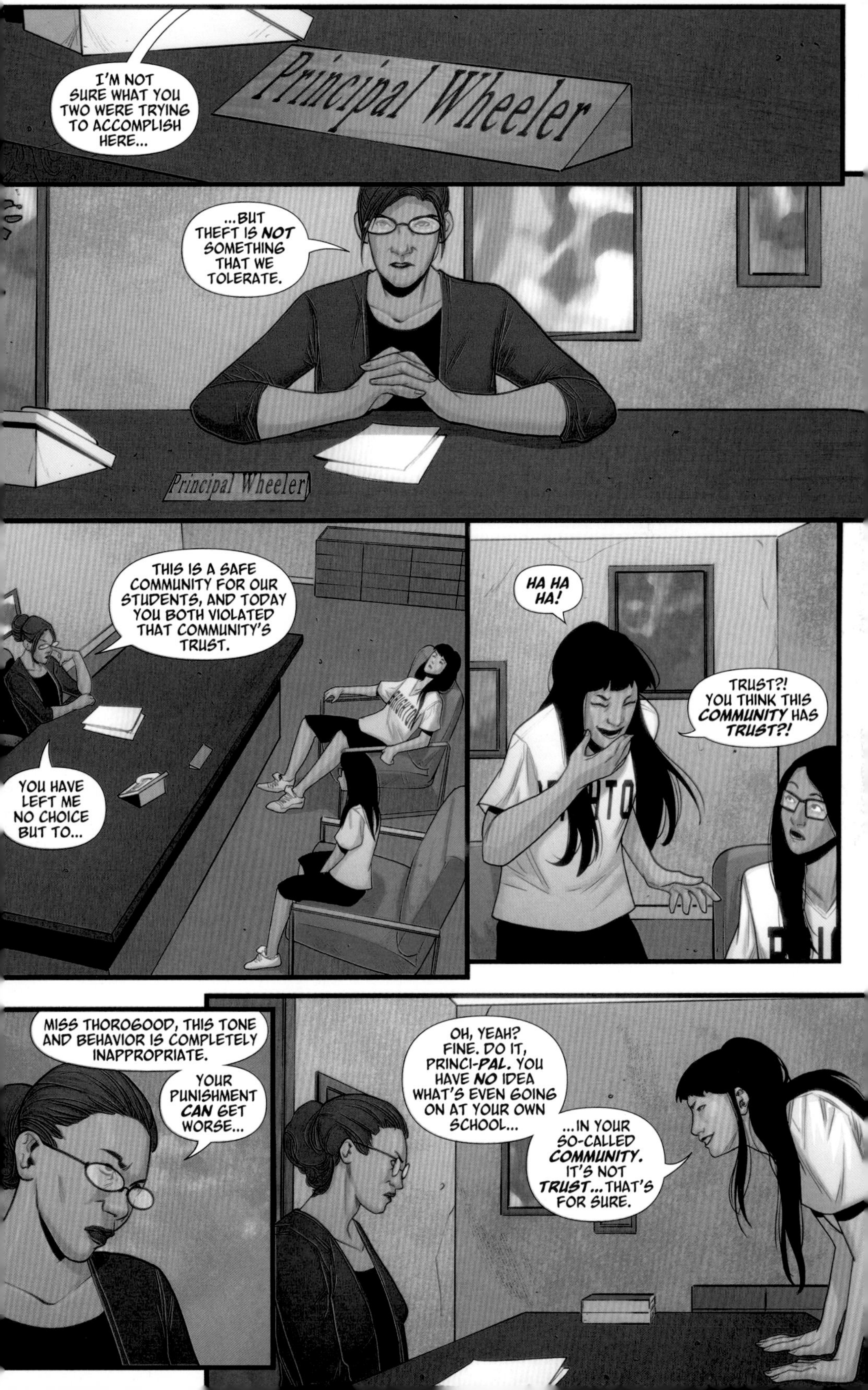

Principal Wheeler
I'M NOT SURE WHAT YOU TWO WERE TRYING TO ACCOMPLISH HERE...
...BUT THEFT IS NOT SOMETHING THAT WE TOLERATE.
Principal Wheeler
THIS IS A SAFE COMMUNITY FOR OUR STUDENTS, AND TODAY YOU BOTH VIOLATED THAT COMMUNITY'S TRUST.
YOU HAVE LEFT ME NO CHOICE BUT TO...
HA HA HA!
TRUST?! YOU THINK THIS COMMUNITY HAS TRUST?!
MISS THOROGOOD, THIS TONE AND BEHAVIOR IS COMPLETELY INAPPROPRIATE.
YOUR PUNISHMENT CAN GET WORSE...
OH, YEAH? FINE. DO IT, PRINCI-PAL. YOU HAVE NO IDEA WHAT'S EVEN GOING ON AT YOUR OWN SCHOOL...
...IN YOUR SO-CALLED COMMUNITY. IT'S NOT TRUST...THAT'S FOR SURE.

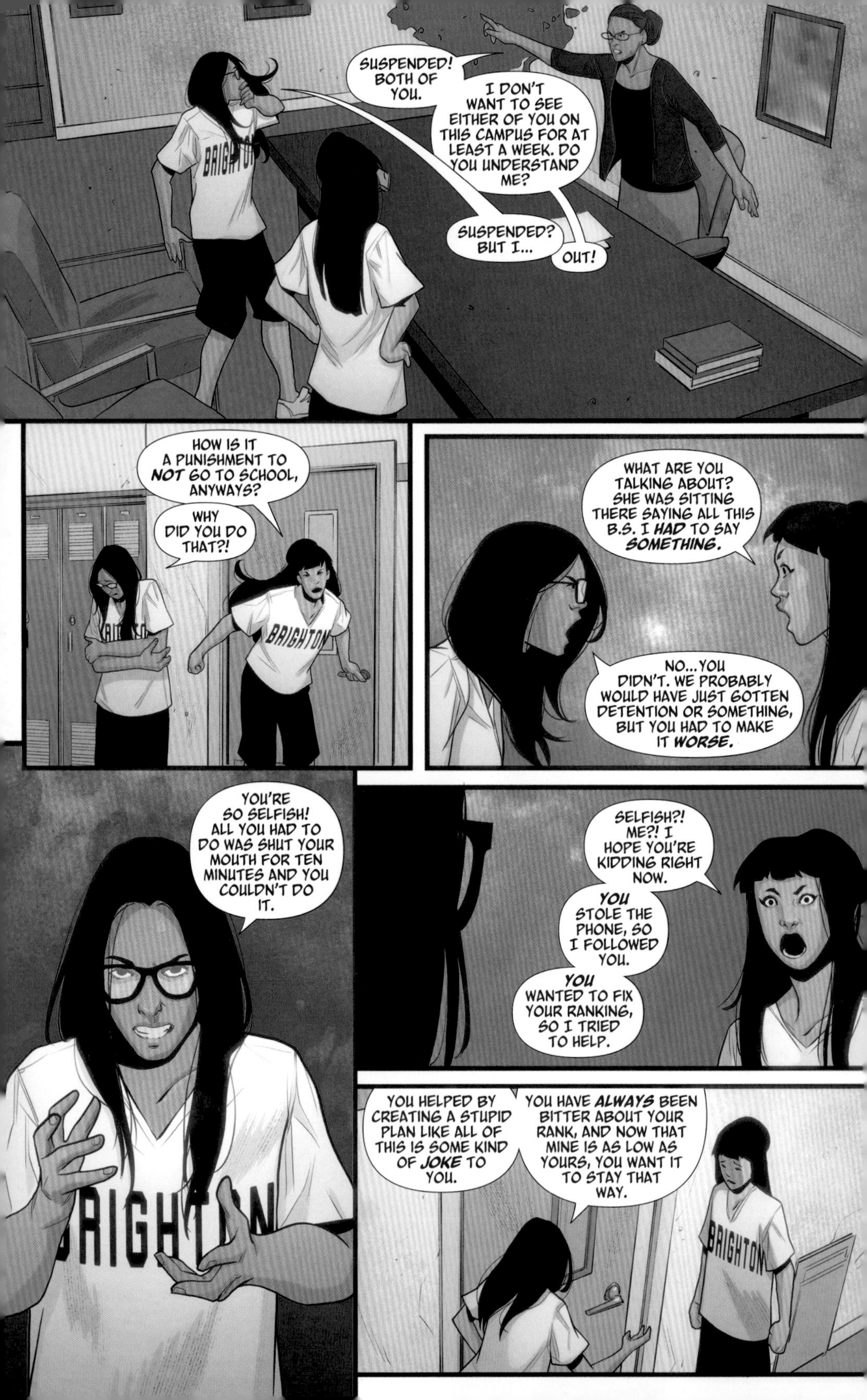
SUSPENDED! BOTH OF YOU.
I DON'T WANT TO SEE EITHER OF YOU ON THIS CAMPUS FOR AT LEAST A WEEK. DO YOU UNDERSTAND ME?
SUSPENDED? BUT I...
OUT!
BRIGHTON
HOW IS IT A PUNISHMENT TO NOT GO TO SCHOOL, ANYWAYS?
WHY DID YOU DO THAT?!
BRIGHTON
WHAT ARE YOU TALKING ABOUT? SHE WAS SITTING THERE SAYING ALL THIS B.S. I HAD TO SAY SOMETHING.
NO...YOU DIDN'T. WE PROBABLY WOULD HAVE JUST GOTTEN DETENTION OR SOMETHING, BUT YOU HAD TO MAKE IT WORSE.
YOU'RE SO SELFISH! ALL YOU HAD TO DO WAS SHUT YOUR MOUTH FOR TEN MINUTES AND YOU COULDN'T DO IT.
SELFISH?! ME?! I HOPE YOU'RE KIDDING RIGHT NOW.
YOU STOLE THE PHONE, SO I FOLLOWED YOU.
YOU WANTED TO FIX YOUR RANKING, SO I TRIED TO HELP.
YOU HELPED BY CREATING A STUPID PLAN LIKE ALL OF THIS IS SOME KIND OF JOKE TO YOU.
YOU HAVE ALWAYS BEEN BITTER ABOUT YOUR RANK, AND NOW THAT MINE IS AS LOW AS YOURS, YOU WANT IT TO STAY THAT WAY.
BRIGHTON

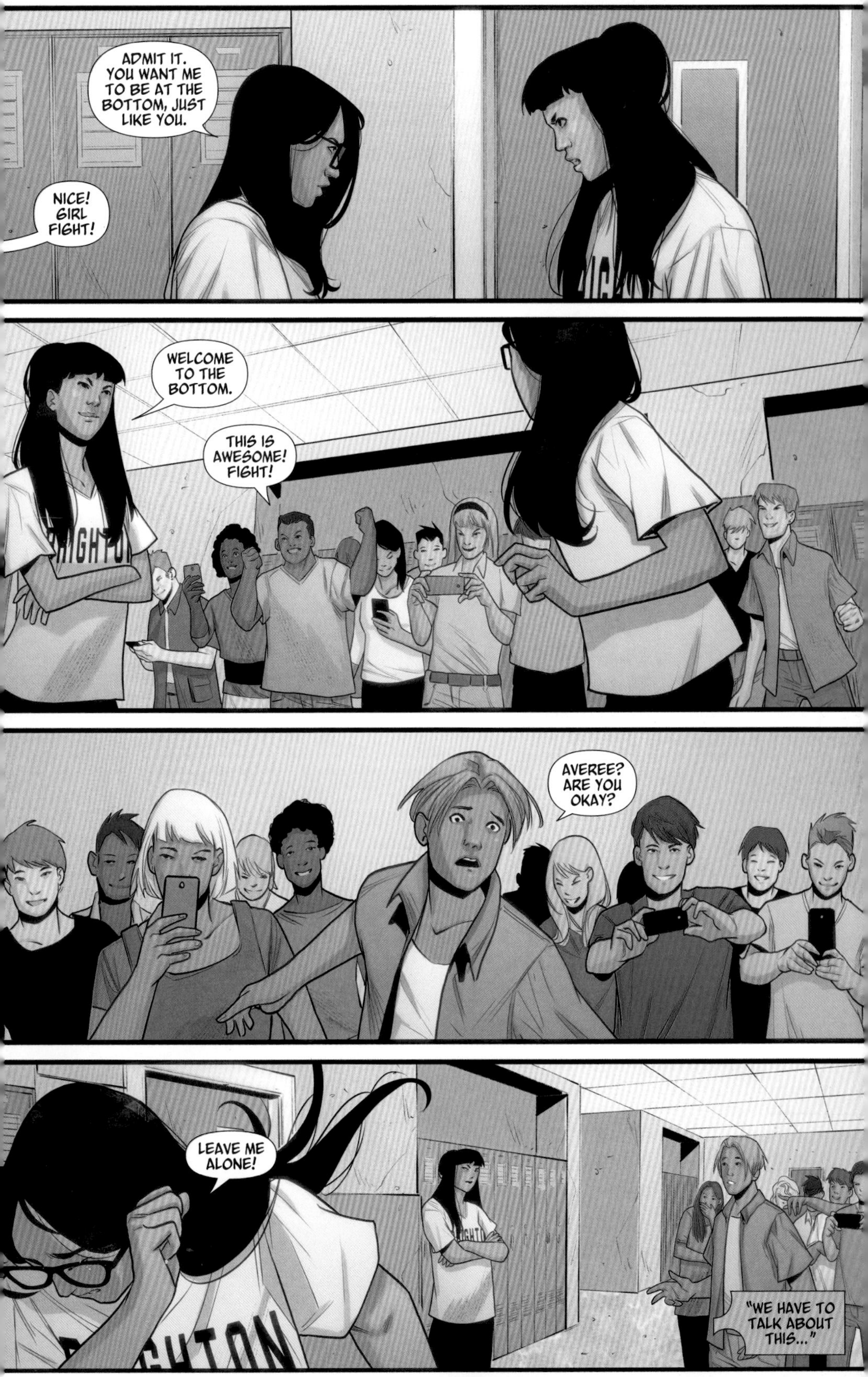
ADMIT IT. YOU WANT ME TO BE AT THE BOTTOM, JUST LIKE YOU.
NICE! GIRL FIGHT!
WELCOME TO THE BOTTOM.
THIS IS AWESOME! FIGHT!
AVEREE? ARE YOU OKAY?
LEAVE ME ALONE!
"WE HAVE TO TALK ABOUT THIS..."

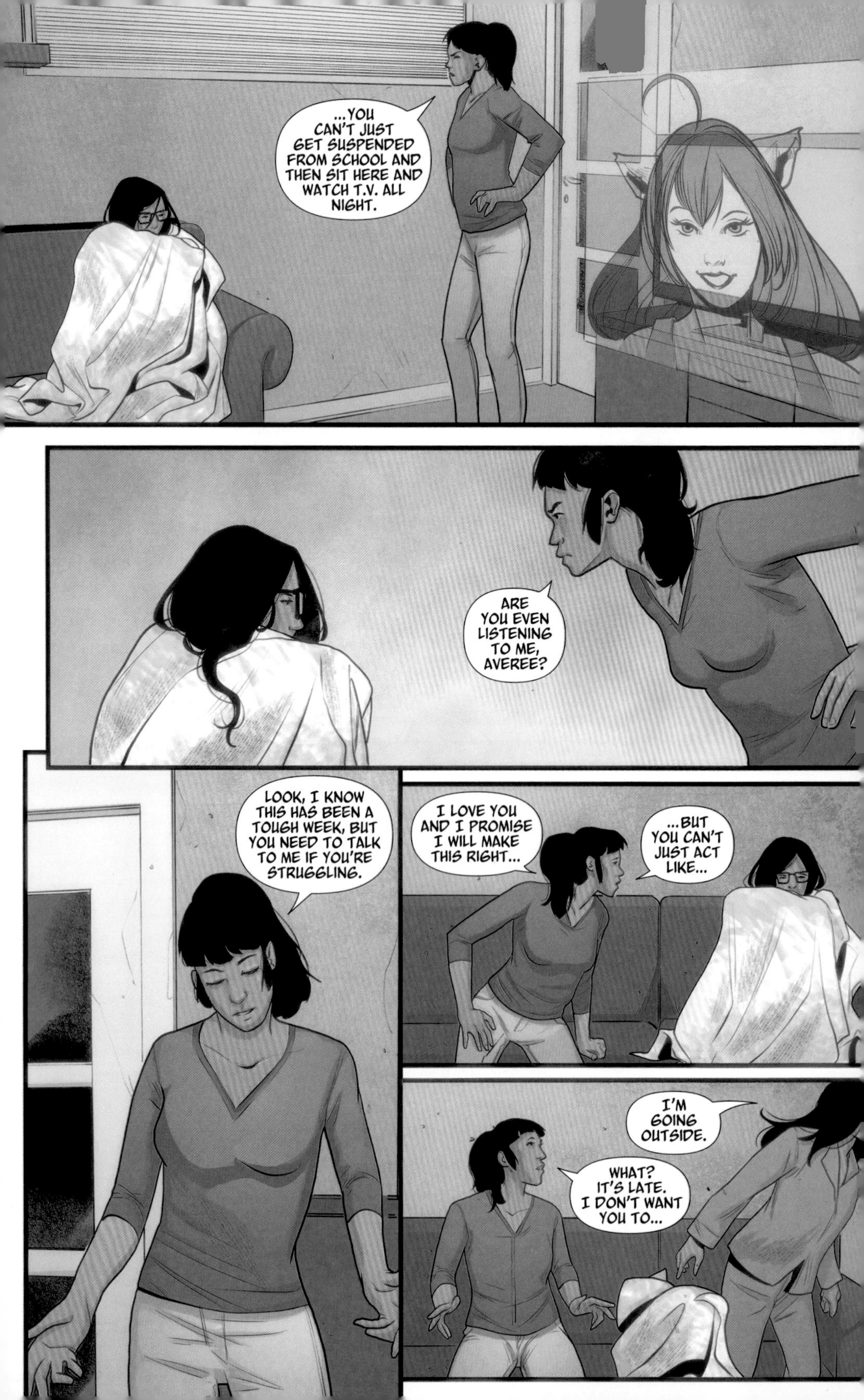
...YOU CAN'T JUST GET SUSPENDED FROM SCHOOL AND THEN SIT HERE AND WATCH T.V. ALL NIGHT.
ARE YOU EVEN LISTENING TO ME, AVEREE?
LOOK, I KNOW THIS HAS BEEN A TOUGH WEEK, BUT YOU NEED TO TALK TO ME IF YOU'RE STRUGGLING.
I LOVE YOU AND I PROMISE I WILL MAKE THIS RIGHT...
...BUT YOU CAN'T JUST ACT LIKE...
I'M GOING OUTSIDE.
WHAT? IT'S LATE. I DON'T WANT YOU TO...

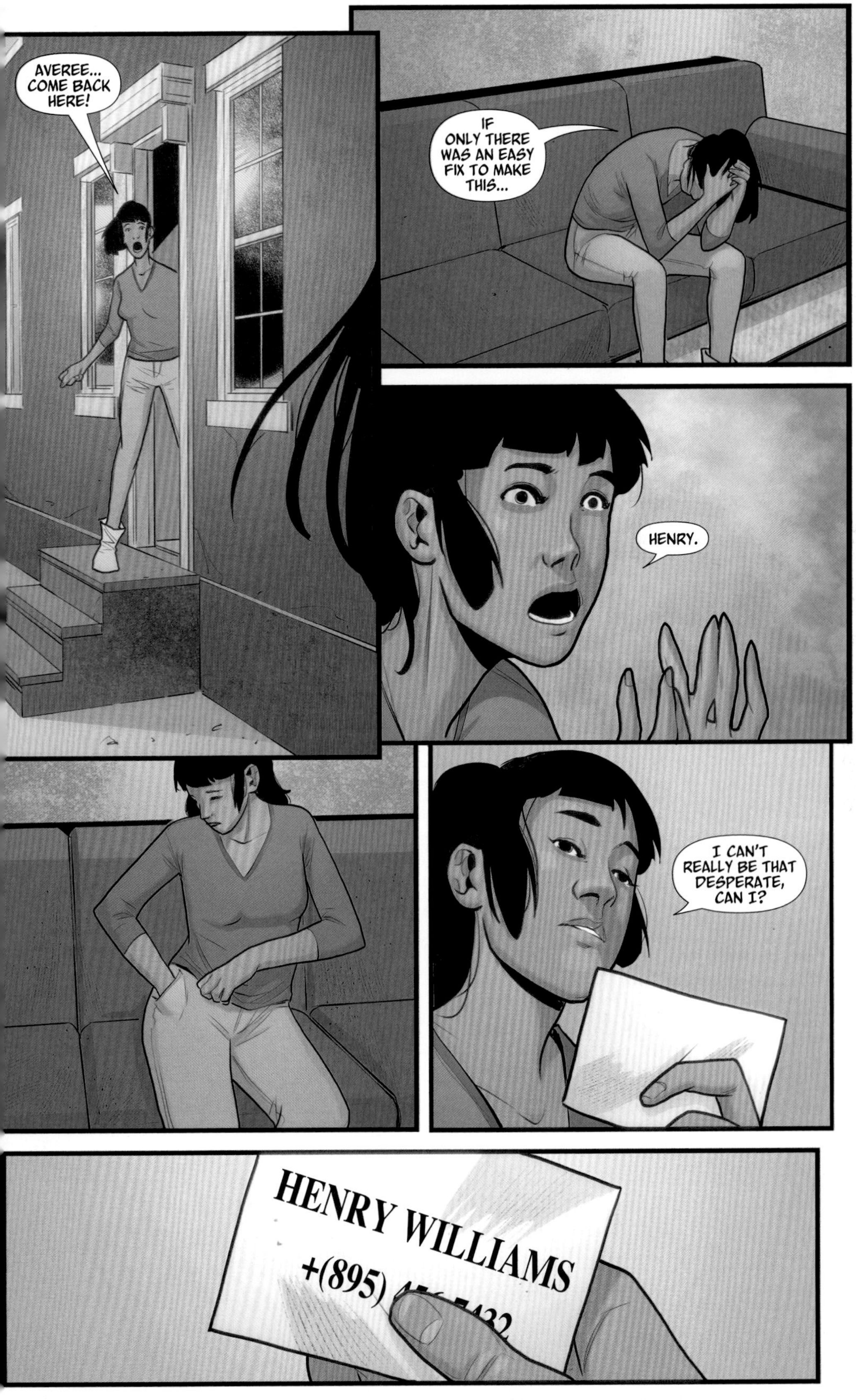
AVEREE... COME BACK HERE!
IF ONLY THERE WAS AN EASY FIX TO MAKE THIS...
HENRY.
I CAN'T REALLY BE THAT DESPERATE, CAN I?
HENRY WILLIAMS
+(895)

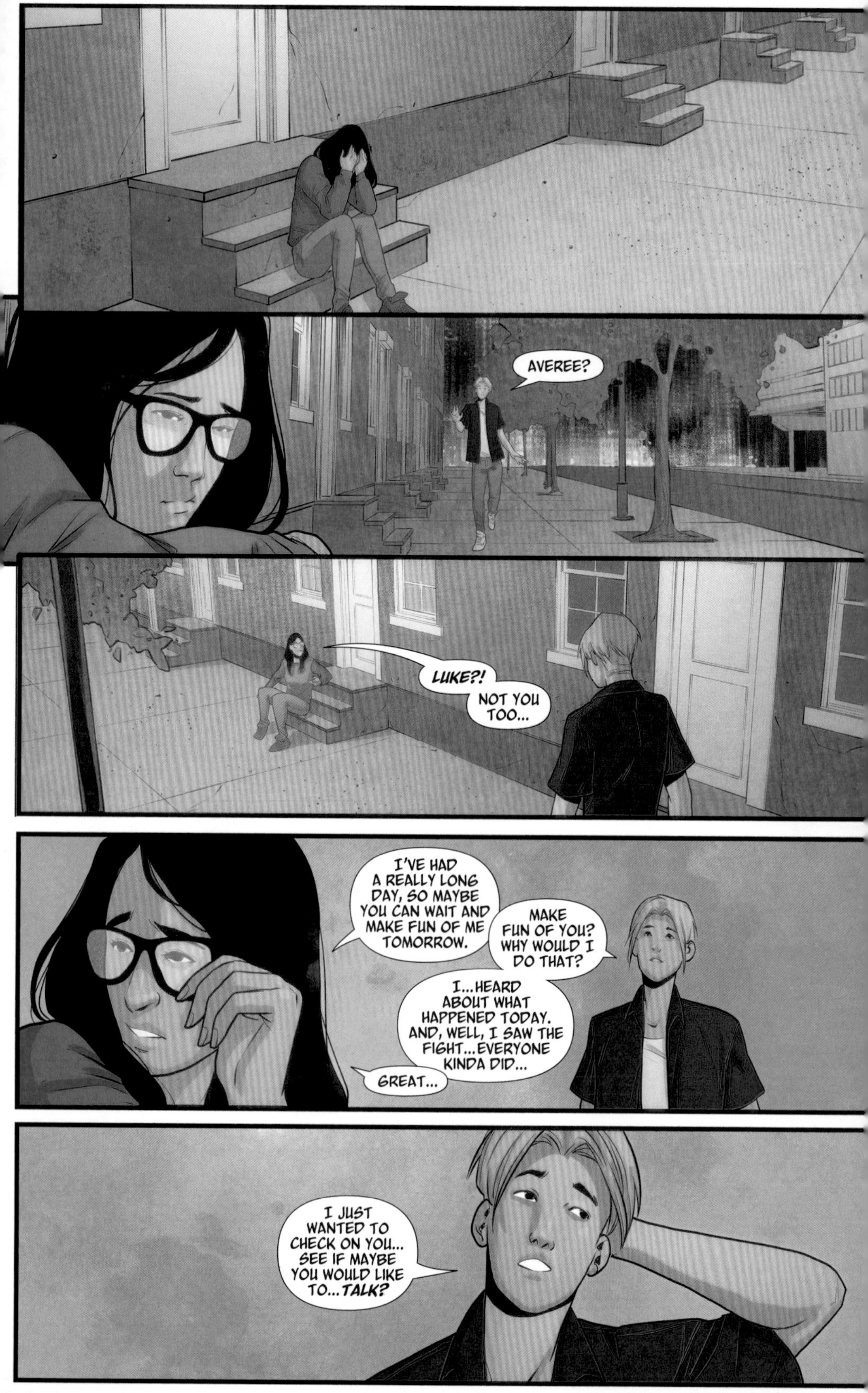
AVEREE?
LUKE?! NOT YOU TOO...
I'VE HAD A REALLY LONG DAY, SO MAYBE YOU CAN WAIT AND MAKE FUN OF ME TOMORROW.
MAKE FUN OF YOU? WHY WOULD I DO THAT?
I...HEARD ABOUT WHAT HAPPENED TODAY. AND, WELL, I SAW THE FIGHT...EVERYONE KINDA DID...
GREAT...
I JUST WANTED TO CHECK ON YOU... SEE IF MAYBE YOU WOULD LIKE TO...TALK?

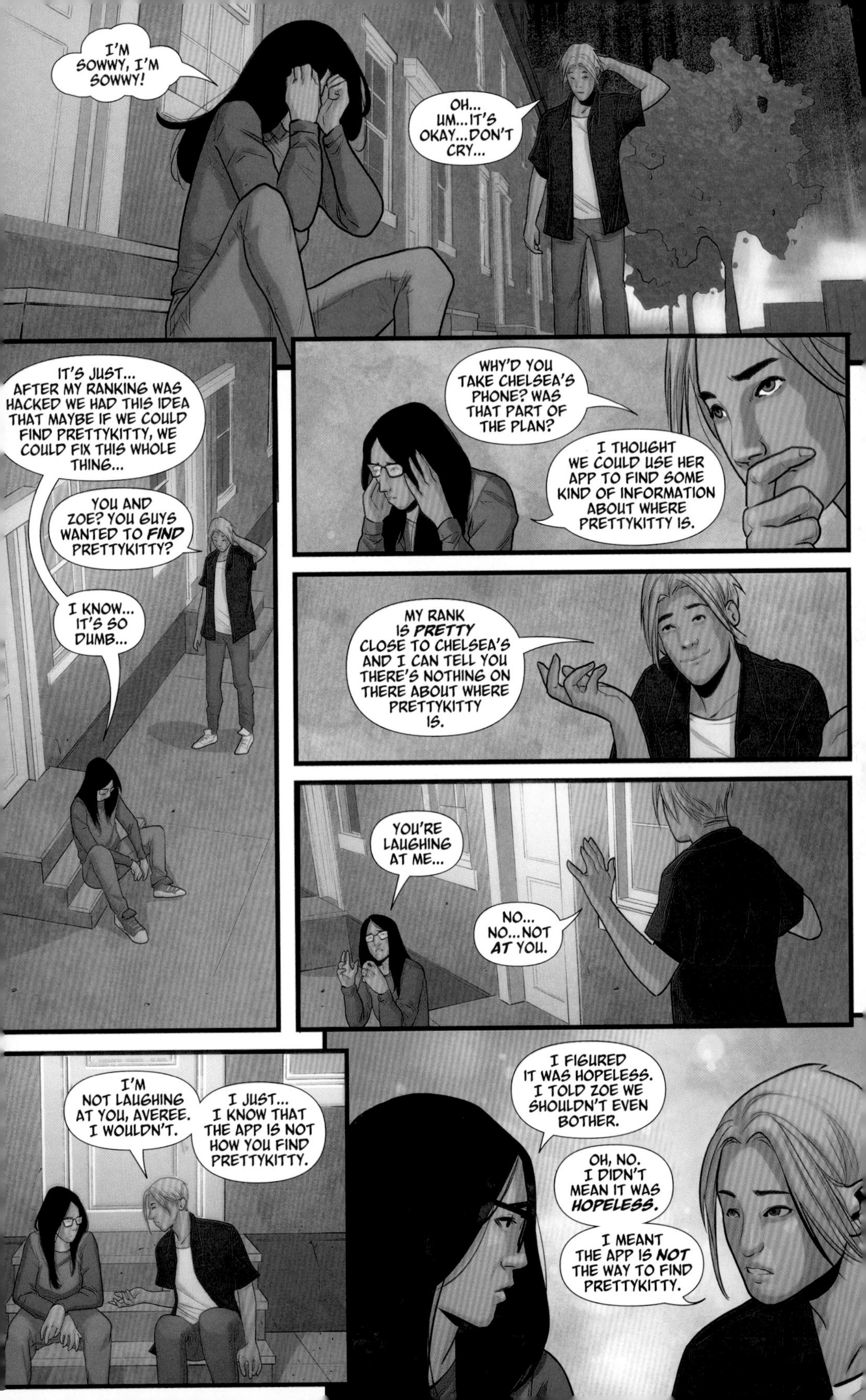
I'M SOWWY, I'M SOWWY!
OH... UM...IT'S OKAY...DON'T CRY...
IT'S JUST... AFTER MY RANKING WAS HACKED WE HAD THIS IDEA THAT MAYBE IF WE COULD FIND PRETTYKITTY, WE COULD FIX THIS WHOLE THING...
YOU AND ZOE? YOU GUYS WANTED TO *FIND* PRETTYKITTY?
I KNOW... IT'S SO DUMB...
WHY'D YOU TAKE CHELSEA'S PHONE? WAS THAT PART OF THE PLAN?
I THOUGHT WE COULD USE HER APP TO FIND SOME KIND OF INFORMATION ABOUT WHERE PRETTYKITTY IS.
MY RANK IS *PRETTY* CLOSE TO CHELSEA'S AND I CAN TELL YOU THERE'S NOTHING ON THERE ABOUT WHERE PRETTYKITTY IS.
YOU'RE LAUGHING AT ME...
NO... NO...NOT *AT* YOU.
I'M NOT LAUGHING AT YOU, AVEREE. I WOULDN'T.
I JUST... I KNOW THAT THE APP IS NOT HOW YOU FIND PRETTYKITTY.
I FIGURED IT WAS HOPELESS. I TOLD ZOE WE SHOULDN'T EVEN BOTHER.
OH, NO. I DIDN'T MEAN IT WAS *HOPELESS.*
I MEANT THE APP IS *NOT* THE WAY TO FIND PRETTYKITTY.

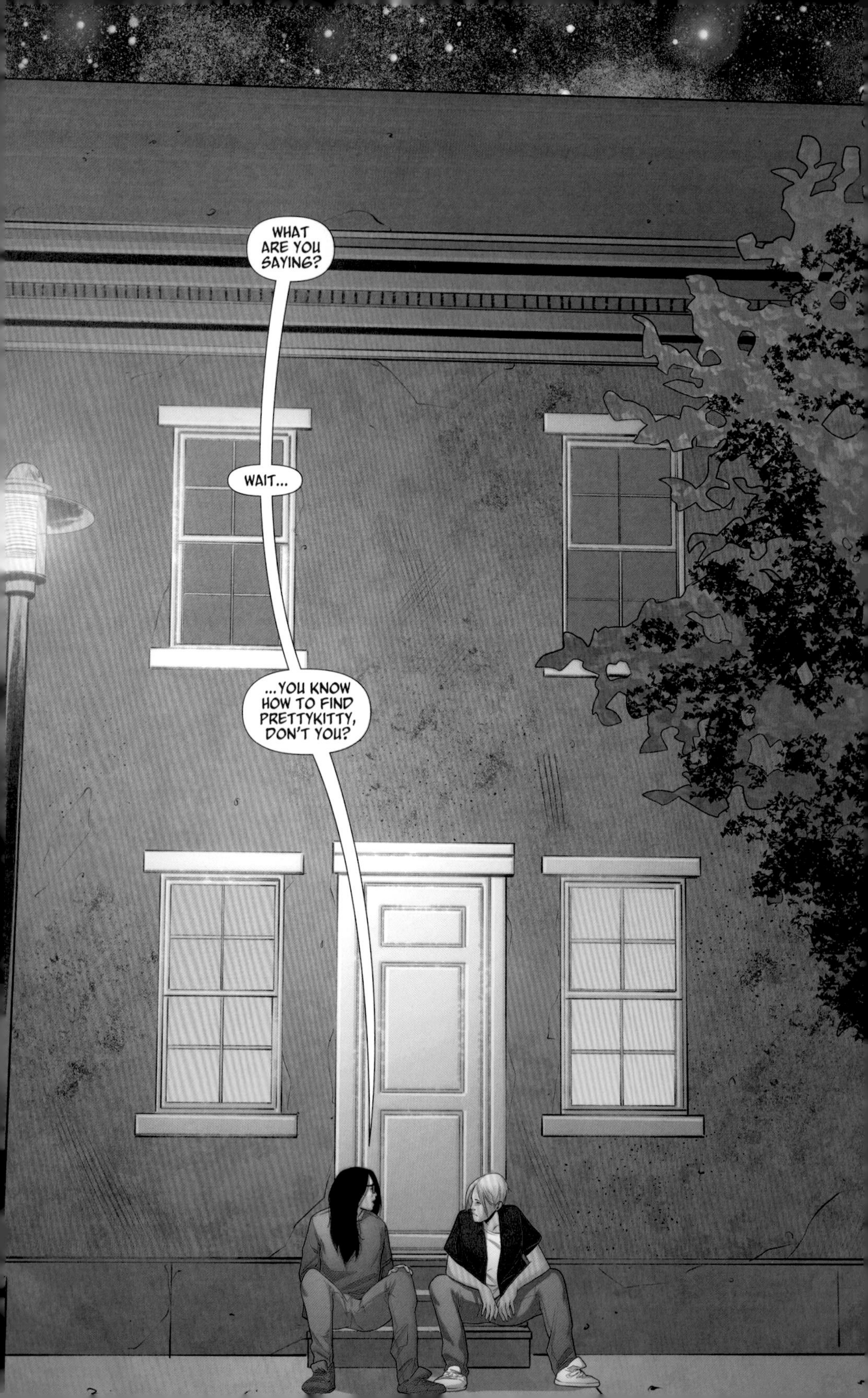
WHAT ARE YOU SAYING?
WAIT...
...YOU KNOW HOW TO FIND PRETTYKITTY, DON'T YOU?

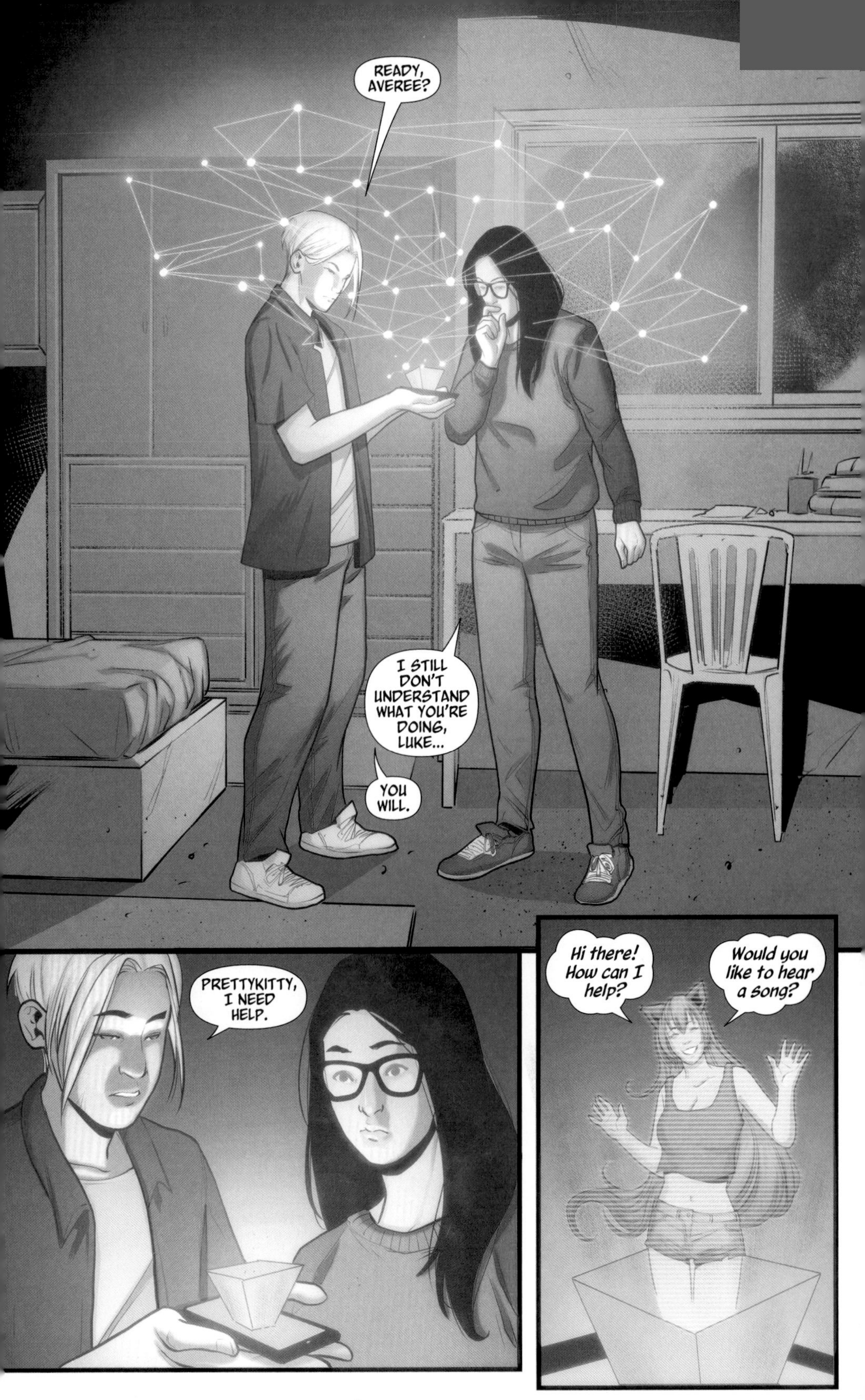
READY, AVEREE?
I STILL DON'T UNDERSTAND WHAT YOU'RE DOING, LUKE...
YOU WILL.
PRETTYKITTY, I NEED HELP.
Hi there! How can I help?
Would you like to hear a song?

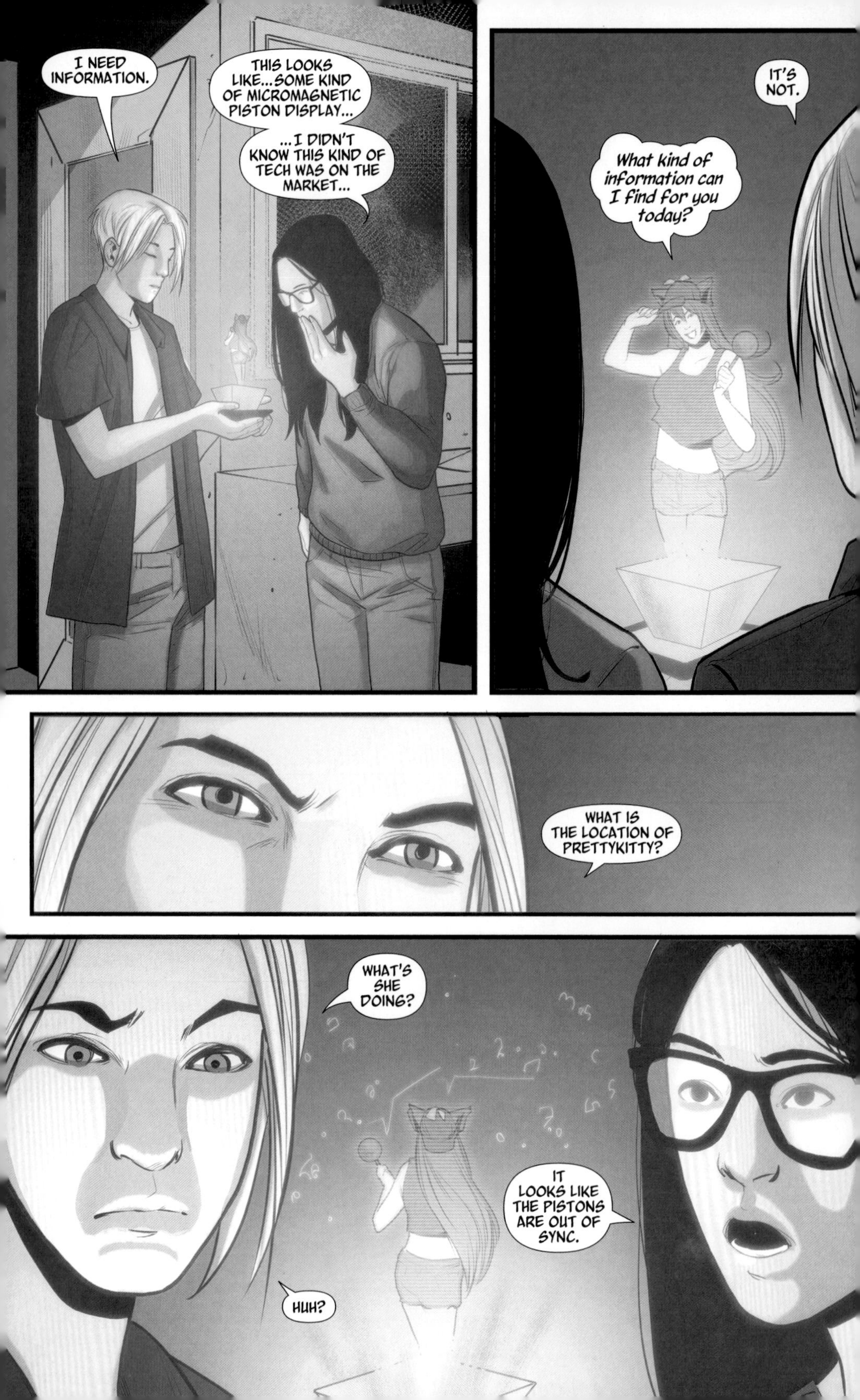
I NEED INFORMATION.
THIS LOOKS LIKE...SOME KIND OF MICROMAGNETIC PISTON DISPLAY...
...I DIDN'T KNOW THIS KIND OF TECH WAS ON THE MARKET...
IT'S NOT.
What kind of information can I find for you today?
WHAT IS THE LOCATION OF PRETTYKITTY?
WHAT'S SHE DOING?
IT LOOKS LIKE THE PISTONS ARE OUT OF SYNC.
HUH?

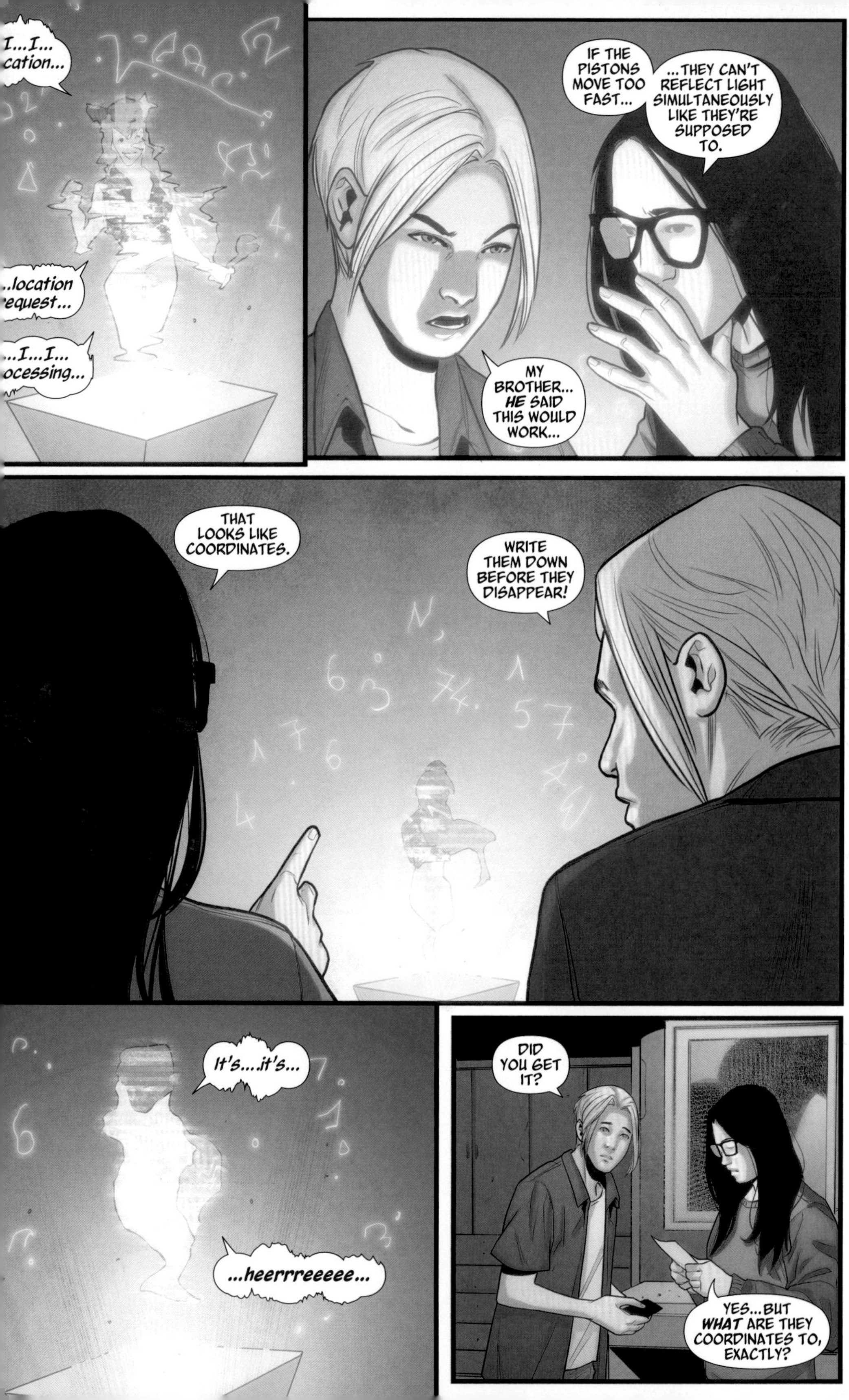

I...I... cation...
...location request...
...I...I... ocessing...
IF THE PISTONS MOVE TOO FAST...
...THEY CAN'T REFLECT LIGHT SIMULTANEOUSLY LIKE THEY'RE SUPPOSED TO.
MY BROTHER... HE SAID THIS WOULD WORK...
THAT LOOKS LIKE COORDINATES.
WRITE THEM DOWN BEFORE THEY DISAPPEAR!
It's....it's...
...heerrreeeee...
DID YOU GET IT?
YES...BUT WHAT ARE THEY COORDINATES TO, EXACTLY?

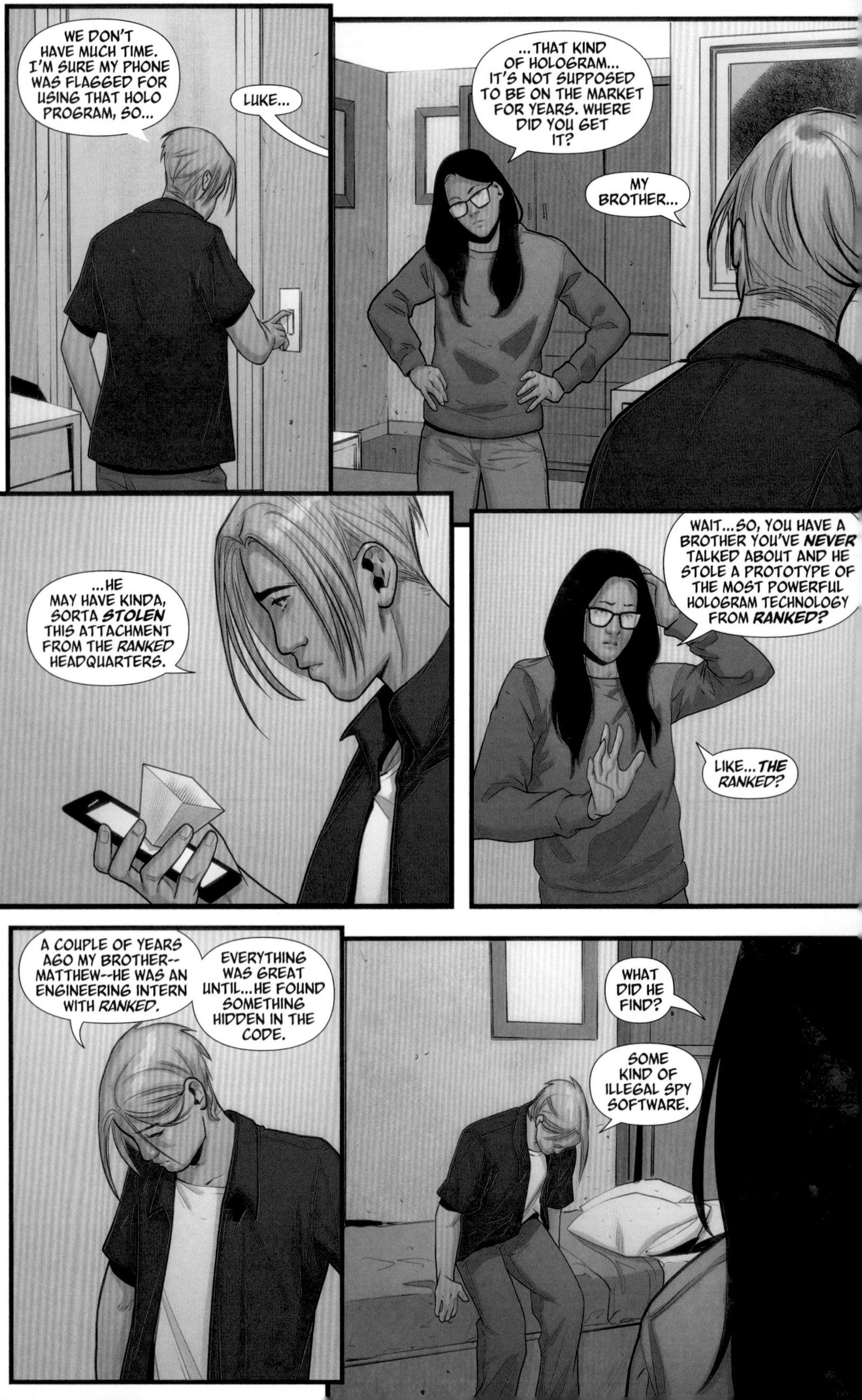
WE DON'T HAVE MUCH TIME. I'M SURE MY PHONE WAS FLAGGED FOR USING THAT HOLO PROGRAM, SO...
LUKE...
...THAT KIND OF HOLOGRAM... IT'S NOT SUPPOSED TO BE ON THE MARKET FOR YEARS. WHERE DID YOU GET IT?
MY BROTHER...
...HE MAY HAVE KINDA, SORTA STOLEN THIS ATTACHMENT FROM THE RANKED HEADQUARTERS.
WAIT...SO, YOU HAVE A BROTHER YOU'VE NEVER TALKED ABOUT AND HE STOLE A PROTOTYPE OF THE MOST POWERFUL HOLOGRAM TECHNOLOGY FROM RANKED?
LIKE...THE RANKED?
A COUPLE OF YEARS AGO MY BROTHER--MATTHEW--HE WAS AN ENGINEERING INTERN WITH RANKED.
EVERYTHING WAS GREAT UNTIL...HE FOUND SOMETHING HIDDEN IN THE CODE.
WHAT DID HE FIND?
SOME KIND OF ILLEGAL SPY SOFTWARE.

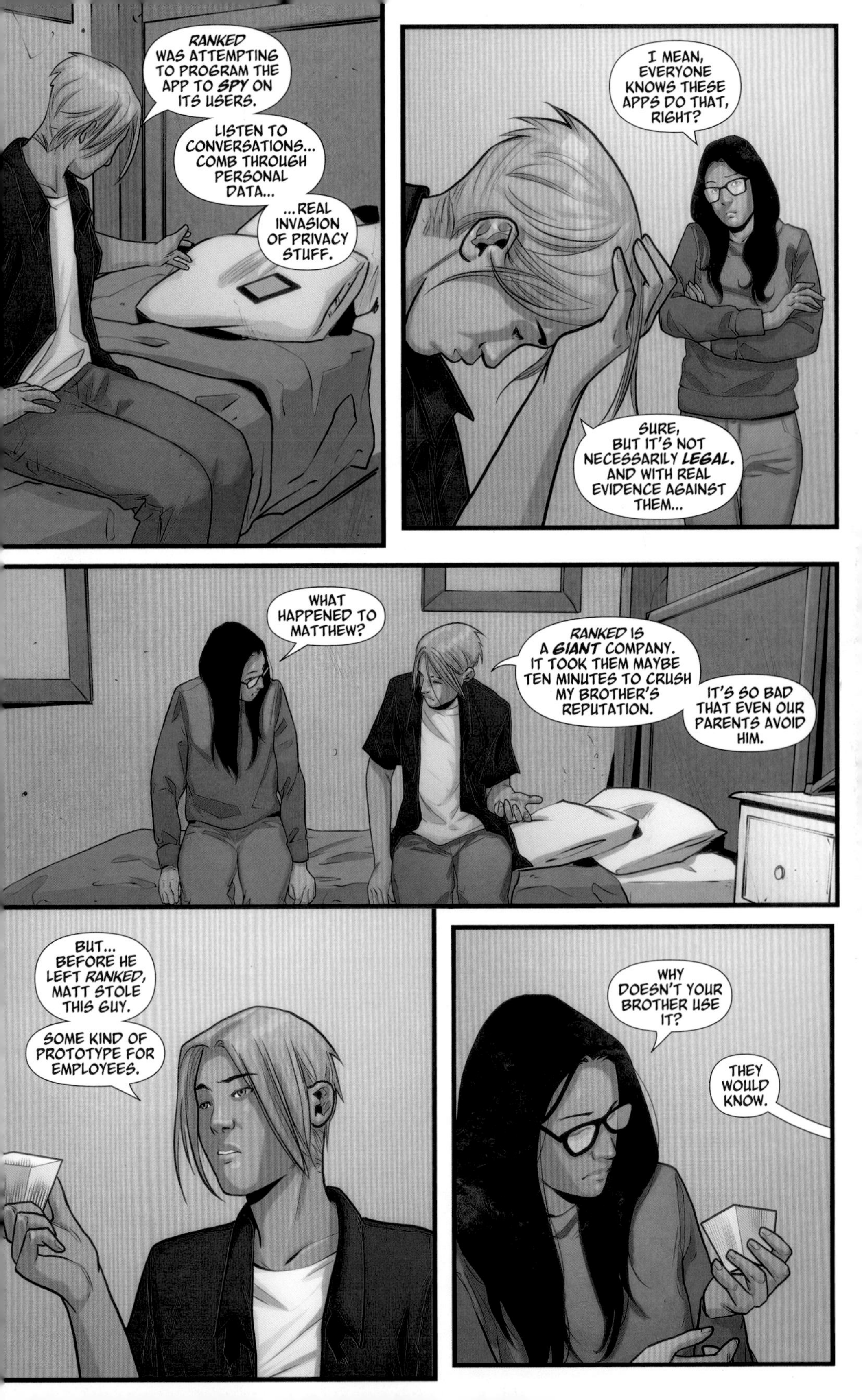
RANKED WAS ATTEMPTING TO PROGRAM THE APP TO SPY ON ITS USERS.
LISTEN TO CONVERSATIONS... COMB THROUGH PERSONAL DATA...
...REAL INVASION OF PRIVACY STUFF.
I MEAN, EVERYONE KNOWS THESE APPS DO THAT, RIGHT?
SURE, BUT IT'S NOT NECESSARILY LEGAL. AND WITH REAL EVIDENCE AGAINST THEM...
WHAT HAPPENED TO MATTHEW?
RANKED IS A GIANT COMPANY. IT TOOK THEM MAYBE TEN MINUTES TO CRUSH MY BROTHER'S REPUTATION.
IT'S SO BAD THAT EVEN OUR PARENTS AVOID HIM.
BUT... BEFORE HE LEFT RANKED, MATT STOLE THIS GUY.
SOME KIND OF PROTOTYPE FOR EMPLOYEES.
WHY DOESN'T YOUR BROTHER USE IT?
THEY WOULD KNOW.

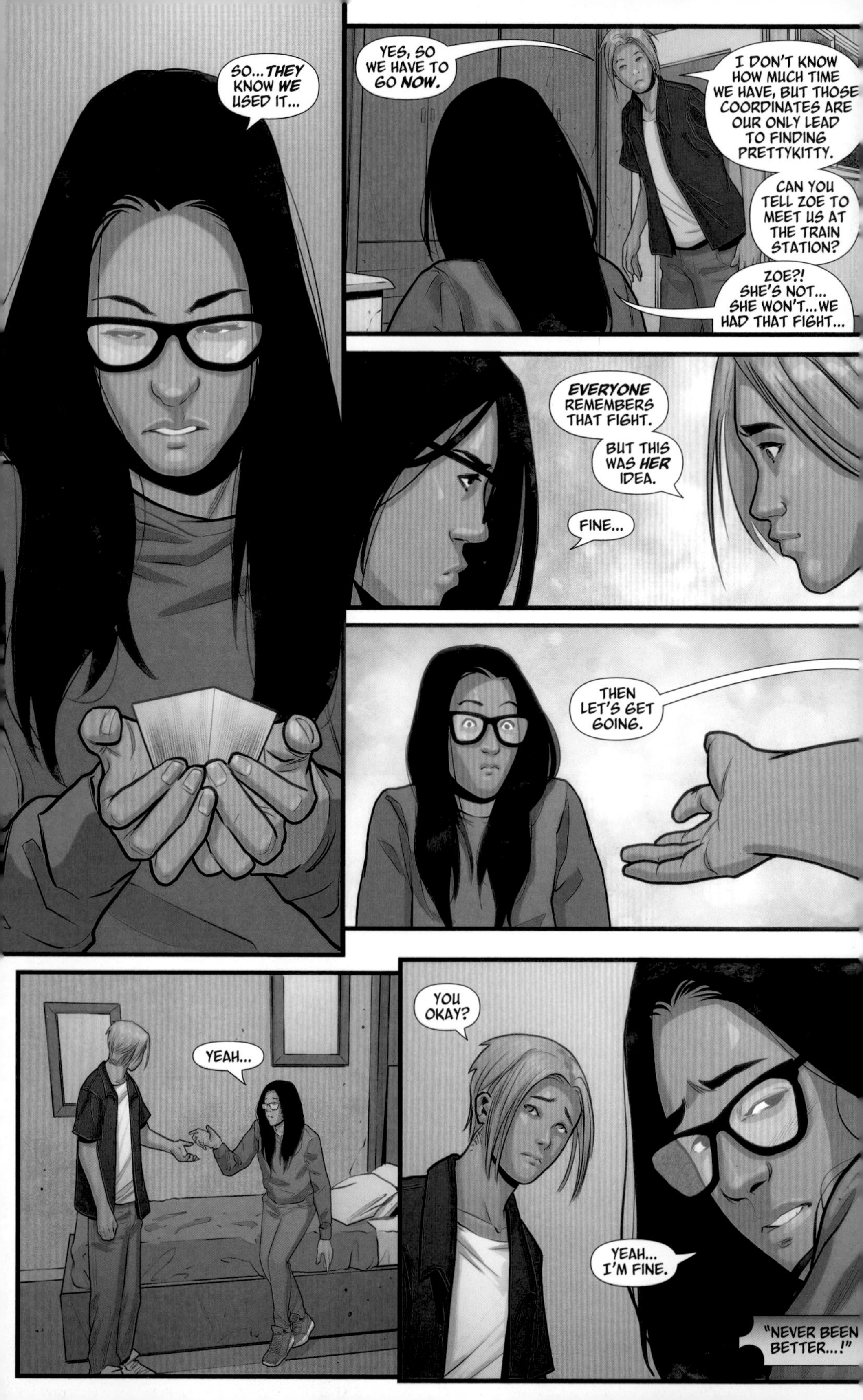
SO...THEY KNOW WE USED IT...
YES, SO WE HAVE TO GO NOW.
I DON'T KNOW HOW MUCH TIME WE HAVE, BUT THOSE COORDINATES ARE OUR ONLY LEAD TO FINDING PRETTYKITTY.
CAN YOU TELL ZOE TO MEET US AT THE TRAIN STATION?
ZOE?! SHE'S NOT... SHE WON'T...WE HAD THAT FIGHT...
EVERYONE REMEMBERS THAT FIGHT.
BUT THIS WAS HER IDEA.
FINE...
THEN LET'S GET GOING.
YEAH...
YOU OKAY?
YEAH... I'M FINE.
"NEVER BEEN BETTER...!"

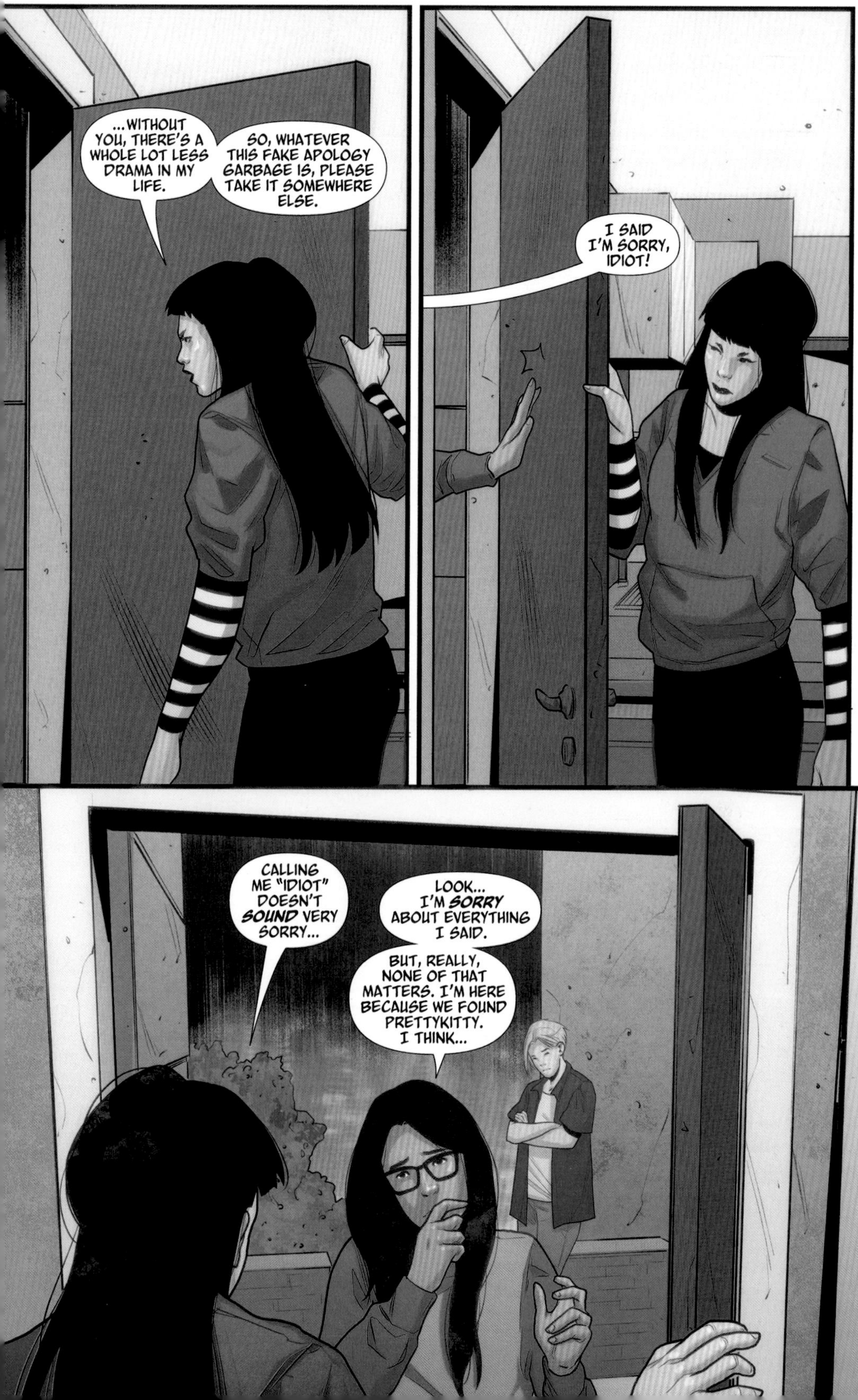
...WITHOUT YOU, THERE'S A WHOLE LOT LESS DRAMA IN MY LIFE.
SO, WHATEVER THIS FAKE APOLOGY GARBAGE IS, PLEASE TAKE IT SOMEWHERE ELSE.
I SAID I'M SORRY, IDIOT!
CALLING ME "IDIOT" DOESN'T *SOUND* VERY SORRY...
LOOK... I'M *SORRY* ABOUT EVERYTHING I SAID.
BUT, REALLY, NONE OF THAT MATTERS. I'M HERE BECAUSE WE FOUND PRETTYKITTY. I THINK...

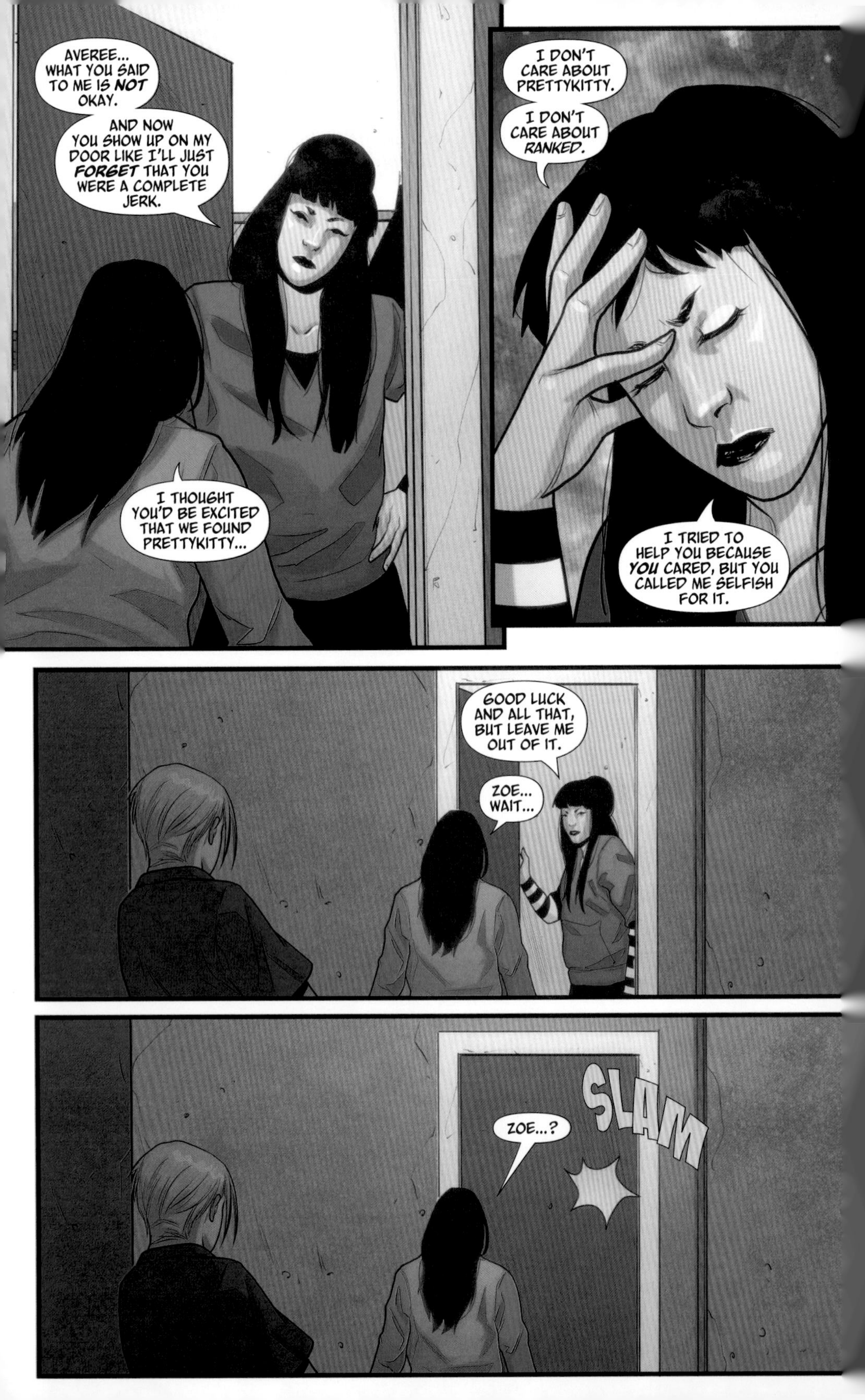
AVEREE... WHAT YOU SAID TO ME IS **NOT** OKAY.
AND NOW YOU SHOW UP ON MY DOOR LIKE I'LL JUST **FORGET** THAT YOU WERE A COMPLETE JERK.
I THOUGHT YOU'D BE EXCITED THAT WE FOUND PRETTYKITTY...
I DON'T CARE ABOUT PRETTYKITTY.
I DON'T CARE ABOUT *RANKED*.
I TRIED TO HELP YOU BECAUSE **YOU** CARED, BUT YOU CALLED ME SELFISH FOR IT.
GOOD LUCK AND ALL THAT, BUT LEAVE ME OUT OF IT.
ZOE... WAIT...
SLAM
ZOE...?

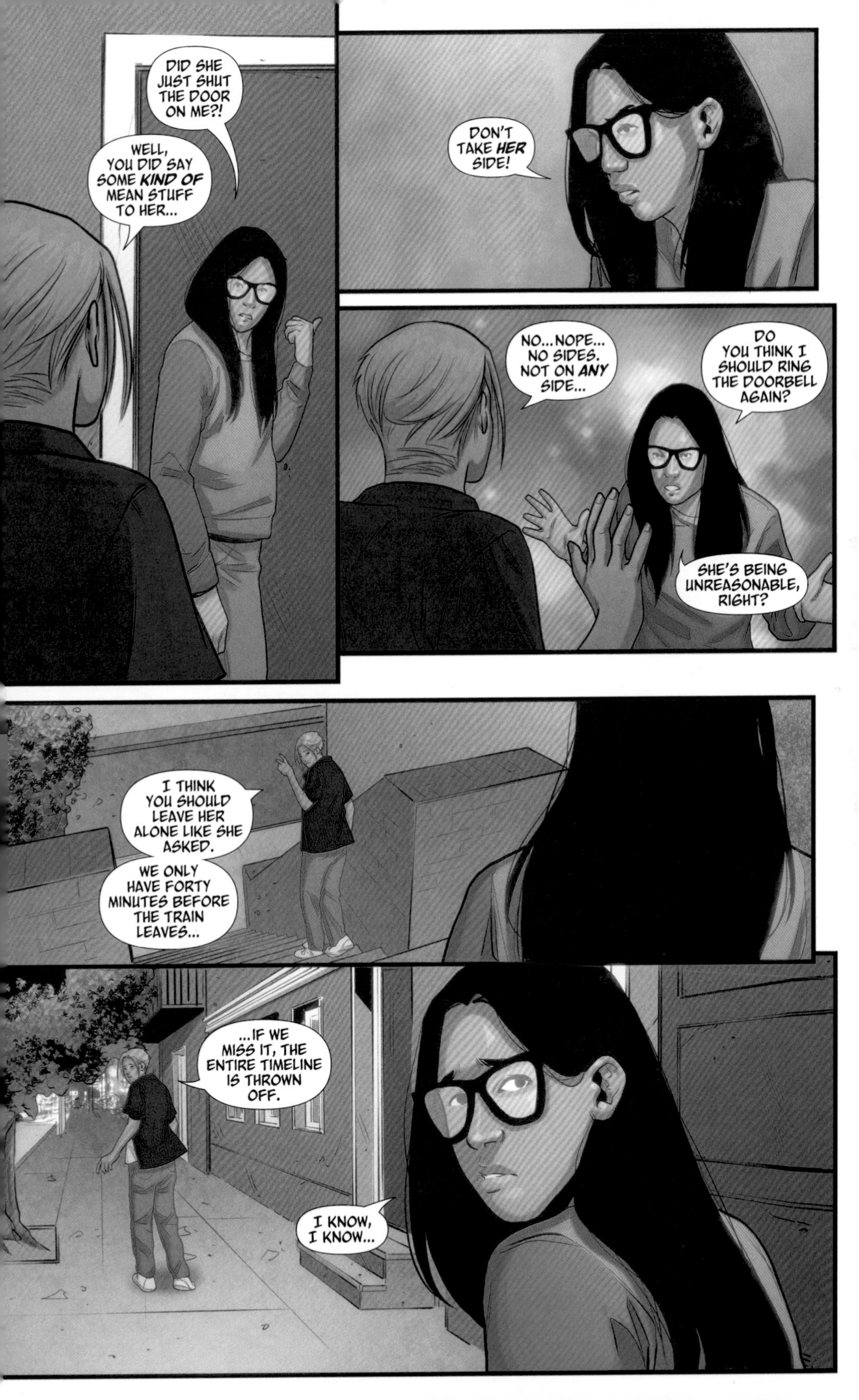
DID SHE JUST SHUT THE DOOR ON ME?!
WELL, YOU DID SAY SOME KIND OF MEAN STUFF TO HER...
DON'T TAKE HER SIDE!
NO... NOPE... NO SIDES. NOT ON ANY SIDE...
DO YOU THINK I SHOULD RING THE DOORBELL AGAIN?
SHE'S BEING UNREASONABLE, RIGHT?
I THINK YOU SHOULD LEAVE HER ALONE LIKE SHE ASKED.
WE ONLY HAVE FORTY MINUTES BEFORE THE TRAIN LEAVES...
...IF WE MISS IT, THE ENTIRE TIMELINE IS THROWN OFF.
I KNOW, I KNOW...

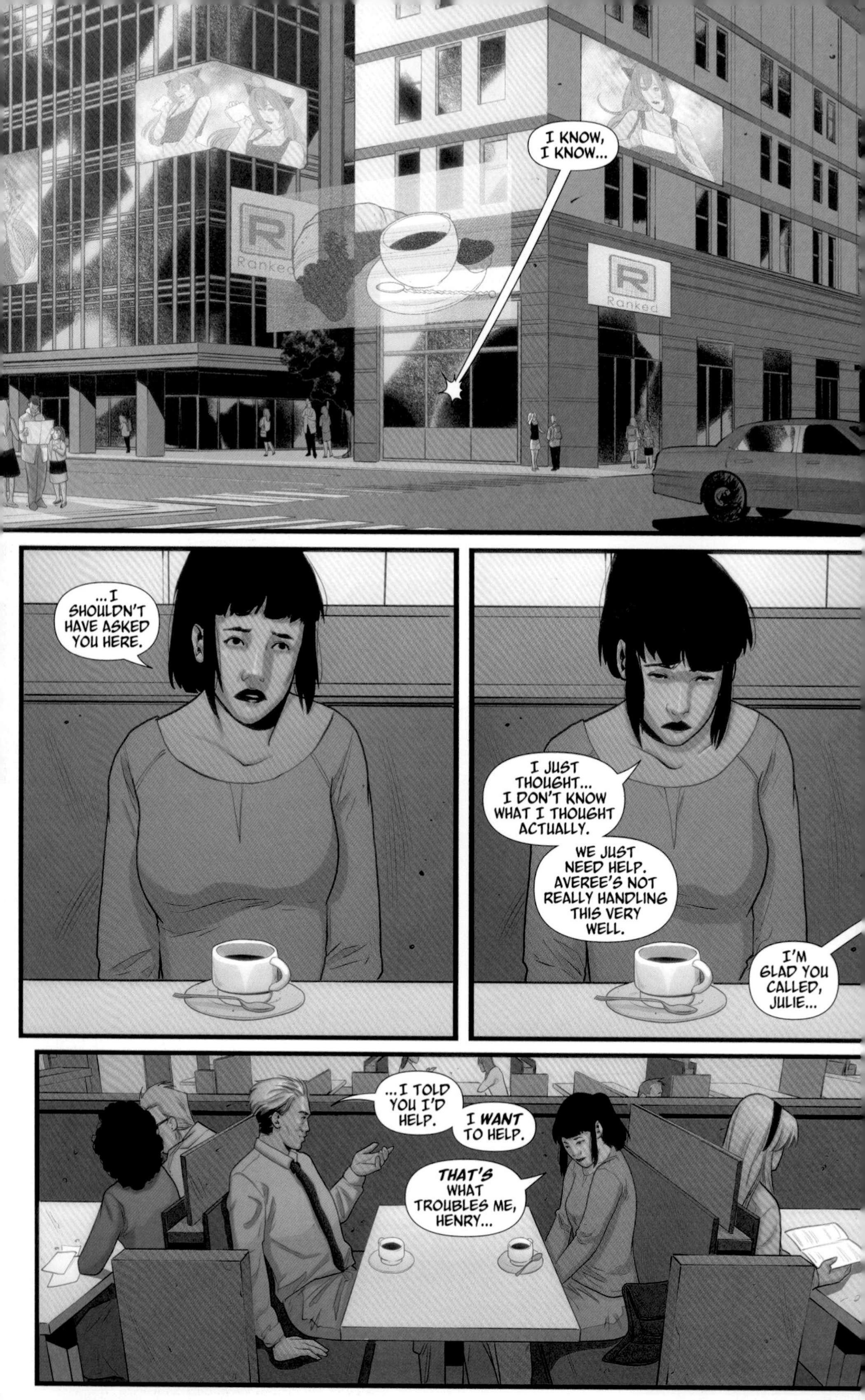
I KNOW, I KNOW...
Ranked
...I SHOULDN'T HAVE ASKED YOU HERE.
I JUST THOUGHT... I DON'T KNOW WHAT I THOUGHT ACTUALLY.
WE JUST NEED HELP. AVEREE'S NOT REALLY HANDLING THIS VERY WELL.
I'M GLAD YOU CALLED, JULIE...
...I TOLD YOU I'D HELP.
I *WANT* TO HELP.
THAT'S WHAT TROUBLES ME, HENRY...

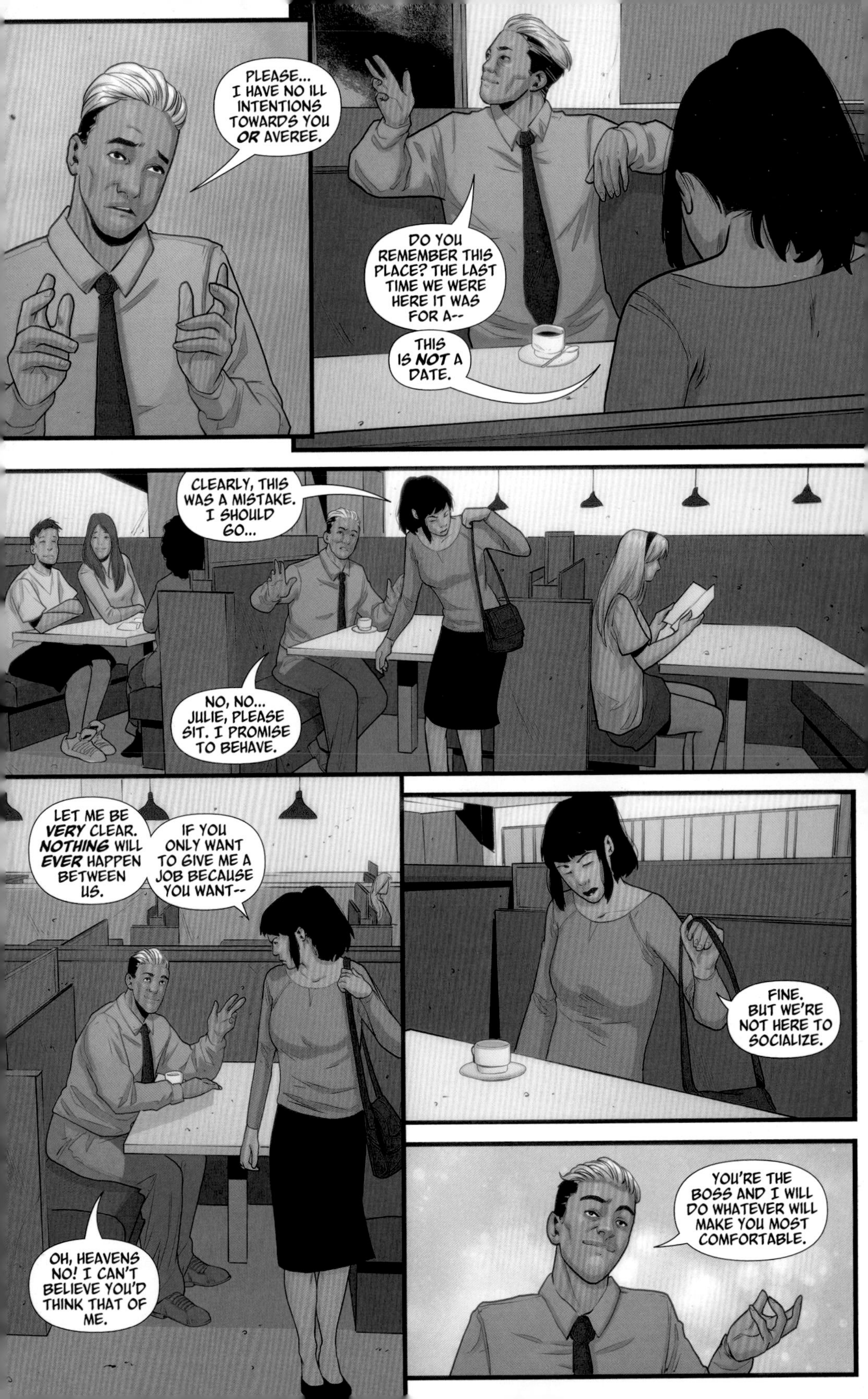
PLEASE... I HAVE NO ILL INTENTIONS TOWARDS YOU OR AVEREE.
DO YOU REMEMBER THIS PLACE? THE LAST TIME WE WERE HERE IT WAS FOR A--
THIS IS NOT A DATE.
CLEARLY, THIS WAS A MISTAKE. I SHOULD GO...
NO, NO... JULIE, PLEASE SIT. I PROMISE TO BEHAVE.
LET ME BE VERY CLEAR. NOTHING WILL EVER HAPPEN BETWEEN US.
IF YOU ONLY WANT TO GIVE ME A JOB BECAUSE YOU WANT--
OH, HEAVENS NO! I CAN'T BELIEVE YOU'D THINK THAT OF ME.
FINE. BUT WE'RE NOT HERE TO SOCIALIZE.
YOU'RE THE BOSS AND I WILL DO WHATEVER WILL MAKE YOU MOST COMFORTABLE.

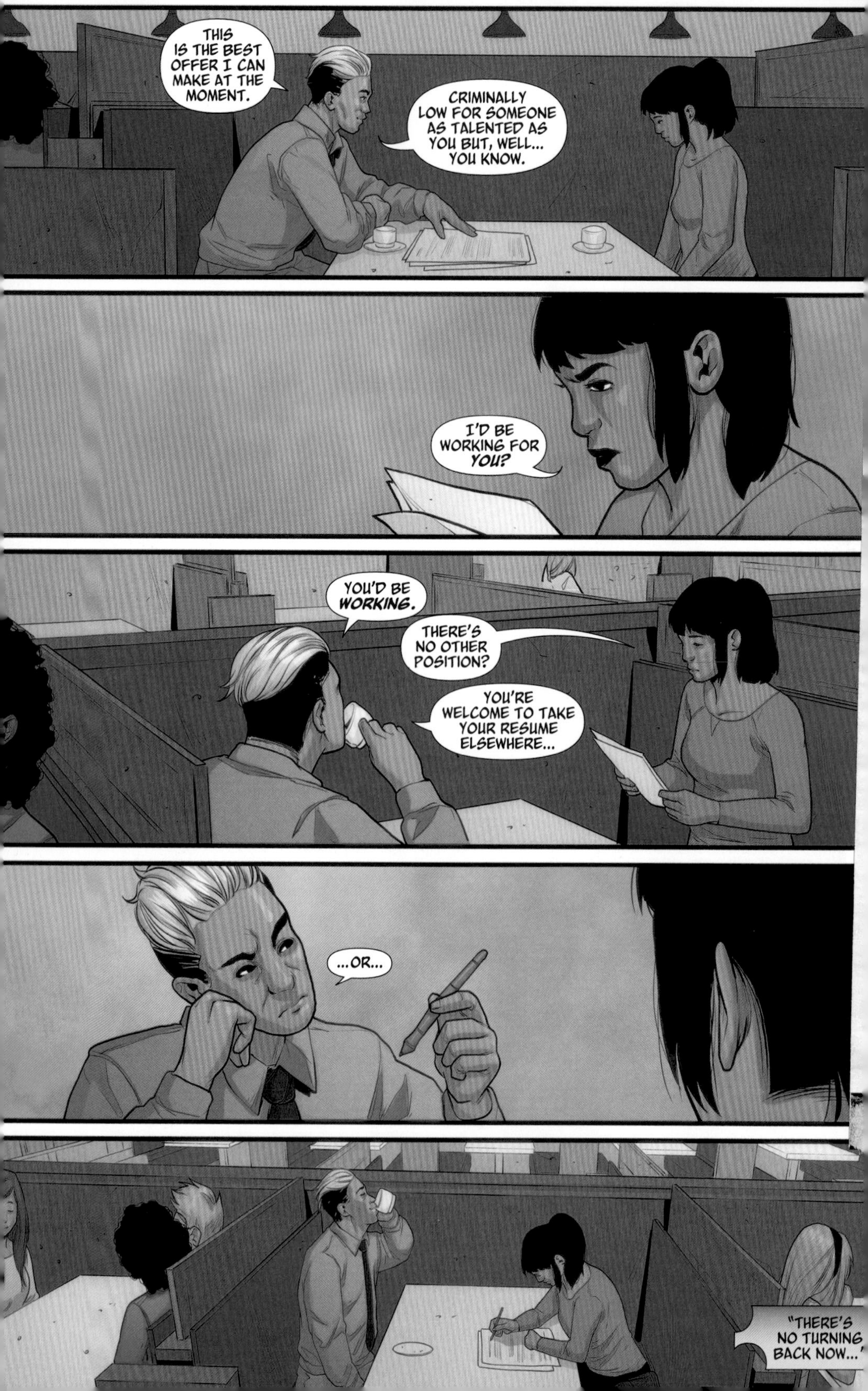
THIS IS THE BEST OFFER I CAN MAKE AT THE MOMENT.
CRIMINALLY LOW FOR SOMEONE AS TALENTED AS YOU BUT, WELL... YOU KNOW.
I'D BE WORKING FOR *YOU?*
YOU'D BE *WORKING.*
THERE'S NO OTHER POSITION?
YOU'RE WELCOME TO TAKE YOUR RESUME ELSEWHERE...
...OR...
"THERE'S NO TURNING BACK NOW..."

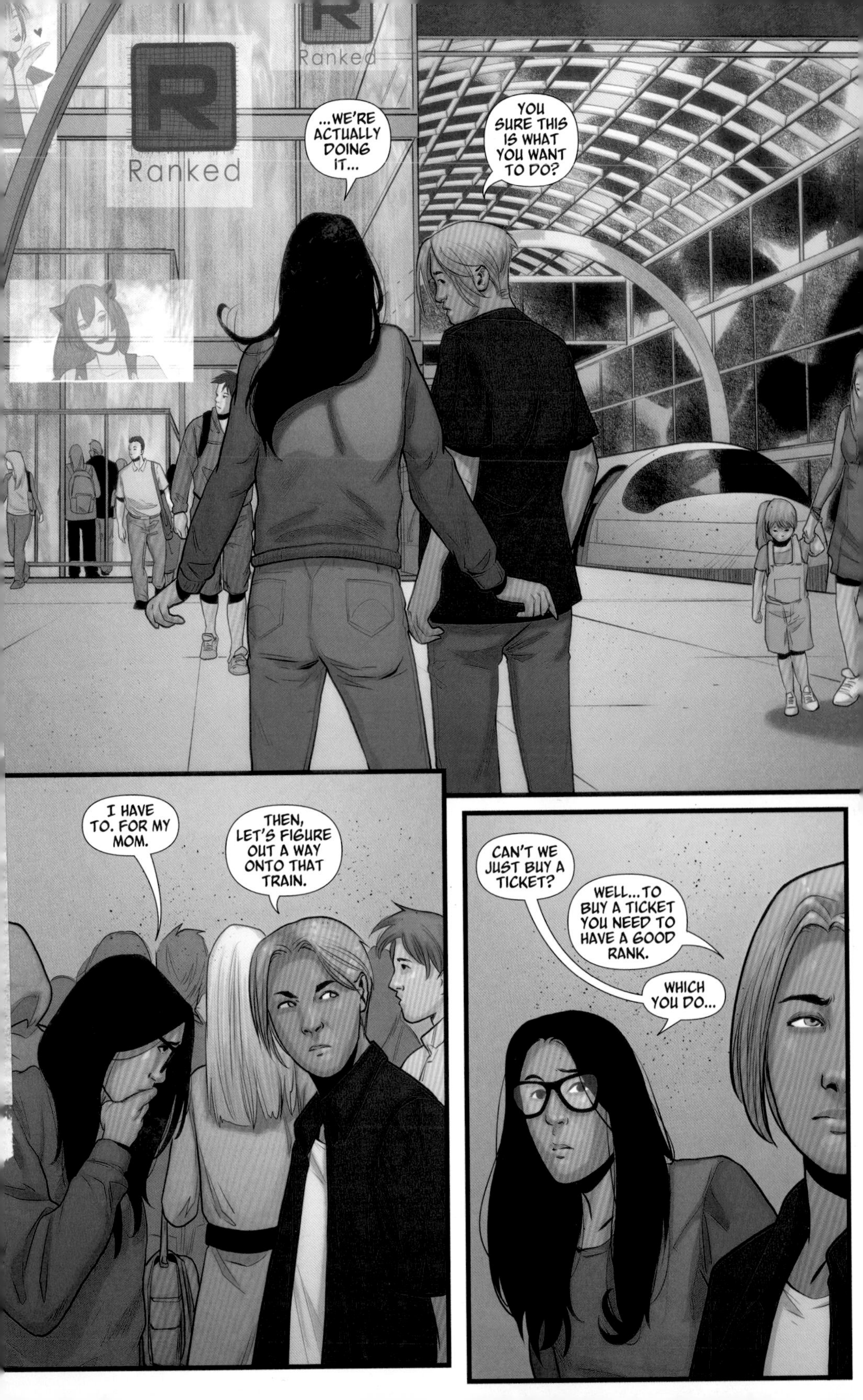
Ranked
Ranked
...WE'RE ACTUALLY DOING IT...
YOU SURE THIS IS WHAT YOU WANT TO DO?
I HAVE TO. FOR MY MOM.
THEN, LET'S FIGURE OUT A WAY ONTO THAT TRAIN.
CAN'T WE JUST BUY A TICKET?
WELL...TO BUY A TICKET YOU NEED TO HAVE A GOOD RANK.
WHICH YOU DO...

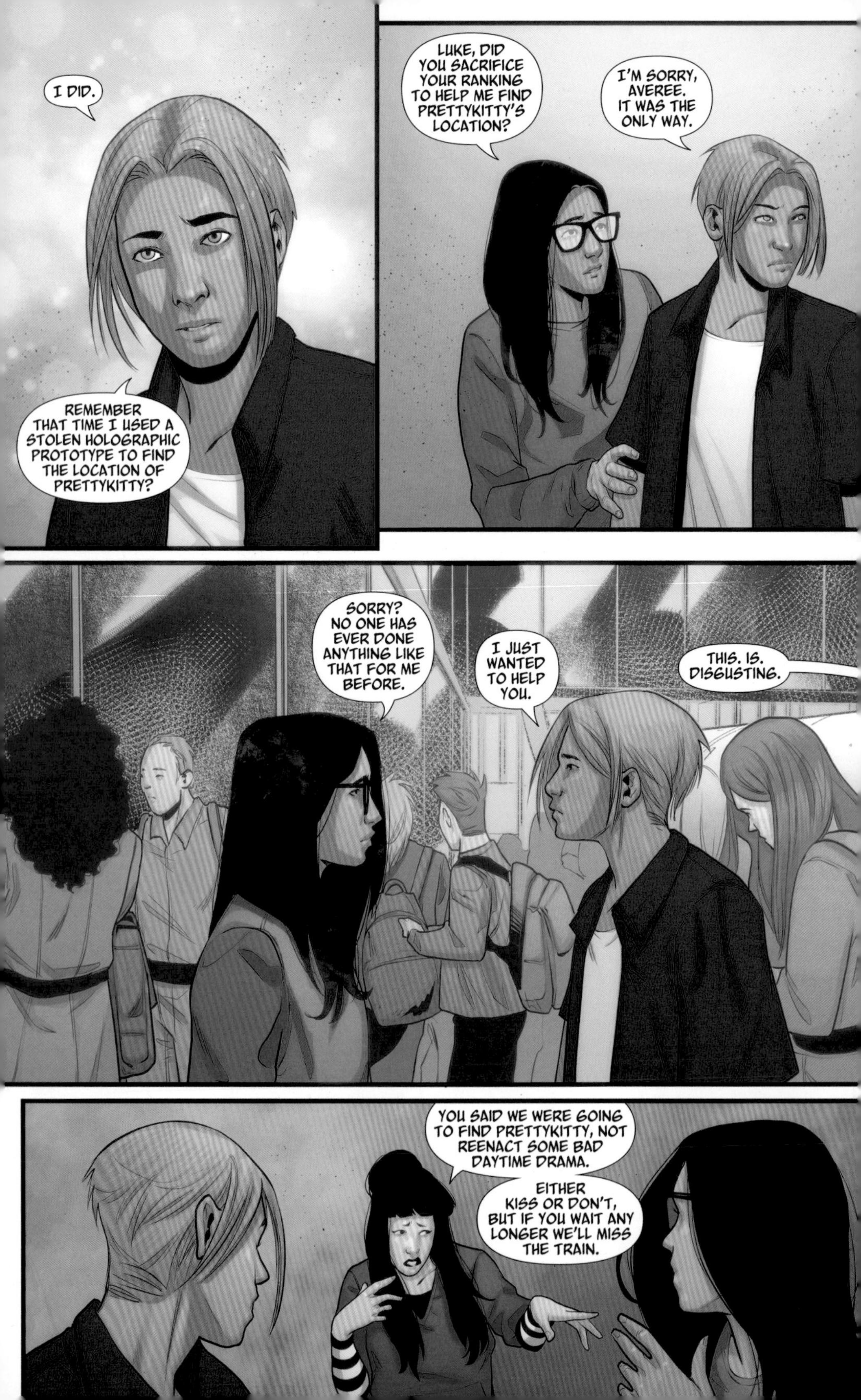

I DID.
REMEMBER THAT TIME I USED A STOLEN HOLOGRAPHIC PROTOTYPE TO FIND THE LOCATION OF PRETTYKITTY?
LUKE, DID YOU SACRIFICE YOUR RANKING TO HELP ME FIND PRETTYKITTY'S LOCATION?
I'M SORRY, AVEREE. IT WAS THE ONLY WAY.
SORRY? NO ONE HAS EVER DONE ANYTHING LIKE THAT FOR ME BEFORE.
I JUST WANTED TO HELP YOU.
THIS. IS. DISGUSTING.
YOU SAID WE WERE GOING TO FIND PRETTYKITTY, NOT REENACT SOME BAD DAYTIME DRAMA.
EITHER KISS OR DON'T, BUT IF YOU WAIT ANY LONGER WE'LL MISS THE TRAIN.

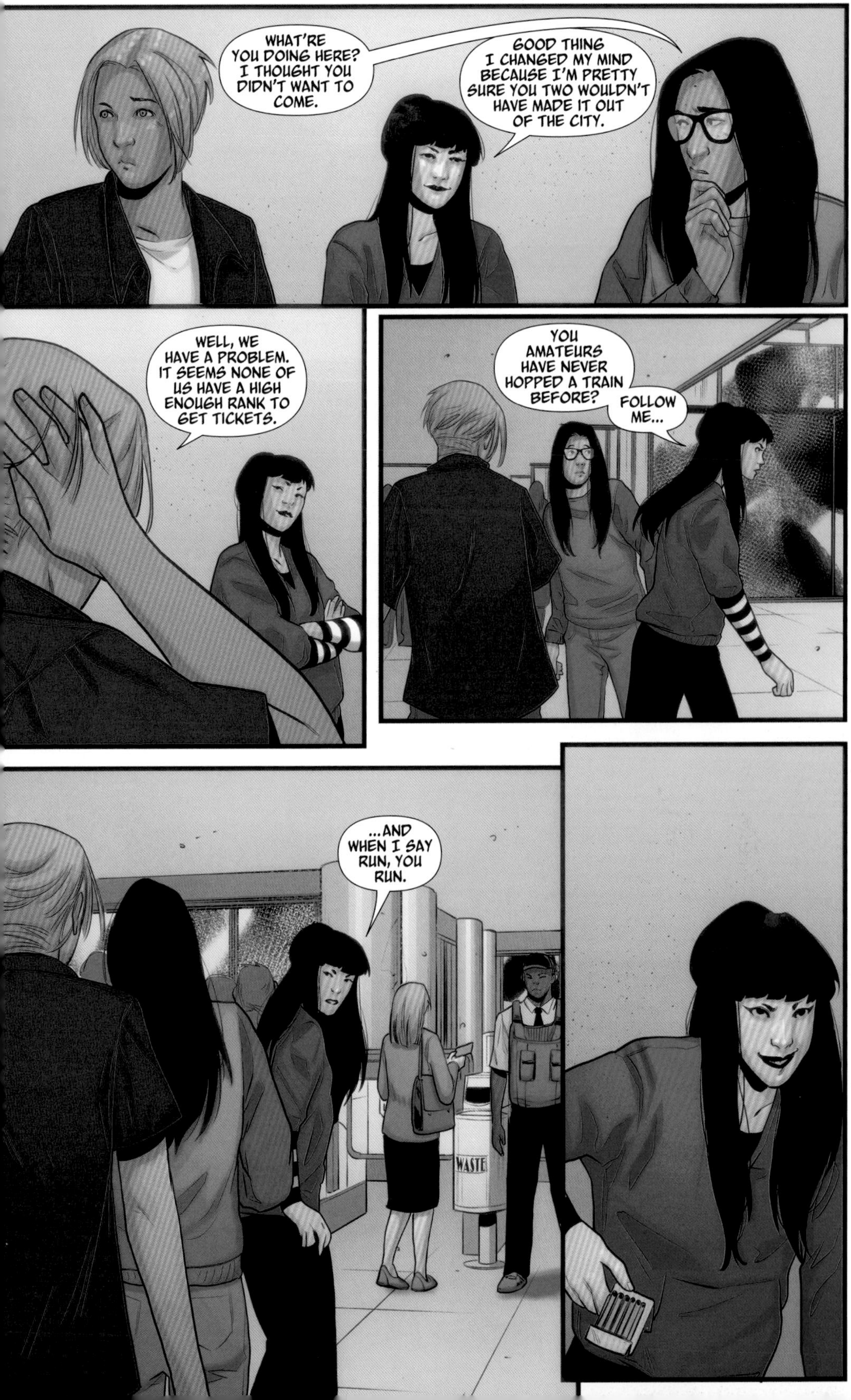

WHAT'RE YOU DOING HERE? I THOUGHT YOU DIDN'T WANT TO COME.
GOOD THING I CHANGED MY MIND BECAUSE I'M PRETTY SURE YOU TWO WOULDN'T HAVE MADE IT OUT OF THE CITY.
WELL, WE HAVE A PROBLEM. IT SEEMS NONE OF US HAVE A HIGH ENOUGH RANK TO GET TICKETS.
YOU AMATEURS HAVE NEVER HOPPED A TRAIN BEFORE?
FOLLOW ME...
...AND WHEN I SAY RUN, YOU RUN.
WASTE

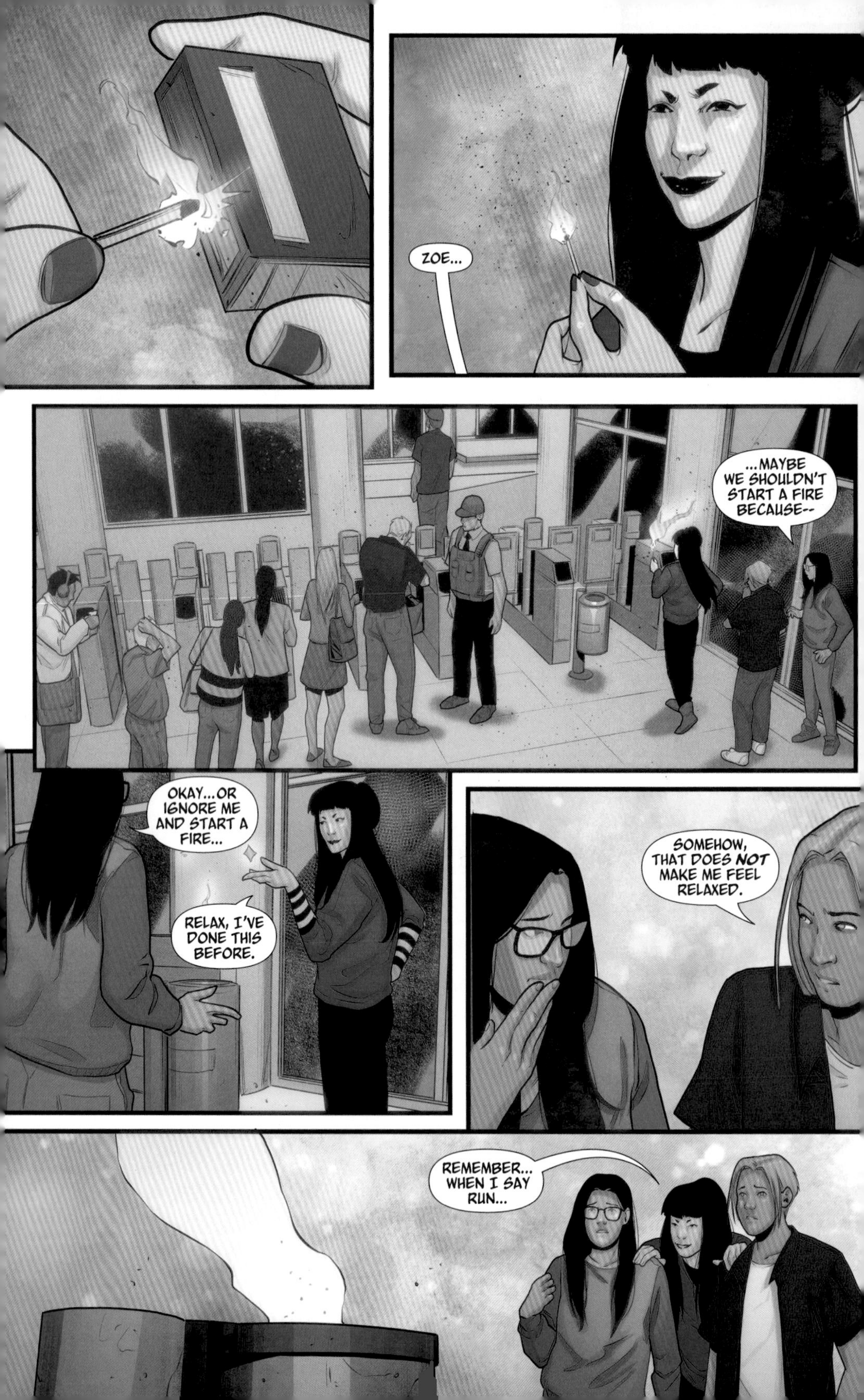
ZOE...
...MAYBE WE SHOULDN'T START A FIRE BECAUSE--
OKAY...OR IGNORE ME AND START A FIRE...
RELAX, I'VE DONE THIS BEFORE.
SOMEHOW, THAT DOES **NOT** MAKE ME FEEL RELAXED.
REMEMBER... WHEN I SAY RUN...

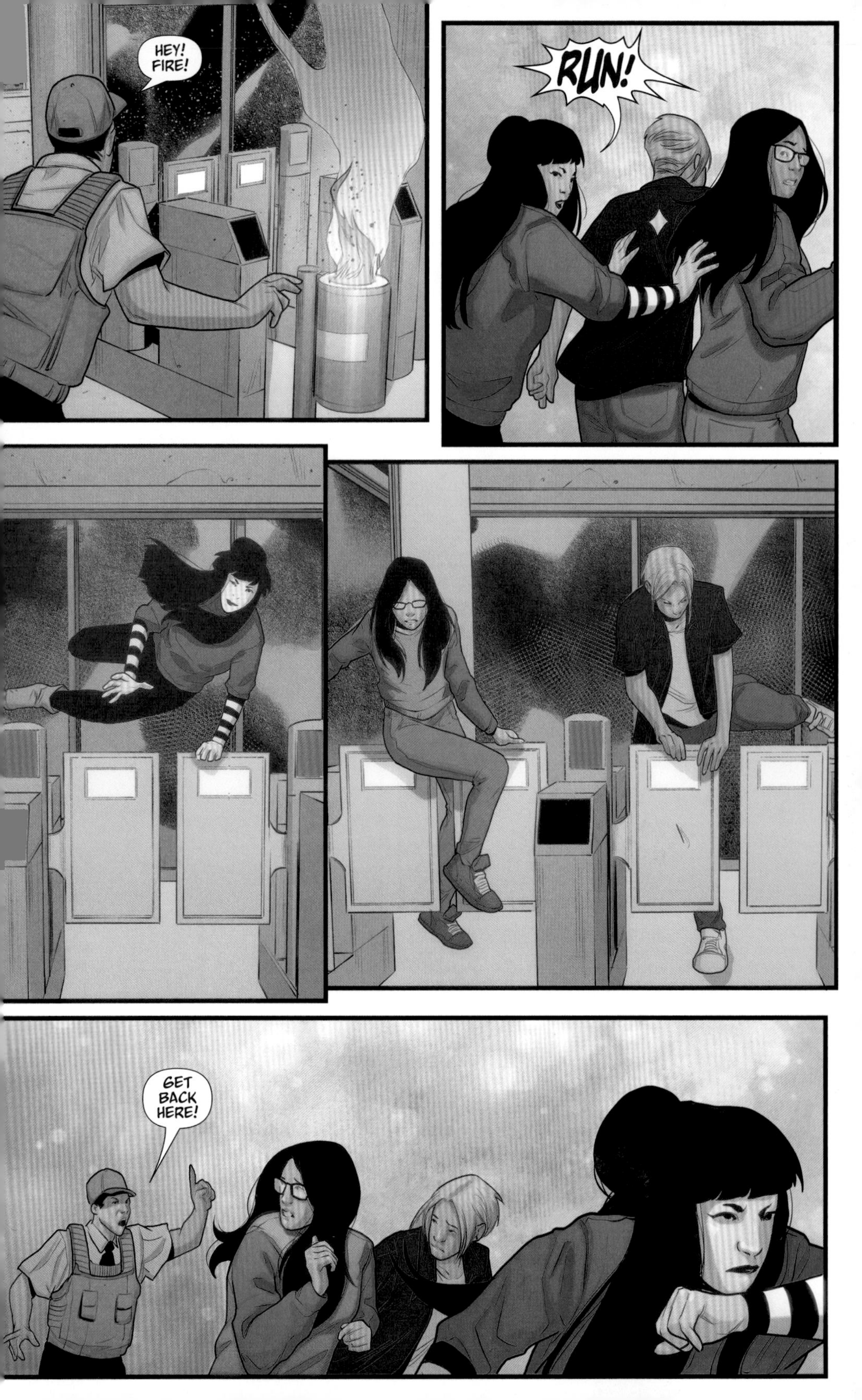
HEY! FIRE!
RUN!
GET BACK HERE!

HEY! STOP THAT TRAIN!

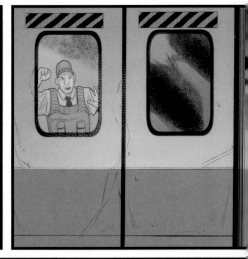

I'LL FIND YOU!

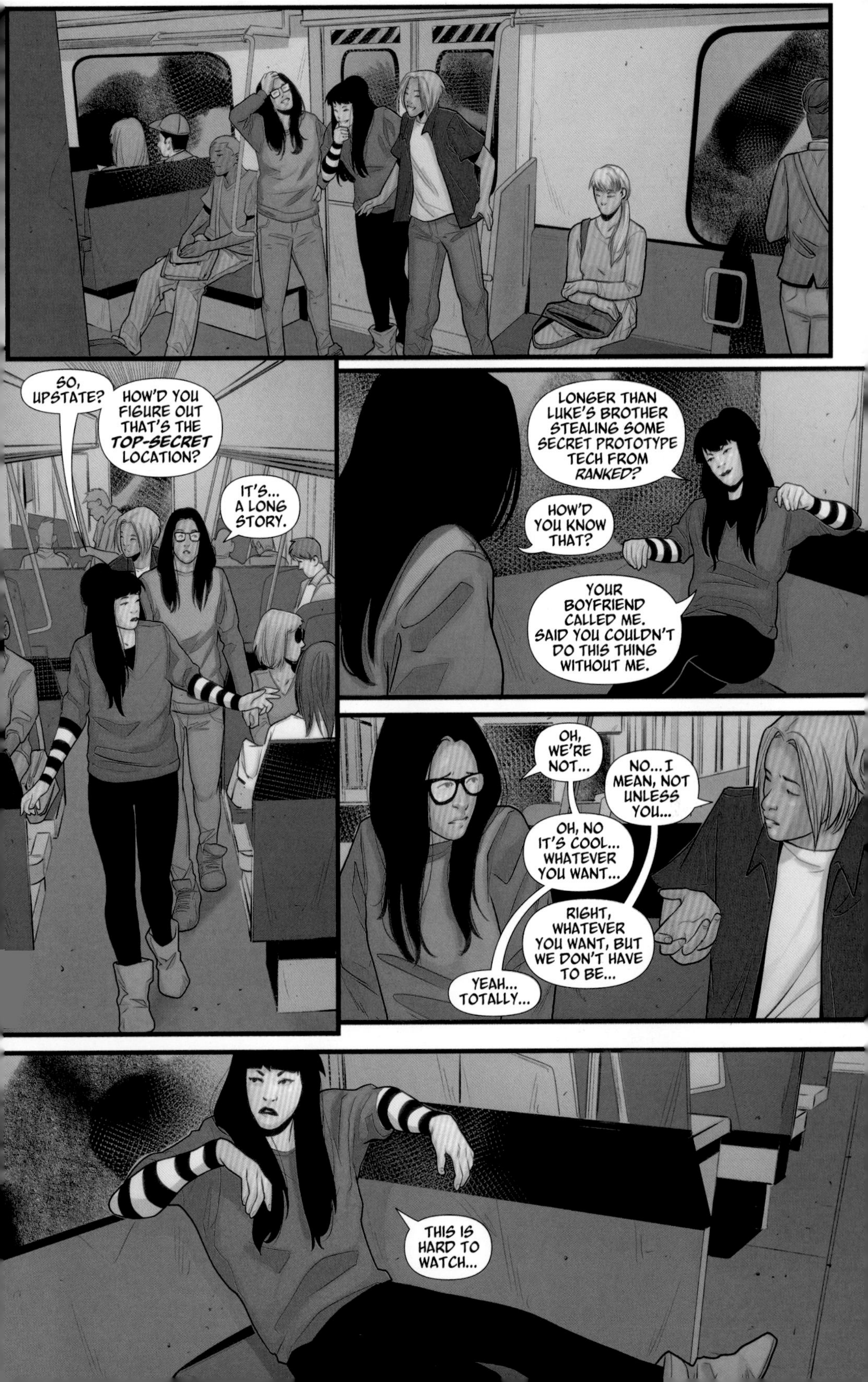
SO, UPSTATE?
HOW'D YOU FIGURE OUT THAT'S THE TOP-SECRET LOCATION?
IT'S... A LONG STORY.
LONGER THAN LUKE'S BROTHER STEALING SOME SECRET PROTOTYPE TECH FROM RANKED?
HOW'D YOU KNOW THAT?
YOUR BOYFRIEND CALLED ME. SAID YOU COULDN'T DO THIS THING WITHOUT ME.
OH, WE'RE NOT...
NO... I MEAN, NOT UNLESS YOU...
OH, NO IT'S COOL... WHATEVER YOU WANT...
RIGHT, WHATEVER YOU WANT, BUT WE DON'T HAVE TO BE...
YEAH... TOTALLY...
THIS IS HARD TO WATCH...

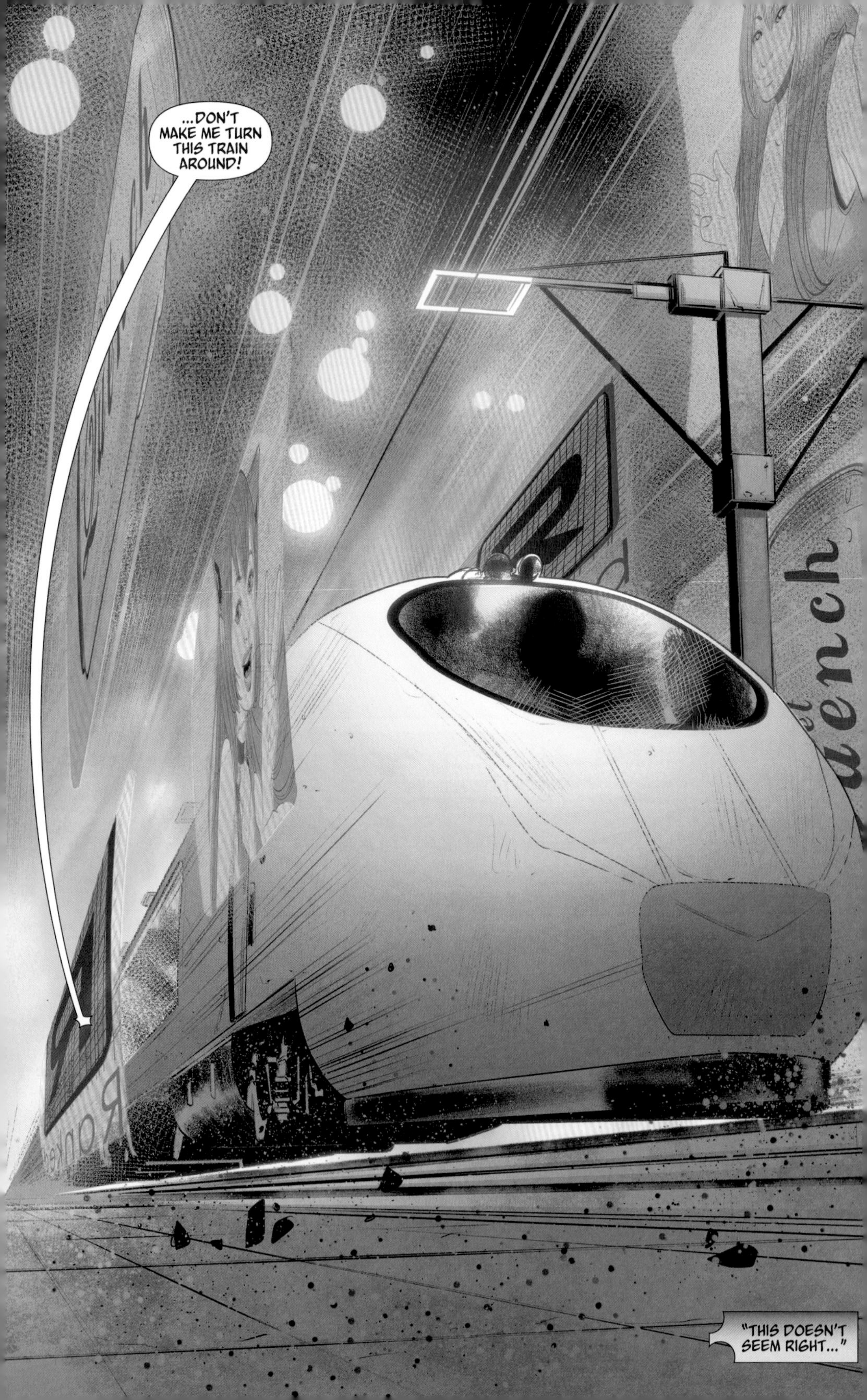
...DON'T MAKE ME TURN THIS TRAIN AROUND!
"THIS DOESN'T SEEM RIGHT..."

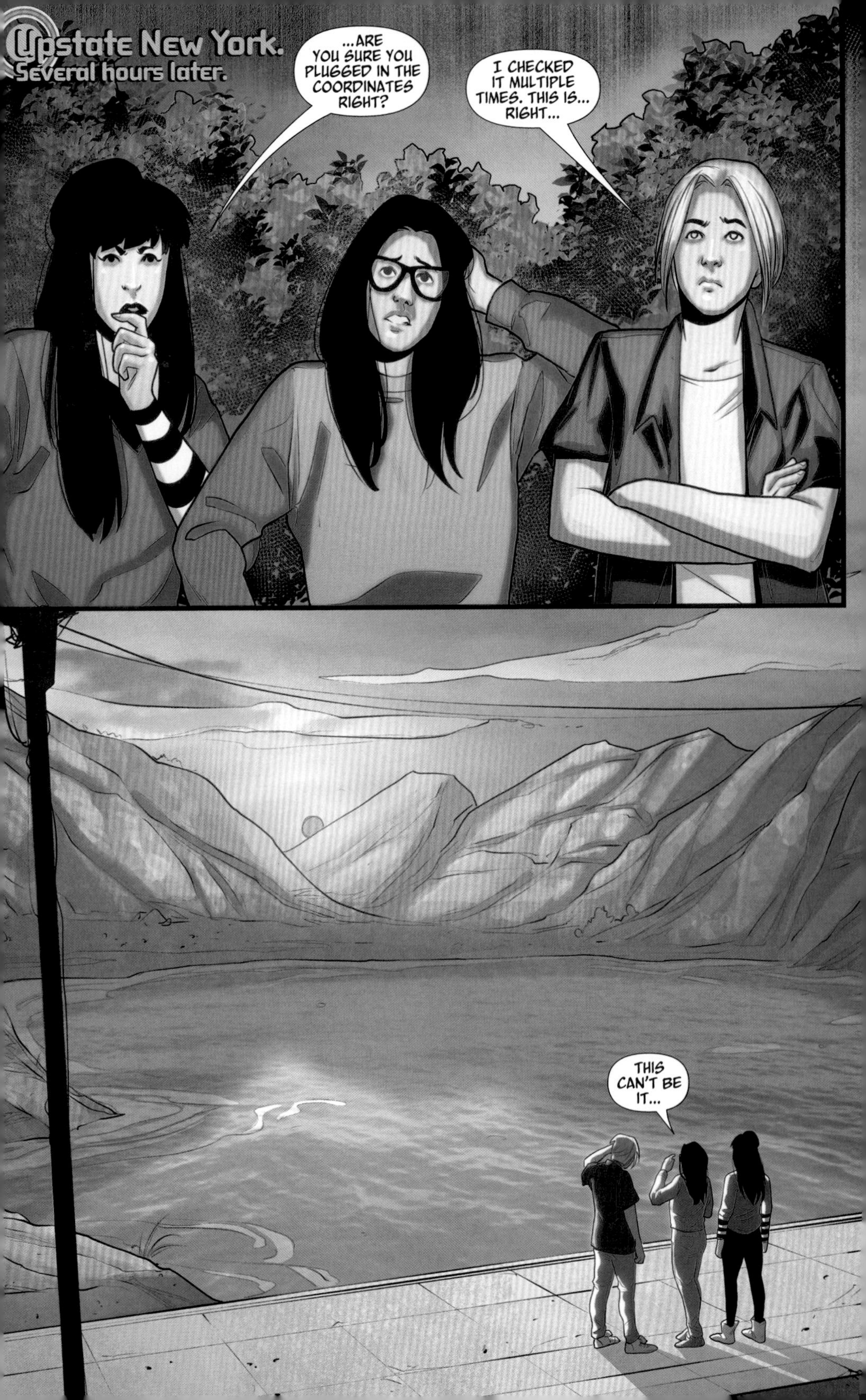
Upstate New York.
Several hours later.
...ARE YOU SURE YOU PLUGGED IN THE COORDINATES RIGHT?
I CHECKED IT MULTIPLE TIMES. THIS IS... RIGHT...
THIS CAN'T BE IT...

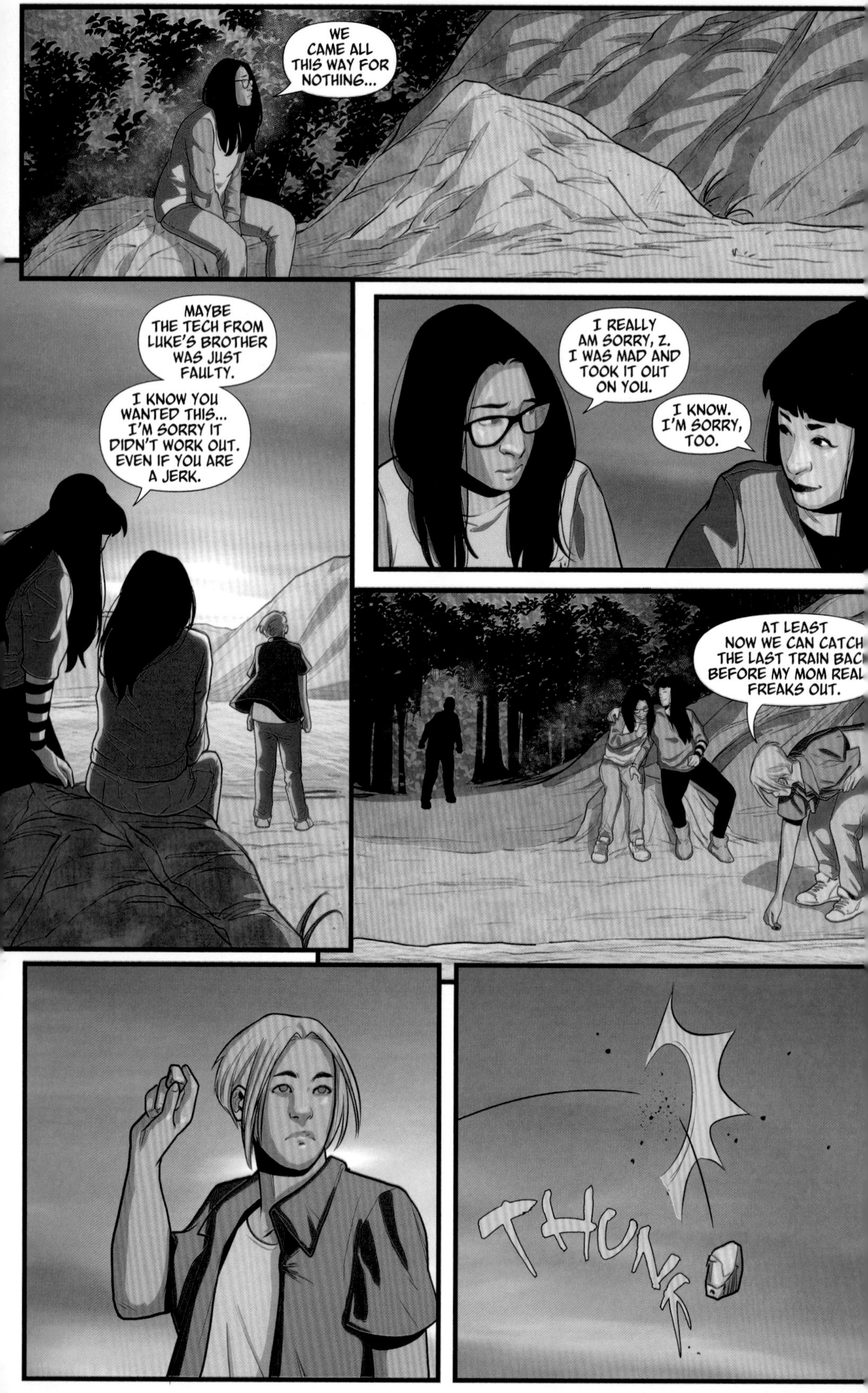
WE CAME ALL THIS WAY FOR NOTHING...
MAYBE THE TECH FROM LUKE'S BROTHER WAS JUST FAULTY.
I KNOW YOU WANTED THIS... I'M SORRY IT DIDN'T WORK OUT. EVEN IF YOU ARE A JERK.
I REALLY AM SORRY, Z. I WAS MAD AND TOOK IT OUT ON YOU.
I KNOW. I'M SORRY, TOO.
AT LEAST NOW WE CAN CATCH THE LAST TRAIN BACK BEFORE MY MOM REAL FREAKS OUT.
THUNK

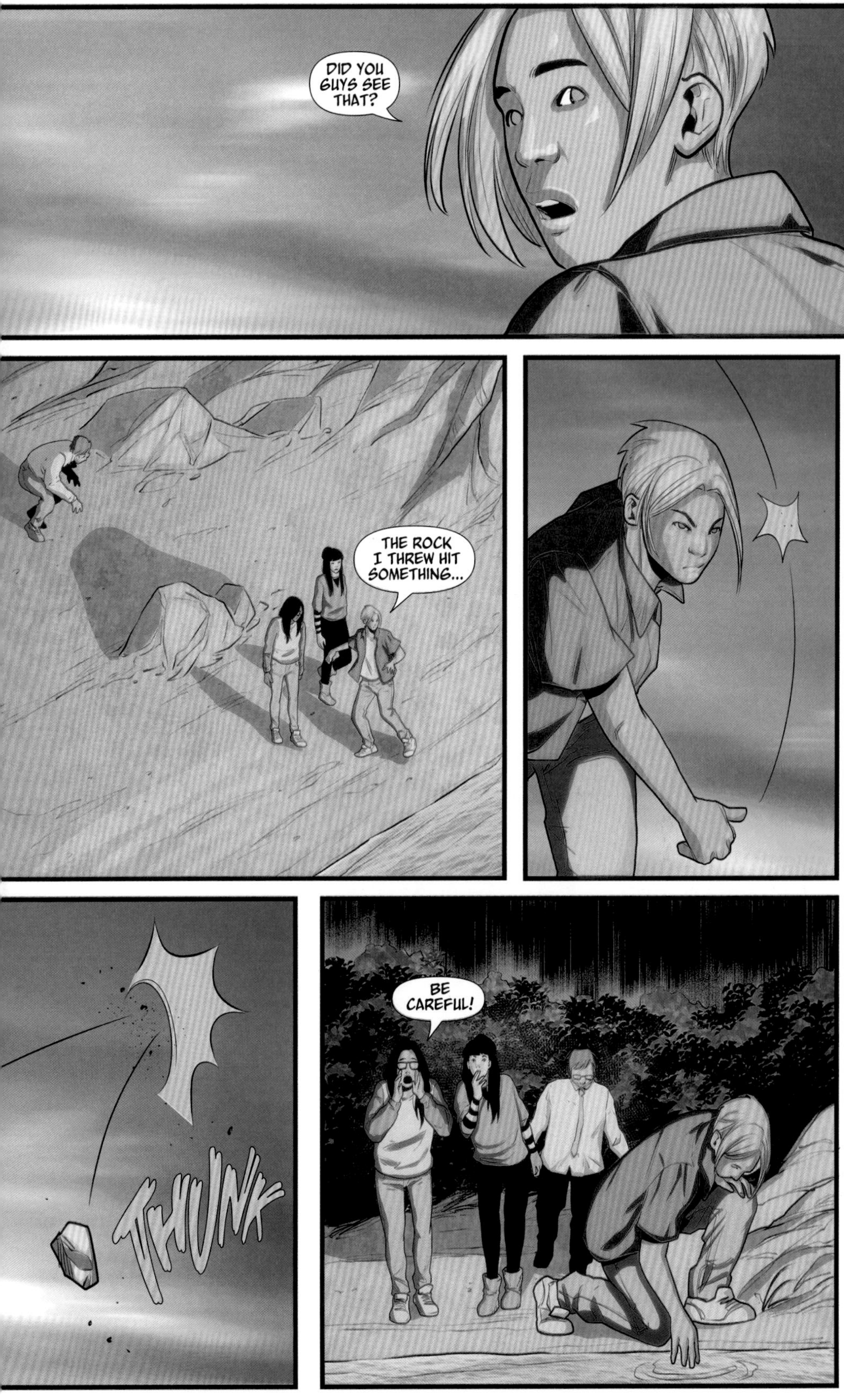
DID YOU GUYS SEE THAT?
THE ROCK I THREW HIT SOMETHING...
THUNK
BE CAREFUL!

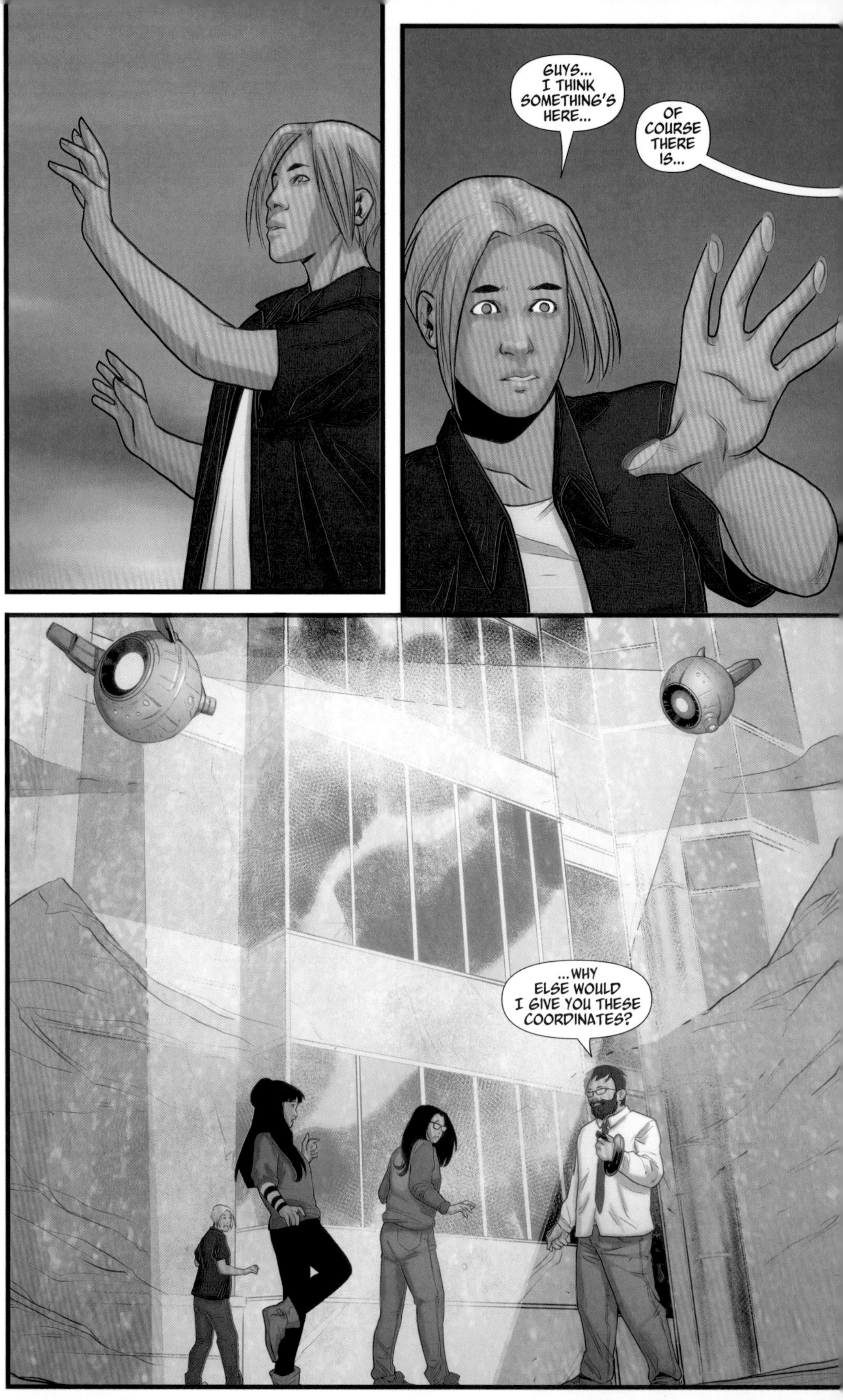
GUYS... I THINK SOMETHING'S HERE...
OF COURSE THERE IS...
...WHY ELSE WOULD I GIVE YOU THESE COORDINATES?

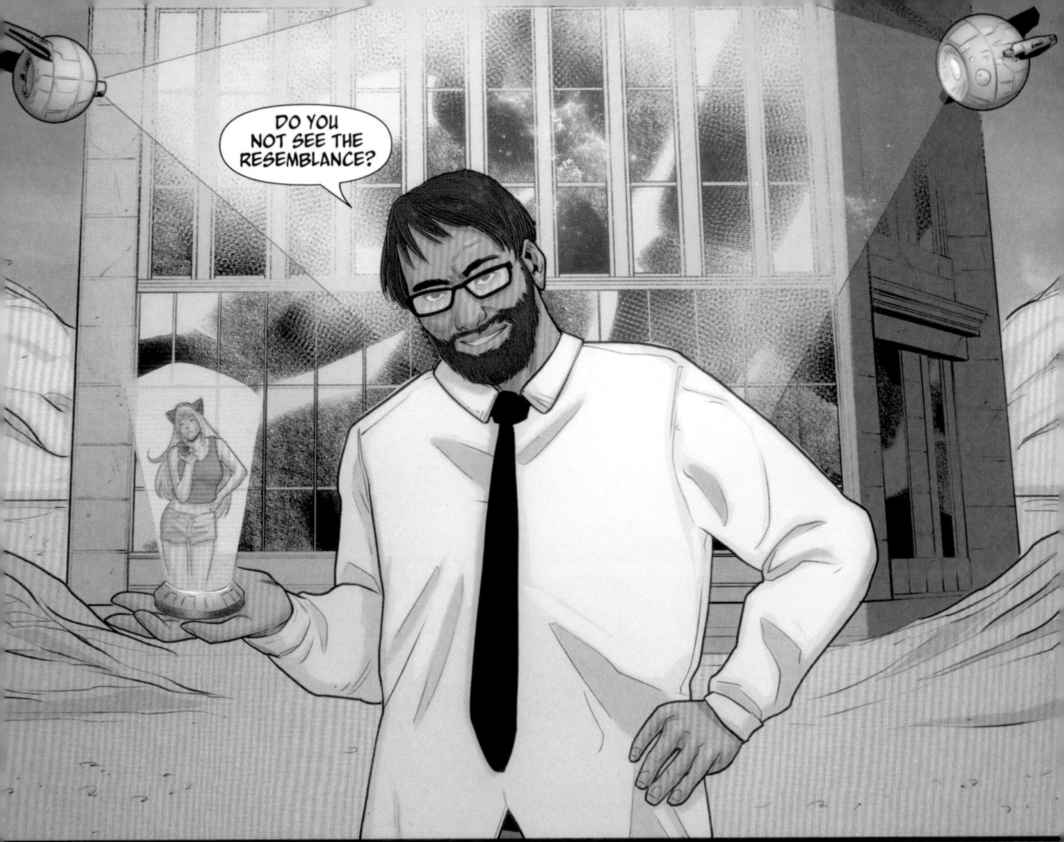
DO YOU NOT SEE THE RESEMBLANCE?

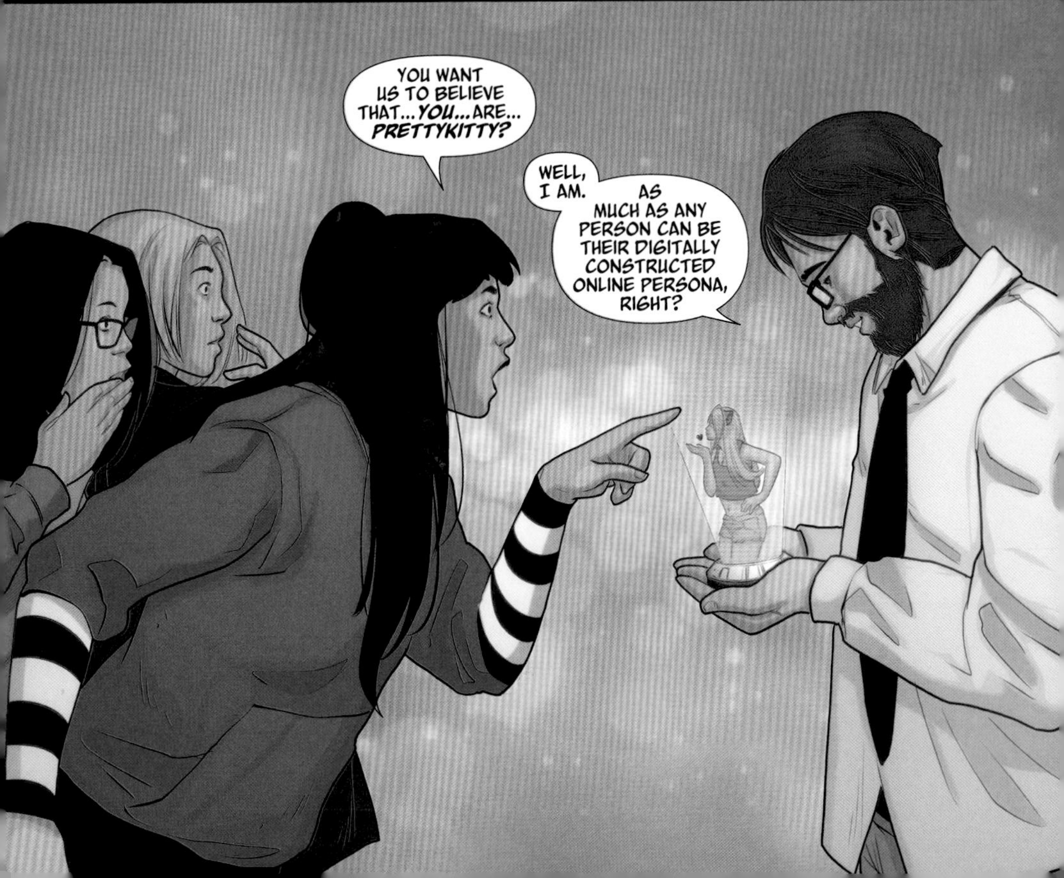
YOU WANT US TO BELIEVE THAT...YOU...ARE... PRETTYKITTY?
WELL, I AM.
AS MUCH AS ANY PERSON CAN BE THEIR DIGITALLY CONSTRUCTED ONLINE PERSONA, RIGHT?

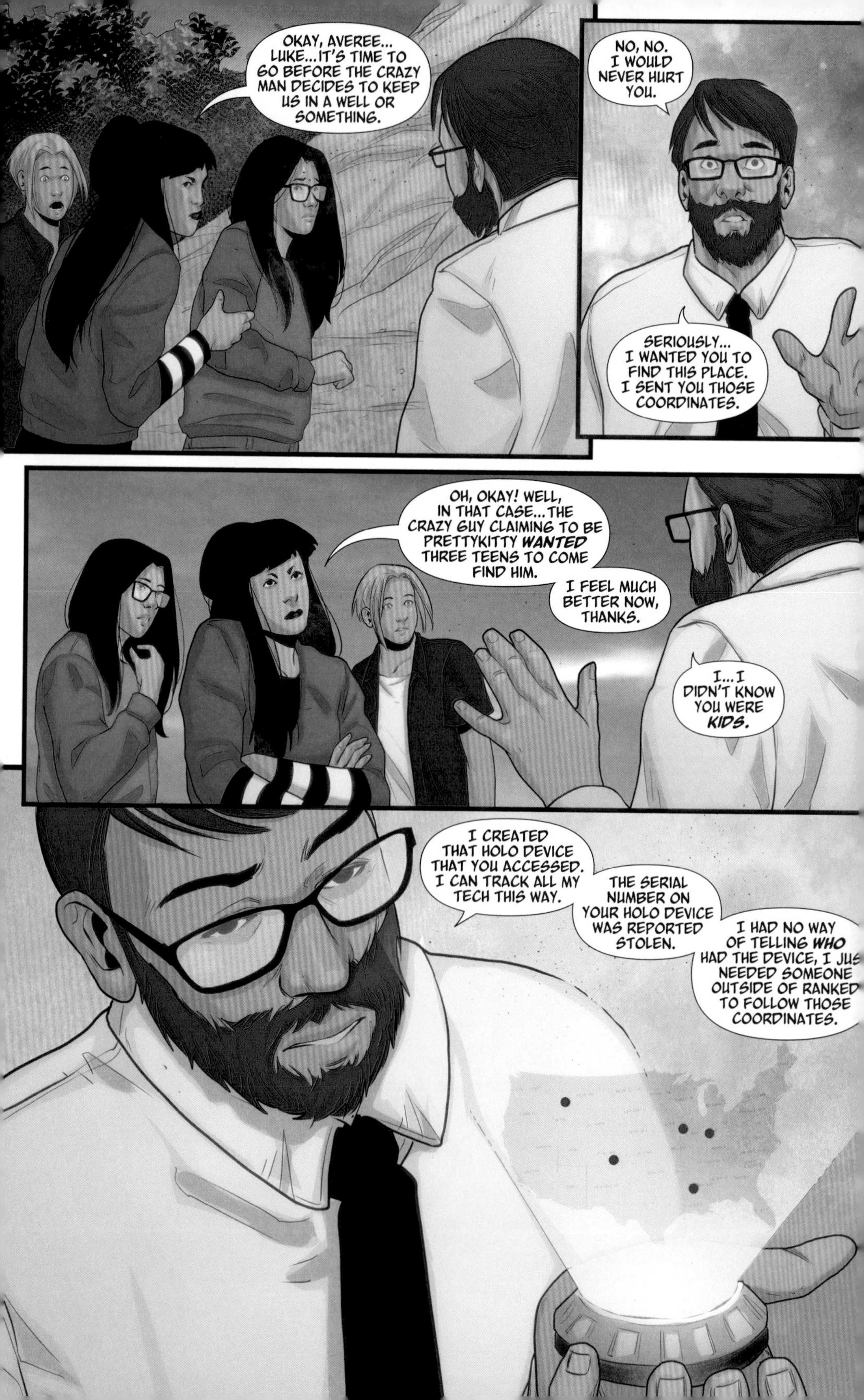
OKAY, AVEREE... LUKE...IT'S TIME TO GO BEFORE THE CRAZY MAN DECIDES TO KEEP US IN A WELL OR SOMETHING.
NO, NO. I WOULD NEVER HURT YOU.
SERIOUSLY... I WANTED YOU TO FIND THIS PLACE. I SENT YOU THOSE COORDINATES.
OH, OKAY! WELL, IN THAT CASE... THE CRAZY GUY CLAIMING TO BE PRETTYKITTY *WANTED* THREE TEENS TO COME FIND HIM.
I FEEL MUCH BETTER NOW, THANKS.
I... I DIDN'T KNOW YOU WERE *KIDS.*
I CREATED THAT HOLO DEVICE THAT YOU ACCESSED. I CAN TRACK ALL MY TECH THIS WAY.
THE SERIAL NUMBER ON YOUR HOLO DEVICE WAS REPORTED STOLEN.
I HAD NO WAY OF TELLING *WHO* HAD THE DEVICE, I JUS NEEDED SOMEONE OUTSIDE OF RANKED TO FOLLOW THOSE COORDINATES.

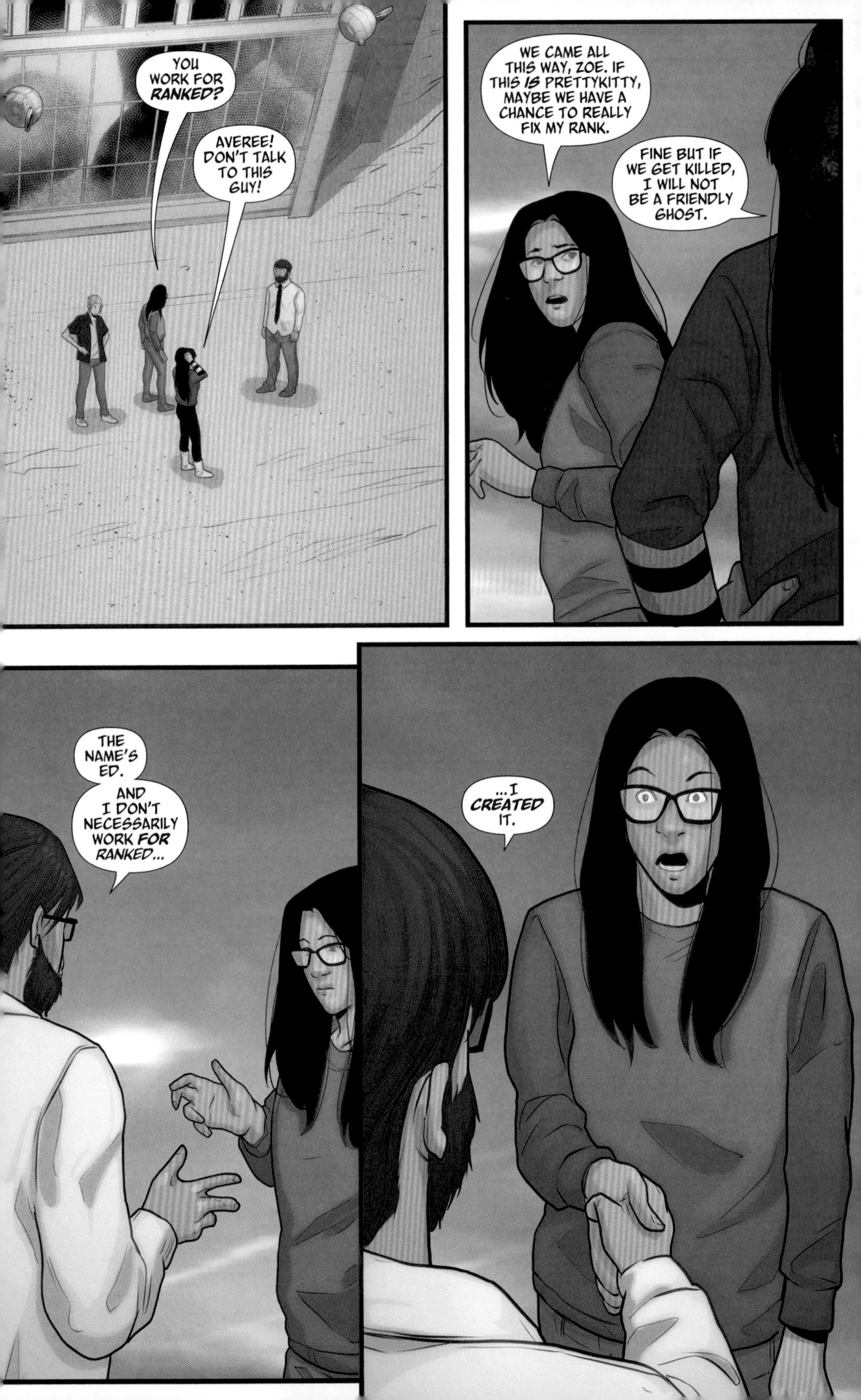
YOU WORK FOR RANKED?
AVEREE! DON'T TALK TO THIS GUY!
WE CAME ALL THIS WAY, ZOE. IF THIS IS PRETTYKITTY, MAYBE WE HAVE A CHANCE TO REALLY FIX MY RANK.
FINE BUT IF WE GET KILLED, I WILL NOT BE A FRIENDLY GHOST.
THE NAME'S ED.
AND I DON'T NECESSARILY WORK FOR RANKED...
...I CREATED IT.

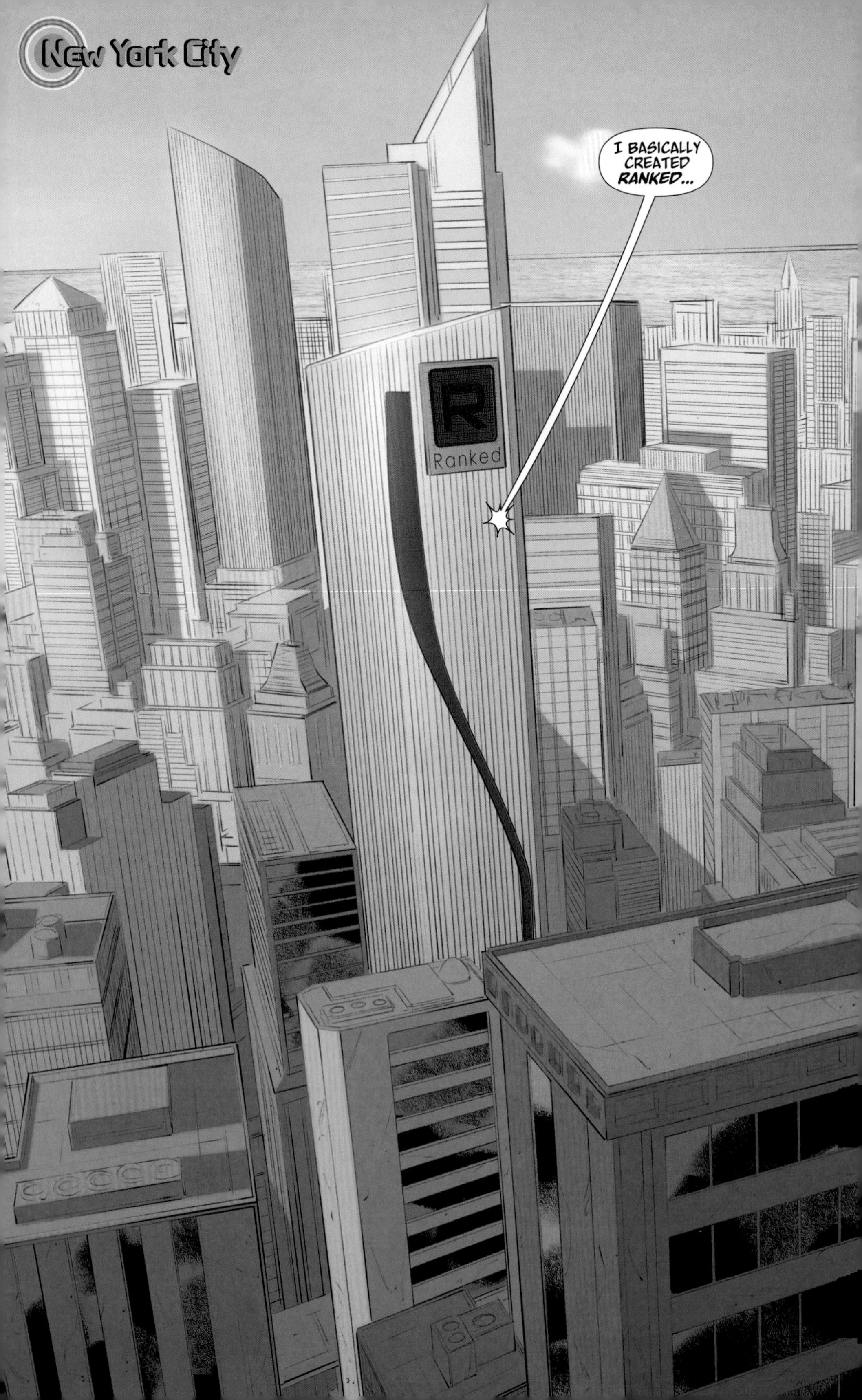
New York City
I BASICALLY CREATED RANKED...
Ranked

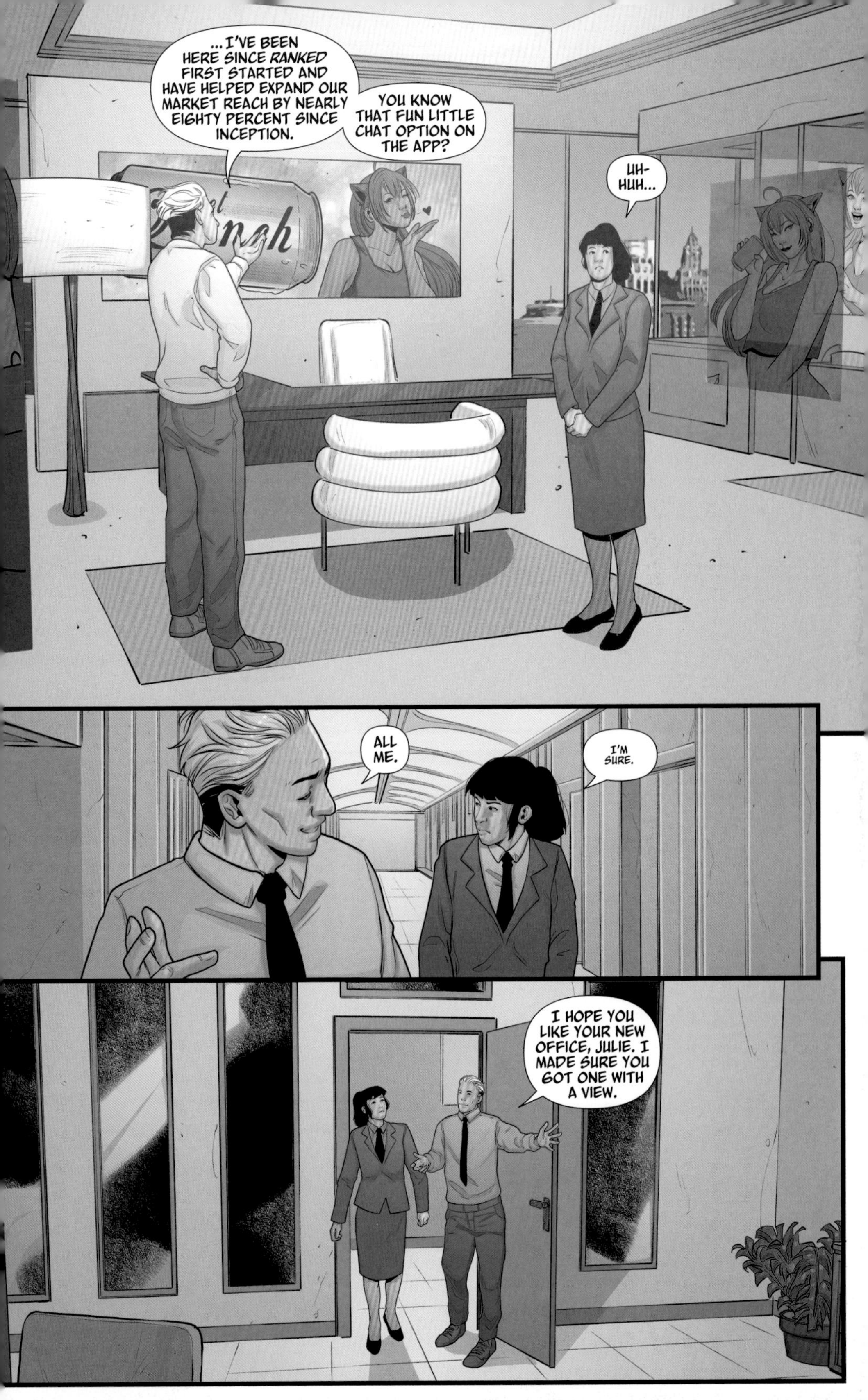
...I'VE BEEN HERE SINCE *RANKED* FIRST STARTED AND HAVE HELPED EXPAND OUR MARKET REACH BY NEARLY EIGHTY PERCENT SINCE INCEPTION.
YOU KNOW THAT FUN LITTLE CHAT OPTION ON THE APP?
UH-HUH...
ALL ME.
I'M SURE.
I HOPE YOU LIKE YOUR NEW OFFICE, JULIE. I MADE SURE YOU GOT ONE WITH A VIEW.

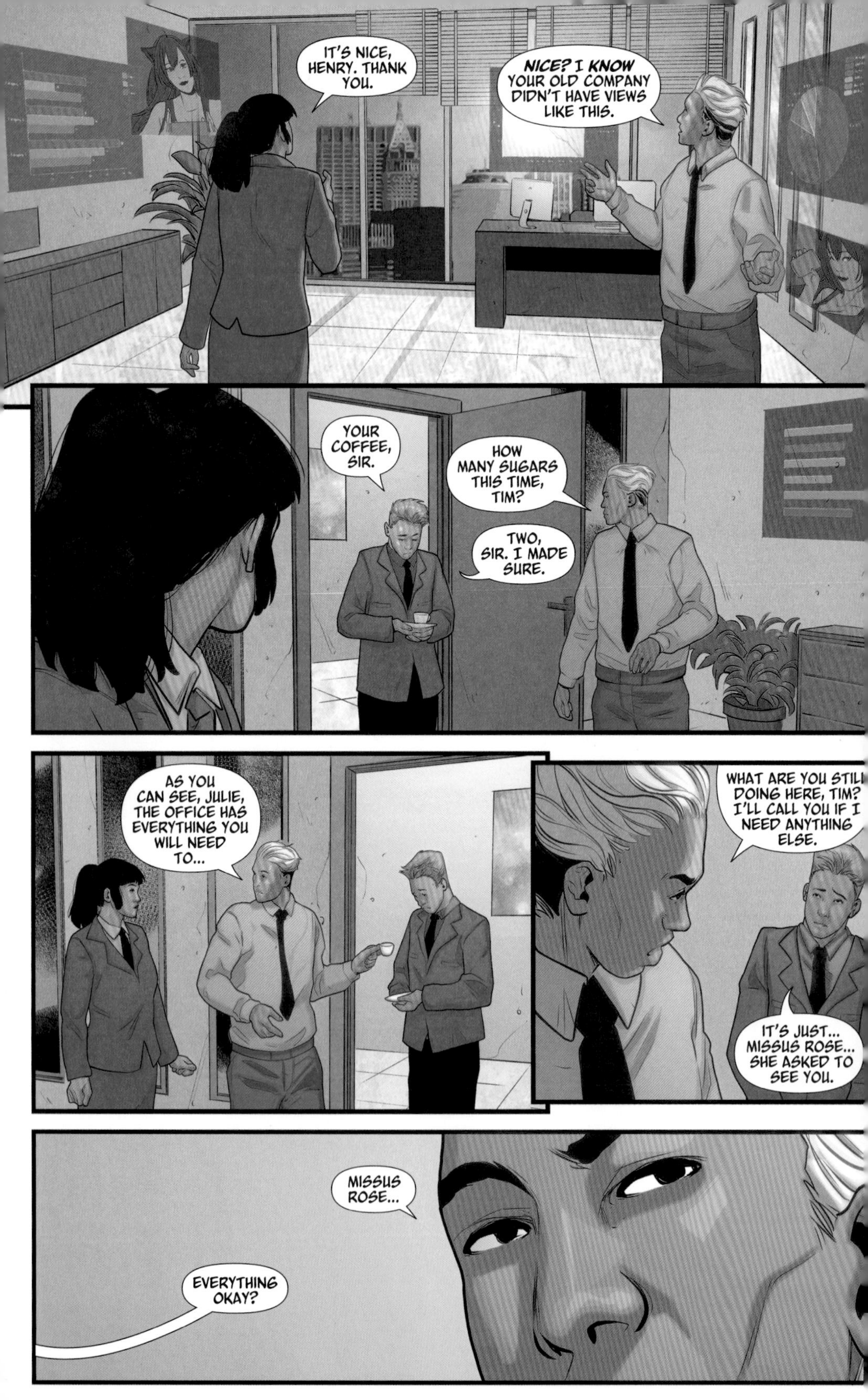
IT'S NICE, HENRY. THANK YOU.
NICE? I KNOW YOUR OLD COMPANY DIDN'T HAVE VIEWS LIKE THIS.
YOUR COFFEE, SIR.
HOW MANY SUGARS THIS TIME, TIM?
TWO, SIR. I MADE SURE.
AS YOU CAN SEE, JULIE, THE OFFICE HAS EVERYTHING YOU WILL NEED TO...
WHAT ARE YOU STILL DOING HERE, TIM? I'LL CALL YOU IF I NEED ANYTHING ELSE.
IT'S JUST... MISSUS ROSE... SHE ASKED TO SEE YOU.
MISSUS ROSE...
EVERYTHING OKAY?

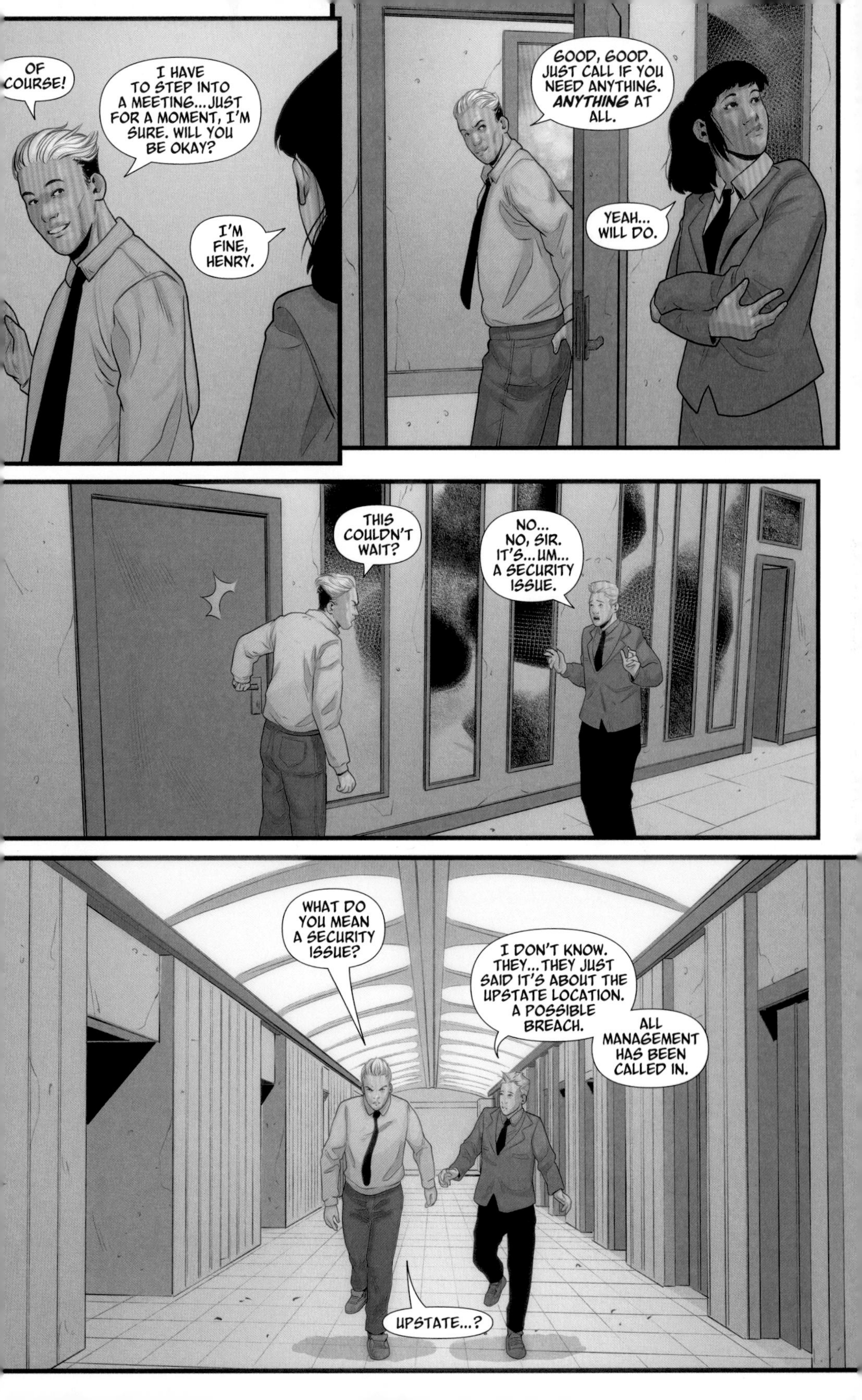
OF COURSE!
I HAVE TO STEP INTO A MEETING...JUST FOR A MOMENT, I'M SURE. WILL YOU BE OKAY?
I'M FINE, HENRY.
GOOD, GOOD. JUST CALL IF YOU NEED ANYTHING. ANYTHING AT ALL.
YEAH... WILL DO.
THIS COULDN'T WAIT?
NO... NO, SIR. IT'S...UM... A SECURITY ISSUE.
WHAT DO YOU MEAN A SECURITY ISSUE?
I DON'T KNOW. THEY...THEY JUST SAID IT'S ABOUT THE UPSTATE LOCATION. A POSSIBLE BREACH.
ALL MANAGEMENT HAS BEEN CALLED IN.
UPSTATE...?

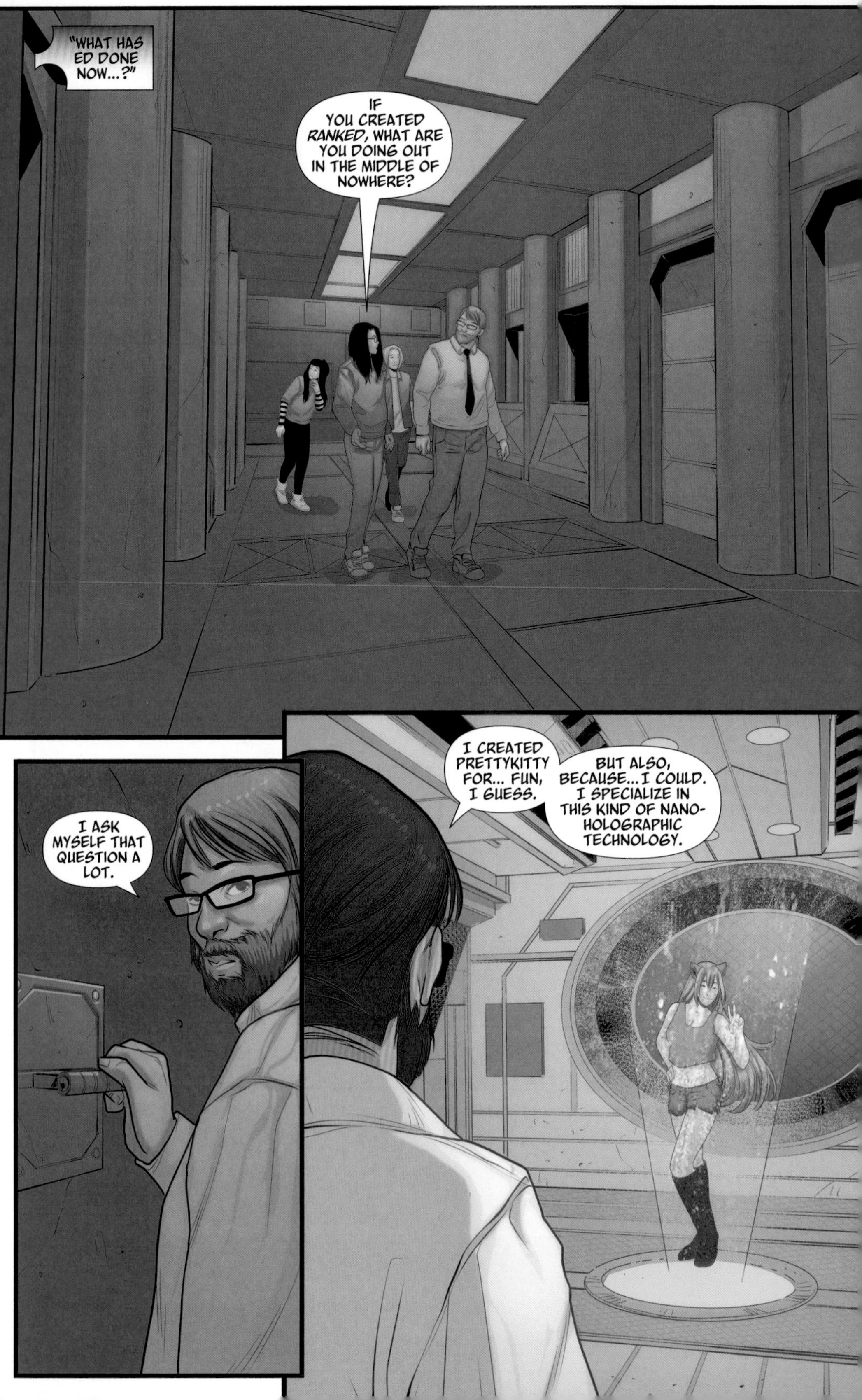
"WHAT HAS ED DONE NOW...?"
IF YOU CREATED RANKED, WHAT ARE YOU DOING OUT IN THE MIDDLE OF NOWHERE?
I ASK MYSELF THAT QUESTION A LOT.
I CREATED PRETTYKITTY FOR... FUN, I GUESS.
BUT ALSO, BECAUSE...I COULD. I SPECIALIZE IN THIS KIND OF NANO-HOLOGRAPHIC TECHNOLOGY.

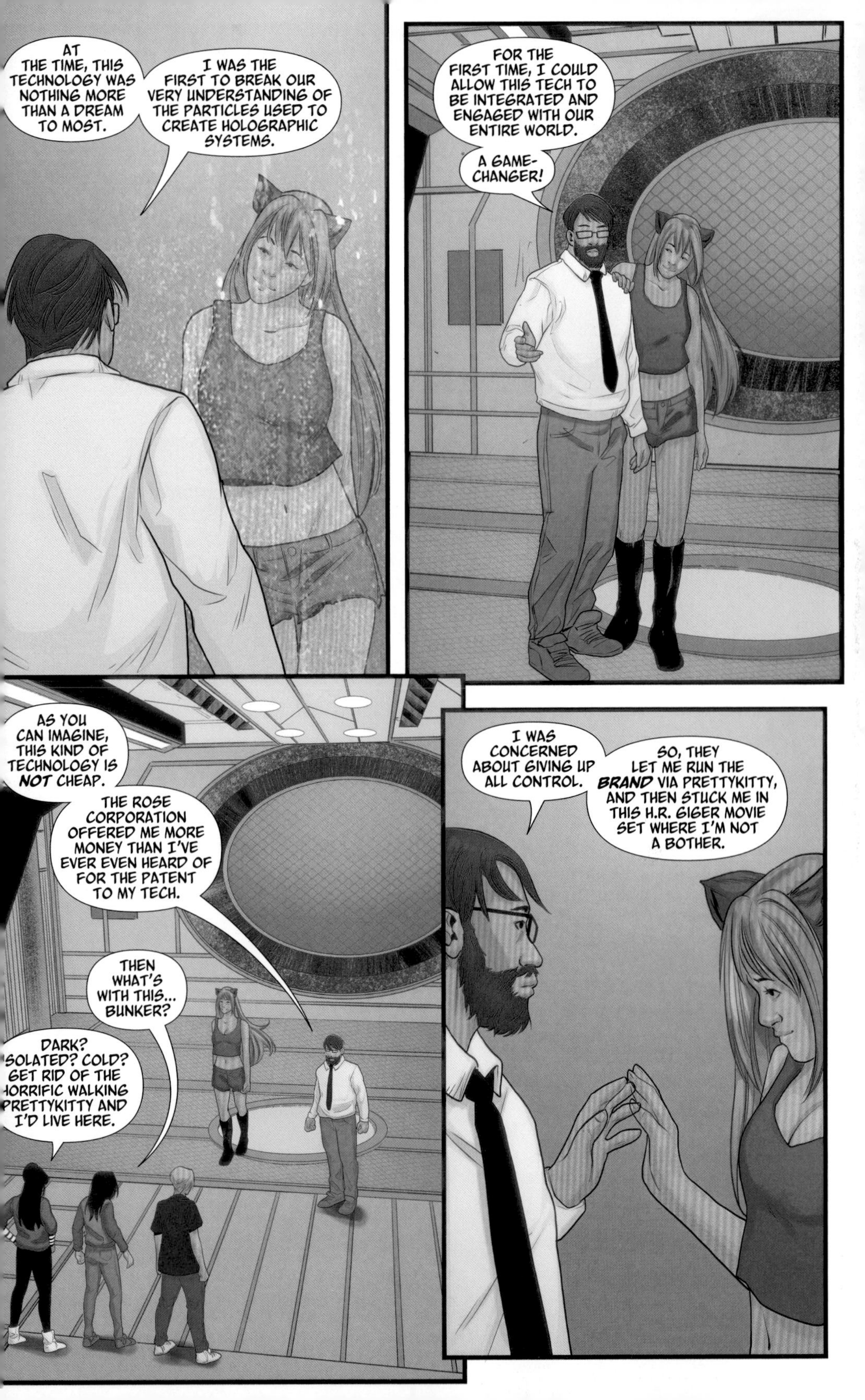

AT THE TIME, THIS TECHNOLOGY WAS NOTHING MORE THAN A DREAM TO MOST.
I WAS THE FIRST TO BREAK OUR VERY UNDERSTANDING OF THE PARTICLES USED TO CREATE HOLOGRAPHIC SYSTEMS.
FOR THE FIRST TIME, I COULD ALLOW THIS TECH TO BE INTEGRATED AND ENGAGED WITH OUR ENTIRE WORLD.
A GAME-CHANGER!
AS YOU CAN IMAGINE, THIS KIND OF TECHNOLOGY IS ***NOT*** CHEAP.
THE ROSE CORPORATION OFFERED ME MORE MONEY THAN I'VE EVER EVEN HEARD OF FOR THE PATENT TO MY TECH.
THEN WHAT'S WITH THIS... BUNKER?
DARK? SOLATED? COLD? GET RID OF THE HORRIFIC WALKING PRETTYKITTY AND I'D LIVE HERE.
I WAS CONCERNED ABOUT GIVING UP ALL CONTROL.
SO, THEY LET ME RUN THE ***BRAND*** VIA PRETTYKITTY, AND THEN STUCK ME IN THIS H.R. GIGER MOVIE SET WHERE I'M NOT A BOTHER.

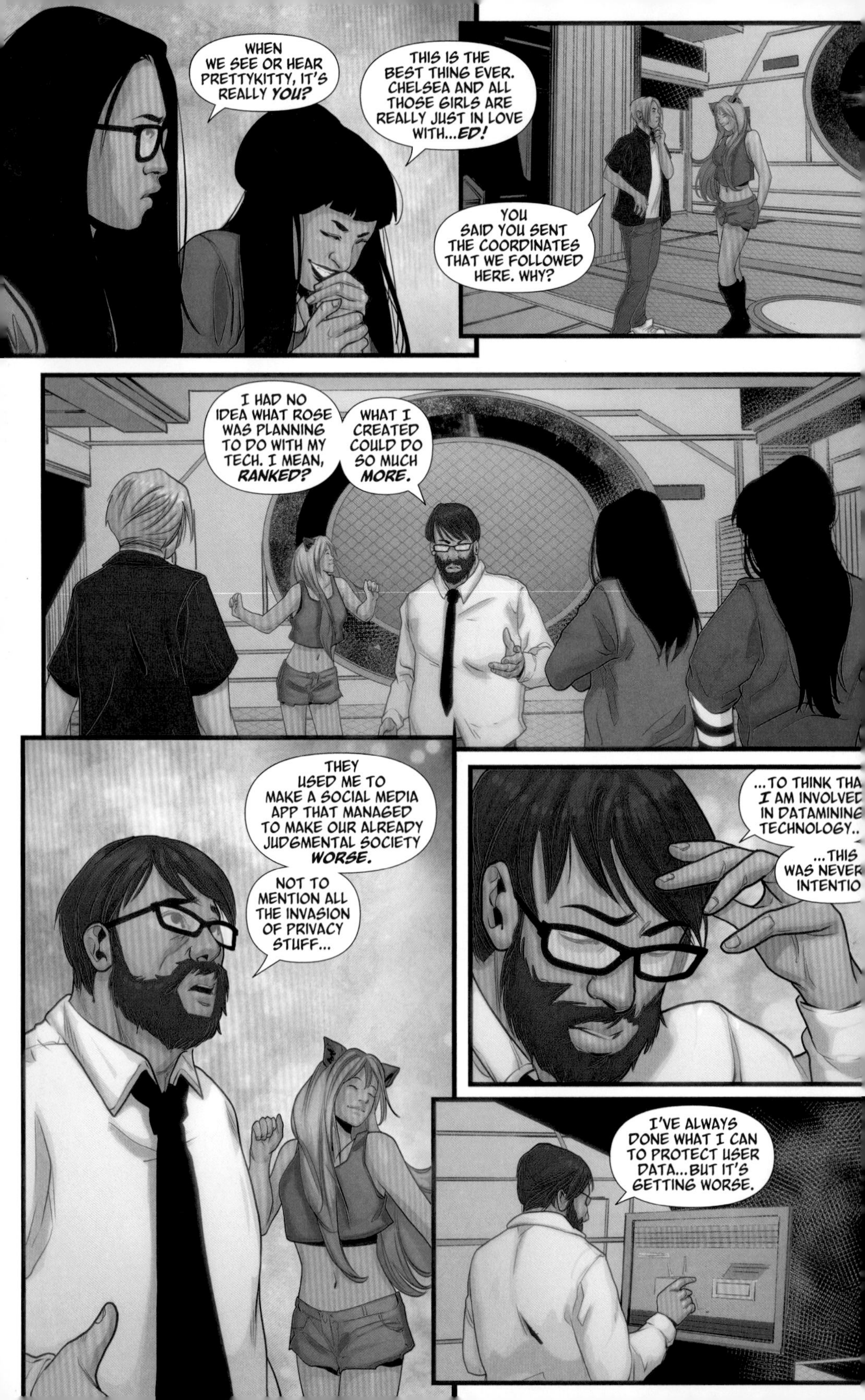
WHEN WE SEE OR HEAR PRETTYKITTY, IT'S REALLY *YOU?*
THIS IS THE BEST THING EVER. CHELSEA AND ALL THOSE GIRLS ARE REALLY JUST IN LOVE WITH...*ED!*
YOU SAID YOU SENT THE COORDINATES THAT WE FOLLOWED HERE. WHY?
I HAD NO IDEA WHAT ROSE WAS PLANNING TO DO WITH MY TECH. I MEAN, *RANKED?*
WHAT I CREATED COULD DO SO MUCH *MORE.*
THEY USED ME TO MAKE A SOCIAL MEDIA APP THAT MANAGED TO MAKE OUR ALREADY JUDGMENTAL SOCIETY *WORSE.*
NOT TO MENTION ALL THE INVASION OF PRIVACY STUFF...
...TO THINK THA *I* AM INVOLVED IN DATAMINING TECHNOLOGY..
...THIS WAS NEVER INTENTIO
I'VE ALWAYS DONE WHAT I CAN TO PROTECT USER DATA...BUT IT'S GETTING WORSE.

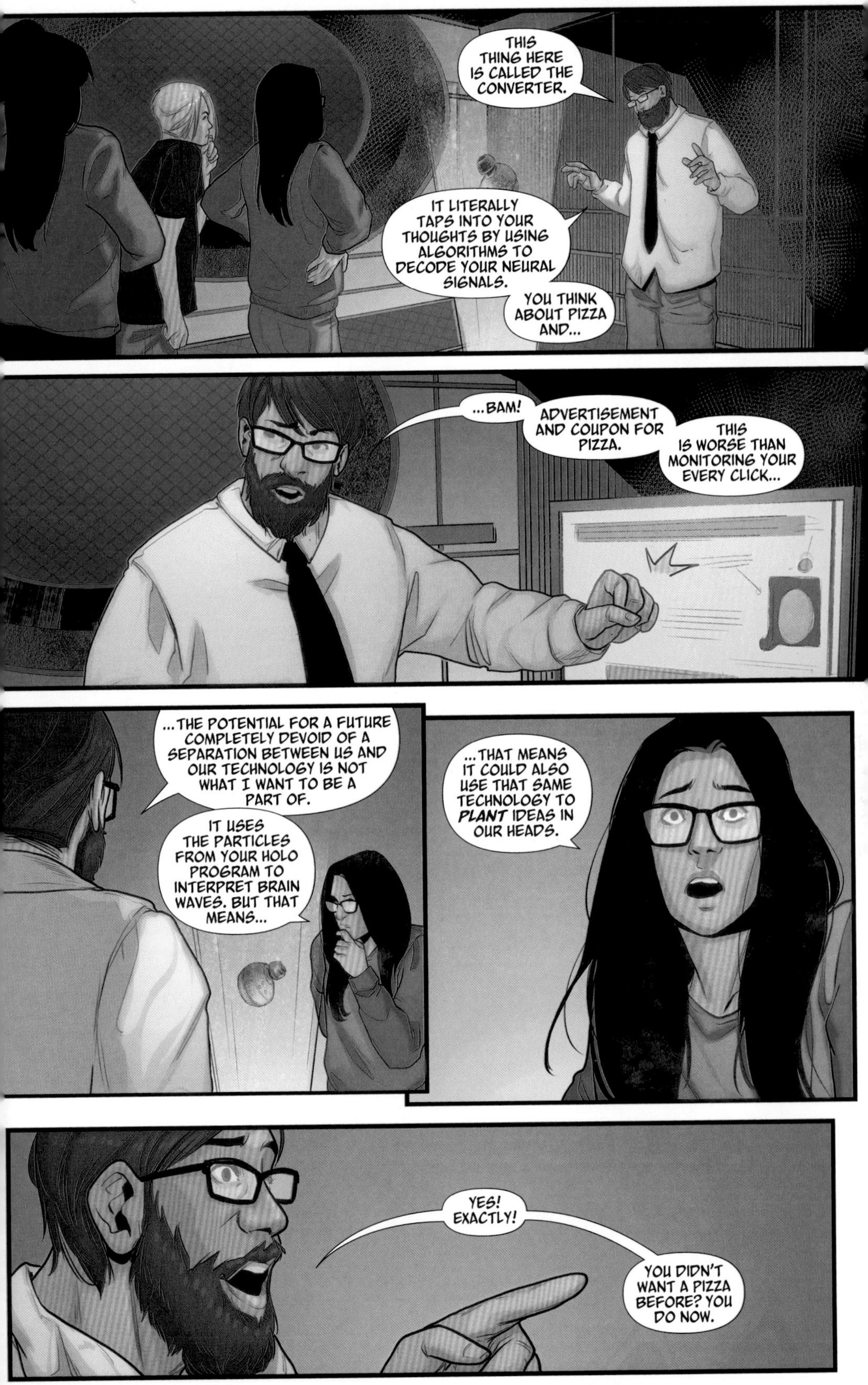
THIS THING HERE IS CALLED THE CONVERTER.
IT LITERALLY TAPS INTO YOUR THOUGHTS BY USING ALGORITHMS TO DECODE YOUR NEURAL SIGNALS.
YOU THINK ABOUT PIZZA AND...
...BAM!
ADVERTISEMENT AND COUPON FOR PIZZA.
THIS IS WORSE THAN MONITORING YOUR EVERY CLICK...
...THE POTENTIAL FOR A FUTURE COMPLETELY DEVOID OF A SEPARATION BETWEEN US AND OUR TECHNOLOGY IS NOT WHAT I WANT TO BE A PART OF.
IT USES THE PARTICLES FROM YOUR HOLO PROGRAM TO INTERPRET BRAIN WAVES. BUT THAT MEANS...
...THAT MEANS IT COULD ALSO USE THAT SAME TECHNOLOGY TO *PLANT* IDEAS IN OUR HEADS.
YES! EXACTLY!
YOU DIDN'T WANT A PIZZA BEFORE? YOU DO NOW.

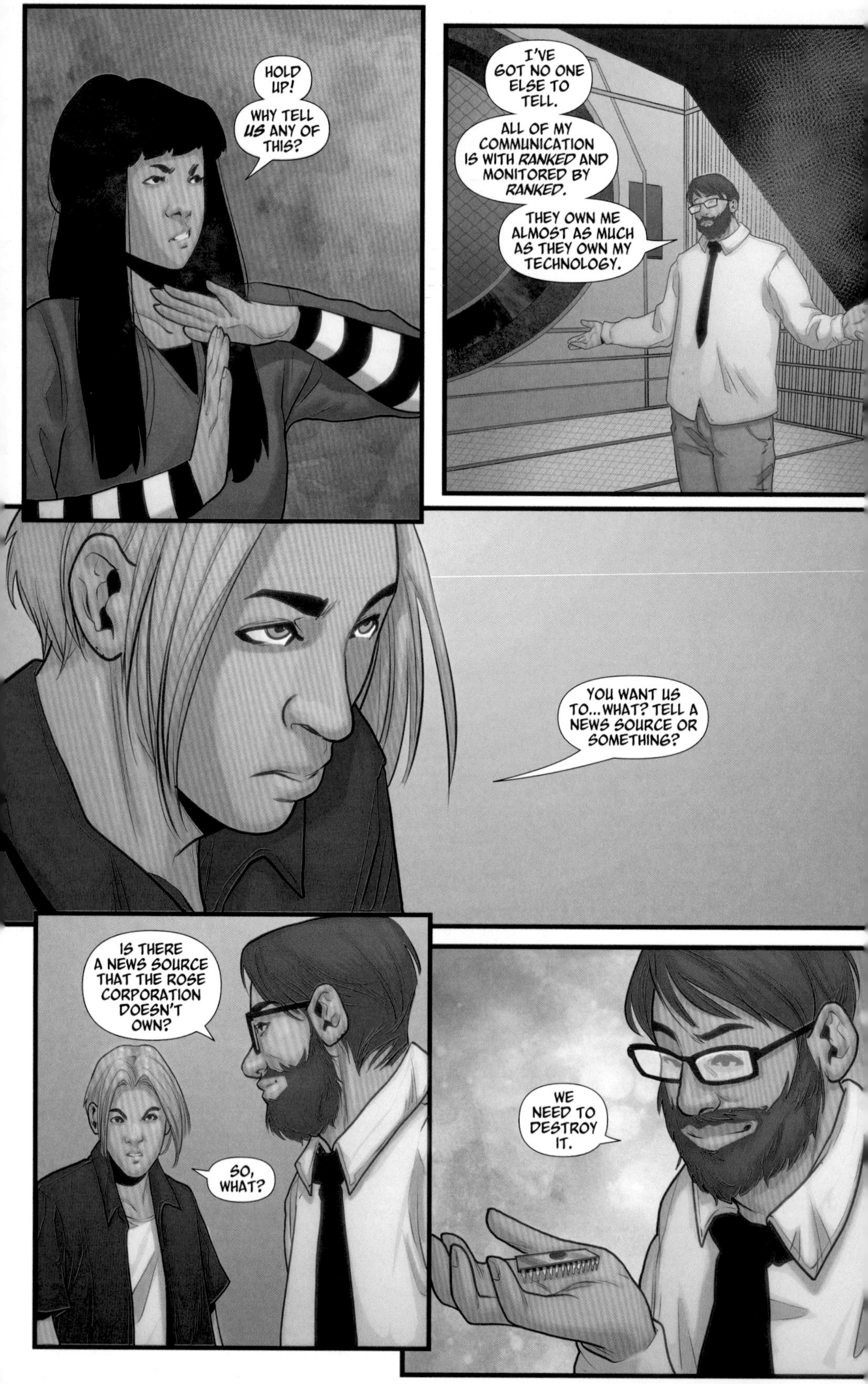
HOLD UP!
WHY TELL *US* ANY OF THIS?
I'VE GOT NO ONE ELSE TO TELL.
ALL OF MY COMMUNICATION IS WITH *RANKED* AND MONITORED BY *RANKED*.
THEY OWN ME ALMOST AS MUCH AS THEY OWN MY TECHNOLOGY.
YOU WANT US TO...WHAT? TELL A NEWS SOURCE OR SOMETHING?
IS THERE A NEWS SOURCE THAT THE ROSE CORPORATION DOESN'T OWN?
SO, WHAT?
WE NEED TO DESTROY IT.

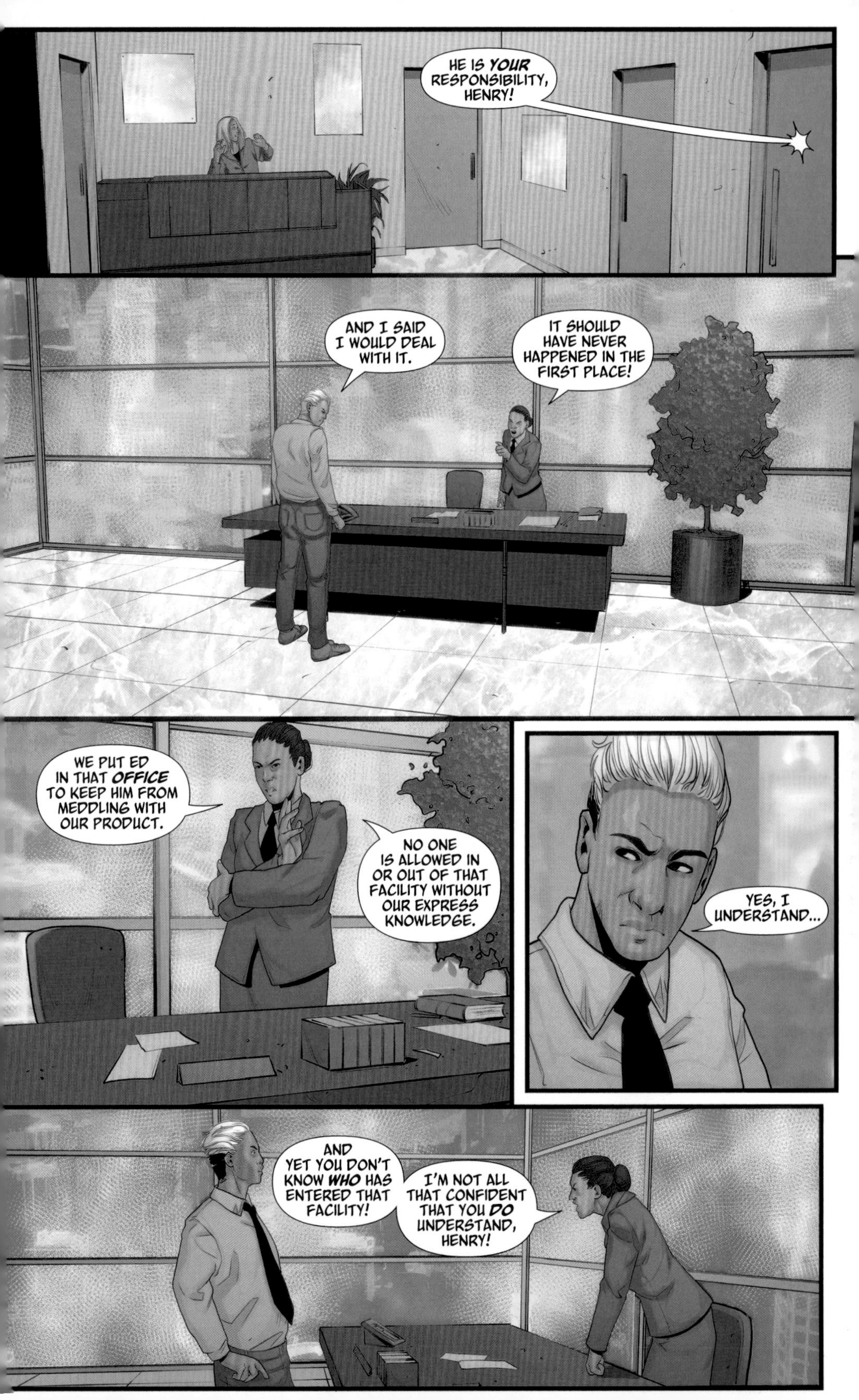
HE IS YOUR RESPONSIBILITY, HENRY!
AND I SAID I WOULD DEAL WITH IT.
IT SHOULD HAVE NEVER HAPPENED IN THE FIRST PLACE!
WE PUT ED IN THAT OFFICE TO KEEP HIM FROM MEDDLING WITH OUR PRODUCT.
NO ONE IS ALLOWED IN OR OUT OF THAT FACILITY WITHOUT OUR EXPRESS KNOWLEDGE.
YES, I UNDERSTAND...
AND YET YOU DON'T KNOW WHO HAS ENTERED THAT FACILITY!
I'M NOT ALL THAT CONFIDENT THAT YOU DO UNDERSTAND, HENRY!

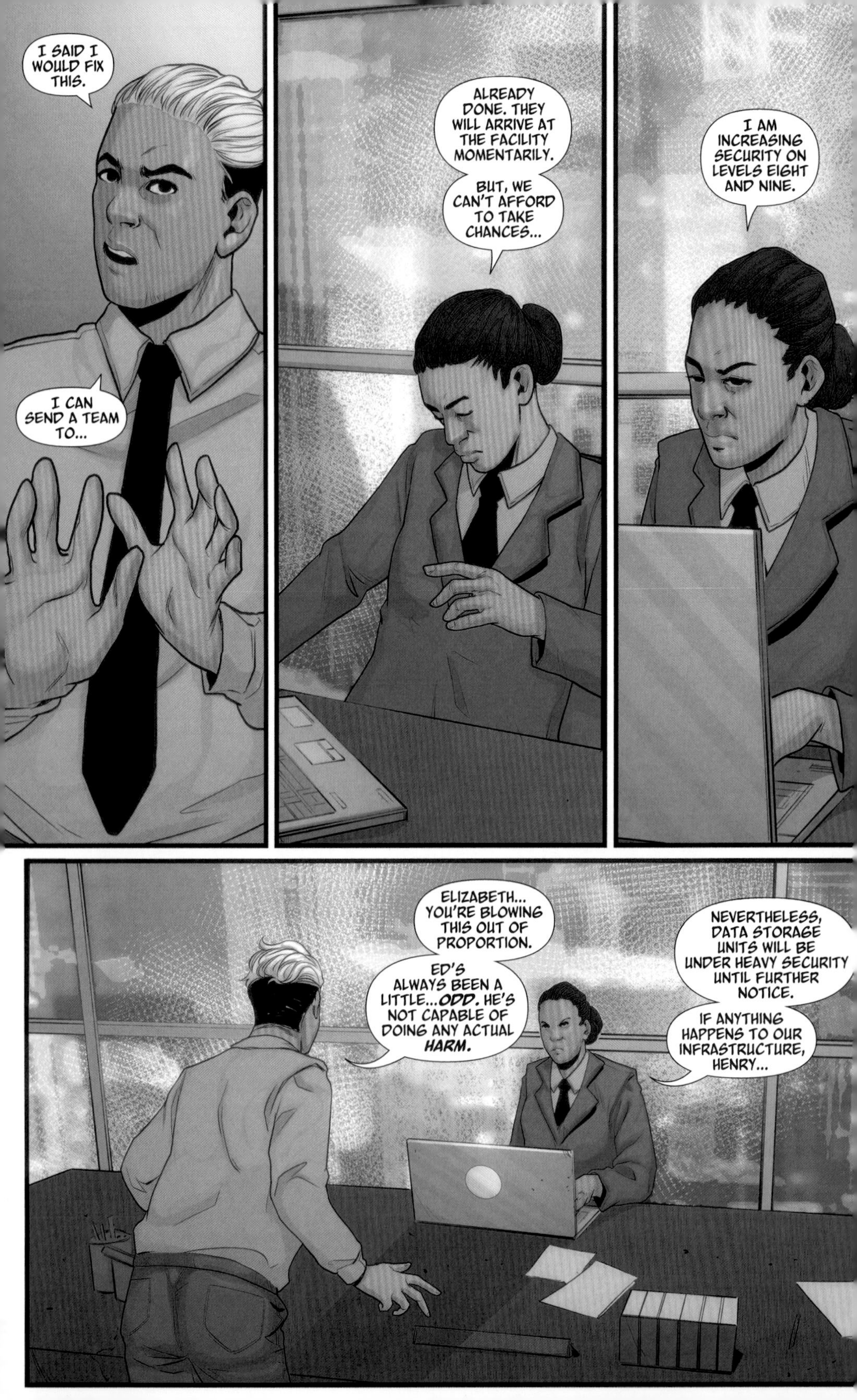
I SAID I WOULD FIX THIS.
I CAN SEND A TEAM TO...
ALREADY DONE. THEY WILL ARRIVE AT THE FACILITY MOMENTARILY.
BUT, WE CAN'T AFFORD TO TAKE CHANCES...
I AM INCREASING SECURITY ON LEVELS EIGHT AND NINE.
ELIZABETH... YOU'RE BLOWING THIS OUT OF PROPORTION.
ED'S ALWAYS BEEN A LITTLE...*ODD*. HE'S NOT CAPABLE OF DOING ANY ACTUAL **HARM**.
NEVERTHELESS, DATA STORAGE UNITS WILL BE UNDER HEAVY SECURITY UNTIL FURTHER NOTICE.
IF ANYTHING HAPPENS TO OUR INFRASTRUCTURE, HENRY...

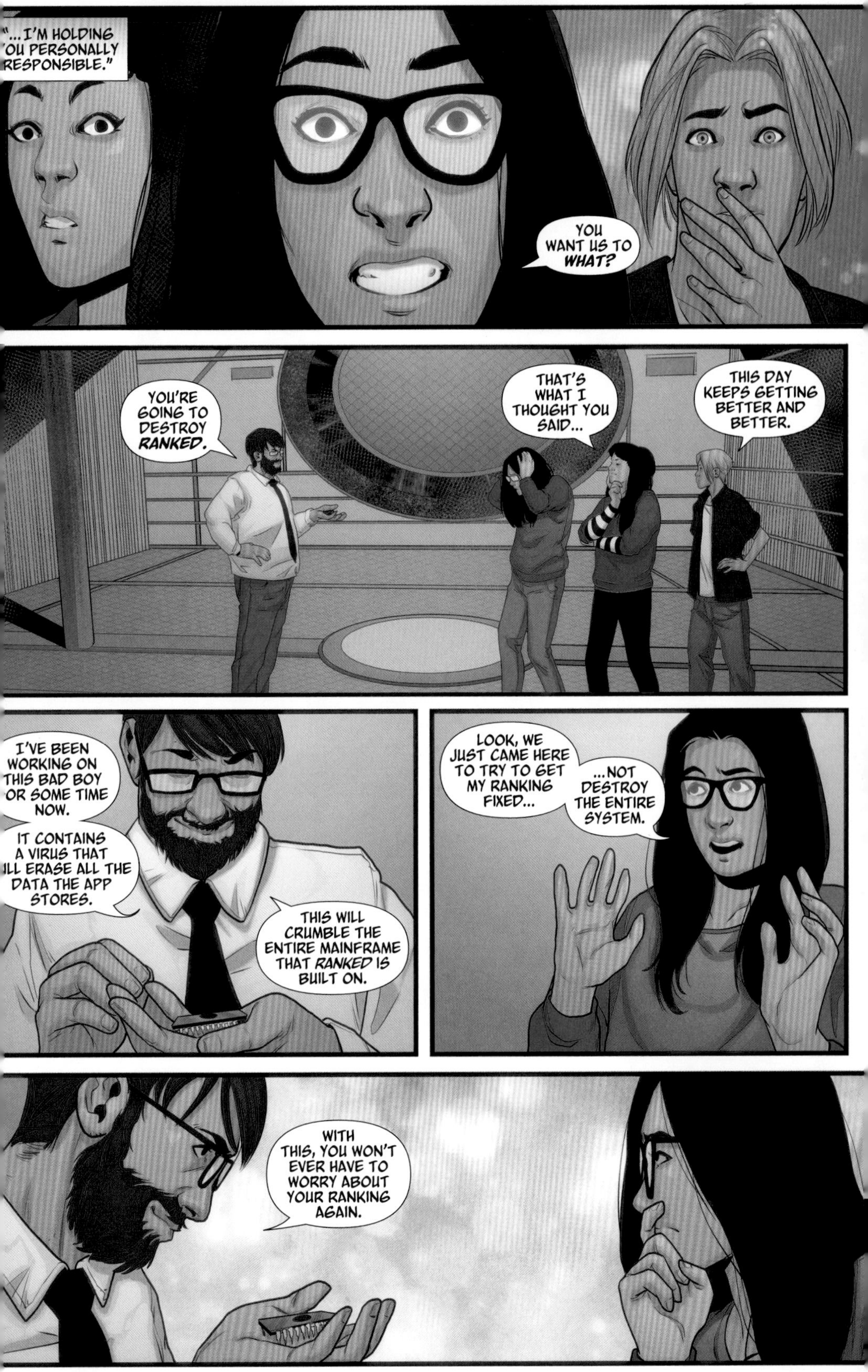
"...I'M HOLDING 'OU PERSONALLY RESPONSIBLE."
YOU WANT US TO *WHAT?*
YOU'RE GOING TO DESTROY *RANKED*.
THAT'S WHAT I THOUGHT YOU SAID...
THIS DAY KEEPS GETTING BETTER AND BETTER.
I'VE BEEN WORKING ON THIS BAD BOY OR SOME TIME NOW.
IT CONTAINS A VIRUS THAT ILL ERASE ALL THE DATA THE APP STORES.
THIS WILL CRUMBLE THE ENTIRE MAINFRAME THAT *RANKED* IS BUILT ON.
LOOK, WE JUST CAME HERE TO TRY TO GET MY RANKING FIXED...
...NOT DESTROY THE ENTIRE SYSTEM.
WITH THIS, YOU WON'T EVER HAVE TO WORRY ABOUT YOUR RANKING AGAIN.

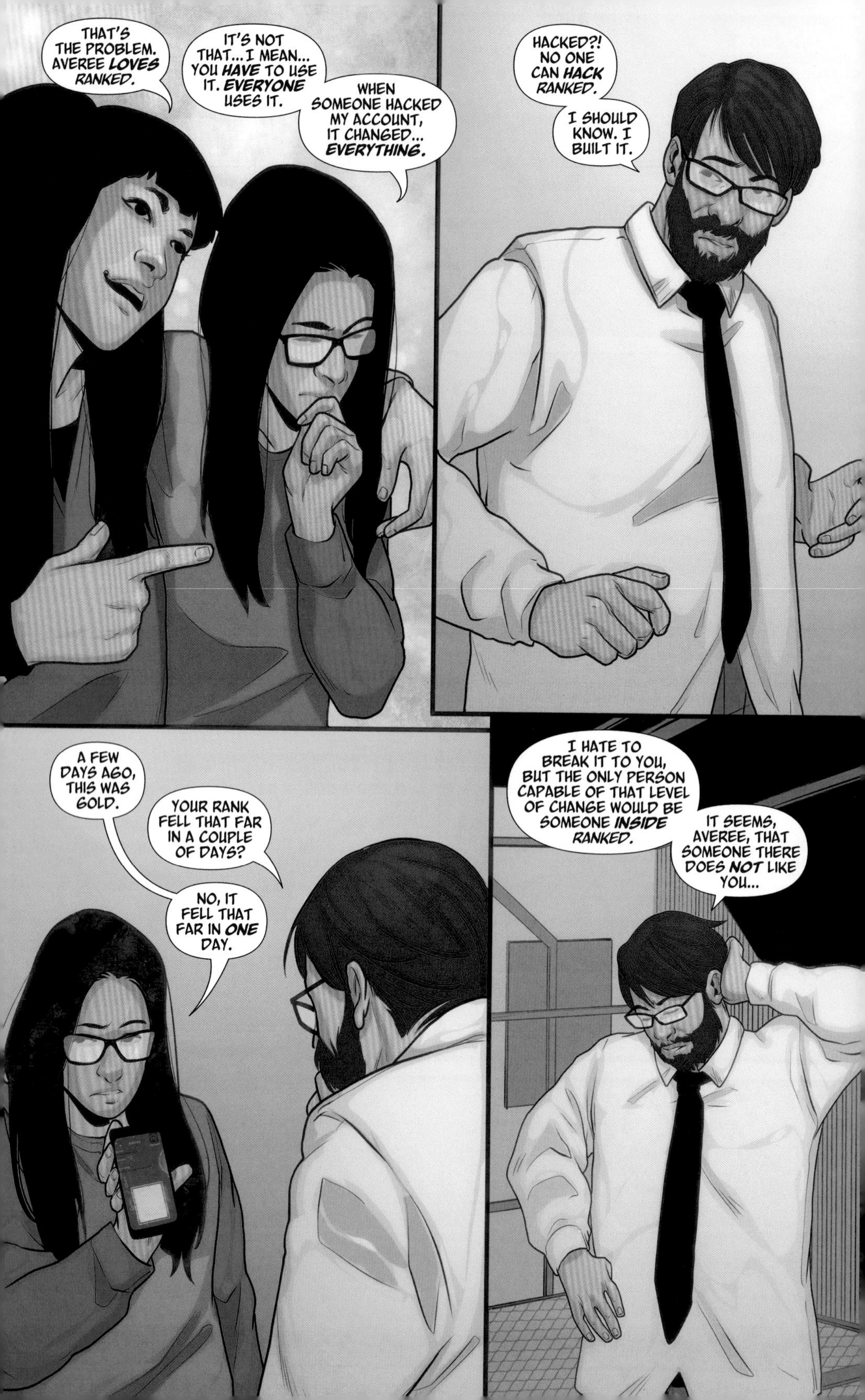
THAT'S THE PROBLEM. AVEREE LOVES RANKED.
IT'S NOT THAT... I MEAN... YOU HAVE TO USE IT. EVERYONE USES IT.
WHEN SOMEONE HACKED MY ACCOUNT, IT CHANGED... EVERYTHING.
HACKED?! NO ONE CAN HACK RANKED.
I SHOULD KNOW. I BUILT IT.
A FEW DAYS AGO, THIS WAS GOLD.
YOUR RANK FELL THAT FAR IN A COUPLE OF DAYS?
NO, IT FELL THAT FAR IN ONE DAY.
I HATE TO BREAK IT TO YOU, BUT THE ONLY PERSON CAPABLE OF THAT LEVEL OF CHANGE WOULD BE SOMEONE INSIDE RANKED.
IT SEEMS, AVEREE, THAT SOMEONE THERE DOES NOT LIKE YOU...

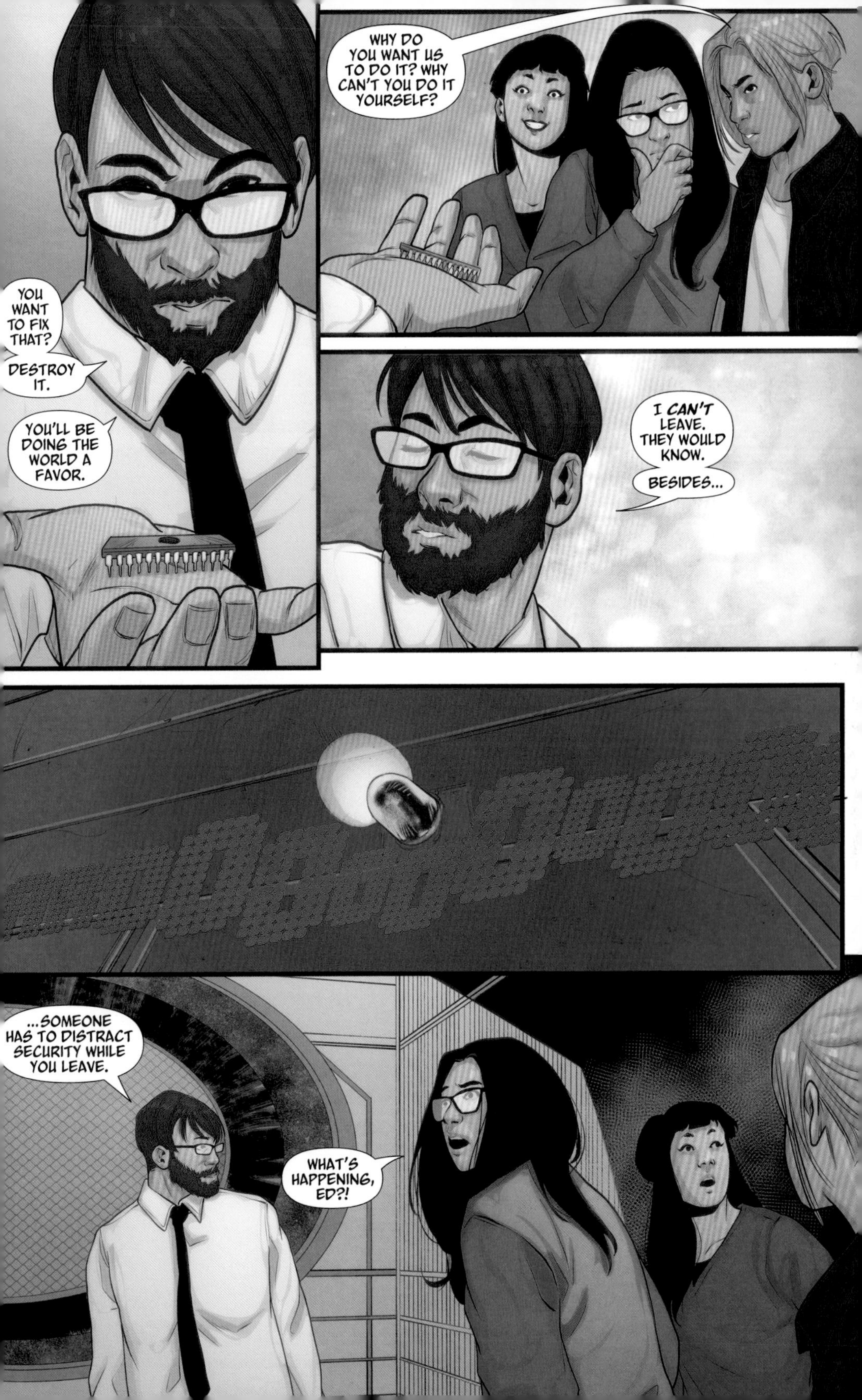

YOU WANT TO FIX THAT?
DESTROY IT.
YOU'LL BE DOING THE WORLD A FAVOR.
WHY DO YOU WANT US TO DO IT? WHY CAN'T YOU DO IT YOURSELF?
I *CAN'T* LEAVE. THEY WOULD KNOW.
BESIDES...
...SOMEONE HAS TO DISTRACT SECURITY WHILE YOU LEAVE.
WHAT'S HAPPENING, ED?!

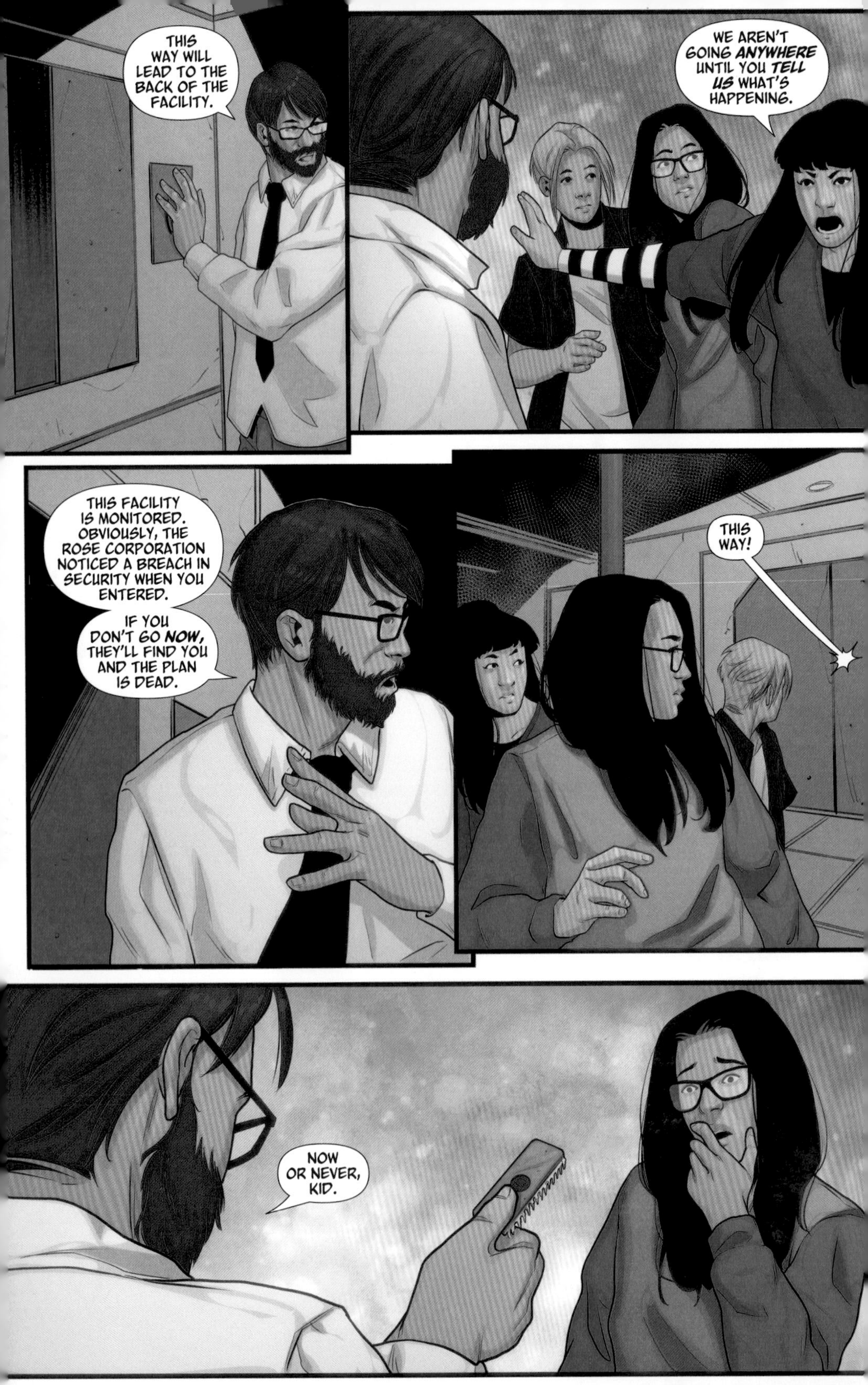

THIS WAY WILL LEAD TO THE BACK OF THE FACILITY.
WE AREN'T GOING **ANYWHERE** UNTIL YOU **TELL US** WHAT'S HAPPENING.
THIS FACILITY IS MONITORED. OBVIOUSLY, THE ROSE CORPORATION NOTICED A BREACH IN SECURITY WHEN YOU ENTERED.
IF YOU DON'T GO **NOW,** THEY'LL FIND YOU AND THE PLAN IS DEAD.
THIS WAY!
NOW OR NEVER, KID.

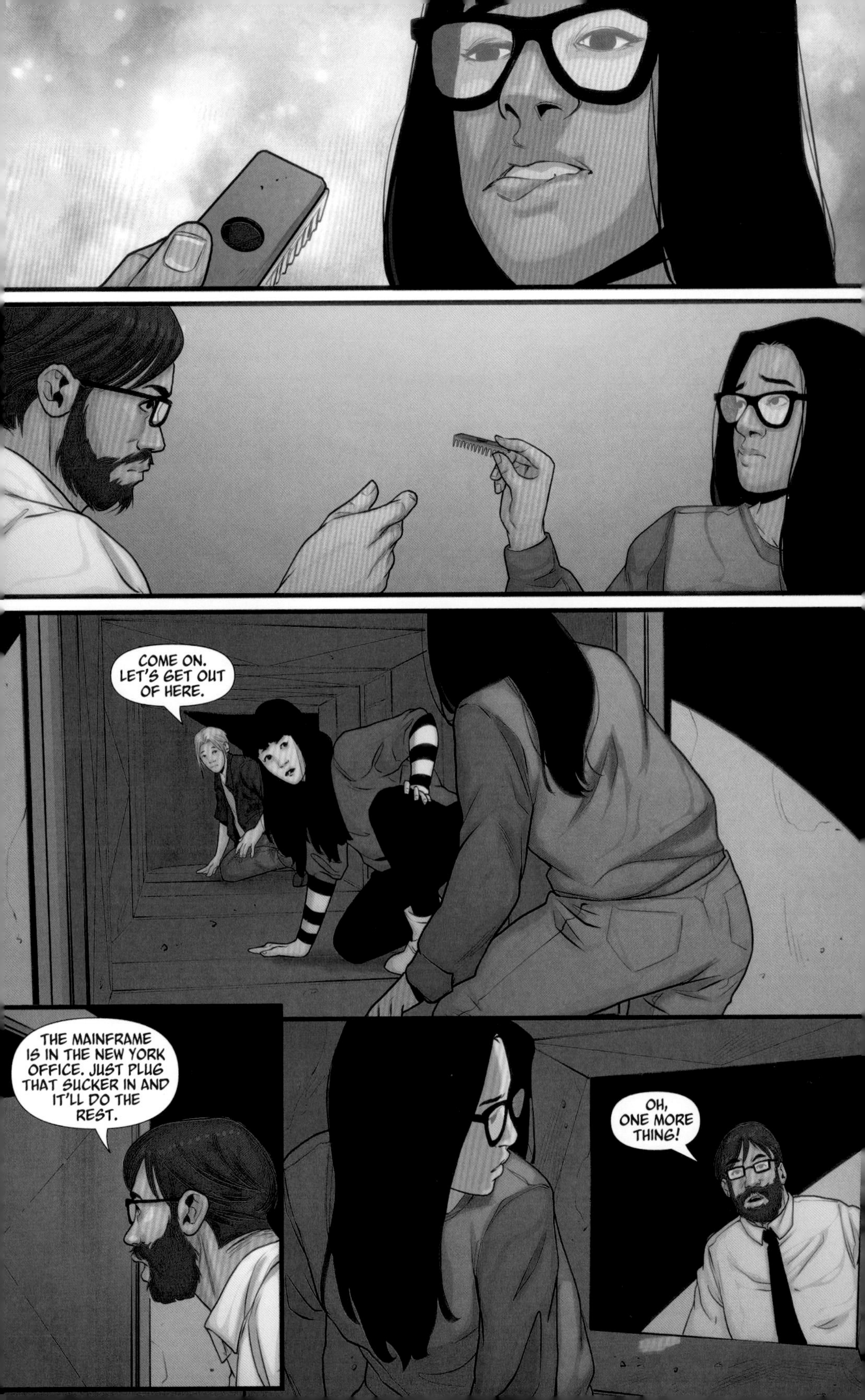
COME ON. LET'S GET OUT OF HERE.
THE MAINFRAME IS IN THE NEW YORK OFFICE. JUST PLUG THAT SUCKER IN AND IT'LL DO THE REST.
OH, ONE MORE THING!

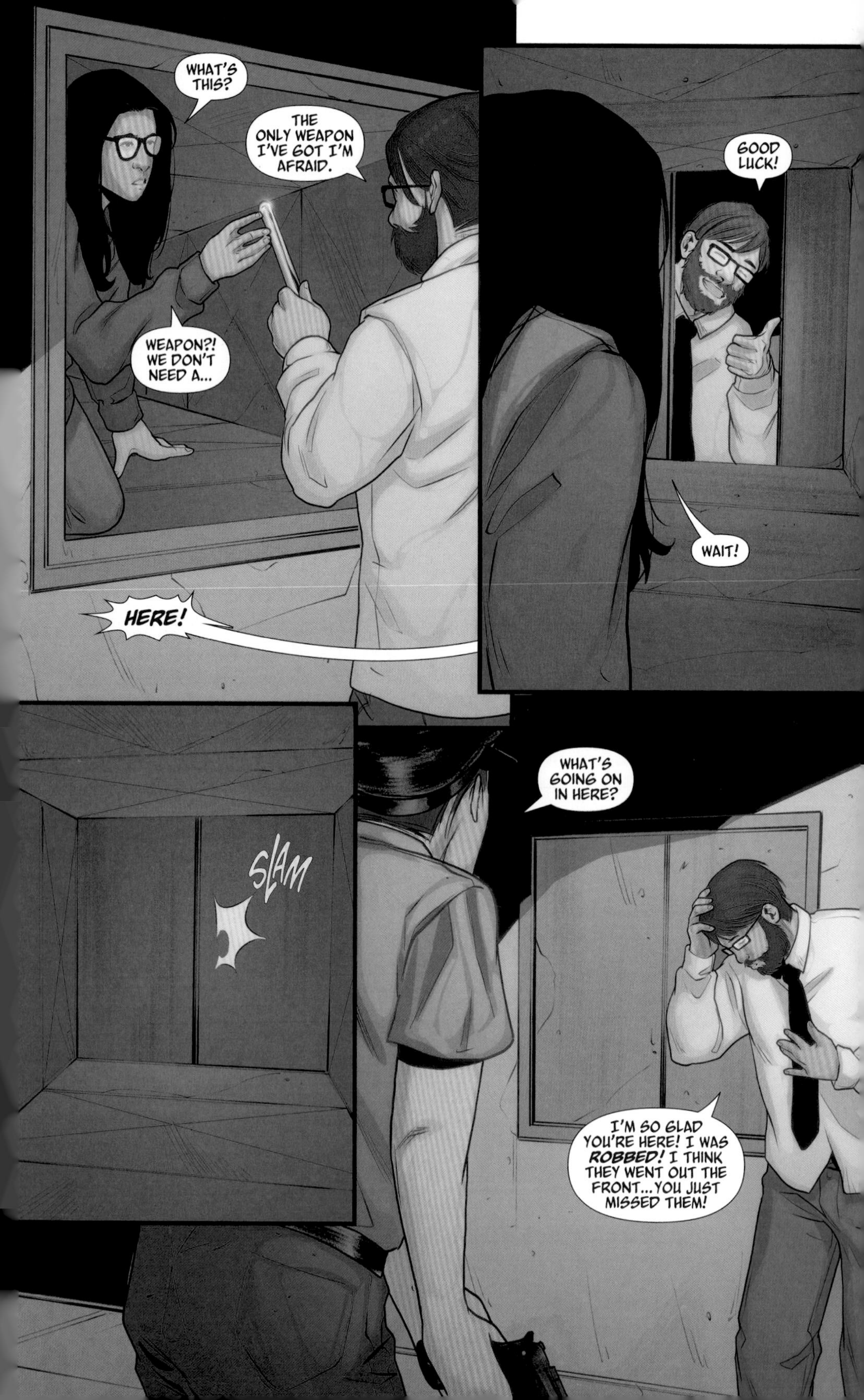
WHAT'S THIS?
THE ONLY WEAPON I'VE GOT I'M AFRAID.
WEAPON?! WE DON'T NEED A...
HERE!
GOOD LUCK!
WAIT!
SLAM
WHAT'S GOING ON IN HERE?
I'M SO GLAD YOU'RE HERE! I WAS ROBBED! I THINK THEY WENT OUT THE FRONT...YOU JUST MISSED THEM!

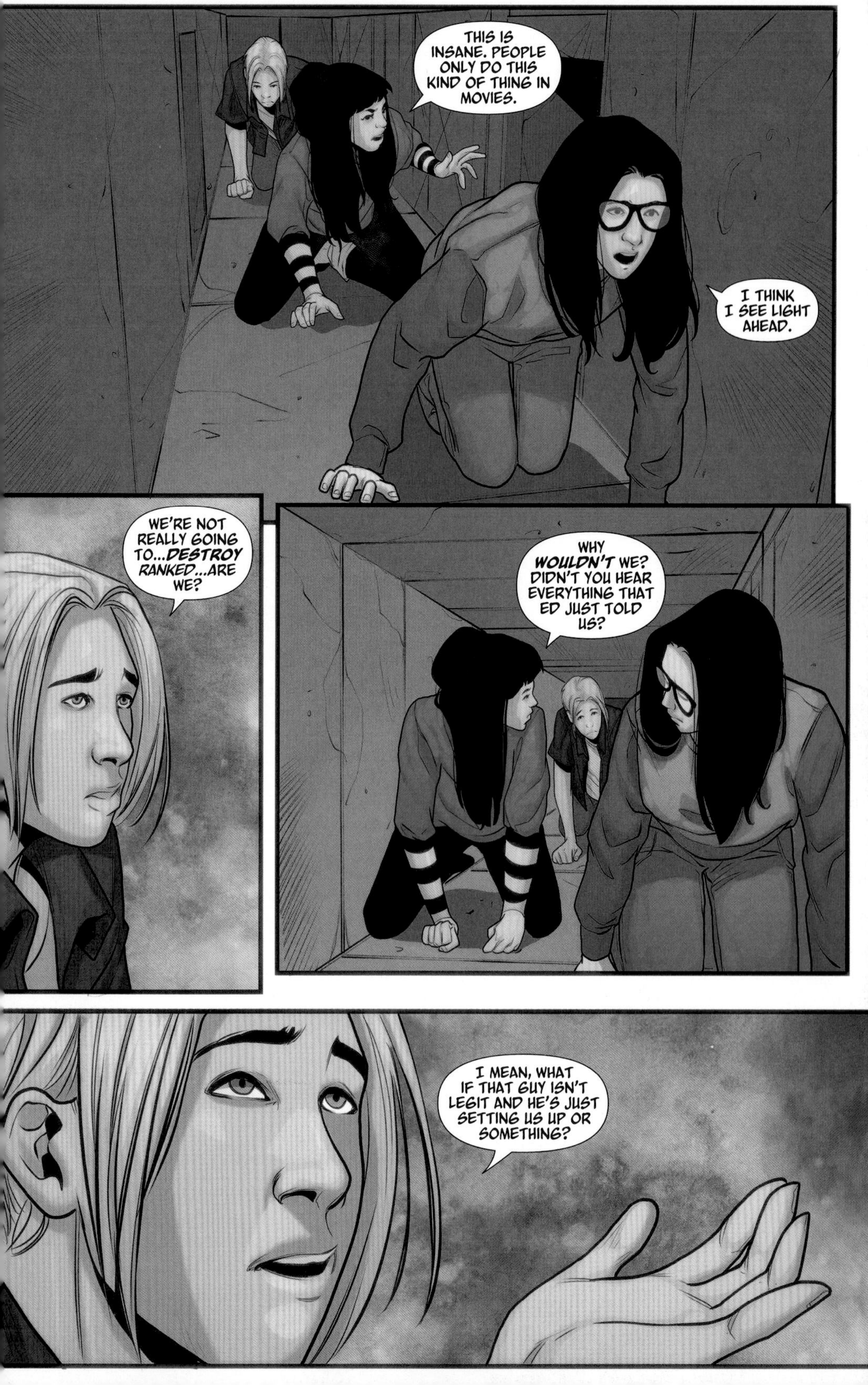
THIS IS INSANE. PEOPLE ONLY DO THIS KIND OF THING IN MOVIES.
I THINK I SEE LIGHT AHEAD.
WE'RE NOT REALLY GOING TO...*DESTROY* RANKED...ARE WE?
WHY *WOULDN'T* WE? DIDN'T YOU HEAR EVERYTHING THAT ED JUST TOLD US?
I MEAN, WHAT IF THAT GUY ISN'T LEGIT AND HE'S JUST SETTING US UP OR SOMETHING?

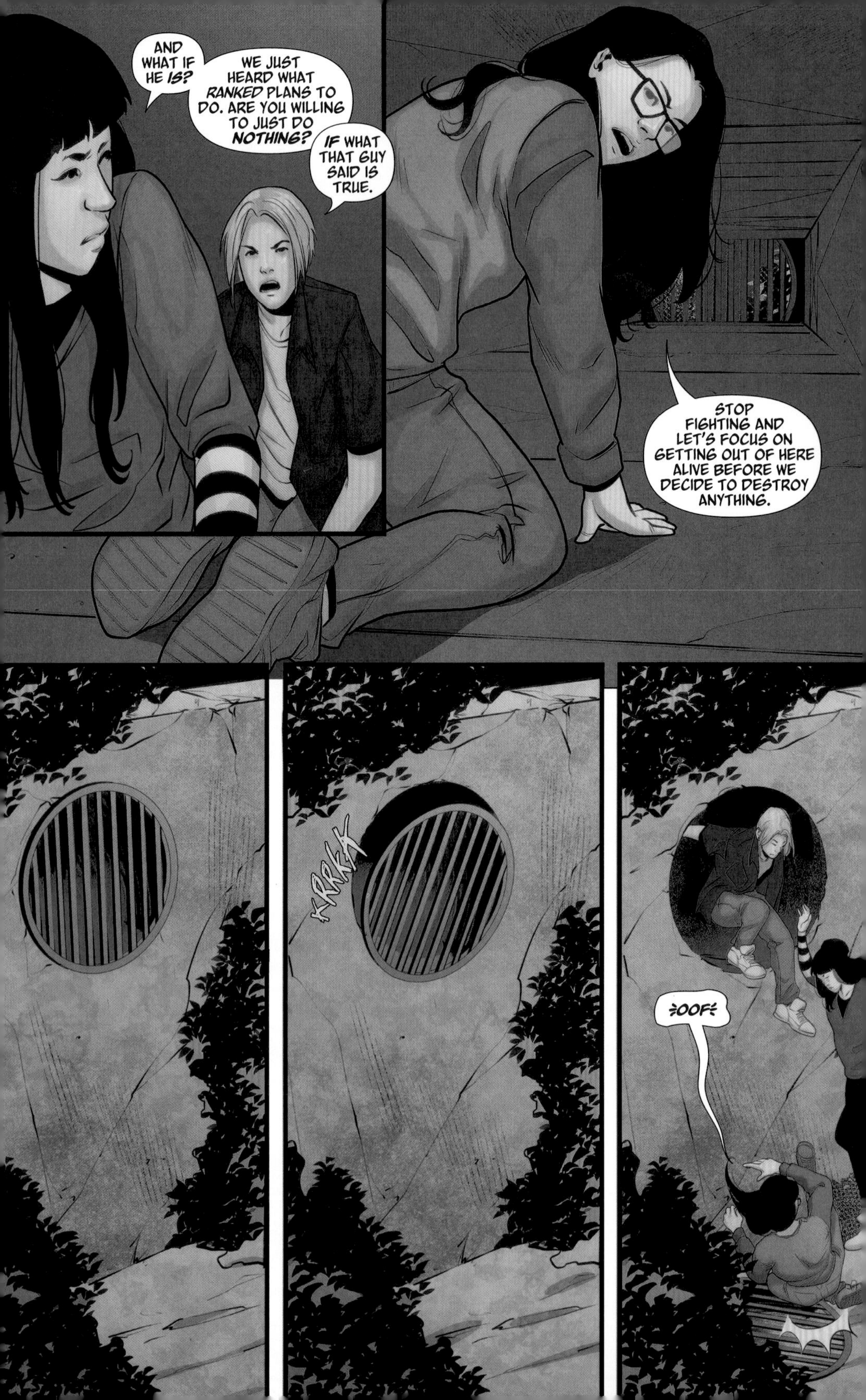
AND WHAT IF HE IS?
WE JUST HEARD WHAT RANKED PLANS TO DO. ARE YOU WILLING TO JUST DO NOTHING?
IF WHAT THAT GUY SAID IS TRUE.
STOP FIGHTING AND LET'S FOCUS ON GETTING OUT OF HERE ALIVE BEFORE WE DECIDE TO DESTROY ANYTHING.
KRRKK
OOF

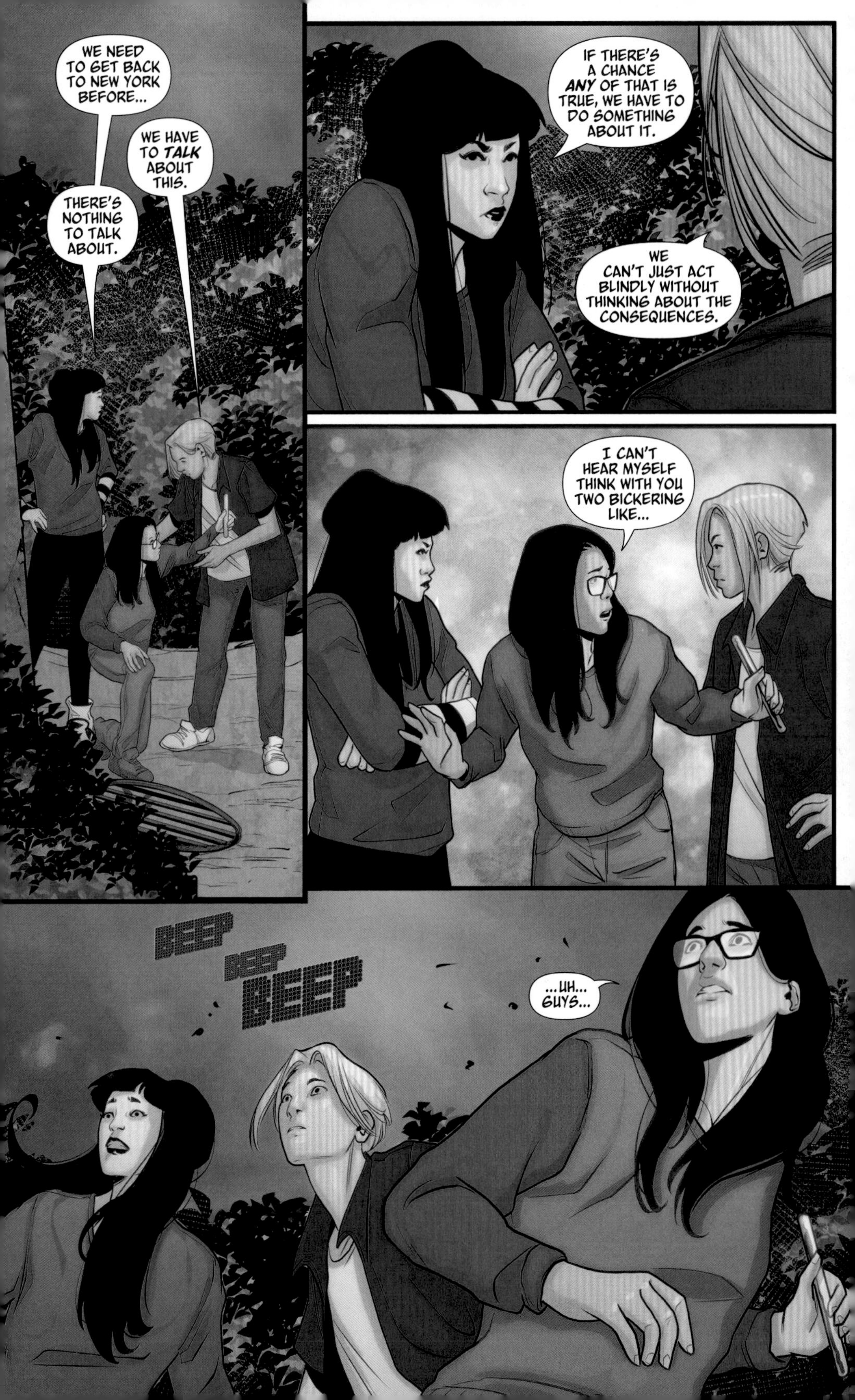
WE NEED TO GET BACK TO NEW YORK BEFORE...
WE HAVE TO TALK ABOUT THIS.
THERE'S NOTHING TO TALK ABOUT.
IF THERE'S A CHANCE ANY OF THAT IS TRUE, WE HAVE TO DO SOMETHING ABOUT IT.
WE CAN'T JUST ACT BLINDLY WITHOUT THINKING ABOUT THE CONSEQUENCES.
I CAN'T HEAR MYSELF THINK WITH YOU TWO BICKERING LIKE...
BEEP
BEEP
BEEP
...UH... GUYS...

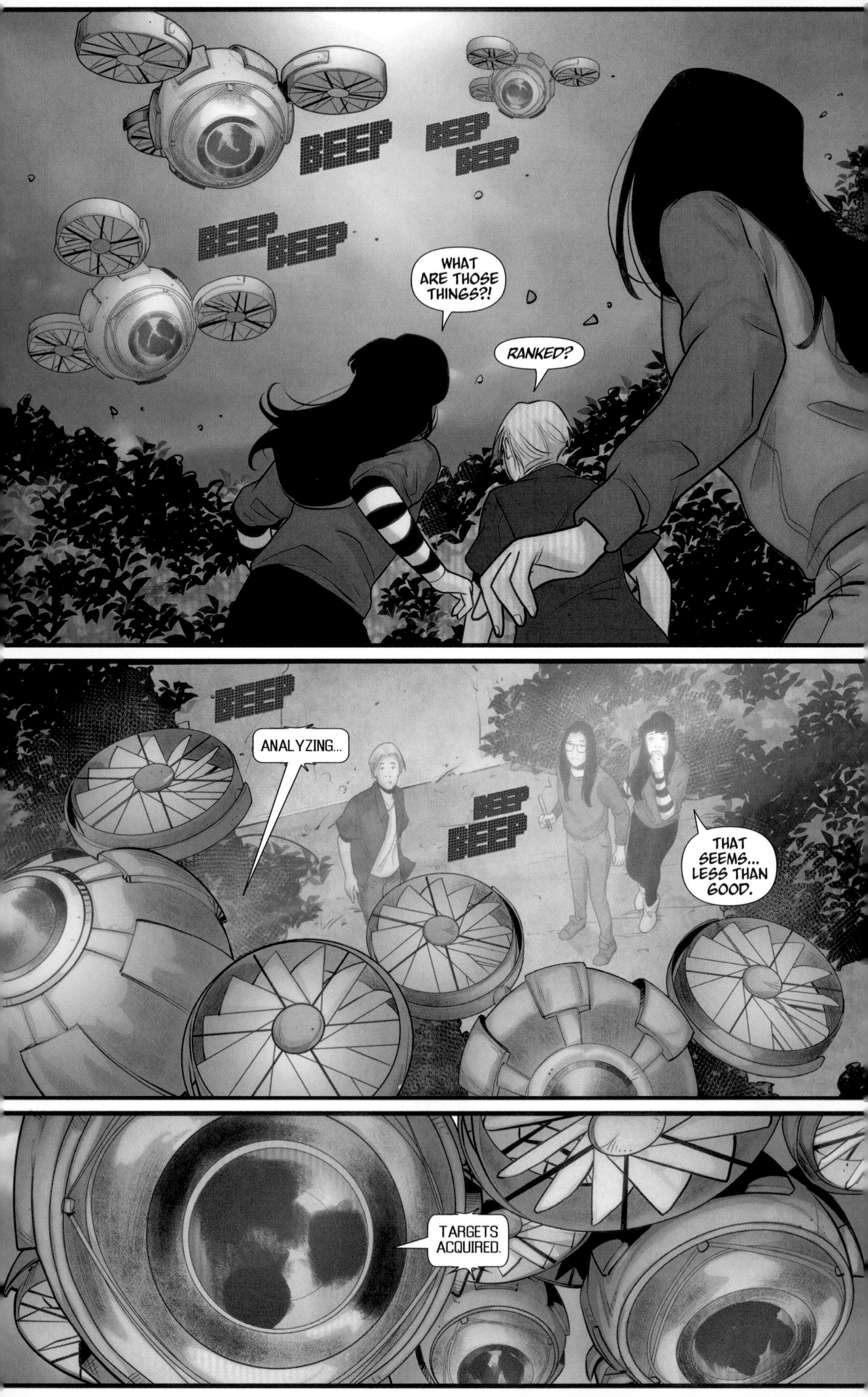
BEEP
BEEP BEEP
BEEP BEEP
WHAT ARE THOSE THINGS?!
RANKED?
BEEP
ANALYZING...
BEEP BEEP
THAT SEEMS... LESS THAN GOOD.
TARGETS ACQUIRED.

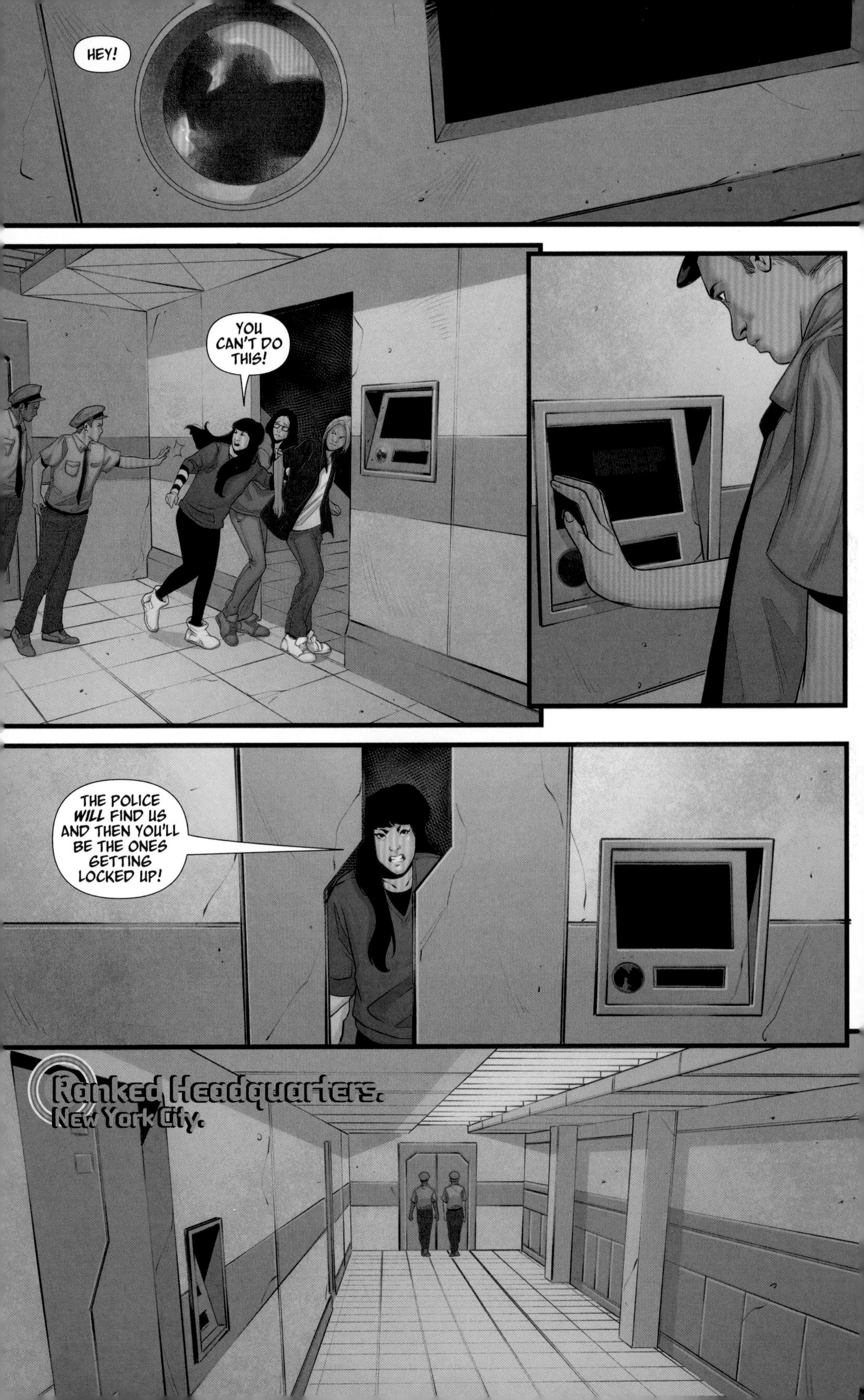
HEY!
YOU CAN'T DO THIS!
THE POLICE *WILL* FIND US AND THEN YOU'LL BE THE ONES GETTING LOCKED UP!
Ranked Headquarters.
New York City.

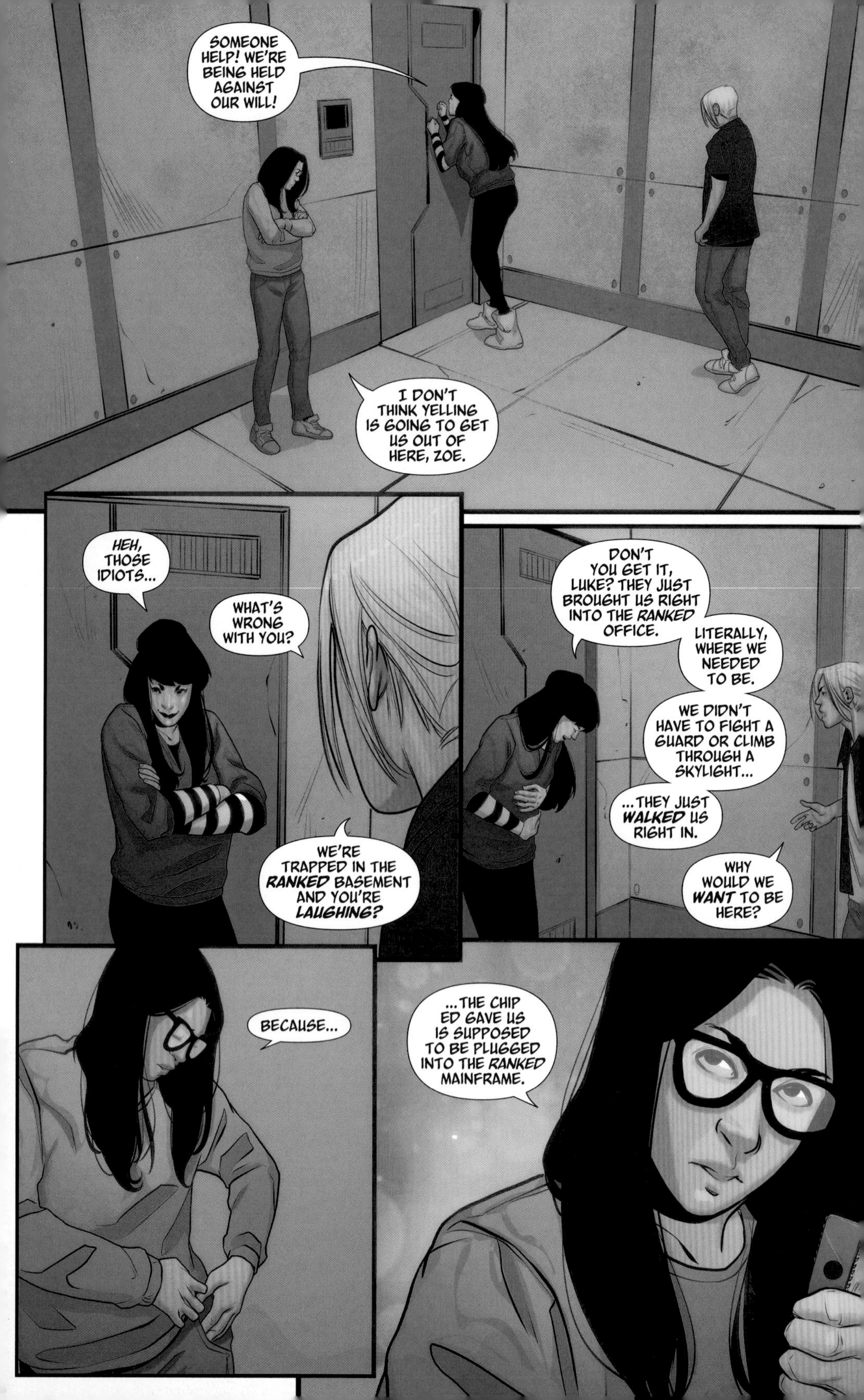

SOMEONE HELP! WE'RE BEING HELD AGAINST OUR WILL!
I DON'T THINK YELLING IS GOING TO GET US OUT OF HERE, ZOE.
HEH, THOSE IDIOTS...
WHAT'S WRONG WITH YOU?
WE'RE TRAPPED IN THE *RANKED* BASEMENT AND YOU'RE *LAUGHING?*
DON'T YOU GET IT, LUKE? THEY JUST BROUGHT US RIGHT INTO THE *RANKED* OFFICE.
LITERALLY, WHERE WE NEEDED TO BE.
WE DIDN'T HAVE TO FIGHT A GUARD OR CLIMB THROUGH A SKYLIGHT...
...THEY JUST *WALKED* US RIGHT IN.
WHY WOULD WE *WANT* TO BE HERE?
BECAUSE...
...THE CHIP ED GAVE US IS SUPPOSED TO BE PLUGGED INTO THE *RANKED* MAINFRAME.

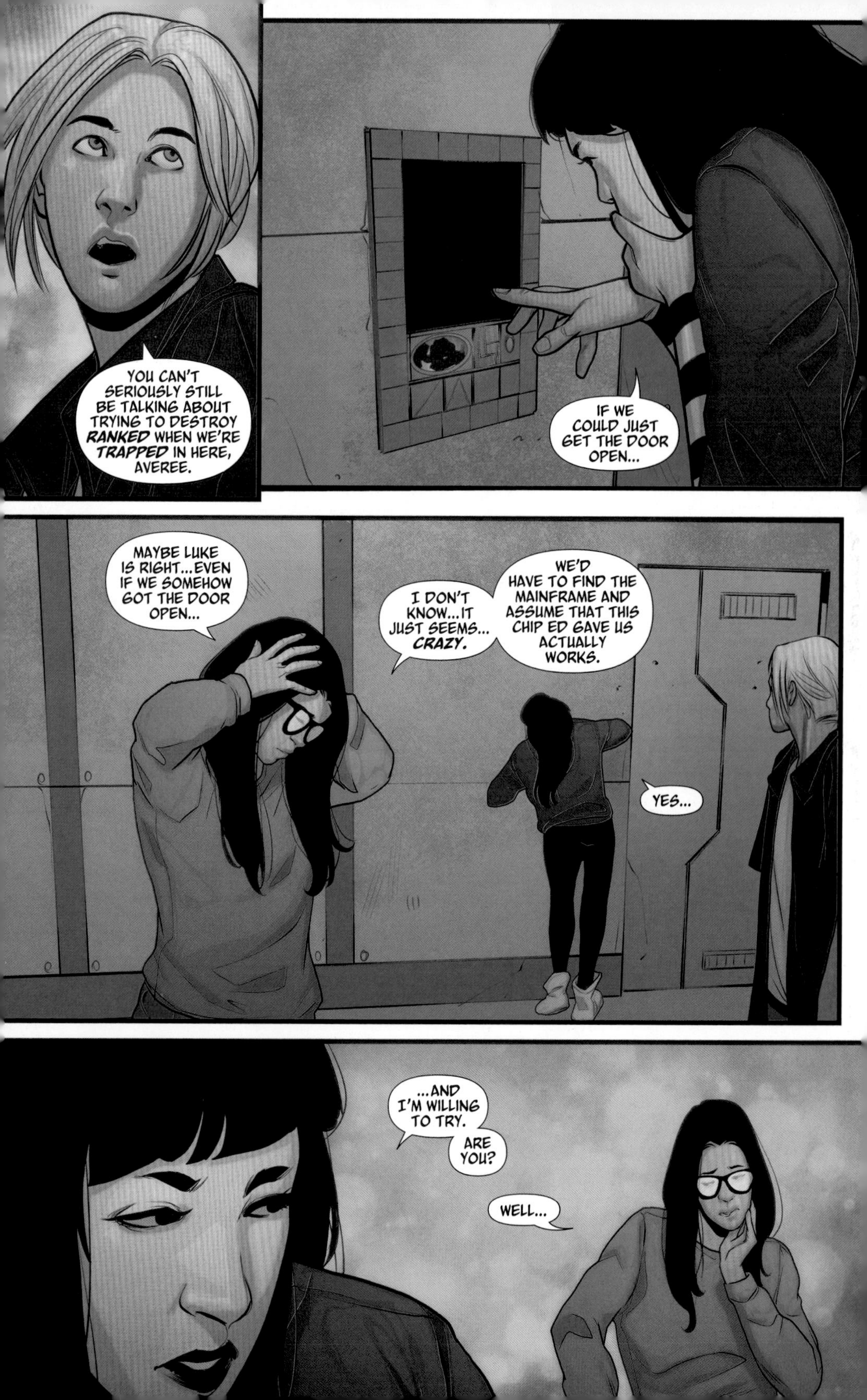
YOU CAN'T SERIOUSLY STILL BE TALKING ABOUT TRYING TO DESTROY RANKED WHEN WE'RE TRAPPED IN HERE, AVEREE.
IF WE COULD JUST GET THE DOOR OPEN...
MAYBE LUKE IS RIGHT...EVEN IF WE SOMEHOW GOT THE DOOR OPEN...
WE'D HAVE TO FIND THE MAINFRAME AND ASSUME THAT THIS CHIP ED GAVE US ACTUALLY WORKS.
I DON'T KNOW...IT JUST SEEMS... CRAZY.
YES...
...AND I'M WILLING TO TRY.
ARE YOU?
WELL...

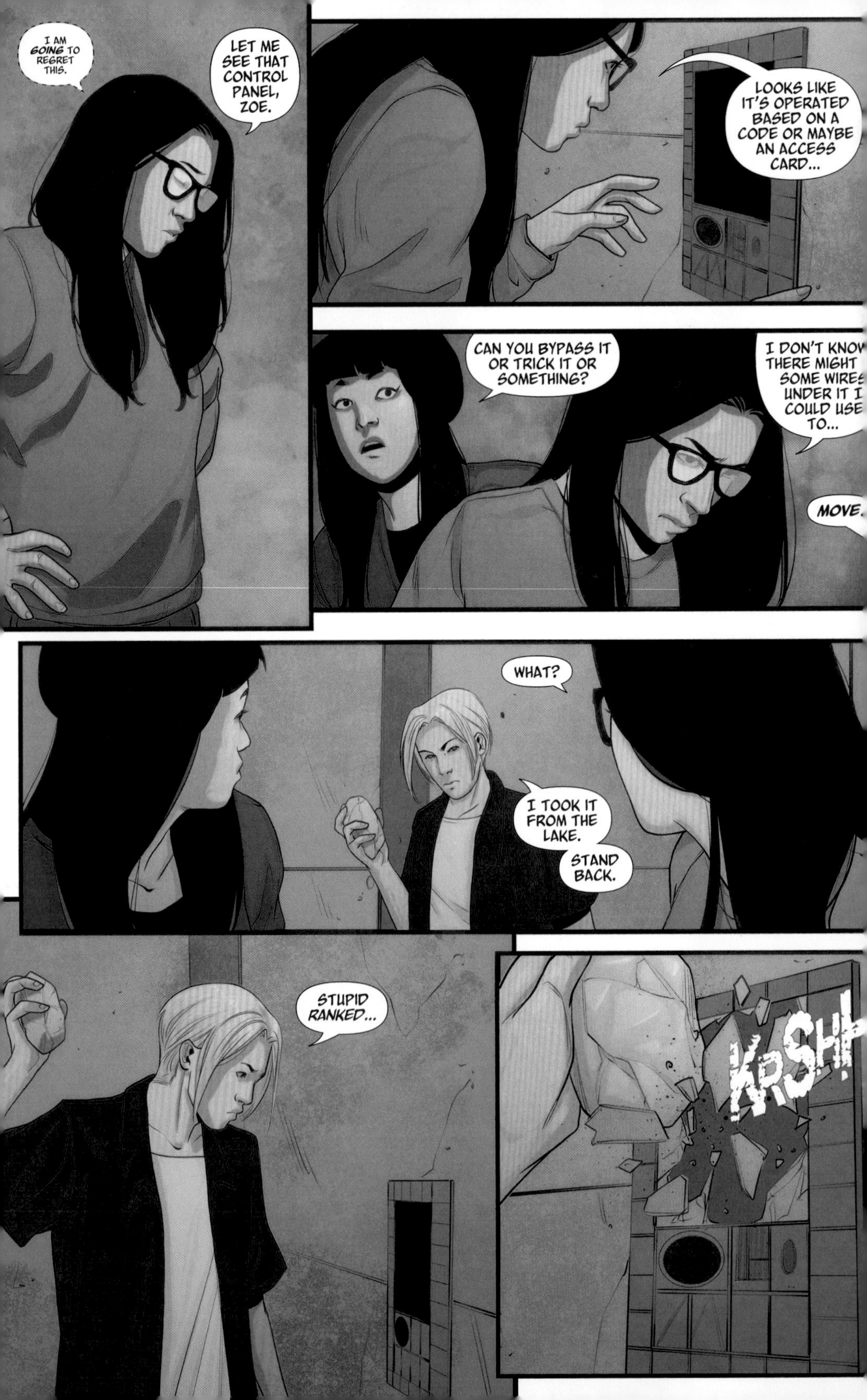
I AM GOING TO REGRET THIS.
LET ME SEE THAT CONTROL PANEL, ZOE.
LOOKS LIKE IT'S OPERATED BASED ON A CODE OR MAYBE AN ACCESS CARD...
CAN YOU BYPASS IT OR TRICK IT OR SOMETHING?
I DON'T KNOW THERE MIGHT SOME WIRES UNDER IT I COULD USE TO...
MOVE.
WHAT?
I TOOK IT FROM THE LAKE.
STAND BACK.
STUPID RANKED...
KRSH!

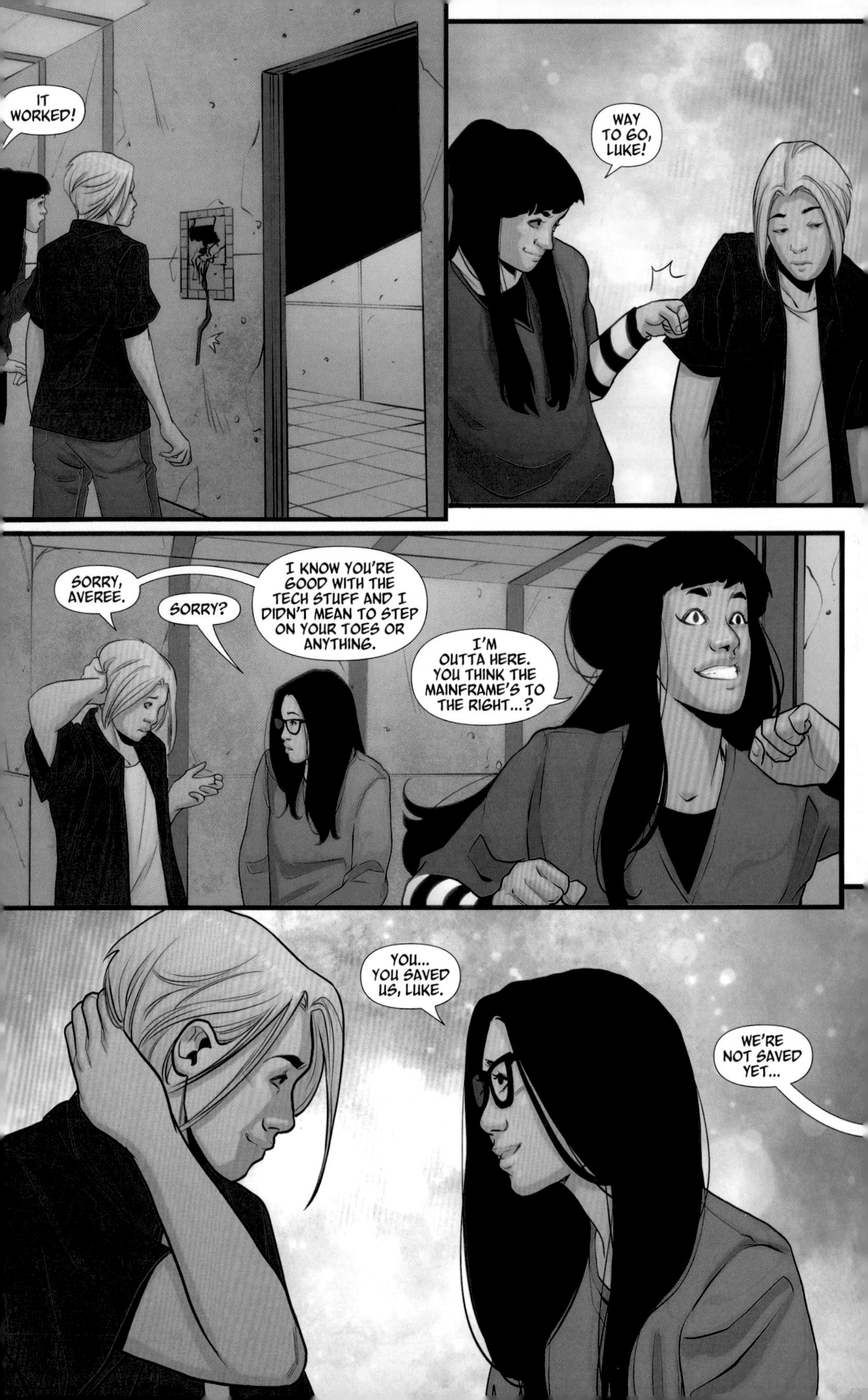
IT WORKED!
WAY TO GO, LUKE!
SORRY, AVEREE.
SORRY?
I KNOW YOU'RE GOOD WITH THE TECH STUFF AND I DIDN'T MEAN TO STEP ON YOUR TOES OR ANYTHING.
I'M OUTTA HERE. YOU THINK THE MAINFRAME'S TO THE RIGHT...?
YOU... YOU SAVED US, LUKE.
WE'RE NOT SAVED YET...

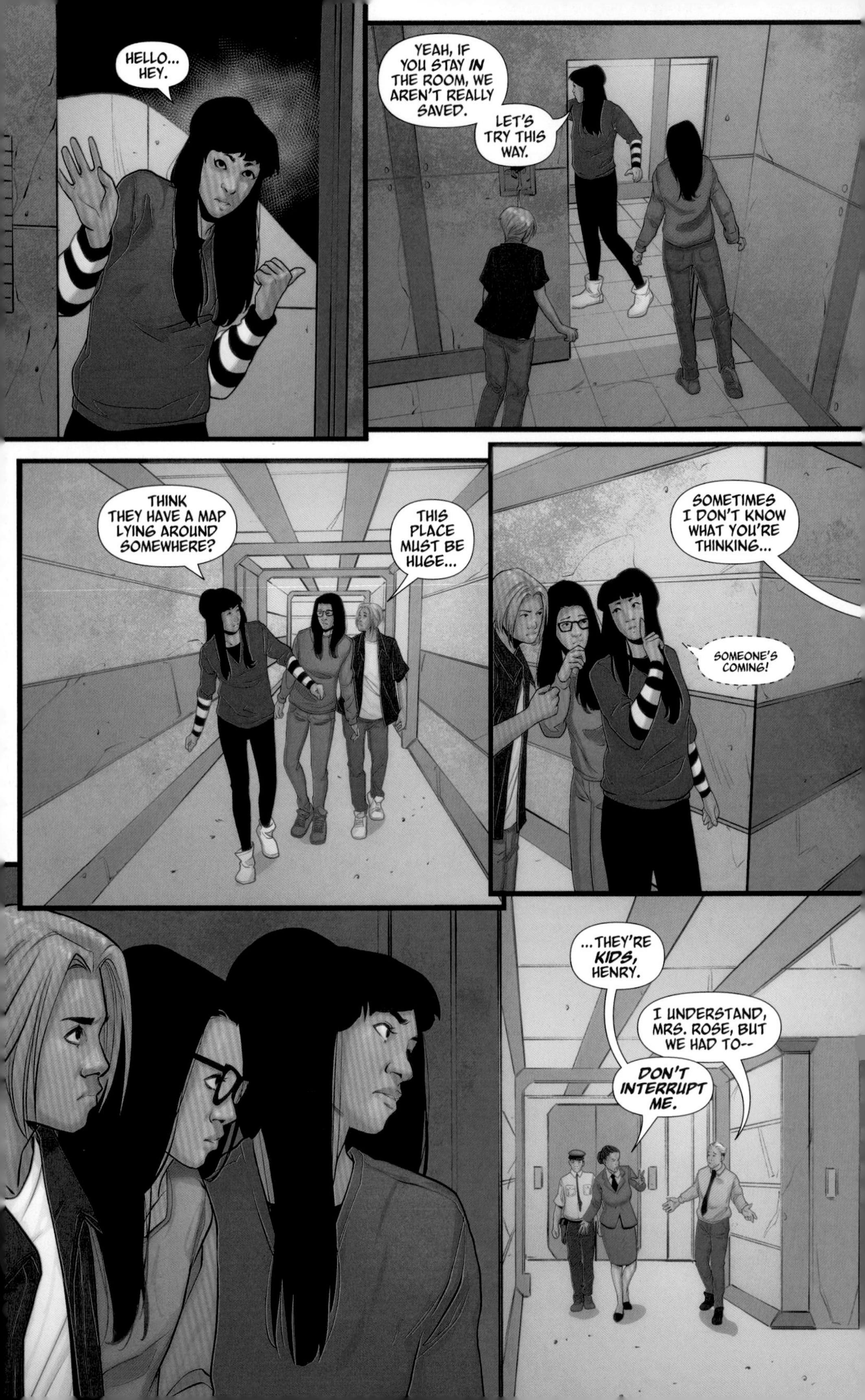
HELLO... HEY.
YEAH, IF YOU STAY IN THE ROOM, WE AREN'T REALLY SAVED.
LET'S TRY THIS WAY.
THINK THEY HAVE A MAP LYING AROUND SOMEWHERE?
THIS PLACE MUST BE HUGE...
SOMETIMES I DON'T KNOW WHAT YOU'RE THINKING...
SOMEONE'S COMING!
...THEY'RE KIDS, HENRY.
I UNDERSTAND, MRS. ROSE, BUT WE HAD TO--
DON'T INTERRUPT ME.

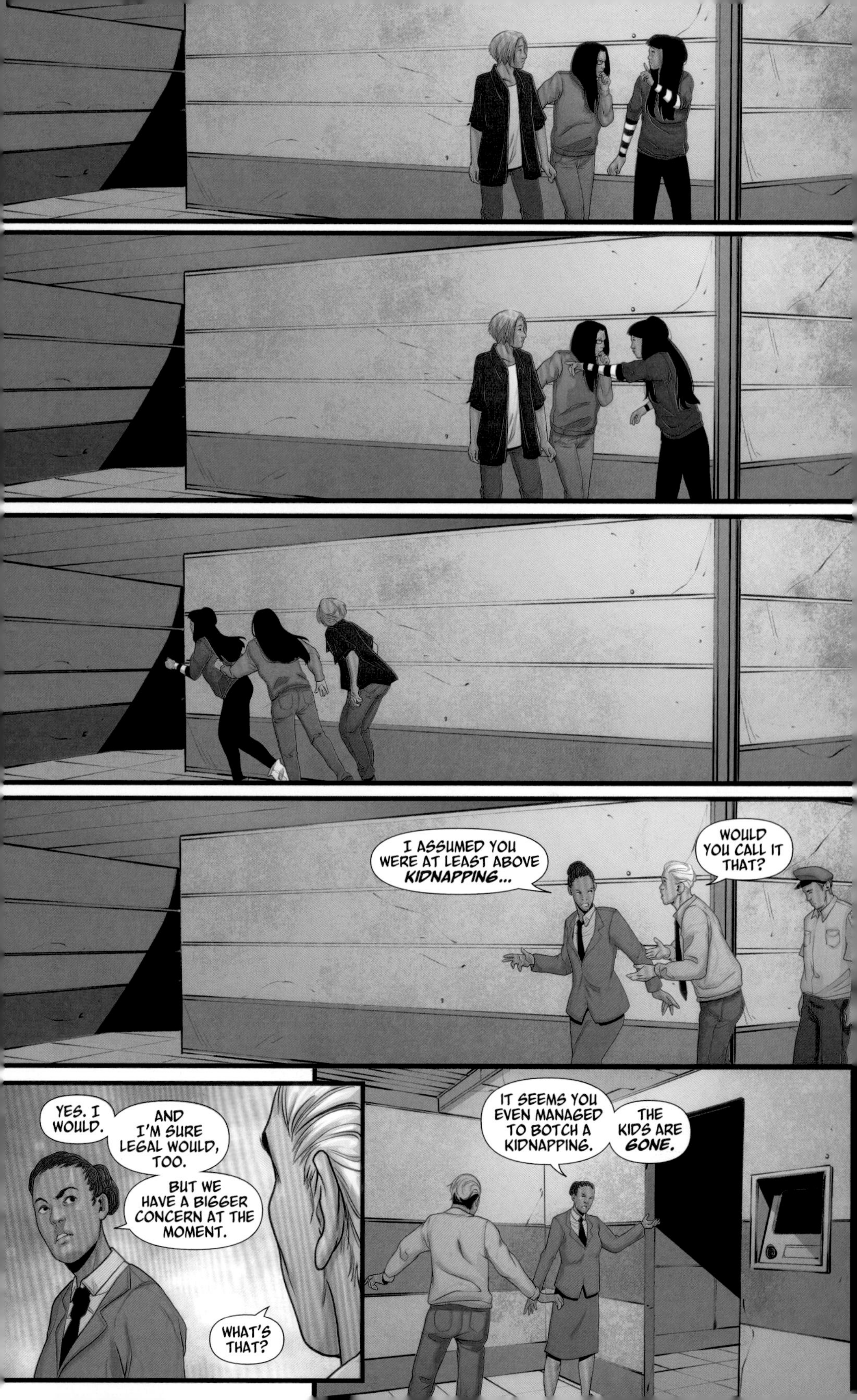
I ASSUMED YOU WERE AT LEAST ABOVE KIDNAPPING...
WOULD YOU CALL IT THAT?
YES. I WOULD.
AND I'M SURE LEGAL WOULD, TOO.
BUT WE HAVE A BIGGER CONCERN AT THE MOMENT.
WHAT'S THAT?
IT SEEMS YOU EVEN MANAGED TO BOTCH A KIDNAPPING.
THE KIDS ARE GONE.

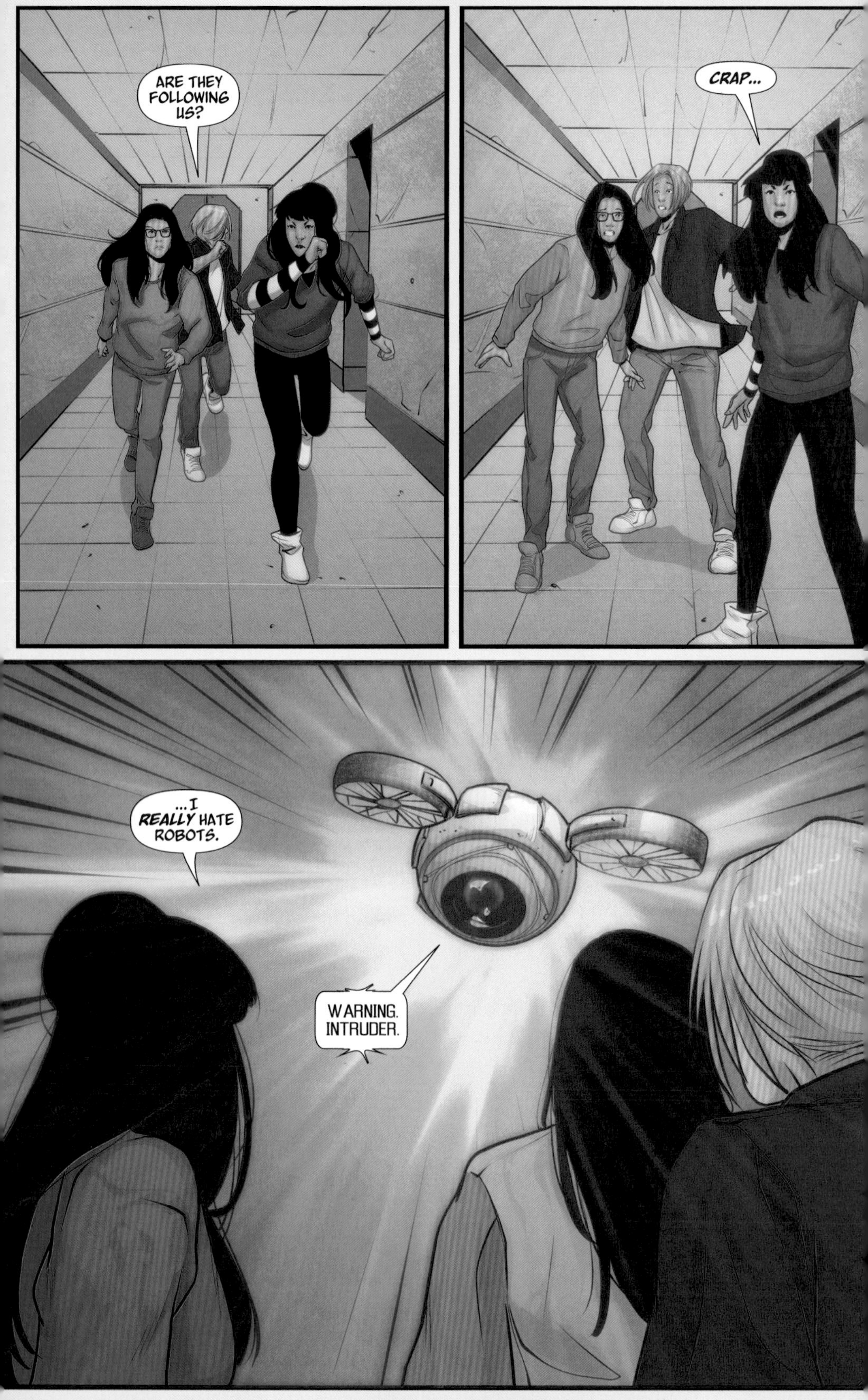
ARE THEY FOLLOWING US?
CRAP...
...I *REALLY* HATE ROBOTS.
WARNING. INTRUDER.

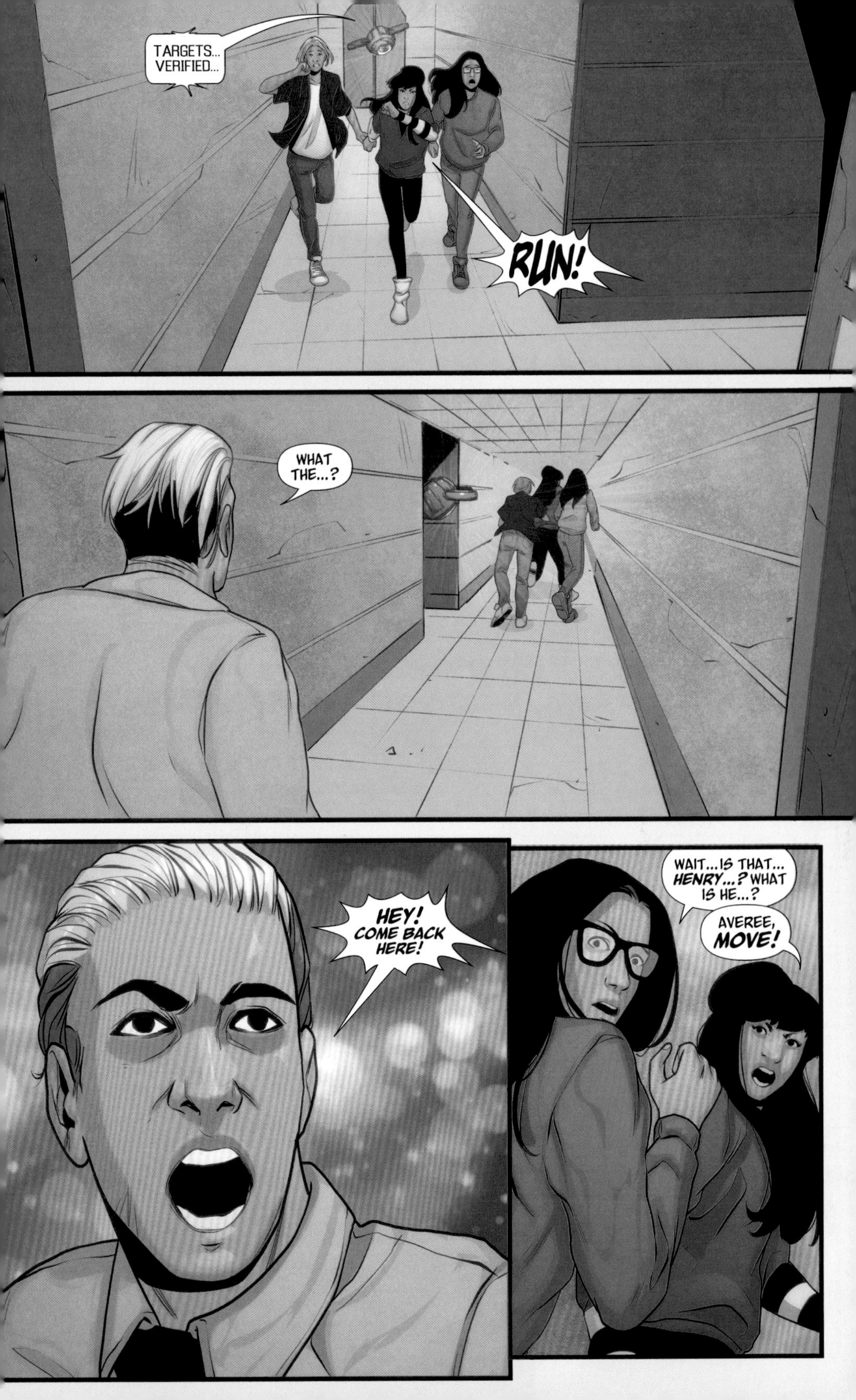

TARGETS... VERIFIED...
RUN!
WHAT THE...?
HEY! COME BACK HERE!
WAIT...IS THAT... HENRY...? WHAT IS HE...?
AVEREE, MOVE!

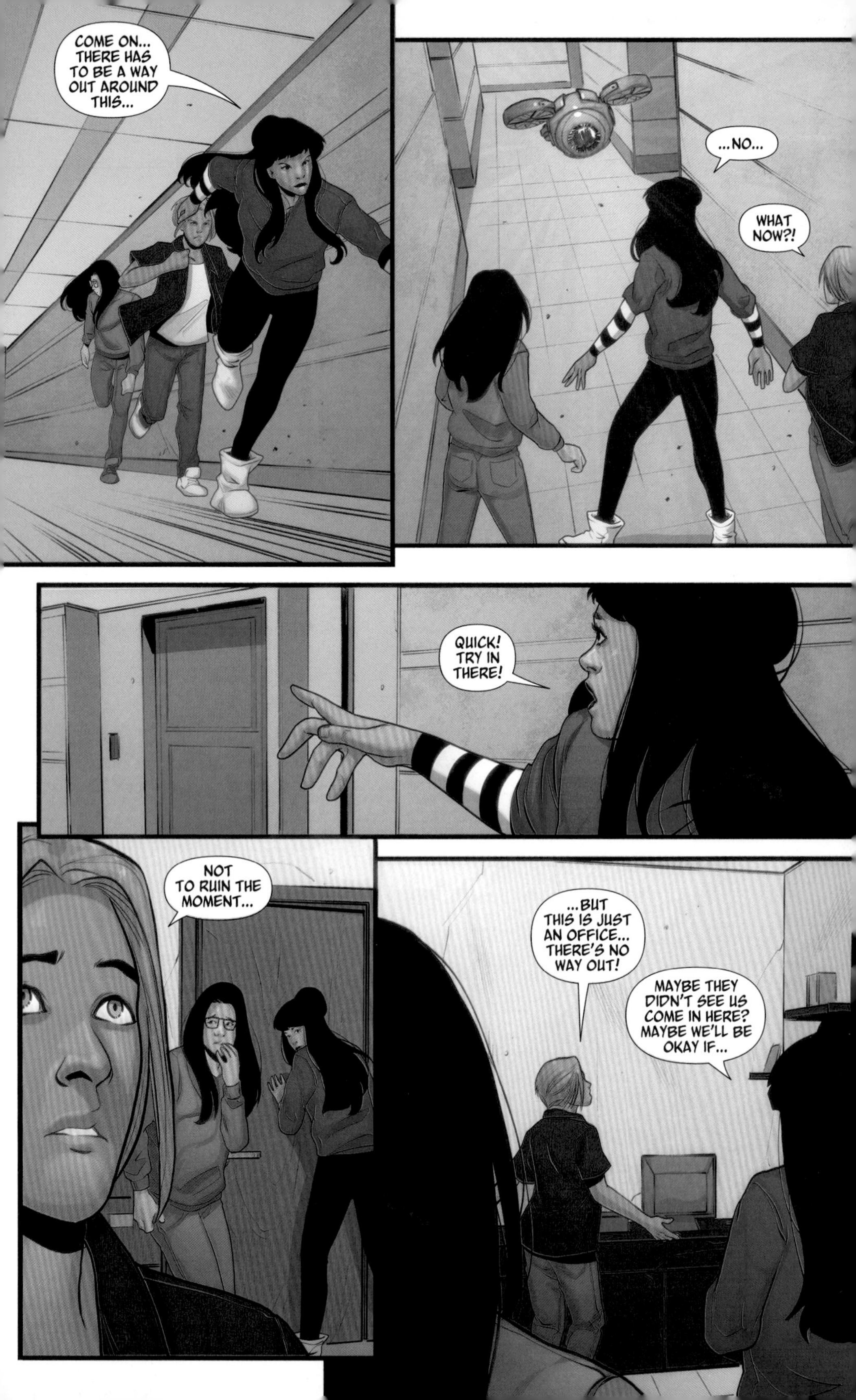
COME ON... THERE HAS TO BE A WAY OUT AROUND THIS...
...NO...
WHAT NOW?!
QUICK! TRY IN THERE!
NOT TO RUIN THE MOMENT...
...BUT THIS IS JUST AN OFFICE... THERE'S NO WAY OUT!
MAYBE THEY DIDN'T SEE US COME IN HERE? MAYBE WE'LL BE OKAY IF...

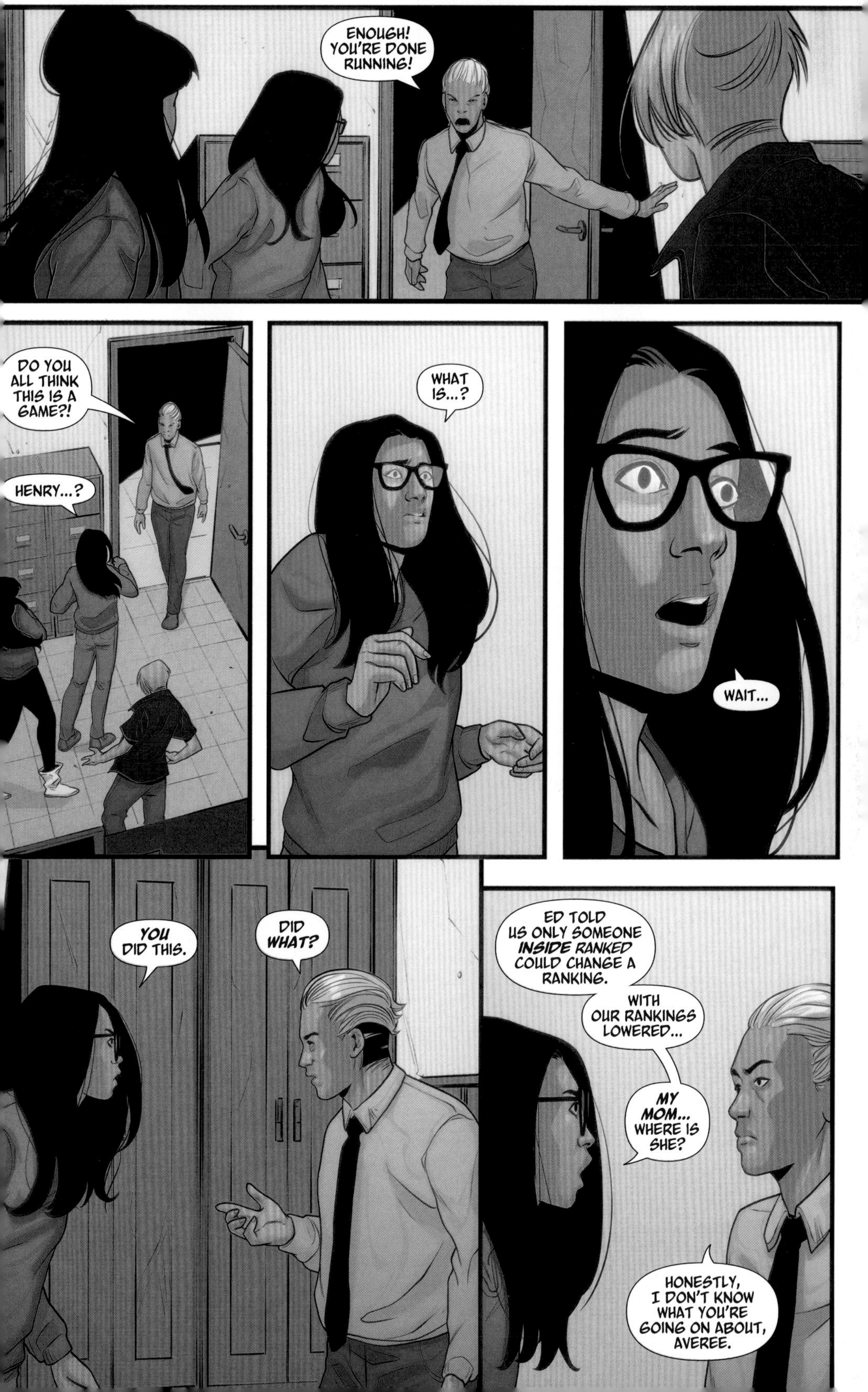
ENOUGH! YOU'RE DONE RUNNING!
DO YOU ALL THINK THIS IS A GAME?!
HENRY...?
WHAT IS...?
WAIT...
YOU DID THIS.
DID WHAT?
ED TOLD US ONLY SOMEONE INSIDE RANKED COULD CHANGE A RANKING.
WITH OUR RANKINGS LOWERED...
MY MOM... WHERE IS SHE?
HONESTLY, I DON'T KNOW WHAT YOU'RE GOING ON ABOUT, AVEREE.

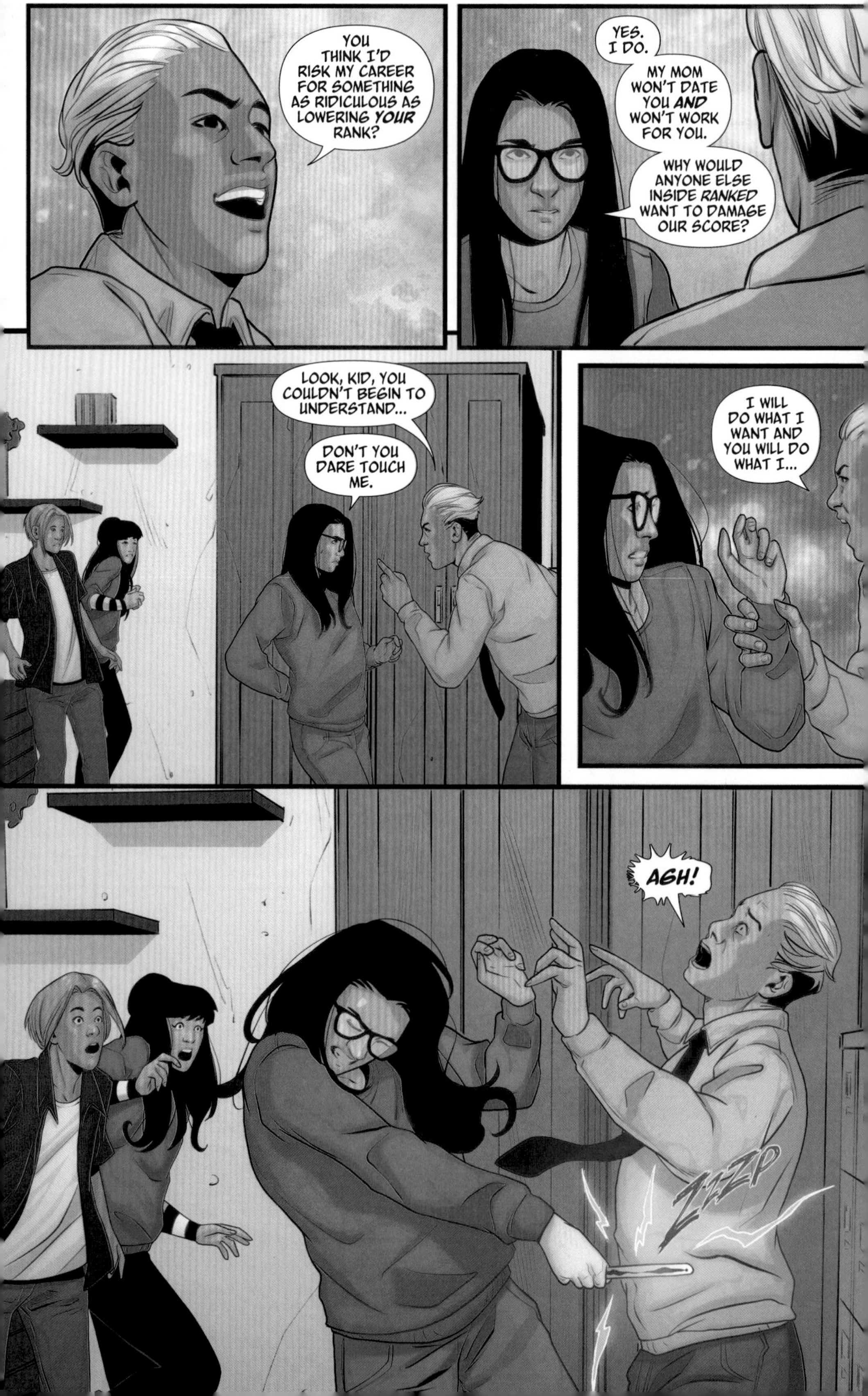
YOU THINK I'D RISK MY CAREER FOR SOMETHING AS RIDICULOUS AS LOWERING *YOUR* RANK?
YES. I DO.
MY MOM WON'T DATE YOU *AND* WON'T WORK FOR YOU.
WHY WOULD ANYONE ELSE INSIDE *RANKED* WANT TO DAMAGE OUR SCORE?
LOOK, KID, YOU COULDN'T BEGIN TO UNDERSTAND...
DON'T YOU DARE TOUCH ME.
I WILL DO WHAT I WANT AND YOU WILL DO WHAT I...
AGH!
ZZZZP

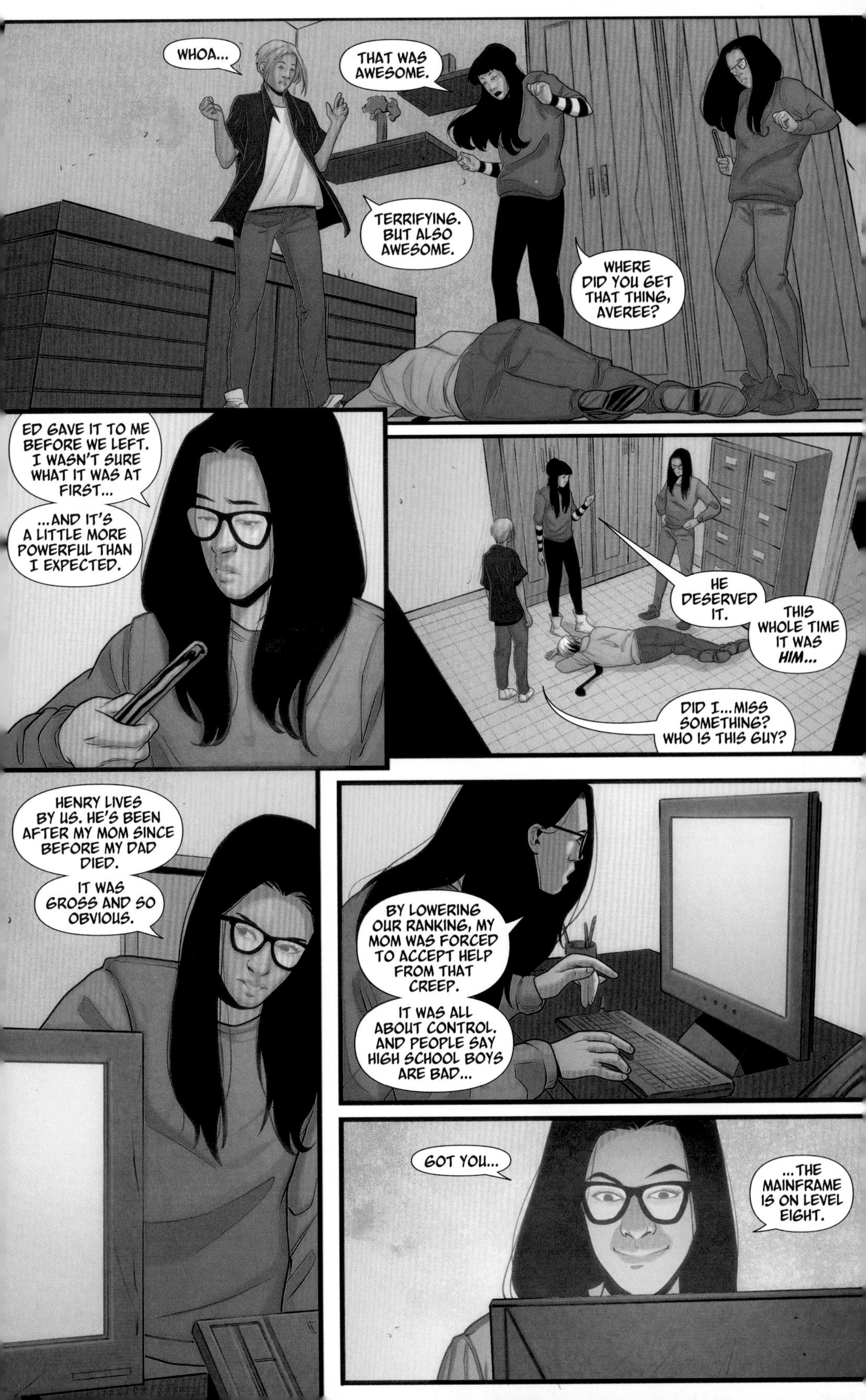
WHOA...
THAT WAS AWESOME.
TERRIFYING. BUT ALSO AWESOME.
WHERE DID YOU GET THAT THING, AVEREE?
ED GAVE IT TO ME BEFORE WE LEFT. I WASN'T SURE WHAT IT WAS AT FIRST...
...AND IT'S A LITTLE MORE POWERFUL THAN I EXPECTED.
HE DESERVED IT.
THIS WHOLE TIME IT WAS *HIM*...
DID I...MISS SOMETHING? WHO IS THIS GUY?
HENRY LIVES BY US. HE'S BEEN AFTER MY MOM SINCE BEFORE MY DAD DIED.
IT WAS GROSS AND SO OBVIOUS.
BY LOWERING OUR RANKING, MY MOM WAS FORCED TO ACCEPT HELP FROM THAT CREEP.
IT WAS ALL ABOUT CONTROL. AND PEOPLE SAY HIGH SCHOOL BOYS ARE BAD...
GOT YOU...
...THE MAINFRAME IS ON LEVEL EIGHT.

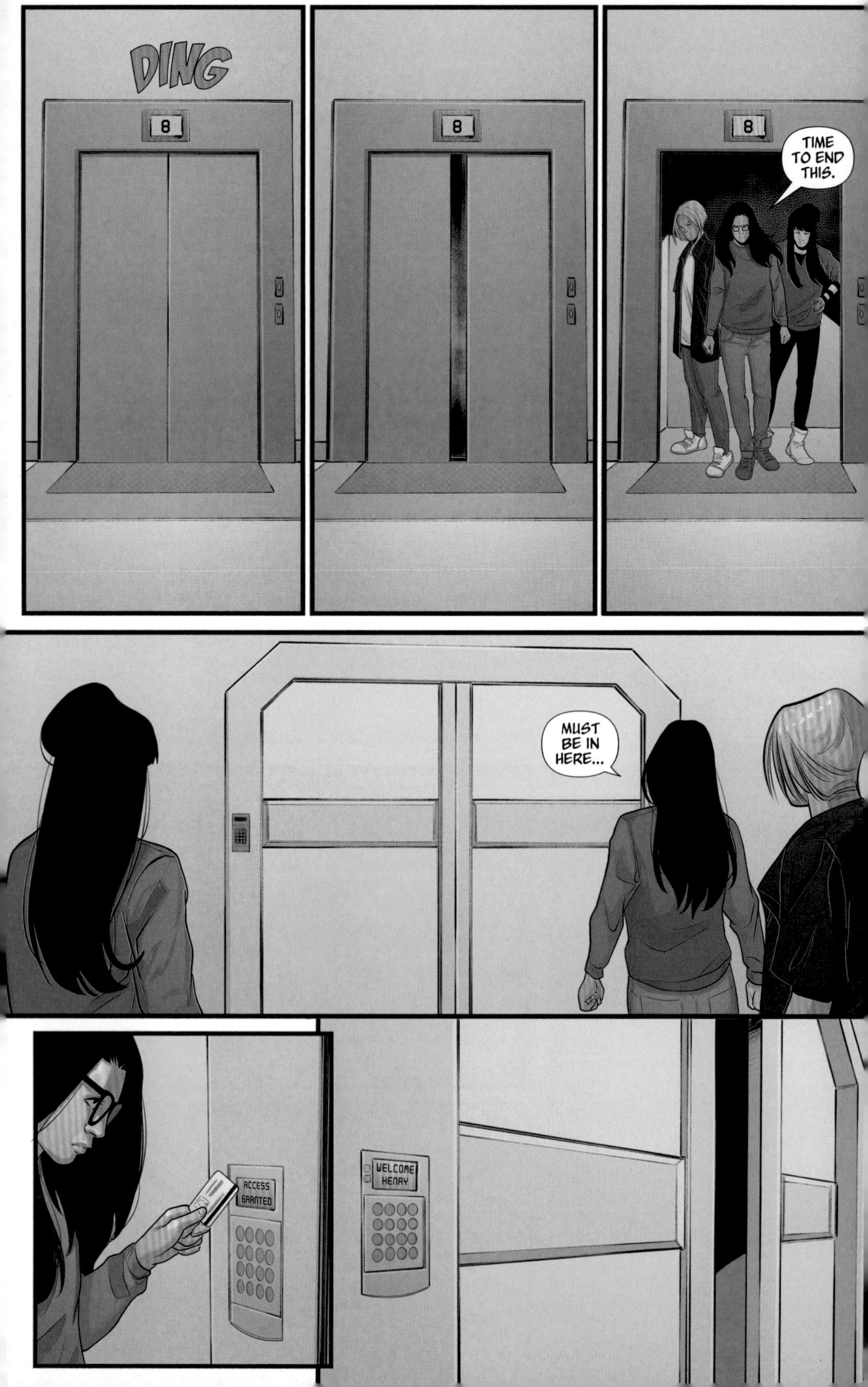
DING
TIME TO END THIS.
MUST BE IN HERE...
ACCESS GRANTED
WELCOME HENRY

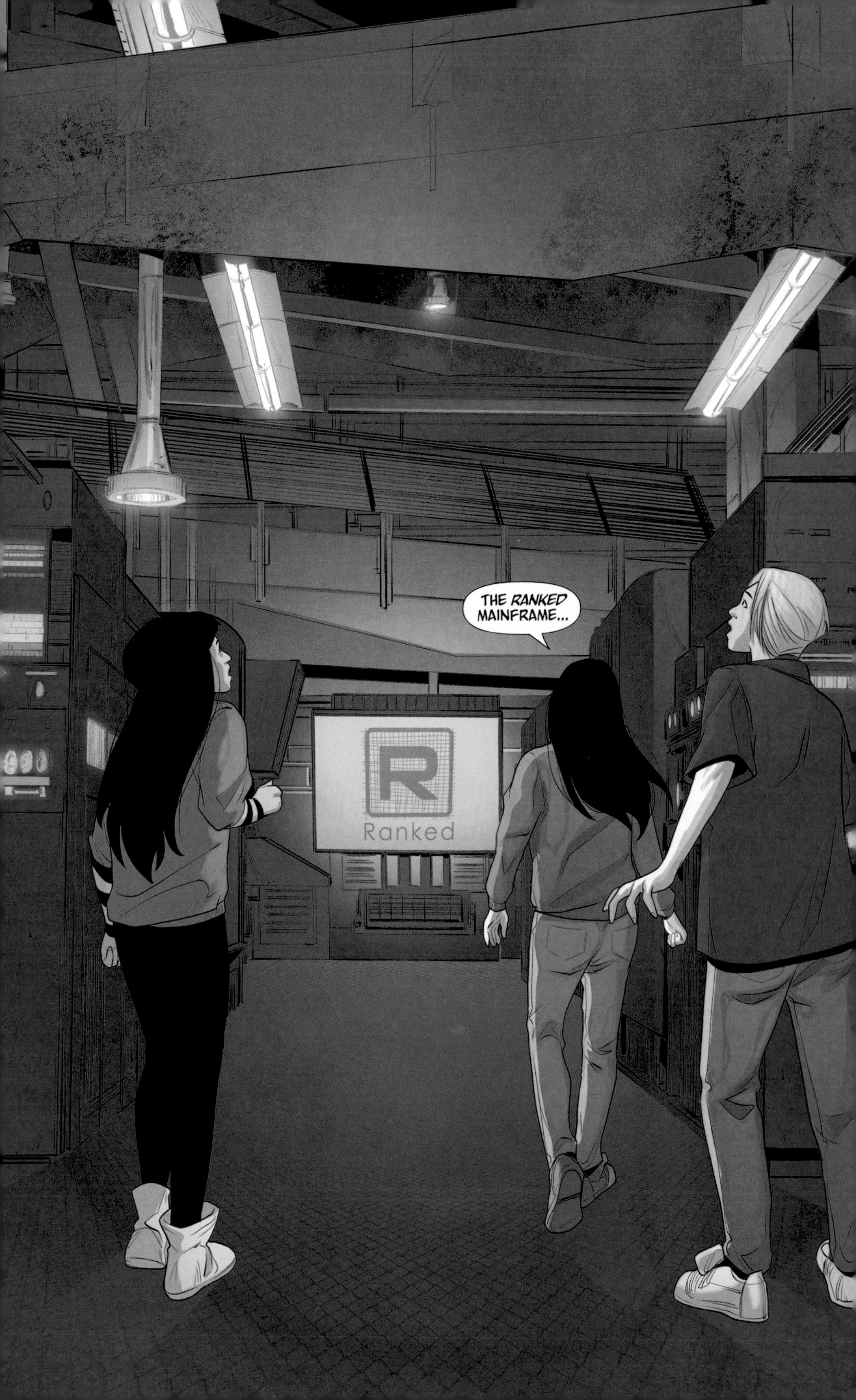
THE RANKED MAINFRAME...
Ranked

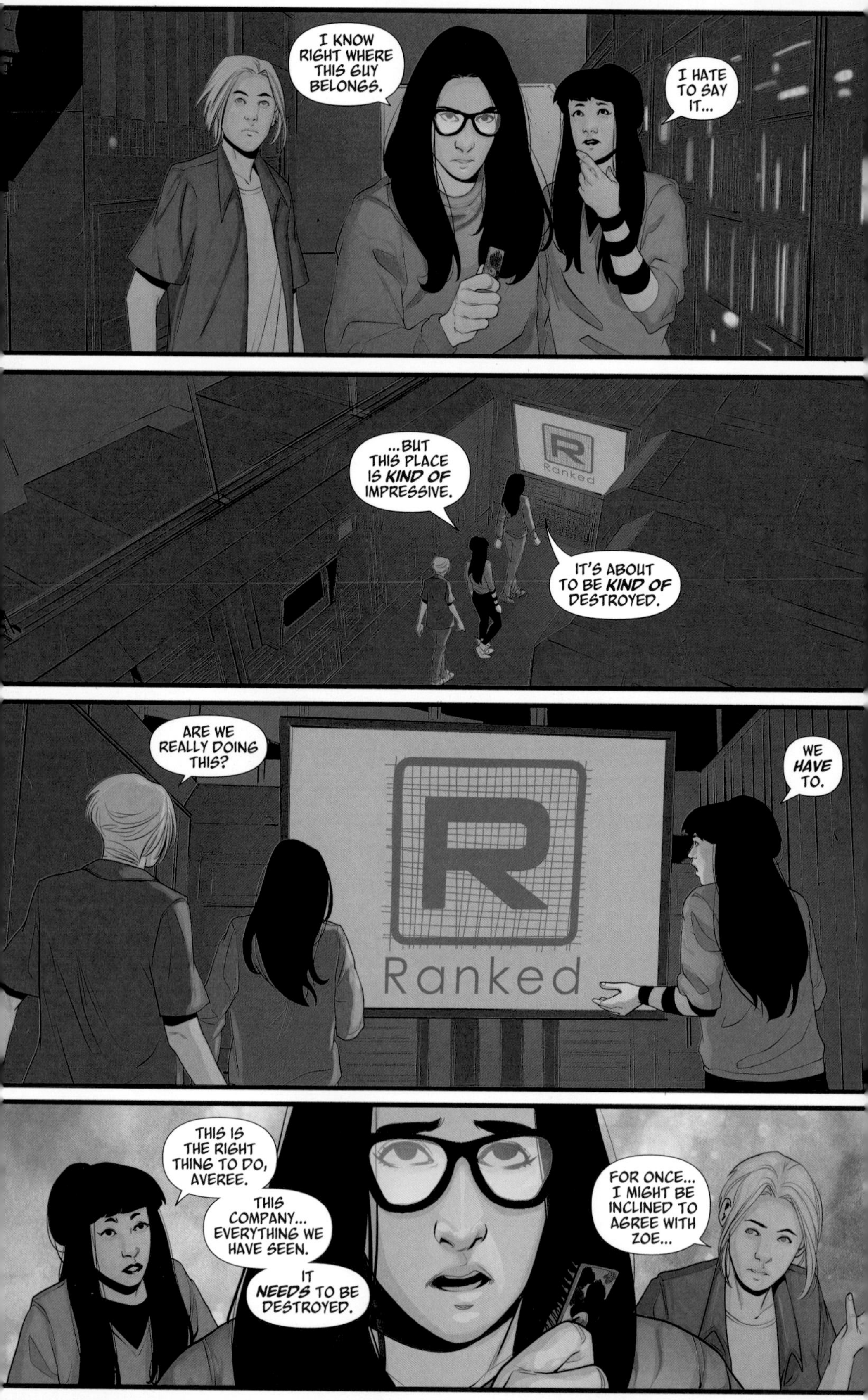
I KNOW RIGHT WHERE THIS GUY BELONGS.
I HATE TO SAY IT...
...BUT THIS PLACE IS *KIND OF* IMPRESSIVE.
IT'S ABOUT TO BE *KIND OF* DESTROYED.
Ranked
ARE WE REALLY DOING THIS?
WE *HAVE* TO.
Ranked
THIS IS THE RIGHT THING TO DO, AVEREE.
THIS COMPANY... EVERYTHING WE HAVE SEEN.
IT *NEEDS* TO BE DESTROYED.
FOR ONCE... I MIGHT BE INCLINED TO AGREE WITH ZOE...

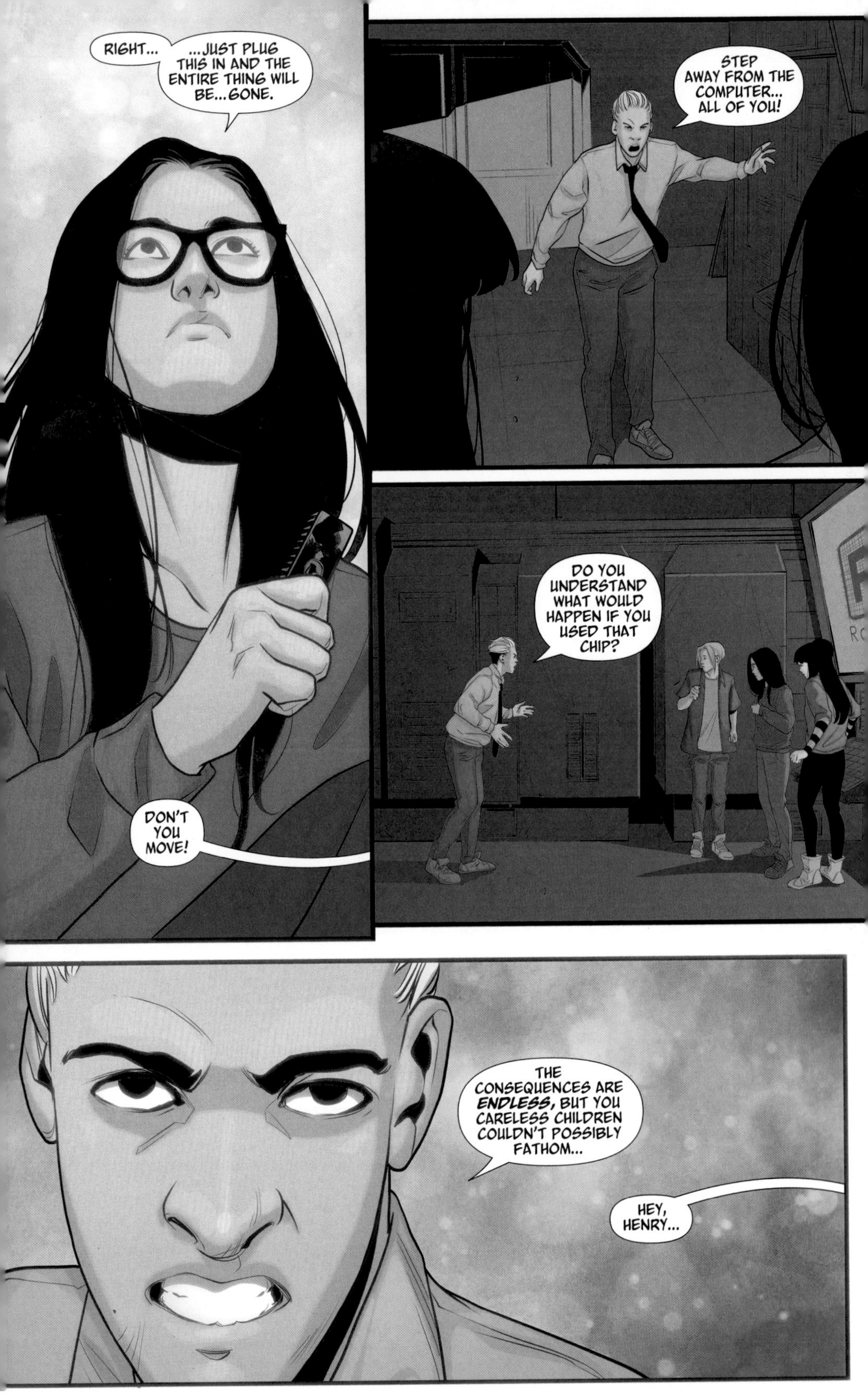
RIGHT...
...JUST PLUG THIS IN AND THE ENTIRE THING WILL BE...GONE.
STEP AWAY FROM THE COMPUTER... ALL OF YOU!
DON'T YOU MOVE!
DO YOU UNDERSTAND WHAT WOULD HAPPEN IF YOU USED THAT CHIP?
THE CONSEQUENCES ARE ENDLESS, BUT YOU CARELESS CHILDREN COULDN'T POSSIBLY FATHOM...
HEY, HENRY...

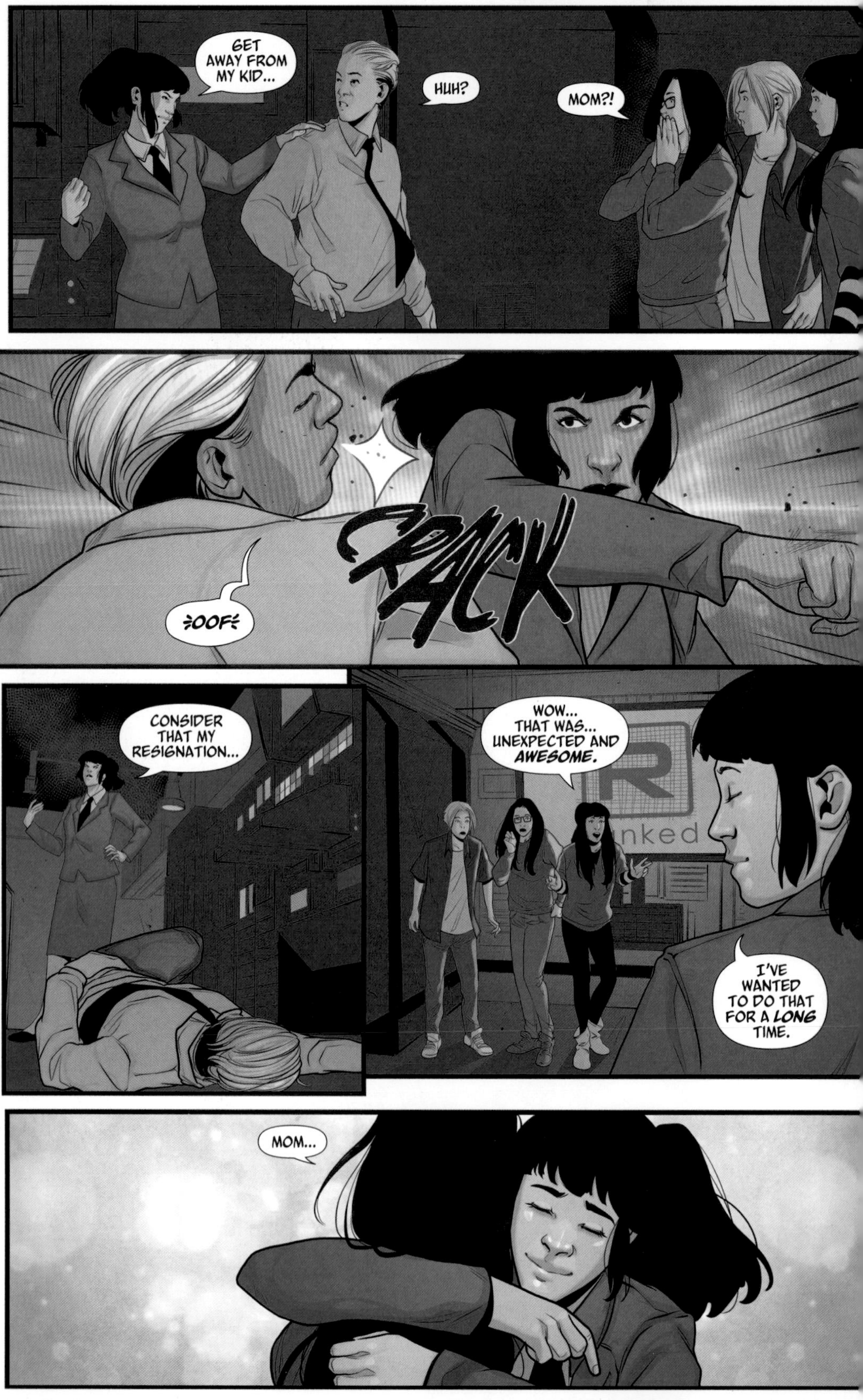
GET AWAY FROM MY KID...
HUH?
MOM?!
OOF
CRACK
CONSIDER THAT MY RESIGNATION...
WOW... THAT WAS... UNEXPECTED AND AWESOME.
I'VE WANTED TO DO THAT FOR A LONG TIME.
MOM...

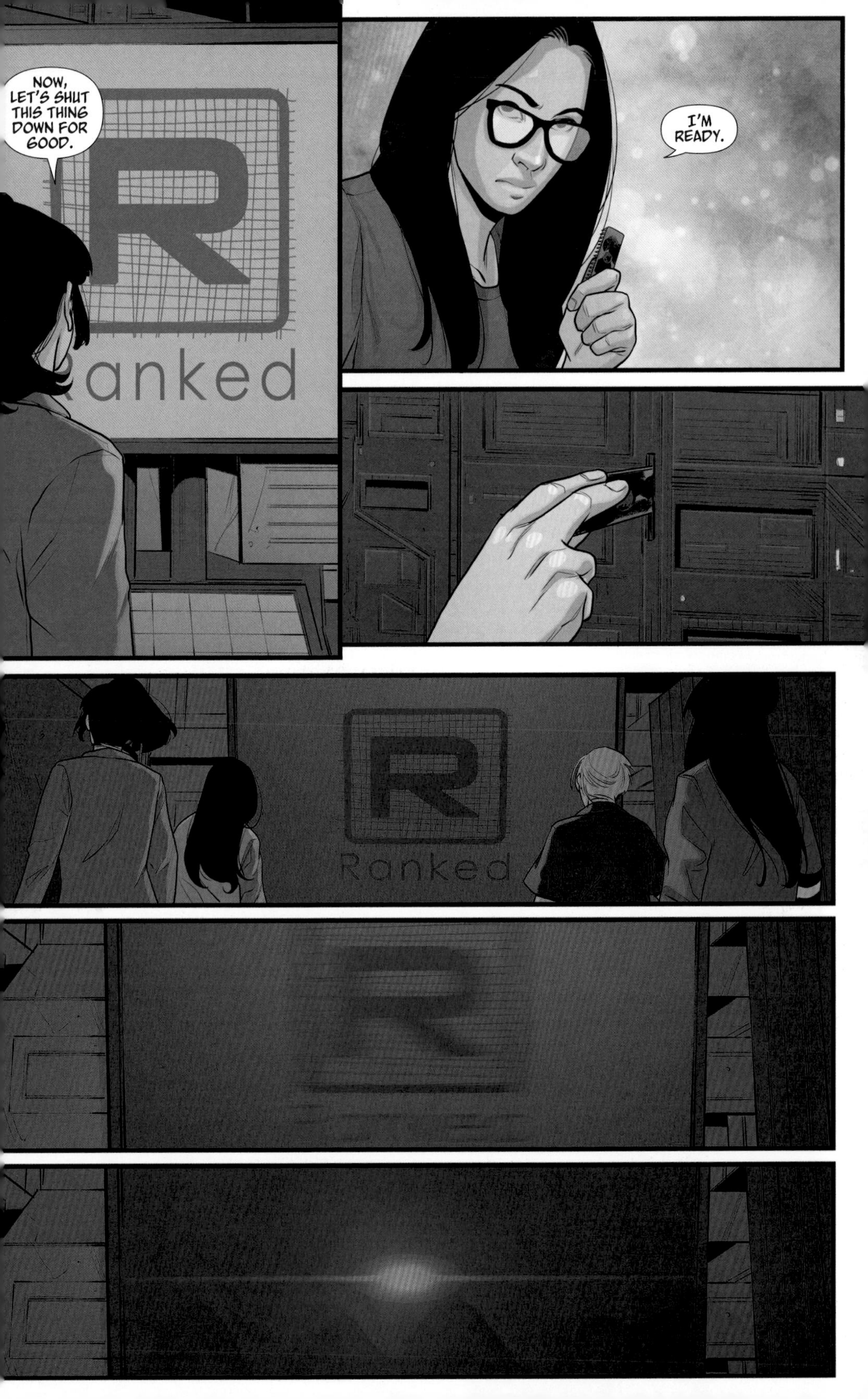
NOW, LET'S SHUT THIS THING DOWN FOR GOOD.
Ranked
I'M READY.
Ranked

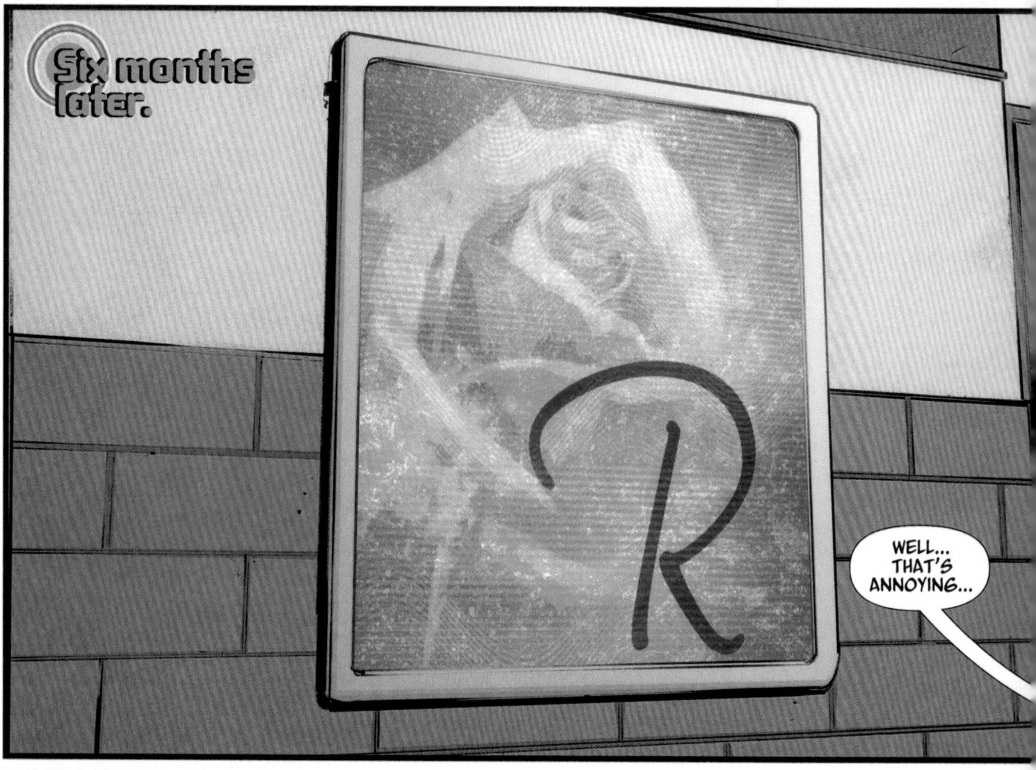
Six months later.
WELL... THAT'S ANNOYING...

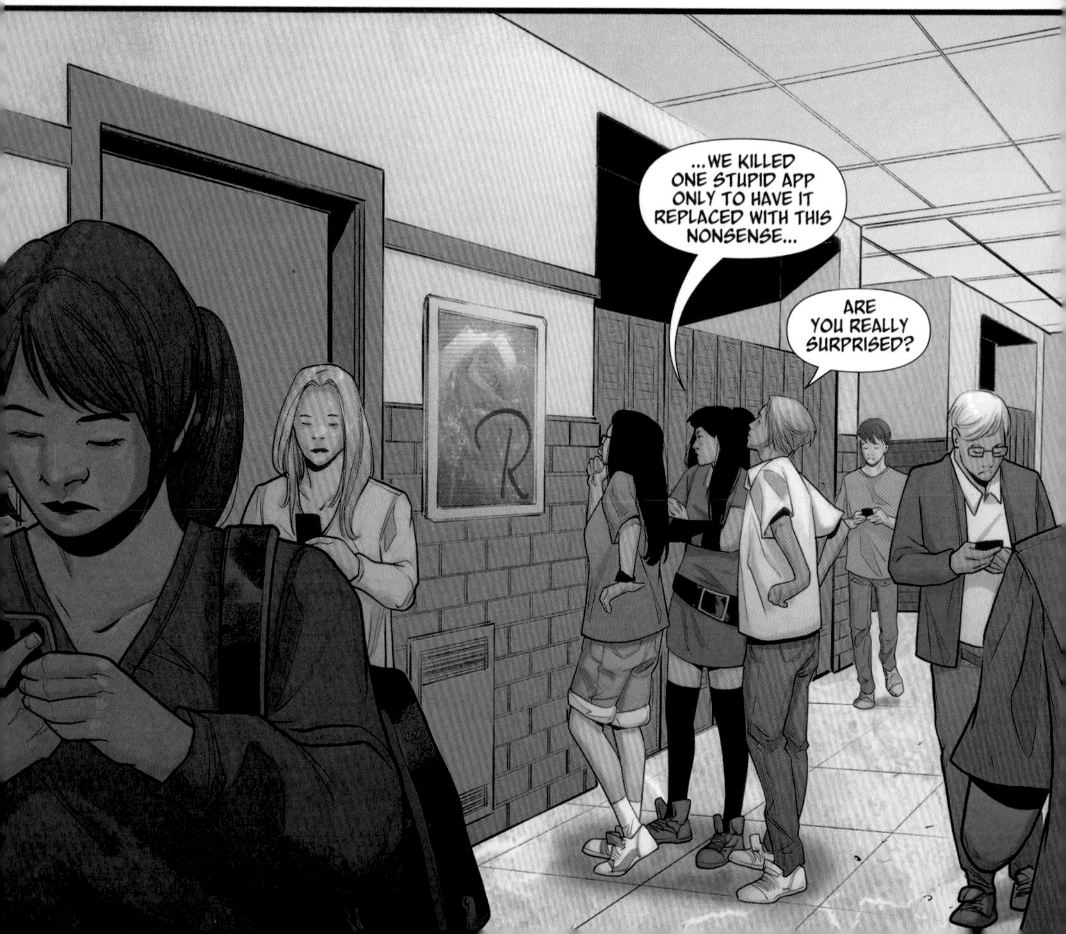
...WE KILLED ONE STUPID APP ONLY TO HAVE IT REPLACED WITH THIS NONSENSE...
ARE YOU REALLY SURPRISED?

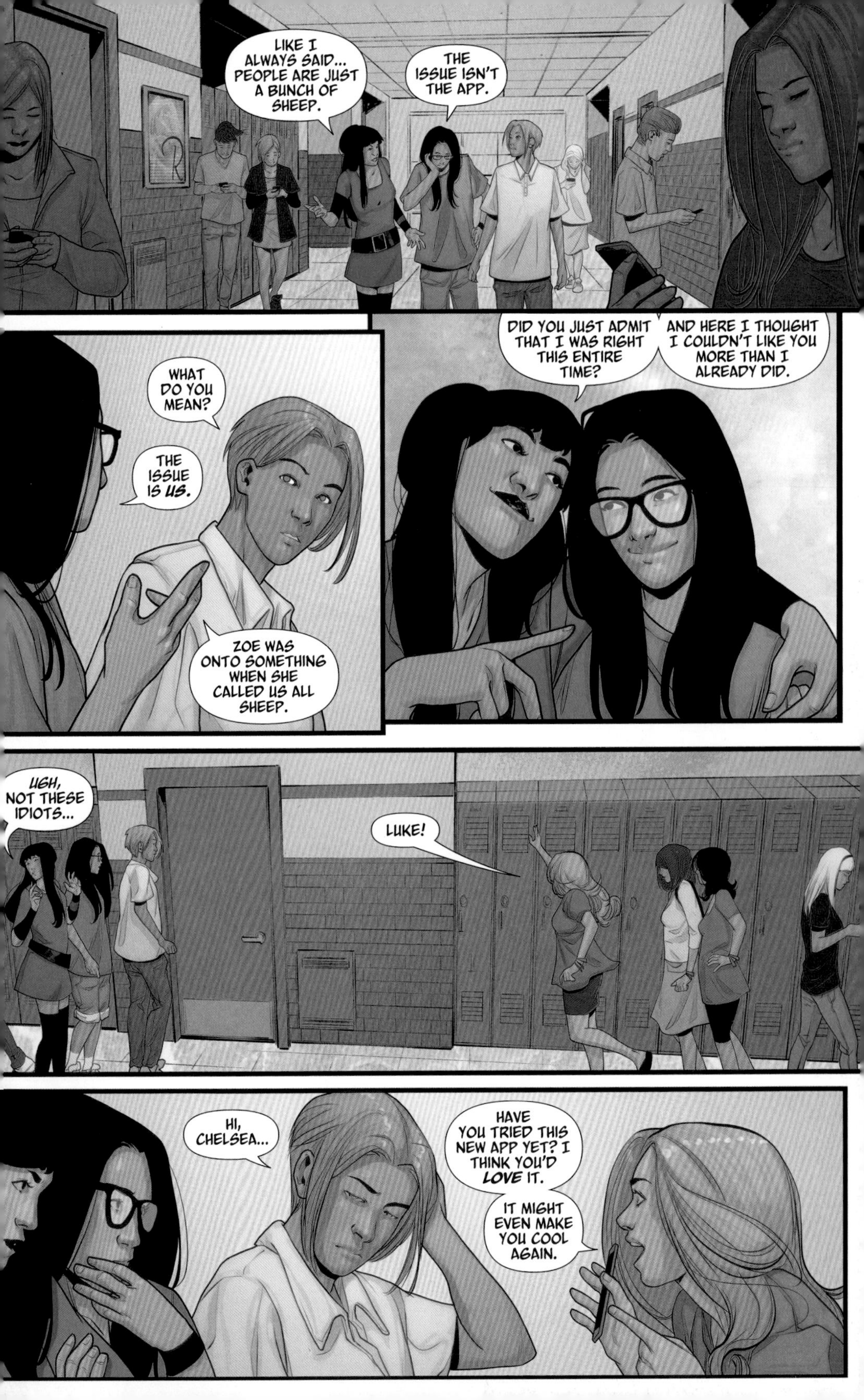
LIKE I ALWAYS SAID... PEOPLE ARE JUST A BUNCH OF SHEEP.
THE ISSUE ISN'T THE APP.
WHAT DO YOU MEAN?
THE ISSUE IS *US*.
ZOE WAS ONTO SOMETHING WHEN SHE CALLED US ALL SHEEP.
DID YOU JUST ADMIT THAT I WAS RIGHT THIS ENTIRE TIME?
AND HERE I THOUGHT I COULDN'T LIKE YOU MORE THAN I ALREADY DID.
UGH, NOT THESE IDIOTS...
LUKE!
HI, CHELSEA...
HAVE YOU TRIED THIS NEW APP YET? I THINK YOU'D *LOVE* IT.
IT MIGHT EVEN MAKE YOU COOL AGAIN.

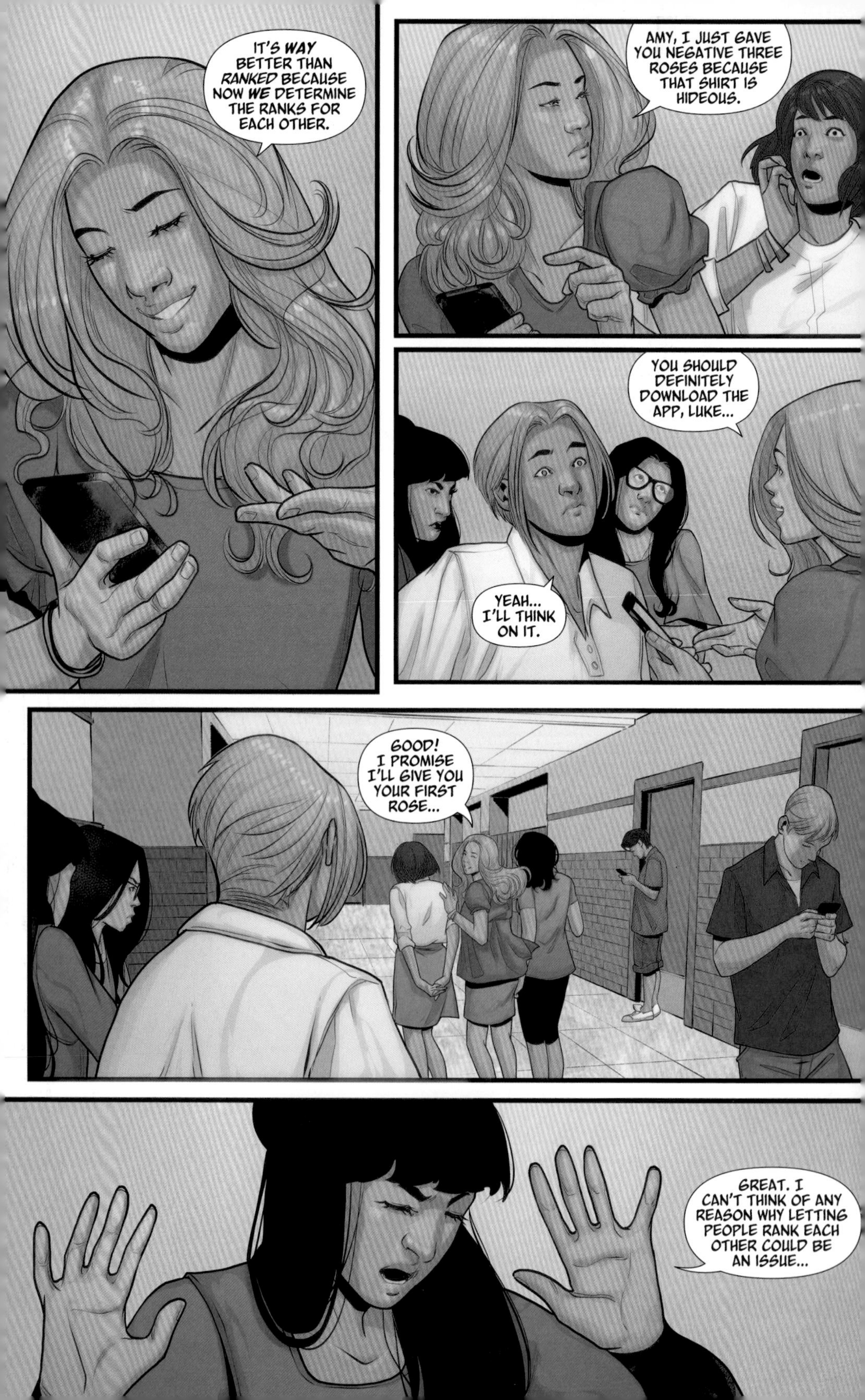
IT'S WAY BETTER THAN RANKED BECAUSE NOW WE DETERMINE THE RANKS FOR EACH OTHER.
AMY, I JUST GAVE YOU NEGATIVE THREE ROSES BECAUSE THAT SHIRT IS HIDEOUS.
YOU SHOULD DEFINITELY DOWNLOAD THE APP, LUKE...
YEAH... I'LL THINK ON IT.
GOOD! I PROMISE I'LL GIVE YOU YOUR FIRST ROSE...
GREAT. I CAN'T THINK OF ANY REASON WHY LETTING PEOPLE RANK EACH OTHER COULD BE AN ISSUE...

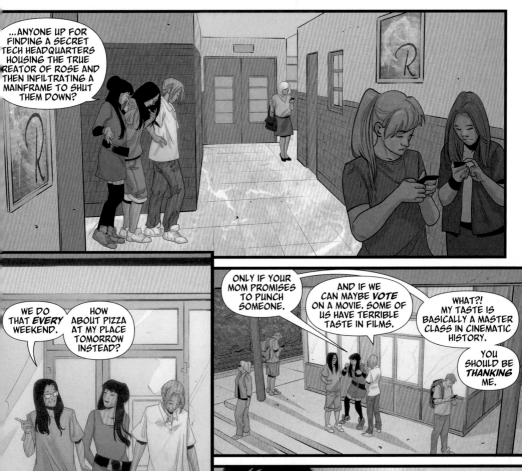

...ANYONE UP FOR FINDING A SECRET TECH HEADQUARTERS HOUSING THE TRUE CREATOR OF ROSE AND THEN INFILTRATING A MAINFRAME TO SHUT THEM DOWN?

WE DO THAT *EVERY* WEEKEND.

HOW ABOUT PIZZA AT MY PLACE TOMORROW INSTEAD?

ONLY IF YOUR MOM PROMISES TO PUNCH SOMEONE.

AND IF WE CAN MAYBE *VOTE* ON A MOVIE. SOME OF US HAVE TERRIBLE TASTE IN FILMS.

WHAT?! MY TASTE IS BASICALLY A MASTER CLASS IN CINEMATIC HISTORY.

YOU SHOULD BE *THANKING* ME.

YOU TWO PICK THE MOVIE AND I'LL SEE YOU TOMORROW.

WHERE'RE YOU GOING?

GOTTA HANG WITH MY MOM. PROMISED HER WE'D DO SOMETHING JUST US TONIGHT.

TELL HER WE SAID HI!

WILL DO! SEE YOU TOMORROW!

"IT'S ALL FALLING APART..."

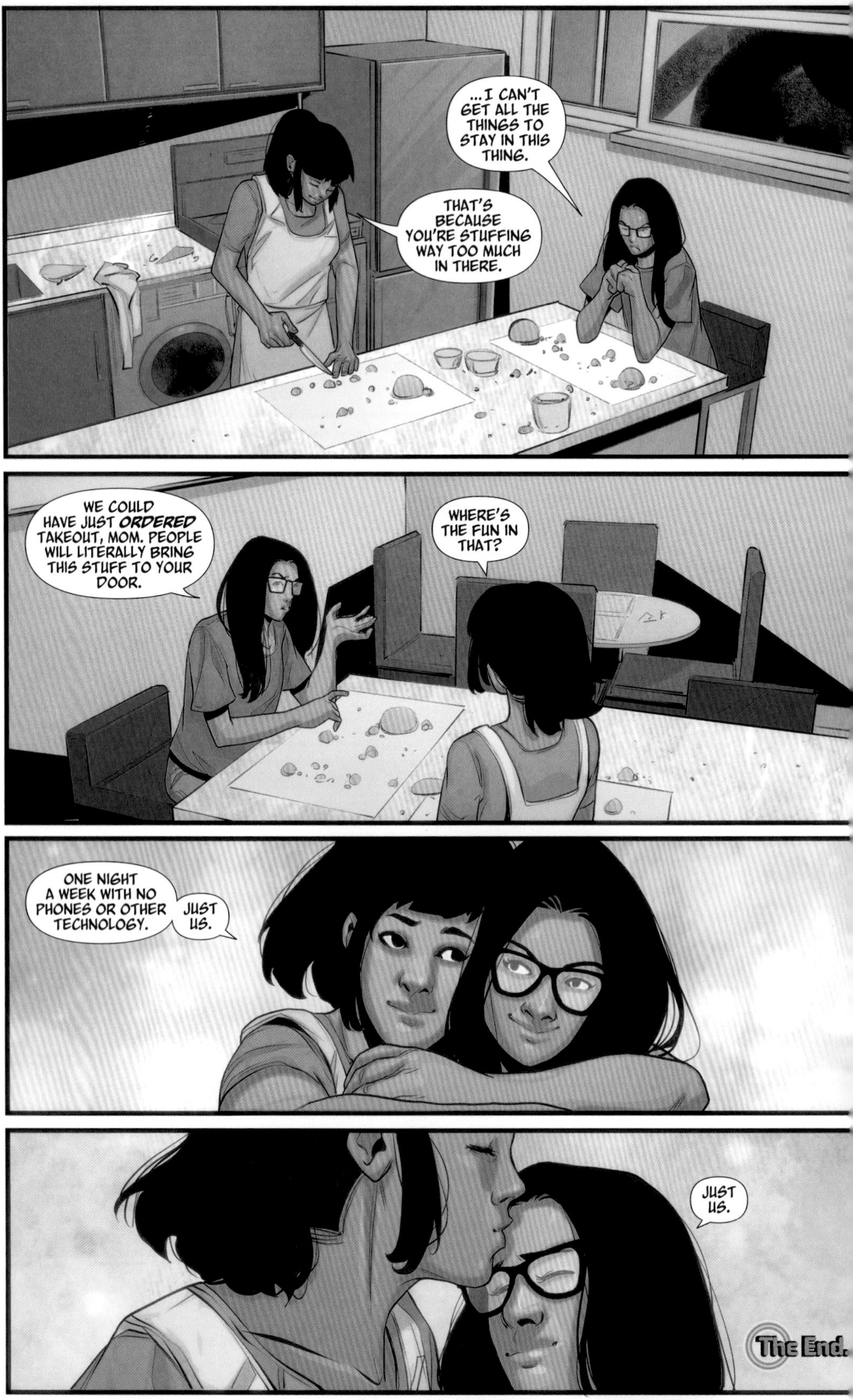
...I CAN'T GET ALL THE THINGS TO STAY IN THIS THING.
THAT'S BECAUSE YOU'RE STUFFING WAY TOO MUCH IN THERE.
WE COULD HAVE JUST *ORDERED* TAKEOUT, MOM. PEOPLE WILL LITERALLY BRING THIS STUFF TO YOUR DOOR.
WHERE'S THE FUN IN THAT?
ONE NIGHT A WEEK WITH NO PHONES OR OTHER TECHNOLOGY.
JUST US.
JUST US.
The End.

Stephanie Phillips is an American writer known for comics and graphic novels such as *Butcher of Paris* and *A Man Among Ye*. Her stories and comics have appeared with DC, AfterShock, Dark Horse, Heavy Metal, Top Cow/Image, Black Mask Studios and more. Stephanie earned her MA in English from the University of South Florida and is currently a PhD candidate in rhetoric and composition while teaching writing courses at the University at Buffalo.

Dave Johnson is an Eisner award-winning artist working on cover art for DC, Marvel, Dark Horse, Dynamite, IDW, and more. He may be best known for his cover work on the noir Vertigo series, *100 Bullets* and his Eisner-nominated work on the critically acclaimed DC Elseworlds miniseries *Superman: Red Son*. Along with comics, Dave is also the co-creator of the Cartoon Network animated series *Ben 10*.

Marika Cresta is an Italian artist born in Terni in 1988. She enrolled at Sapienza Università di Roma and graduated with a degree in architecture in 2015.

An avid learner, Marika is also a graduate of the Scuola Internazionale Comics di Roma where she stayed on for post-graduate work after receiving her diploma.

Her first published work was in 2016, a well-received short story in the book *Yamazaki 18 Years Apocrypha* (Manfont Publishing). That same year, she debuted on the foreign market scene with a story in *Grimm Tales of Terror Holiday Special* for Zenescope Entertainment. Then she worked for Lion Forge on *Summit* for the Catalyst Prime universe.

Scouted by Marvel's talent crew at Lucca Comics & Games, an annual convention in Lucca, Italy, Marika was brought on as a new artist to work on such iconic titles as *Power Pack X-Men* and *Dr Aphra*.